THE
SERPENTINE
ROAD

PAUL MENDELSON

Constable • London

CONSTABLE

First published in Great Britain in 2015 by Constable

This paperback edition published in Great Britain in 2016 by Constable

A CIP catalogue record for this book
is available from the British Library.

UK ISBN: 978-1-47211-138-8 (paperback)

Typesetting and design in Bembo by Photoprint, Torquay
Printed and bound in Great Britain by
CPI Group (UK) Ltd, Croydon CR0 4YY

Papers used by Constable are from well-managed forests
and other responsible sources

MIX
Paper from
responsible sources
FSC® C104740

Constable
is an imprint of
Little, Brown Book Group
Carmelite House
50 Victoria Embankment
London EC4Y 0DZ

An Hachette UK Company
www.hachette.co.uk

www.littlebrown.co.uk

AUTHOR'S NOTE

The actions of the Azanian People's Liberation Army (APLA) and the events surrounding the attack at the Heidelberg Tavern in Cape Town on 31 December 1993 are fact; the bombing of the Victoria Drinking Hall is fictitious.

Similarly, there are many real addresses and places within this story, but some are imagined. The opinions of some of the characters about real people involved in contemporary South African history, whether alive or dead, are those of the character alone – this is a fictional story.

'Metro' police officers act within the centre of Cape Town alone, and are primarily there to reassure residents and tourists of their safety, dealing with by-law infringements, traffic offences and community policing. The SAPS are the general police service throughout the country.

Oranjezicht is a residential area just above the CBD of Cape Town on the lower slopes of Table Mountain, affording panoramic views of Cape Town waterfront from one side and the near vertical face of Table Mountain on the other.

Paul Mendelson

PROLOGUE

January 1994

He stares, aghast, at the smoking void where the façade of the Victoria Drinking Hall had stood for the previous sixty years. Above and beyond the ruin, Devil's Peak is shrouded in fast moving dark cloud and rain falls sporadically but hard, diagonally across the taped-off streets onto ambulance men and police officers surrounding the scene.

South African Police Captain Vaughn de Vries can make out eight blanket-covered mounds in human form, laid out side by side in rows four deep, and feels his fists clench, jaw tighten. The smell of cooking meat is not the sweet *braai* smoke of the summer just ending, but acrid, choking. Twenty-three days before, he attended the Heidelberg Tavern bombing, not one kilometre away. To the whites of Cape Town, this is a senseless atrocity. He and his fellow officers had watched silently at the station, bile rising, Nelson Mandela walking from Victor Verster Prison amidst the cheering throng, the now inevitable path for South Africa indelibly signposted: elections, black majority rule, President Mandela; the end, many believe, of their cherished country. Yet, three years on, dates for elections set, world watching, still the APLA, armed wing of the Pan African Congress, targets innocent civilians at churches and bars. This is the second within the suburb

1

of Observatory: four dead at the Heidelberg, at least eight here; students, adults and the elderly; white and black and coloured.

He hears his name barked:

'Captain de Vries. Take that vehicle, follow me. We have information on the suspects' escape route. Move.'

De Vries salutes, sprints to the van, sees another officer jump into the passenger seat, guns the engine, follows in the wake of the huge police van and his commanding officer, Major Kobus Nel, who breaks through the cordon, heads up towards Main Road and takes a sharp left towards Rondebosch. De Vries's vehicle howls as he accelerates up the hill, moans as he turns. He catches glimpses of rubberneckers, covered against the rain and wind, but ashen faced, their white complexions sickly green in the faltering dusk and flickering street lamps.

He turns to his passenger.

'Who are you?'

'Constable Mitchell Smith, sir, Rondebosch.'

'De Vries, Captain, Observatory. You know my CO, Major Nel?'

Smith shouts above the engine noise: 'No, sir.'

'Taskmaster. Do as he says; don't think for yourself. You get it?'

The vehicle ahead pushes through red robots at the hospital junction, bears left and drops down onto Settlers Way, crosses four lanes, accelerates onto the N2 freeway. On the vehicle radio, they can hear shouted directions in a mixture of English and Afrikaans, hysterical and contradictory, barely comprehensible beneath a blanket of interference and static. De Vries discerns Nel's bark above the cacophony:

'Khayelitsha, Pama Road . . . Grey building.'

The rain is falling harder now, without respite, driven across the freeway by the gusting wind: a sharp summer cold front hitting town. The sky is now completely dark but for a pale halo of light around the mountains on the horizon; the freeway lights are out.

As they pass the cooling towers and head towards DF Malan airport, the front tyres lose traction momentarily and De Vries struggles to regain control.

'Shit. Keep a lookout for them ahead. I can't keep up in this *kak* fucker.'

De Vries struggles with the gearbox, wills the vehicle on, steers hard into the buffeting wind. There are few other vehicles on the road, a dangerous enough stretch without the hazardous conditions. As they pass under one of the new pedestrian bridges, built to prevent the squatter camp dwellers from trying to cross six lanes of fast-moving traffic, De Vries looks up: the squatters have been dropping lumps of concrete onto cars beneath them; half a dozen individual fatal incidents; a huge pile-up had cost seven lives just five weeks back.

The road rises as they pass the end of the runway, the airport itself quiet and dark. Already, De Vries knows, more people arrive in South Africa as sanctions are lifted and the pariah state is re-welcomed back into the world. What kind of country will it be that raises its head amongst its peers?

Suddenly, Smith shouts: 'Left turn ahead. Left, left, left.'

De Vries swerves onto the slip road, the back of the van slides outwards and he struggles to steer into the spin and bring the vehicle under control, hears Smith gasp at his side. Ahead, in what seems like thick, fast-moving mist, De Vries can see the larger police vehicle pulling away from him again, thinks he will lose it, squints through the windscreen barely cleared by the stuttering wipers. Everything is *opgefok* in this outfit, nothing works, nothing functions. What a country we're going to give them; economy fucked, infrastructure crumbling, people starving. Beneath the roar of the rain on the roof and the engine straining, he mouths the words: 'But, for fuck's sake, we're giving it to you, so don't go fucking killing our people or we'll fucking kill you back.'

* * *

He sees the vehicle pull off the tarmac surface, catches up with it, watches jiggling rear lights as both vehicles thunder along the rough unsurfaced road, tyres in potholes throwing up orange-brown ejaculations of mud. Ahead of them, at a deserted crossroads, a damp grey dwelling constructed of breeze blocks and corrugated iron sits dripping in the white light of a single lamp post, and a metallic green Ford Escort stands nose first in a partially fenced front yard.

De Vries can see Nel and three other white officers, armed and squatting behind their vehicle. Smith winds down the passenger side window, struggles against the oozing stiffness of the old mechanism.

'Across the way there,' Nel orders in his deep, strident voice, eyes blazing, sweat on his upper lip. 'De Vries, stay by your vehicle, take the sightlines across the crossroads, keep anyone else out of the scene. You,' he points the muzzle of his handgun at Smith. 'I want you at the perimeter of the yard to this shit-hole. Check the green car, guard our backs. You got it?'

They acknowledge the orders, watch Nel back off, keeping low, order his men to follow him. De Vries knows them all: Mike de Groot, Sheldon Rich, Johan Esau. There is another in the driver's seat, could be Joey Swanepoel, left to guard the vehicle, keep the engine running.

De Vries climbs out of the van, draws his weapon, holds it in both hands, balances it on the roof of the van; he scans 270 degrees, sees no one. This is not a night to be out on the street, not a time to be taunting the armed white policemen, high on a righteous mission. Smith has taken his place at the corner of the tiny plot. De Vries sees him feel the bonnet of the green Ford, check the doors, open the boot, shake his head.

Shouts from inside the dwelling; a shot, screams, then a dozen rounds like frenzied drum beats, a woman's wails. De Vries swings around, his weapon pointed at the doorway. He can see Smith squatting behind the green car, weapon primed, hears more shouts, a woman begging, imploring; then swearing, Nel's shout, two final shots – an epilogue. A minute flash of silver catches his eye at the side of the shack; a semblance of movement. He thinks he makes out a figure. He raises his gun, aware his hands are wet from rain and sweat, the muzzle shaking. Another movement, perhaps a scraping sound, a high-pitched, almost whispered command. He tightens his grip, feels the trigger bite into the joint of his index finger. Something tells him not to fire: it is a child, children. He tilts his head. The rain makes him blink, re-focus; he sees eyes stare back at him; too small, too low to be an adult. With his left hand, he pushes down the muzzle of his gun, squints, discerns nothing but the sound of heavy raindrops beginning to fall again on the tin-roofed shacks around him. If he has seen children – seen any living animal – it, or they, have run away down the narrow alley between the two rows of shacks and tiny houses, beneath the sagging lines which steal electricity from the looming pylons at the end of the encampment, into the maze of the dark and filthy township.

He looks across to see Nel and the three officers exit the building, senses more than sees shock and fear on the faces of the young subordinates, their legs weak.

'Next junction, grey house. Go.'

De Vries does not know whether this is an order to him or to Nel's men. He watches them stumble into the vehicle, the sound of the engine revving, back-firing, jolting into gear. It passes De Vries, turns again onto the main thoroughfare and heads away, thick fumes in its wake.

5

De Vries looks over to Smith, still crouching. He turns full circle, scanning the shacks and passages, sees no movement, scurries across to the van, crouches next to him.

De Vries is dry-mouthed:

'What happened?'

'I dunno.'

'What did you see?'

'Nothing. Nothing.'

'You see anyone come out the back, the side of the shack there?'

'No.' Smith turns around, looks down the alleyway, shakes his head. He stares at De Vries, mouth agape, panting.

'Wait here. Cover me.'

Keeping low, De Vries jumps the broken chain fence around the yard, runs to the front door, jams his back against the wall, primes his weapon, glances inside the building. He takes a deep breath, ducks inside.

The rain on the tin roof is like a thousand gunshots, the bitter stench of fresh blood clashes with the warm smoky air, thick with sweat and urine. The interior is lit only by a fading hurricane lamp atop a pile of firewood, a faint orange glimmer from a fire against the back wall. To his right, deep, dark blood oozes from the bodies of an old man and woman sprawled on a thin, stained mattress; ahead of him, in front of the fire, a young girl lies face up, her head encased in a solid helmet of hair matted in blood; to his left, two adults, he thinks maybe in their late thirties or early forties, lean against one other, heads touching, one with half his face blown away, the other riddled with bullets. In their agony, they seem to have embraced, arms around each other, ankles crossed.

De Vries fights back vomit in his chest, takes short staccato breaths, squeezes his eyes shut yet forces himself to picture each body, each face. He searches for weapons, sees none. He makes himself step forward, pushes aside debris with his foot and with the muzzle of his gun. Still he finds nothing.

He backs out, reaches the cooler, heavy air and breathes it into his lungs; he remembers where he is and what he has seen, swings around and sees only Constable Smith, alert yet somehow mesmerized, pointing his gun at him. He meets his stare, drops to one knee and checks around him. Still there is no sign of life on the streets. He pulls himself up, scurries towards Smith and the green vehicle.

'What is it?'

'Something set them off. Firefight. Five down in there.'

Smith swallows.

'Blacks?'

'*Ja.*'

'We follow Major Nel?'

De Vries hesitates.

'No.'

'Sir?'

'We go back to Obs. Back to the station.'

He rises, pulls Smith's sleeve, scampers back to their own van, fights to get the engine started, pulls away, swings around, heads back in the direction from which they have come.

Above the sound of the straining engine, Smith shouts:

'What happened?'

De Vries grits his teeth, fights the stench in his nostrils, keeps watch either side of the road, alert for ambush; he says nothing.

What happened?

Wrong house, wrong car, wrong information – if there ever was any. Trigger happy, angry, vengeful policemen, sick of the struggle, sick of seeing their own cut down, sick of the weather. Out of control commanding officer venting his hatred, his frustration that at the end of years of toil, decades of faith in the system, those above have capitulated; lashing out at anyone without answers, anyone black . . .

What happened?

'Don't know,' De Vries says.

Kobus Nel is scarcely older than him, but he is broad and balding, and very fit, his muscular arms filling out his rain-and-sweat soaked uniform. De Vries is taller, but he is thin and lean, his hair still buzz-cropped, army-style. He is back on home territory in Observatory, but he has been away for two years and is newly posted to the station.

The changing rooms are located in an old stone building covered by corrugated asbestos roofing. The rain thuds against it. It is cold and damp and, mid-shift, empty. De Vries has showered under the sputtering tepid streams, torn between remaining to face his CO or getting out and going home, and facing him the following day. He is absentmindedly toweling himself down when he hears the door slam and Nel's voice boom. Nel runs down the narrow corridor of lockers, pushes him hard in the chest. He stumbles back, falls over a low wooden bench, hurtles against the far wall of lockers, causing a crash of metallic thunder. He scrambles to his feet, naked, heart pumping.

'Come here, De Vries.' Nel points at the ground in front of him. Vaughn stands straight, winded and shocked. They are alone and De Vries can smell the liquor on the man's breath, senses the unstoppable determination in his posture; that his will cannot be challenged. De Vries looks up at the grey lights.

'De Vries. Where the fuck were you?'

'Sir?'

Nel shoves him again, forcing him back.

'We moved from the house in Pama Road to further locations. You were our back-up.' He stamps forward, shoves De Vries hard;

another thunder-clap of bone on metal locker-front. 'Where were you?' He shoves again, until De Vries' back hits the lockers; a cymbal cacophony echoes. 'And Constable Smith?'

De Vries unconsciously switches to military mode, barks his answers, loud and staccato.

'Understood we were to remain in situ, guard the scene, sir.'

Nel has him trapped at the end of the row. He slams his fist into the locker door next to De Vries's ear.

'No, Captain, you cowardly fucker. You fucking left that scene, abandoned your unit and slunk back here. What if we had encountered resistance?'

'I misunderstood your orders, sir.'

Nel is shaking now; his gloved hand shoots for De Vries's neck. Vaughn feels the cold, clammy leather on his windpipe, knows he has only seconds to decide whether to fight back. Nel smashes the locker door with his other fist, releases his grip on De Vries's neck, stands back. De Vries realizes that the physical threat is bluster, that Nel's anger is diminishing, mutating into a different mood.

'Your report on my desk before you leave the station. Make sure it's right. You understand?' He takes a small step away from De Vries. 'Check what Constable Smith writes, counter-sign it and leave it with yours. You have a duty, Captain. Fulfill it and this is over.'

De Vries prevents his head from nodding automatically; he stands still, ignores his heart pounding in his chest, feels control returning to his limbs. Imperceptibly, he draws himself taller.

'What do you want in my report, sir?'

Nel stares at him, his pale eyes focused.

'Nothing that brings disrepute to this station, to my command. I make myself clear?'

De Vries stands taller. His shaking has abated, his nakedness forgotten.

9

'What role did those people play, sir, the people who are now dead, in the incident at the Victoria?'

'That is not your business. You report what you saw. Only what you saw, not what you think you saw.'

'I saw,' De Vries says.

There is a beat of silence before Nel comprehends, recoils. De Vries sees him re-evaluate the threat he poses. Nel lowers his voice, comes back towards him.

'I am the commanding officer, De Vries. What you believe you saw makes no difference. There are four witnesses who will recount what occurred. We were threatened at gunpoint by men and women who harboured terrorists. We defended ourselves, confiscated weapons. No one will recall differently.' He backs away and then struts towards De Vries anew.

'One word from me and you're gone. When the new regime comes to power they will exploit any weakness to gain control. So, you decide, De Vries. Stay with us, or be our enemy. See how many friends you have then. You won't live to see the new fucking *kaffir* South Africa.'

'I'll see it rather than start a bloodbath.'

'*Ja*, that is what you would do. You and fucking De Klerk and the Nats who've sold every one of us down the fucking river. And that fucking *kaffir* terrorist, fucking saboteur, Mandela. You think he will bring peace to this country? He's a fucking bomb-maker. You think men like me will let him become the fucking messiah?'

Kobus Nel struts in a circle, still blocking De Vries's exit. He is shrieking.

'You know what will happen? The police force is over; they'll disband it because there'll be no fucking rule of law. They're going to take our jobs, our houses, our land, destroy everything we have done to build this country into the great nation that we are. They're going to fuck us all up, and with the whole world watching, cowards like you are going to let them.'

De Vries baulks, knows that over brandy and cokes with his friends he has drunkenly debated the future, acquiesced to the ugly fears of his colleagues, the hateful proselytization, but he has never fully accepted it. His new wife, Suzanne, younger and more enlightened, more informed, has tempered his insistent gnawing fears and argued to accept the inevitable, to gauge a reaction, not to allow knee-jerk ignorance to rule his heart, and to believe in hope for their daughter's future in the new Republic of South Africa.

De Vries says quietly:

'You know what's frightening about people like you? I am angry, I feel betrayed, fear for my country, but you know what? You make me sound so fucking reasonable.'

Nel laughs bitterly, shakes his head.

'We're all fucked, whatever you pathetic liberals, you fucking apologists think, but I'm warning you, you threaten my future and I will bring you down. So, right now, you better do your duty, Captain. Don't do it for yourself. Do it for your wife and child.'

He turns, and in the split second Nel's back is to him, the thought comes to De Vries to jump the man, to bring him down, to beat the life out of him.

When the door to the locker room finally closes, leaving him alone, he bows his head, his weight still on the steel doors against which he had been trapped. He pretends that he hasn't yet decided what he will do but, deep inside, he already knows. He wonders whether the shame will allow him even to stand upright to leave this place, to dress, to type up his lies and cajole the frightened Constable Mitchell Smith, to walk through the station to the exit, to travel home to his wife and baby.

PART ONE

3 April 2015

Colonel de Vries rides De Waal Drive as far as the Mill Street slip road, sees one plane of the tower blocks in the CBD bright with white sun, the Waterfront lit by watery rays of sunrise, turns left up towards the face of the dark Mountain, encounters only gradations of grey, from grey tarmac, through the thick layer of smoke, up the staggered, unending growth of mountain, to dark white cloud above it. He guns the puny engine up the steep incline, inhaling rich, choking smoke through the ventilators, presses on, almost in darkness, awaiting the moment when he crests the deep haze and finds daylight again. He locates the turnoff onto Serpentine Road, swings the car parallel to the coastline. The smoke follows him, lies on his rear window. For three months now, the fires have blazed. More of the famous posters have appeared on billboards, those which scold and beg simultaneously, the design decades old, a cartoon for adults: the vast, delicate Springbok head, wide eyes anguished, naïve, painted flames behind it, a tear falling from its eye. The fawn, engulfed by pathos, pleads: 'Only YOU can stop bush and veldt fires.'

He finds Park Terrace, draws up short of the misty blue flashing lights ahead of him, swings open the car door, feeling the wind take it away from him, and struggles to slam it shut. Behind him, the eponymous little park at the road's end with its Umbrella

15

Pines seems unscathed, and he sees no flames from the foot of the Mountain where the fire must have blazed during the night. He turns back, walks with the wind, engulfed in smoke, towards the scene.

'Fucking fires,' he mutters, cupping his hands around the tip of a new cigarette, emerging choking into the square of marked police vehicles. The cylinder ignites and he draws deeply. He turns to a uniformed cop, flashes his ID.

'Day doesn't begin till the poison meets my lungs.' He waves the cigarette at the officer between the 'v' of his fingers, strides on through the haze towards the house wrapped in police tape. He pauses, takes two further drags, flicks the butt into the gutter and spits on the road. He trots up the stairs, passes through a wide front door, sees a group of Cape Town Central officers in the palatial hallway.

'Who thinks they are in charge here?'

The men shuffle to face him, fall silent. He hears footsteps on the wide staircase, suspended seemingly in midair, wide plains of white marble tapering down to the ground floor. Two sets of cheap shoes, crisply pressed grey trousers, white shirts and navy ties appear in fifteen centimetre degrees. The taller man, a broad black African, fit and muscular, snorts, tilts his chin at De Vries.

'Of course it would be one of you.'

De Vries meets his eye.

'Who are you?'

'Nkosi. Lieutenant Sam Nkosi.' He holds out his hand.

'Step outside with me, Lieutenant.' De Vries turns from the proffered hand, walks back to the front door, onto the street. As he passes the wide mirror in the hallway, he sees the eyes of the other officers turn towards to Nkosi.

De Vries waits, stares up at the mountain, his back to the property. When he hears footsteps behind him, he turns.

16

'I am Colonel de Vries of the Special Crimes Unit . . .' He observes Nkosi's blank reaction. 'If you know who I am, your attitude is misjudged. If you don't, then I'm telling you now, Lieutenant: I'm taking this case from you.'

'I know that,' Nkosi says.

'Where are you from?'

'Central.'

'Before that?'

'Pretoria.'

'Nobody likes this system. But it works. Chalk it up to experience. What do I need to know about the scene?'

'I have walked it with my Sergeant to check it. We have touched nothing.'

'I hope not.'

'Been done right.'

'Good. I'll base my opinion of you on your word. Give me a card?'

Nkosi shakes his head.

'I don't have one. I have been here six months and they still have not been printed.'

'Write down your cell-phone number, Lieutenant, in case we need you. Then take your men away. Tell them no one discusses the scene. I rely on you to enforce that order. You understand?'

'Yes.'

De Vries looks past him, involuntarily taps his right foot.

'Don't make me say it, Lieutenant.'

Nkosi's eyes remain blank.

'Yes, sir.'

As the Cape Town Central officers leave, they stare at him. He knows his reputation and he judges that they wear the anticipated expressions: curiosity, fear, some little distain. De Vries scrutinizes each of them, coloured and black officers, makes them lower their eyes. Finally, Nkosi appears, walks slowly down the stairs and pauses in front of him.

'You might want to talk to me, sir.'

'Might I? Why?'

'I know who the victim is.'

De Vries snorts.

'So do I.'

'I met her a week ago.'

'She say who wanted her dead?'

'No.'

'Then, Lieutenant, we will talk.' He looks at a small sheet of folded paper in Nkosi's hand. 'Your contact details?'

Nkosi hands it to him, shakes his head, moves on to an unmarked car.

De Vries turns behind him and nods at the Scene of Crime team. When they are inside, De Vries walks over to his Warrant Officer, Don February, who stands by the gate which leads down the side of the property to the terraced garden.

'Those Central guys all go upstairs?'

'Not when I arrived, sir. Just the Lieutenant and one other officer. Before that, the same officer and his partner, who answered the original call. But, maybe before I got here . . . ?'

'You tell the Lieutenant that I was coming?'

'Just that a senior officer from Special Crimes was coming. Not your name.'

'Why not?'

'I do not like the reaction when I say your name.'

De Vries smiles. His Inspector's wit is dryer than the Karoo.

'So you bought yourself a moment of respite . . .'

'A senior officer thinks he is leading a case and then it is snatched away by some elite unit. It is no wonder that it breeds resentment.'

18

'He should be glad of the break. That's what our unit is for: take the tough ones and leave more officers available.'

'Even you said nobody likes the system.'

'I lied,' De Vries says. 'I like it.'

In the hallway, they dress in blue disposable boiler suits, over-boots and latex gloves. Although the house is full of people, there is a chapel-like hush. Don February speaks in a whisper.

'Down the stairs is the kitchen and a casual living space, which leads onto the pool deck and garden. There is no evidence that anyone went there. The doors are barred and locked. Everything happened up here.'

They begin to climb the white staircase.

'Did she live alone?'

'Miss Holt? I do not know. It is a big house for one woman only.'

Don studies his notes.

'Miss Taryn Holt, aged thirty-eight. She has been identified as the victim by the live-in maid, her ID, photographs of her in the house. But, I think I have heard that name . . .?'

'Taryn Holt inherited her father's company a few years back. Holt Industries is a major heavy-industrial player in Southern Africa. She's richer than your Uncle Bob Mugabe.'

Don rolls his eyes.

'I have not heard of Holt Industries.'

'Me neither, till an hour back. Plenty of big, successful companies operating under the radar. She isn't involved, but she owns most of it.'

They reach the upstairs landing and, immediately, De Vries can see through the expansive dual-level living space to a huge wall of floor-to-ceiling sliding doors which open to a breathtaking panorama over the city, the Waterfront and Table Bay. The shards of silver sunlight paint lines of smoky perspective over the scene until sea and sky merge on some unseen horizon.

A crime scene technician is bent over the lock on an open door in the corner of the room, another is searching the cream carpet for debris. Everything, De Vries thinks, is very bare, very pale. He looks at the large bronze sculpture on a cream marble plinth: a lioness attacks a wildebeest. De Vries feels that he has seen this scene before, in the same style, but cannot place where. He looks at the large paintings on the walls. They are mainly bright abstracts, garish and vulgar amidst the pure white, but there is one darker portrait of a black African woman. She stares proudly out from the canvas, demands that her gaze be met.

'What else?'

'There are many staff members, but they all travel in each day. There is one live-in maid. She has a room at the bottom of the garden. She called us early this morning. I have not spoken with her yet, but she told dispatch that she thought she heard something in the garden, went outside and looked up at the main house to see the terrace door in the corner open. As the alarm had not sounded, she came into the house to check that everything was all right. Her call to the station was logged at 5.14 a.m.'

'And the victim?'

Don February turns, retraces his steps to the hallway and then gestures towards the door at the end of the long broad corridor.

'She is in the final door to the right – the master bedroom.'

De Vries begins to walk towards it.

'It is not nice.'

De Vries pushes the door gently with the back of his gloved hand. It is heavy, but opens smoothly and silently. Ahead of him, he sees the same view of the sea through wide windows. To his right, a crime scene officer is on his knees taking samples from the legs of an antique bureau; to his left, a vulgar display of modern art: still life with blood. He catches his breath. The bedroom: white walls, white carpet, a big broad bed encased in a polished yellow-wood frame – spattered in pink and red, pock-marked in sticky almost-black tar. Like some horrendous Jackson Pollack canvas, everything emanates from the explosion on the bed. There is blood on two walls, on the ornate polished-wood headboard, on the ceiling. A parallelogram of sunshine hits the bed, illuminating her long matted hair, making the droplets of blood on the walls in the corner of the room sparkle.

He turns to Don.

'Can we approach?'

Don turns back to the crime scene officer, who nods at him.

De Vries pads forward gingerly, aware that he is now amidst the mire of blood.

The woman's body is sprawled across the end of the mattress, her torso atop it, her legs hanging over the end at a strange angle. Her left foot rests lightly on the carpet; her right a few centi-metres above it, floating stiffly. She is naked.

He leans close to her head, starts to squat, peers through the sticky hair to the side of her face, half of a mask, a rictus of agony. He swallows hard. There is something in her mouth: a bulbous brown growth.

De Vries takes a pen from his jacket pocket, points at the object.

'What is that?'

Don February says: 'I do not know.'

'I'm not going to take it out, Vaughn . . .' De Vries looks up and turns towards the new voice. It is Steve Ulton, the Crime Scene Leader, a man De Vries respects. 'But, I suspect that it is a dildo. A black dildo.'

'Part of the attack?'

'I doubt it. Not my job to opine on C.O.D. but clearly she has been shot several times.'

De Vries nods.

'So this . . . Dildo. This is something else?'

21

'I would say so.'

'The scene is staged?'

Ulton smiles. 'Unless she just happened to be sitting on the edge of her bed with a huge rubber dick in her mouth, then, *ja*, I'd say so.'

De Vries regrets his clumsy question; his head is already full of ideas, jostling with the new information every glance at the scene provides.

'Okay.'

'You want to work backwards?'

'You ready already?'

'Work in progress, thinking aloud . . .'

De Vries nods.

'Look at the wooden headboard . . .' They turn to it; each tries to avoid running their eyes over the body on the bed, none succeed. It is ornately carved wood, almost like tangled branches, yet highly polished and a rich light brown colour. Using a ballpoint pen, he indicates an area about a quarter of the way across. 'Look here. You can see that there are deep abrasions here . . .' He leans over the bed without coming into contact with it and points again, this time to scratch marks about a quarter of the way from the opposite side. 'The same here.'

'What are they?'

'I will take samples and examine them further; if necessary the entire bed can be taken away. However, judging from their position mainly behind and to some extent to the side of each wooden strut, I would say they are marks from where rope or cuffs were tied to the bed-head. I've seen this before, both in completely innocent contexts and more sinister ones.'

Don February says quietly: 'Completely innocent?'

De Vries glances sideways at him. Ulton stands straight, arches his back. 'Innocent in terms of being consensual.'

Don nods imperceptibly, keeps his head low.

Ulton takes a pace backwards, faces Taryn Holt.

'If you look at the wrists of the victim, you will see that there are no abrasions, no obvious evidence of being bound in the past.'

'So, what does that mean?'

'Possibly nothing. The pathologist will examine the victim for signs of sexual attack, but there isn't anything immediate to suggest that there was anything of a penetrative sexual angle to the attack – apart from the dildo, and that is likely to have been inserted post-mortem.'

De Vries frowns. The information is detailed and revealing, but it seems irrelevant to the murder itself.

Ulton turns and walks slowly to the doorway.

'The door closes automatically. The mechanism is balanced very finely. Very high quality workmanship. If the victim was unaware of the presence of an intruder, he – or she – could approach down the corridor without being noticed.'

He indicates the corridor.

'We've examined the carpet along here. There are indistinct footprints all over the place. I doubt we'll find anything but, since the bedroom windows are all sealed, we can assume that the attacker walked along this corridor, both to and from the scene.'

Ulton exits the bedroom and slowly retraces his footsteps back to the living area. It seems to De Vries even bigger than before, hollow and devoid of identity and personality, unconnected somehow with its owner.

'The lock on this far window has been tampered with. He might have got in from the terrace through there.'

'Might?'

Ulton tilts his head. 'Just a preliminary observation. I'm in doubt that the tampering occurred from the outside.' He turns back to De Vries. 'There's no physical evidence we've found so far that leads us to the weapon and, obviously, no sign of the weapon itself.'

'One assailant?'

'Nothing, yet, to suggest otherwise.'

De Vries is frustrated. None of Ulton's responses mean anything.

'Timing? I know you'll be guessing . . .'

'Preliminary readings suggest eight to ten hours. Don't quote me. The maid found her body just after five, so work it out yourself . . . It's eight fifteen now. Between ten last night and one this morning. Because of the maid, we got here quickly, Vaughn.'

De Vries stares at him a moment longer, expectant.

'Aren't you going to ask?' Ulton says.

De Vries shrugs.

'I can't be certain but I'd say that the weapon was a nine milli-metre. She was shot at least five times. There are no shells. The shooter took the time and trouble to collect them.'

'Planned actions . . .'

'Yes.'

'That makes things more complicated. Anything else?'

'That's it for now,' Ulton tells him. 'They'll take the body when you're finished here and I'll see you back in town.'

'*Ja*. Give me ten more minutes, then you can take her,' De Vries says. 'Glad it's you working this.'

Ulton turns and descends the stairs to the main hallway. In the distance, De Vries can hear him instructing his team. He turns to Don.

'You want to see the scene again?'

Don hesitates.

'If you think so.'

They walk back to the master bedroom and re-enter the expansive space. The crime scene technician has left now, and they are alone. De Vries lets Don stand next to him. He senses the door

24

closing silently behind him, jumps minutely as it clicks shut. He takes a deep breath and surveys the whole room, taking in everything he can, but knowing that the photographs will always be there to remind him of everything physical. He holds his breath now, in the silence absorbing what he feels. There is no stench of death, just mild wood smoke and the acrid smell of fresh blood. He turns his head to scan the entire suite. It is very stark and impersonal, as if the space is too big for a woman on her own. He wonders whether she chose this style and that it reflects her personality or whether she just called in a designer and came home one day to find it all done. He looks down to his Warrant Officer.

'Any thoughts?'

Don pauses. 'Yes . . . But I do not have words for them yet.'

De Vries stares at him for a moment.

'Then say nothing . . .'

In the hallway, De Vries waits for Don February; he wonders what his Warrant Officer is thinking about as he slowly descends the staircase.

'We should talk to the maid. She still here?'

'Yes,' Don tells him. 'She is downstairs in her quarters, with one of our officers.'

'Okay, I'm going to take a look at the perimeter. Get her ready, will you?'

De Vries finds the entrance-way empty now, trots down the stairs to the street. He pulls out his cigarettes, lights one in cupped hands, walks to the other side of the road and slouches against the low wall of the opposite building. The smoke is diminishing, but it still taints the clear sea-air with a brown-blue haze.

The street-facing façade of the Holt house is white and minimalist. It is a smart new building, probably designed by one of the famous Cape Town architects on what looks like at least two generous mountainside plots. De Vries ambles across the street and climbs the low gate to a set of steep, narrow stone steps lined by large boulders, scrubby windblown trees and lush ferns. He gazes down to a small building at the bottom of the inclined garden, assumes that this is the maid's room. He descends a dozen steps, looks back up at the house. From here, he cannot see the terrace or pool deck and notes that there is no direct access from this path. He scrutinizes the rocks, wonders whether an agile man or woman could climb up them to the terrace. After a while, he convinces himself that they could, reminds himself to ask Steve Ulton whether his team have surveyed this possibility. De Vries shakes his head and turns away: the population are gripped by fear of crime, but they do nothing practical to prevent it, expecting the private security firms to patrol them twenty-four hours a day to protect them.

He stares up at the Mountain. Here, beneath it, the scale of it, so often unprocessed by his brain, is awe-inspiring. All his life, it has stood sentinel. He wonders at the atrocities it has witnessed; what has played out in its gloomy shadow in the last few hours? He thinks about Taryn Holt, wonders, beyond the hastily assembled sheets of biography he has scanned, who she is, and what caused her to be killed so brutally.

He hears a sound below, sees Don walking up the steps, taking one at a time, quickly, but deliberately.

'What is it?'

Don waits until he is one step beneath De Vries, their disparate heights over-emphasized. He speaks quietly: 'I would like permission to interview her. In her room.'

De Vries tilts his head.

'Why?'

'She is very shocked and I think . . . You always say to play to our strengths. I think she will talk to me.'

'Rather than to me?'

Don pauses.

'Maybe.'

De Vries smiles.

'Go on then.'

He watches Don take the steps down carefully, looks back up to the house and then follows his Warrant Officer, stopping a few steps from the bottom. Then, repeatedly glancing back up at the house, he climbs them again, one by one. About halfway up, there is a view of the house, and he can see the open door at the far end of the bank of windows from the living area. This is the lowest point of her quarters from which the maid could see that a window was open; he wonders why she would come this far up the staircase in the middle of the night.

As he walks back up to the main house, he searches for lights, but finds only cheap solar lanterns widely spaced along the length of the steps. He squats down and examines the one nearest the house. It is old and worn, and he doubts that it works. He looks away, looks at nothing, his mind already full of questions.

'You have everything up and running . . . ?'

'Within five hours of the initial call.'

Director Henrik du Toit nods slowly, views De Vries with mild surprise.

Du Toit says: 'Another long weekend ahead.' He watches De Vries shrug. 'The rest of your team may not be so unconcerned.'

'You're right. We should ask people to be more considerate: kill on a Monday.'

Du Toit looks around, through the window which separates De Vries's office from the rest of the squad-room, and back again.

'You almost seem cheerful, Vaughn.'

'You know me, sir. Death enlivens me.'

27

Du Toit does not smile.

'Tell me what we have?'

'The usual nothing. In a few hours, we'll have too much. We think that Taryn Holt was killed between 10 p.m. Thursday and 1 a.m. this morning. No apparent motive. Warrant February spoke with the maid, says she seems loyal and reliable. She's upset, probably for her job, but she says she can't see anything missing. She claims she scarcely slept because of the smoke and the fear that the fires might spread to her street. She heard noises in the night, but put them down to the wind. When she woke at 5 a.m. she decided that she would not sleep, so she walked up through the garden, saw open windows and went to investigate. She found the body, and called it in at 5.14 a.m. Looks like the alarm had not been set. Central were there by 5.35 a.m. and it then came through to our desk. Warrant February was there by 6.40 a.m. I was there thirty minutes later . . .'

'Any trouble with the Central guys?'

'Not really.'

Du Toit leans back.

'You handled it diplomatically?'

'Probably not.'

Du Toit coughs.

'Any thoughts from the scene?'

De Vries scratches his ear.

'You know I don't like doing this . . . She was shot, several times, close range. Maybe there is nothing missing, and then we have a very rich single woman murdered seemingly without motive – until you think about the money.'

Du Toit nods.

'And, I can tell you now: whoever it was, he's not going to leave us anything.'

'Meaning?'

'It doesn't appear spontaneous.'

'Then you're exactly where you should be.' He rises, and De Vries mirrors him. Du Toit moves towards the door of the office, turns back to him.

'Bad timing if this gets complicated.'

'Your leave?'

'A week in Pretoria for some damn conference . . . Then, hard-earned leave. Keep me informed of major developments.'

De Vries nods, and turns to open the door.

Du Toit says:

'You were serious, weren't you? You're pleased you have your murder?'

De Vries gets through the door and turns back, says blankly:

'It's why I get up in the morning.'

Although the building in the centre of town which houses the Special Crimes Unit and Administrative offices was built in the eighties, the Pathology Lab on the lower ground floor looks more like something from the fifties: iron where you might expect aluminium; fluorescent tubes on chains where you might expect recessed LEDs.

De Vries knocks on the office door, lets himself in and glances immediately towards the two desks. One is empty but, behind the other, sits a short, very slim woman wearing a headscarf, head bowed over a keyboard. De Vries instinctively sighs, but she does not raise her head. He waits in silence until she stops tapping, looks up at him.

'Good morning, Doctor.'

Doctor Anna Jafari studies him calmly.

'I am sure it is not. You are disappointed to see me, but that is beyond my control.'

'Not at all . . . That is . . . We have a break on the Holt murder. She was discovered a lot earlier than the murderer might expect. I want to maintain that advantage.'

Doctor Jafari leans back in her chair.

'So, you tell me, Colonel de Vries . . . Shall I move your victim ahead of the four I have in the queue?'

De Vries smiles thinly, tries to stay calm.

'There might be a significant advantage in obtaining PM results quickly.'

'But not with these other victims . . .?'

'I don't know who or what you have to examine today, but I know that I'm here, we have a team assembled and we need information fast.'

Jafari shakes her head slowly.

'You know the procedure. If you want to lobby General Thulani, that is not my concern, but try if you like. Tell him that you want your white victim moved ahead of the four black boys I have here . . .'

De Vries feels the blood pump in his cheeks, attempts to suppress it.

'This unit was set up to deal with priority crimes . . .'

'. . . And, because you are a small unit and your victims are relatively few,' Jafari says, without looking up from her reports, 'we also process certain additional victims in the Central area.'

De Vries sighs, knows that the men she will examine will be victims of drug crime, of gang wars; that what killed them will probably never be discovered, their killers never bought to justice. He takes a deep breath.

'I would appreciate your attention as soon as you possibly can, Doctor. Perhaps you will call my office when you begin?'

Jafari stands up. She is very small.

'I will do that.'

They stand facing one another for a moment. De Vries is the first to turn away.

De Vries wishes he had driven. Don February drives fast and well but, like so many Capetonians, changes lanes constantly. He gains no advantage, but the sour coffee in De Vries's belly slops from side to side. He knows this is not good when he can actually hear it.

'It's bad news we have Jafari.'

Don says: 'Why, sir?'

'She won't do us any favours and, more importantly, if we need her in court, she doesn't stand up well . . .' He chuckles. '. . . Literally – and as an expert witness. She volunteers doubt all the time. She's a defence attorney's wet dream.'

'She has done well though,' Don says. 'A Cape Coloured woman to become a pathologist. That is an achievement.'

De Vries sighs.

'And a Muslim.'

'That's the problem, isn't it, in the new South Africa? She may have done well for someone from her background but she's still not as good as her white counterparts. So, what do we do? Patronize her that she's done okay, or judge her as we would anyone else?'

'Doctor Jafari has passed the exams. She has qualified?'

'The exams, yes. The new exams. Listen, Don, her achievement may be commendable but if she's useless to us, none of that really means anything. The system deteriorates, and it keeps deteriorating.'

Don glances at him.

'You think I'm politically incorrect? You should know: the colour of a man's skin means nothing to me, only how he does his job.'

'. . . Or her job?'

De Vries closes his eyes.

The room is white; sun coruscates through tall windows, bleaching thick white stripes, diamonds of shadow within them cast from the frames of smaller panes of glass. The woman is sitting up in bed, staring out of the window, her left eye bloodshot. She is naked, her nightdress torn to reveal her breasts and vagina. Her stomach is bruised; a scar runs down her thigh. Her expression is blank, mind seemingly empty, the look in her eyes hopeless. De Vries balks.

'Who the fuck would buy this?'

Don February shakes his head slowly, avoiding looking back at the canvas, and steps back from the gallery window.

'Something happened here.' De Vries gestures down the length of the shop-front. The final floor-to-ceiling window is missing and the space is boarded with plywood. In front of it, there are half a dozen refuse sacks; beyond them, broken glass across the pavement and in the gutter. He turns back to Don. 'Ring again.'

Don February presses the bell push once more. They hear nothing from within the darkened gallery.

De Vries looks across Bree Street. This top end of town is in the process of being gentrified: houses and flats are being developed, warehouses converted to offices; design shops and trendy bars form little courtyards. He turns back, cups his hands either side of his eye sockets and pushes his face against the window. Inside, the space is huge. He can just make out the subjects of the big canvases: more nudes. He turns away from the New Worlds Gallery, beckons Don to follow him across the road to the Bree Street Bakery.

At the door, they are welcomed by a young black waitress,

who offers them the choice of sitting inside or upstairs on the balcony above.

'It's shady?'

She nods, and De Vries lets her lead them to the upstairs balcony, which looks back over the road towards the gallery. They sit at a painted metal table set with autumn flowers, order two coffees. It is still far too hot for the time of year – an Indian summer of no end. When the girl returns with their order, De Vries shows her his ID.

'You know the woman who owns that place?' He points at the gallery.

'Taryn? Yes.'

'How well do you know her?'

'She comes here for coffee.'

'She there on her own?'

'No. There's a guy who works with her. Dominic. And a couple of other girls, but I don't see them often.'

'She ever come in here with anyone?'

The waitress considers for a moment.

'Not when I've been on duty. Maybe. I don't know. I've only spoken with her when she's come to take coffee away.'

He gestures across the street.

'Do you know what happened to the window?'

'Don't you?'

'No.'

The woman smiles.

'They opened that new exhibition on Wednesday. You know, with a party and . . . what do you call it . . . ? A private view, for all the rich buyers. But, there is a demonstration, because of the paintings. Have you seen them?'

De Vries nods.

'There is a women's group, and they were protesting . . . And some guy from the church in Saint Jerome Street. It was quiet enough at the start, but then more people arrived and they started singing and chanting and blowing their vuvuzelas. Some heavy guys came out of the gallery and there was a lot of shouting, and then somebody threw a stone, a brick, I don't know, at the window, and all hell breaks loose.'

'What happened then?'

'Your guys turn up . . . You don't know this?'

'Different unit. Did you see Taryn Holt?'

'No.'

De Vries nods at her name badge.

'That you?'

She looks down, smiles.

'Yes.'

'Dayo.' He seems to consider the name. 'Thank you. Before you go, the police: did they talk to you about the demonstration?'

'No.'

She checks both their faces, turns and walks away.

De Vries looks over to Don, silent but aware. De Vries is about to speak when Don says: 'Look, across the road.'

A man is unlocking the front door to the gallery. He slips inside when it is open only a crack and locks it behind him. They finish their coffee and De Vries glances at the little bill slip which came with them, snorts and leaves sixty rand on the saucer.

When they reach the gallery, the lights are still off and there is no sign of the man who entered. De Vries rings the bell, knocks on the glass door firmly. After a few moments, he sees a figure peer at them from the back of the shop. He holds up his ID, shouts:

'Police. Answer the door, please.'

As the figure approaches, De Vries sees that he is a man in his thirties, red-haired, sporting a goatee and a moustache with the ends twirled.

'Are you here about Taryn?' His voice is clipped, a pitch higher than De Vries was expecting. He takes the safety chain off the door.

De Vries says: 'Who are you?'

The man steps back, opens the door for them.

'Dominic van der Merwe. I worked with Taryn. I guess I was the manager here.'

'We need to talk to you.'

'I thought you might.'

He swivels, leads them to a long black desk at the rear of the gallery, gestures for them to sit, walks around it to face them. He presses a switch under the desk and three small lights glow in the ceiling, cast three crisp beams through the floating dust. It is not light which illuminates anything but small circles on the glossy surface of the desk. In the gloom, De Vries observes that the man's eyes are red, his face rigid.

'How did you discover the news, Mr van der Merwe?'

'After the incident on Wednesday night, I was worried about her. They were threatening her . . . Both of us . . . And, when she didn't answer her cell-phone this morning and then she didn't arrive here, I drove round to her house. I saw the scene, spoke to an officer.'

'Who threatened Ms Holt?'

'You know what happened here? We always hire extra security for a private view, because there are wealthy people who come here, park their expensive vehicles outside. On Wednesday, we knew there might be problems. We'd had the pictures up for two days and there were advertisements in the arts press. There'd been phone calls and discussions . . .'

'Who with?'

'I don't know. Taryn spoke to most of them. There were some people from the church in St Jerome Street, some feminists. They

35

saw the pictures, didn't understand them, thought they were attacking women, demeaning them.'

De Vries stands.

'We've only seen the one in the window.'

He walks away from the desk towards the nearest canvas. It is a domestic scene: a woman in a simple, old-fashioned kitchen, standing in front of a sink. She is naked; her black skin glows. On her ankle, there is a strange little box, a red light; De Vries thinks it looks like a control tag. Her ankles and her left wrist also bear signs of having been tied with rope or wire. There is something about her posture which is incredibly evocative: she is a prisoner.

He moves to the next painting. A large black African woman, her head bowed, is tied to a wooden chair, her arms behind her back, ankles tied to the legs. Her nose is bloodied. In the foreground are the backs and buttocks of several broad black men, their skin stained and dusty. Once again, the artist has somehow achieved expression from within the static pose of the woman; she seems empty, almost dead.

De Vries turns back towards the long black desk, but Van der Merwe is standing a few paces behind him.

'Who painted this work?'

'A Mozambican artist: Dazuluka Cele. She paints the exploitation of women in Africa.'

'Exploitation by who?'

Van der Merwe sniffs.

'Men, obviously. Whether it is centuries of tribal bigotry or the murder of Reeva Steenkamp. It makes no difference. Black or white or coloured. It is the plague of Africa.'

And, De Vries thinks, a rehearsed pitch.

'But other people saw the art differently?'

'They judged without knowing the story. I doubt any of them even know the artist is a woman.'

'Does that make any difference?'

Van der Merwe looks at De Vries, uncomprehending.

'Of course. If these pictures were painted by a man, they would mean something completely different.'

De Vries frowns.

'You think so?'

'Of course.'

'Tell me about Miss Holt's role in this gallery. She was the owner, but was she involved in the art?'

'Of course, yes . . .' Van der Merwe beckons De Vries to a giant spot-lit photograph of Taryn Holt, positioned in an alcove close to the gallery entrance.

'You don't know? Taryn was one of the biggest private bene-factors of art and artists in the country. It was her passion.'

De Vries studies the photograph. Taryn Holt is standing beside a brightly coloured canvas. She is wearing a plain full-length white linen dress, her long dark hair swept back from her forehead. She looks very beautiful; the lens loves her. She is smiling, yet there is a disconnect between the expression on her lips and that in her eyes. De Vries stares at her for a long while, discerns that it is the public smile of someone not happy. He wonders whether this is the emotion of the moment, or an enduring truth, poorly hidden.

Van der Merwe says: 'The ability of art to disseminate a mes-sage through the canvas. It is powerful. You can see . . .'

For a moment De Vries thinks he is talking about the photo-graph of Taryn Holt; then he realizes that Van der Merwe is looking at the painting adjoining it. He turns to the man.

'Can you identify any of the protesters on Wednesday night?'

'Only what I told the police officers at the time. A few of the women we had spoken with during the day, the priest from that church.'

'And, before this, had Miss Holt been threatened?'

'No.'

37

'Was there anyone who Miss Holt considered an enemy; any-one who might wish to harm her?'

Van der Merwe stares at the ground for a moment.

'No, I don't think so, but then I knew her here, at work, not in her private life. Taryn was outspoken. She wanted art to make a difference. She believed that it could. She was political and opinionated. Some people did not like that.'

'What people?'

Dominic van der Merwe shrugs.

'I didn't mean anyone in particular.'

De Vries turns away, looks towards the back of the gallery for Don February, but he is not there. Instead, he sees him midway down the far wall, staring up at another huge canvas.

'Sir?'

The tone of the single word carries weight. De Vries strides over to him, follows his gaze up to the painting.

The white woman is face up on a wide bed, her body riven with bullet holes. The blood has turned the surface of the mat-tress deep red. In her mouth, there is a big black phallus. The phallus is over-scaled and the impression of penetration is brutal. De Vries swallows, stands back from the canvas and looks back up at it. On the walls of the bedroom are pictures of young black men; each seems to look down on the victim, their mouths blank, but their eyes full of lust. Again, De Vries is struck by how the tiniest line of paint can convey so much.

'Photograph this,' he tells Don February in a whisper. He turns to Van der Merwe:

'Has this been here all week?'

'Yes. Everything was hung last weekend, with the artist. It is also in the catalogue.'

'I need a catalogue, then.'

He fetches a thick glossy brochure, hands it to De Vries.

'I need you to give Warrant Officer February contact details for the artist . . .'

'Dazuluka Cele . . .'

'Yes, her. And yours, Mr van der Merwe. Where were you yesterday evening?'

'In the Waterkant. Drinks with some friends. We ate at Anatoli's. After that, we went back to a friend's place, Jarvis Street. I stayed over. You want his name as well?'

'For the record . . .' De Vries begins to walk towards the front door. 'Will you re-open the exhibition?'

'I've been thinking. These pictures are about violence against women in South Africa, and that is exactly what Taryn has become. So I think so, yes.'

'And you could still sell some paintings . . .'

Dominic van der Merwe smiles sadly.

'I don't need to. They all sold within an hour. They fought about them out there, and they fought about them in here.'

De Vries stands at the broad table in his incident room, behind him a white board bearing photographs and printed details on the victim. Soon, there will be connections to suspects and other evidence but, for now, it remains predominantly white and empty. Don February is at his side; a further half-dozen officers stand around the table, notepads in front of them.

'To start,' De Vries says. 'We are likely to be without Brigadier du Toit for the duration of this case. So, I'm where the buck stops. If you want to go higher, you can go see General Thulani, but let's try to keep this in-house.'

De Vries knows that it is unlikely anyone would dare risk an audience with Assistant Deputy Provincial Commissioner Thulani, his reputation for disliking the Special Crime Unit hardly a secret, his office kept ice-cold to ensure the brevity of unwanted meetings. He looks up.

'What have we got?' He nods at Ben Thwala, a tall, broad black African officer, who has headed up the house-to-house enquiries.

'The neighbours did not see much of Miss Holt,' Thwala says. 'And only two remember seeing any visitors at any time. If she socialized, she did not invite any of them. The elderly gentleman at number twelve, across from the victim's house diagonally, says that he saw her occasionally leaving in her car, and that she was with a younger Caucasian man on several occasions. He could not give me a description. At number fourteen, there is a family with a teenaged daughter. She was not available, but her mother said that she had seen Miss Holt and that they regularly waved to one another. Otherwise, nothing specific, and nothing at all for the evening and night of Thursday second.'

Don February says: 'According to the gallery manager, Dominic van der Merwe, Miss Holt left the gallery on Thursday at approximately 7 p.m. and told him that she was tired and that she was going straight home.'

De Vries looks around the table.

'So, what we have so far places her at home that evening from, say, 7.15, 7.30 p.m.' He looks over to the one woman in the room. 'Sally?'

'Taryn Holt has a boyfriend of several years: a man called Lee Martin. He's English, a musician, aged thirty-three, been here for the last ten years and lives in a shared house in Woodstock. According to Taryn Holt's supposedly best friend, a Jessica Templeman, they never lived together. Taryn Holt liked being a free agent.'

'Were there other men?'

'I don't know. Miss Templeman claimed that she was Taryn Holt's confidant and that she didn't mention anyone else . . .'

'Any talk of personal or business problems, other threats?'

'None.'

'Any relatives?'

'Both parents deceased. No siblings. As far as I could make out, she didn't have any contact with family. There are no photographs at the house, no correspondence and, although we've only just begun on her cell-phone, no one who seems directly related.'

De Vries nods.

'All right. What do we know about the private view and party on Wednesday night?'

When no one answers, he turns to Don.

'Put someone on that. I want to know who in Metro dealt with it, whether Central Station sent men, and what they knew about the situation. We know about this women's group and the church in St Jerome Street, but we need to know who else was there and whether the subject matter of the art was the only reason there was a disturbance.'

He looks back around the table.

'Anything else? Okay, Don, do your thing. I'm in my office.' He looks back up at Sally Frazer. 'Sally . . . I want to ask you something.' He turns, walks to his glass-walled office and holds the door for her, closes it behind her. He slumps in his chair behind his desk.

'Jessica Templeman. What didn't you like about her?'

Frazer shakes her head, laughs.

'Who told you that?'

'You did. You said she was "supposedly" Taryn Holt's best friend, and that she "claimed" to be her confidant.'

Frazer tilts her head.

'She's not what you would call a sympathetic witness. I mean, I got the impression that she felt I was there to talk about her. I don't know what her relationship with Taryn Holt actually was. I think she bought art off her. Her cell-phone number was the third speed-dial after this Lee Martin and Dominic van der

Merwe – who I knew you were talking to – so I went after Templeman. I said what I said because it was what she said, and it just seemed odd, like she was eager to establish her credentials.'

She laughs. 'I'll be more careful what I say in future.'

De Vries sits up.

'No. What you've told me is what I want to know. I need officers who can form an impression and pass that on to me.'

'Then, good. You'll talk to her too?'

'Maybe. If she wants the attention, we'll give it to her.'

As Frazer leaves his office, a smartly suited man strides quickly across the squad-room towards De Vries's office. He greets De Vries with a firm handshake and nods at Don February, who has followed him into the office. He stands to the side of the desk, his hands placed on the surface.

'The boyfriend, a man called . . .' He looks down at a leather bound folder.

'. . . Lee Martin. He gets a good proportion of the estate. The house plus, ball-park figure, maybe seventy to eighty million cash.' Norman Classon looks up at De Vries and Don February. 'If the motive is money then this Lee Martin is your man.'

Classon is the Senior Attorney attached to the Special Crimes Unit, advising the department on legal matters. Usually, he joins an enquiry as charges are being prepared; De Vries wonders how he has become involved within hours of the start of the investigation.

'. . . English guy, been seeing each other for the last five years. Eighteen months ago, Taryn Holt changes her will to make him the biggest private beneficiary.'

'Does she?'

'Makes him interesting, I would say.'

'We're about to talk to Mr Martin,' De Vries says, glancing at Don February. 'Anything else?'

'The gallery is left to Dominic van der Merwe. She owned the freehold so it is not an insubstantial gift. Some pretty hefty bequests to art institutions. But, that's not really the interesting part.' Classon removes his glasses, studies the lenses, produces a silk handkerchief to wipe them.

'As I think you know, Taryn Holt inherited her father's company, Holt Industries, in 2009. His instructions were quite clear. His daughter was to have no involvement in the running of the company, and was prohibited from selling more than twenty-four per cent of the total company stock. That stock now passes to a trust held by those members of the board indicated within Graeme Holt's will. Taryn Holt's heirs do not get their hands on any part of the actual company.'

Don February asks:

'What is the significance of twenty-four per cent?'

Classon nods.

'Indeed, Warrant February. If Taryn Holt had realised the full twenty-four per cent of stock in Holt Industries, it would still have left her fifty-one per cent of the company. In other words, control remains within the Holt family, or with those who Graeme Holt specified. She was prevented from ever realizing the value of the remainder of her father's company.'

'Did she ever sell any stock?' Don asks.

'Another apposite question. No, she did not. But, apparently, she had made enquiries approximately three months ago about how she would go about the sale of stock if she wished to raise a capital sum.'

'And how much would that have been?'

Classon smiles down at Don.

'Something in the region of five hundred million rand.'

For several seconds, the enormity of the figure silences them.

43

'Why would she want a sum like that?' De Vries asks. 'What could she spend it on?'

'Not known . . .'

'Or not revealed?'

Classon smiles at De Vries.

'That was what Miss Holt's lawyer told me. He had been candid up to that point. I had no reason to doubt him then.'

'I don't believe him,' De Vries says.

'On what grounds?'

'It's my default position with lawyers.'

'I hope,' Classon says quietly, 'that doesn't extend to me?'

There is a discernible beat of silence. Then De Vries says:

'You certainly did well getting all of this so quickly.'

Classon raises his eyebrows.

'It seems that her lawyer had been instructed by the Holt Industries board to co-operate fully with our investigation. But, I agree, such access is . . . unprecedented. I went there to make an initial request. I didn't expect to be handed everything.'

'How did they know anyway?' De Vries says. 'She's not been dead twelve hours . . .'

'I suspect,' Classon replies, 'that an important company like Holt keeps a very close eye on its owner, even if she didn't have day-to-day control.'

'Who there benefits . . . ?'

'At Holt Industries? I can't tell you that.'

'Because you don't know?'

'Yes.'

'Who owns the remaining quarter of the company, sir?' Don asks.

Classon turns to Don.

'As far as I can see, it is shared between the founding partners and their families, most of whom have a representative on the board.'

De Vries says: 'Boardroom tensions?'

'Not as far as I could tell. I did ask. I, of course, am not a policeman.'

'No.' He stares at the lawyer. 'Anyway, well done on the information.'

Classon turns to face De Vries. 'You should know: Director du Toit wants me working this with you, in case things get tricky . . .'

'Things?'

'The case.'

'The case will always get tricky.'

'His exact words were that I was to "stick to you like a limpet".'

De Vries walks to his door, grabs the handle and turns back to Classon.

'Our roles are defined then, Norman. I am the rock; you are the limpet.'

On their way to Woodstock, a call directs them instead to a music venue in town; Lee Martin is rehearsing for a gig that evening. De Vries swoops down the Woodstock slip-road, takes a sharp right over the freeway and re-joins Nelson Mandela Boulevard travelling back into town. In the docks to their right, dwarfing the cranes and warehouses, a gargantuan oil rig is moored for servicing, a dominating industrial silhouette against the silvery opalescence of Table Bay. The mountain fires seem extinguished and once again the sky is deep blue, the temperature rising. The whole peninsula waits for autumn now; for the first rains to rinse the streets and damp down the mountainside. De Vries has his window open, his arm on the ledge, a cigarette burning brightly between two fingers. As they drop down towards the centre of town, he says:

'Have you heard of this place?'

'No.'

'Lived here all my adult life and I still don't know half of it.'

'It is probably new. Places open and close. Things change. Where is it?'

'St George's Cathedral,' De Vries says. 'In the crypt.'

He pushes around the near-stationary traffic, mounts the pavement. He stops in the dense shade of the pollution-stained trees right by the walls of the cathedral, flashes his ID at a perplexed traffic cop, leads Don towards the entrance.

The entrance to the crypt has not changed since De Vries had been here previously. The low Gothic vaulted ceiling encloses a small space displaying blown-up photographs of the famous peace demonstration which started out at the cathedral in 1989 and quickly swelled to many tens of thousands. It made headline news in many countries, and some were to come to see it as the true beginning of the end for the old regime. Both men slow their pace, glance at the images; they have meaning to both of them, though different for each man.

The Crypt music venue has twin glass doors leading on to a short staircase. Even down these steps, the space is only a lower ground floor rather than a true crypt and, through small leaded windows, the street outside can still be glimpsed.

There is no one at the bar, but two musicians on the little stage to their left hold guitars and talk in low voices. One is a tall, rake-thin black African, the other, a handsome white guy with thick curly black hair and a Mediterranean complexion. When they see the policemen, they stop, scrutinize them.

The white guy says: 'We're closed. Can we help you?'

De Vries holds up his ID.

'Lee Martin?'

'He'll be back just now.'

'And you are?'

'Davide Batisse,' and, nodding in the direction of the other man, 'Freddie Kokula.'

'You know why we're here?'

He watches them stiffen momentarily, consciously affect disinterest.

'No.'

'Better that way . . .' De Vries smiles to himself, wonders what they fear. He glances away from them at the sound of a door opening behind him, and sees a very slim, pale man approach from behind the bar area. He takes a step towards him.

'Mr Martin?'

The man nods, and De Vries gestures him away from the stage, towards an alcove table in the furthest corner of the venue. Lee Martin nods, somberly follows De Vries, who invites him to take a corner seat on the banquette. They face each other across the table; Don February stands a few paces away. The venue is small; De Vries speaks in a hushed voice and, even then, imagines his words bounce and echo around the room beneath its low stone arches and alcoves.

'You haven't told your musician friends?'

Martin pouts, shakes his head.

'How long had you and Taryn Holt been together?'

Martin hesitates.

'Maybe five years, but it's not how you think.'

'In what way?'

'This is why I don't talk about it . . .' He looks past De Vries to the stage. 'Who cares now? It doesn't matter.' He shrugs. 'Taryn didn't do relationships. We went out when it suited us. We behaved like a couple when that's what we wanted. Other times, we didn't see each other for weeks . . .'

'When did you last see Miss Holt?'

'Tuesday night. Night before her exhibition opening.'

'You didn't go?'

'No.'

'She ever come here?'

'No.'

'Did Miss Holt discuss with you about being afraid, being threatened?'

'I don't think Taryn ever felt threatened.'

De Vries ponders what Martin means, wonders whether this is a broader description of her character than merely the answer to his question.

'Where were you last night? Between 10 p.m. and 4 a.m.?'

Lee Martin looks down.

'At home. I practised until one of my housemates came in, maybe midnight, then I went to bed.'

'He, or she, see you?'

'We spoke, yeah.'

'And you didn't leave your house?'

'No.'

'You have a car?'

'No.'

'Did Taryn Holt have any other male friends?'

Martin smiles thinly.

'You mean lovers? Of course. That was the point. She didn't see any need to limit herself. When you are someone like her, with such potential and the energy to make it happen, why confine yourself? Why, even, get serious? Anyway, how was she ever to know who wanted her and who just wanted her money?'

'Did you want her money?'

Martin looks disgusted.

'That's a fucking nasty question.'

De Vries says nothing, does not break his stare.

'No, I didn't want her money. I loved Taryn for who she was, how she made me feel. I live in a crummy house in Woodstock with three other mates, drive a scooter ten years old. I've been with Taryn five years: you think if I wanted money, I wouldn't be doing a bit better than I am now?'

'She leave you anything in her will?'

'I've no idea.'

'Did you know the identity of these other boyfriends?'

'No.'

'It bother you?'

'If it did, I didn't have to stay . . .' Martin subsides, nodding gently. 'You took Taryn on her terms. She didn't want a full-time relationship; she didn't believe in monogamy. We were both free to do what we wanted, and we both knew that we had each other when the time came.'

'Every few weeks . . . ?'

'Sometimes. Sometimes every day for a week. That's what it was like.'

'No one you can think of who might wish her harm?'

'No.'

De Vries waits, but Martin says nothing.

'Speak to my Warrant Officer for a few moments, Mr Martin. He'll want the name of your house-mate who you spoke with, some other details. I hope we won't bother you again.'

Lee Martin stands shakily, holds out his hand. De Vries shakes it.

De Vries walks away towards the stage while Don asks his official questions. The two musicians have left and the venue seems deserted. He finds bars and clubs depressing in the daytime: none of the magic of lighting and music to transform the atmosphere from a gloomy lower ground floor room, hung with blue velvet curtains and painted a purple-ish black. He turns, leans against the back of a chair, observes Lee Martin from afar. He is not whom he expected Taryn Holt might go out with, even though he scarcely knows either of them. Martin is sickly pale, thin tattooed arms protruding from the short sleeves of a Fred Perry polo shirt, his jeans like drainpipes. But it is his face which intrigues De Vries; it is slender, with angular cheekbones, a narrow beak of a nose and thin lips. He strikes De Vries as an unattractive man; he makes him wonder what he gave to Taryn Holt.

Taryn Holt leaves him her property, millions of rand in her will. He is her prime beneficiary yet, by his own admission, he seems little more than a regular lover. De Vries ponders whether their relationship was more intense than Martin lets on, or whether her gifts illustrate that there is no one closer in her life than this unassuming man.

He observes their conversation, unable to hear more than an occasional word, and wonders whether Martin is capable of murder and then able to perform innocence so completely. He studies him again, follows the tattoos down his arms, which are stretched out over the table, to clenched hands. At each wrist, he sees a band of barbed wire in blue-green ink and, yet, there is something more. He stands, strolls around the venue and positions himself more closely, leans against a stone pillar. He squints at Martin, studies the marks, sees that around the tattoos, over them somehow, are bruises. He wonders whether to ask him about them, whether they could possibly be relevant, and decides not to.

When Don concludes his procedure, he and Lee Martin stand. Martin proffers his hand again. De Vries watches Don hesitate, and then shake. For a policeman, shaking a hand is to show respect to a suspect, and De Vries does not know whether this is Lee Martin's character or whether it is a ploy. Yet, both he and Don have shaken his hand. He wonders what this reveals about Martin, reveals about them.

★ ★ ★

When they are back in the car, attempting to join the gridlocked traffic at the Church Street junction, De Vries says: 'You'll make sure that's checked? The housemate?'

'Yes, sir.'

'What did you make of him?'

Don February lays down his notebook in his lap.

'I think that he was telling us the truth. You, sir?'

'Pretty much . . . When he said "we", he really meant "she".'

Don glances at him.

'"We" did what "we" wanted; "we" were a couple when "we" liked. I don't think that's how it was.'

'She was in control?'

'It seems that way. If she had other boyfriends, we need to know who they were. Call Sergeant Frazer and get her to check her e-mail, her cell-phone.'

'He said that he had not seen her much in the past few months. Does that suggest that she was in a relationship with someone else?'

'Possibly. Or she was just tired of him. He didn't go to her gallery; she didn't go to his concerts. What did they have in common?'

'Enough for her to leave him a lot of money in her will.'

'Yes . . .' They move off, negotiate two more sets of traffic lights before they are stopped again. Why, De Vries wonders, does an illicit affair within a marriage seem commonplace, almost normal, whereas a mutually agreed open relationship strikes him as peculiar?

Don February says: 'We can eliminate Lee Martin?'

'No.'

'What are you thinking?'

'You see his wrists?'

'The tattoos?'

'No. Not the tattoos. Bruises. Like his wrists had been tied.'

51

Don turns to him.

'I did not see that. The wounds were fresh?'

'Not wounds. Not recent. Almost like shadows. On both wrists. It made me curious.'

'You did not ask him?'

'No . . . What matters now is we tie down what time the housemate saw him and whether that leaves enough time for him to travel to Oranjezicht and back to be relevant.'

'You think he knew he would be in her will?'

'Fifty million is a motive right there. He's living in a shared house, has no money. But, if he did kill her, then he's very good.'

'Good?'

'I was watching him when you were talking to him. He seemed genuinely dazed.'

De Vries jams on the brakes behind a taxi-van which stops without warning. He then sits, indicator on, arm outstretched from the window until another driver lets him into the right-hand lane.

'There was one thing,' he says. 'Some of his behaviour was interesting. How he wanted us on his side. You notice?'

'His body language was open?'

'It was.'

Don tilts his head.

'The handshakes?'

De Vries smiles to himself. Don February, so unassuming he often seems not even to be present, and yet he spots things De Vries has never known another black officer to notice, or to appreciate.

'Yes.'

'I do not understand a man,' Don says vehemently, 'who would take a woman for five years and let her sleep with other men.'

'I don't think he was the one doing the letting.'

'But that is what I mean: it is not masculine behaviour.'

'No.'

'I asked him, at the end, when I had finished with the official questions: did he have other girlfriends . . .'

'He said "no"?' De Vries says.

Don looks at him. 'He said "no".'

'I thought so.'

At Katy's Bowl in Kloof Street, they pick up sandwiches and cold drinks, slide across town from the café to St Jerome Street, park fifty metres down from St Jerome's Chapel and Hall. They eat in a silence De Vries appreciates; it is his Warrant Officer's ability to say nothing that he cherishes. He considers the interviews with Dominic van der Merwe and Lee Martin, realizes that they have defined Taryn Holt more vividly than any number of reports. This is why he personally interviews everyone close to the victim; answers always lie in these interactions.

The hall adjoining the chapel is dark, the wooden doors locked. De Vries leads Don to the entrance porch of the chapel itself. As he pulls open the Gothic arch door, blue frankincense smoke floats past them and into the street.

The small interior is unlit, but for the pale coloured light from the dusty stained-glass panels set into the small, deep window holes, and the Virgin Mary surrounded by candles. The statue seems to hover in the smoke, the haloed candle flames burning points of light in the damp, heavy air. De Vries, who has not been in a church for many years, now finds himself in a second one within the hour. He innately mistrusts peddled stories, prides himself on knowing a liar; he has never heard one word from a pulpit in which he has faith. At least it is cool here.

PAUL MENDELSON

To the right of the altar, a door opens and a priest appears, straight white hair cut crudely above the collar, and bustles down the aisle toward them. Halfway down, he slows, narrows his eyes.

'What do you want?'

De Vries holds up his ID. The man stops and announces from afar:

'I've spoken to you people already. Our action was legal and just. I have nothing further to say.'

The tone is flat. It annoys De Vries.

'Taryn Holt is dead.'

De Vries senses his words travel through thick air, sees the priest recoil.

'Dead?'

'That is why we must speak with you.'

The priest walks slowly towards them, gestures to what looks like a school table and chairs in the corner at the back of the church. He sits first and waits for De Vries and Don to follow him.

De Vries says: 'Who are you?'

'I am Father Jacobus.'

He hears the priest's voice echo around the small chapel, made cold by the damp, thick air. He lowers his voice.

'You work here alone?'

'Apart from the lay volunteers, yes.'

'Did you know Taryn Holt personally? Before you were involved in the demonstration outside her gallery?'

The priest folds his fingers together and stares upwards.

'I did not.'

De Vries pauses, eager to hear what the priest might ask, but the man says nothing, his expression locked.

'Had you met her?'

'Last Monday. I visited her with representatives of the women's group who are based in the hall.'

'Where?'

'At her gallery. On Tuesday, at her home.'

'For what reason?'

'To demand that she cancel her revolting exhibition. To remove the offensive canvas from her shop window.'

'You found it offensive?'

Father Jacobus breathes in deeply.

'It is offensive.'

De Vries stares at him, scrutinizes the certainty in his expression. De Vries lives in a world of evidence and fact; he finds dogma inexplicable.

'What was Miss Holt's response?'

'Freedom of expression, human rights, artistic license. Pornography comes in many guises, and boasts myriad defenders.'

'This is artwork, sir. Paint on canvas. You can turn away if you do not like the subject.'

Jacobus leans forward.

'It is not always easy to turn away from evil. You should know that.'

De Vries stares at him a moment, smiles in the right-hand corner of his mouth.

'We have been told that the pictures were painted by a female artist, protesting against the mistreatment of women in Africa. Is that pornography?'

'The treatment of women is exaggerated. If you see what these African women who claim to be raped are wearing. Most are prostitutes or, if not, they are seeking sexual pleasure.' He flicks his wrist, dismissing the matter. 'In any case, the process behind the pictures is irrelevant; the images are an affront to God, disturbing to children and to all impressionable minds.'

De Vries finds Jacobus hubristic and pompous but represses the urge to challenge him, knows that he must not become distracted.

'Why did you speak with her twice?'

'I wanted to lodge a final plea. I went to her home, hoping that, alone, she might see reason . . .' He stares past De Vries, into the dark, small cavern of his church.

'Did you threaten Miss Holt?'

'Threaten? We do not threaten.'

De Vries raises his eyebrows. Jacobus continues:

'We explained that we would picket the gallery, attend the opening from the street, that our vigil would not be broken. That is what we did. Ours was a peaceful protest.'

'Apart from you and members of this women's group, who else demonstrated?'

'A few I did not recognize . . .'

'And did you hear threats or intimidation?'

'No.'

'Did you see who threw the brick which broke one of the gallery's windows?'

'No.'

'Did you see or speak to Miss Holt after talking with her at her home?'

'No.'

De Vries follows Jacobus's skewed focus, sees Don scrutinizing him.

'Did she invite you into her house?'

'She did. I did not sit. My reasoned request was quickly denied. I left.'

'You didn't return at a later stage?'

'That would have served no purpose.'

'How did you travel to visit her?'

Jacobus looks up.

'What do you mean?'

'How did you get to her house? Did you drive?'

'I walked.'

'From here?'

Jacobus nods. De Vries wonders how far from Taryn Holt's house they might be now, wonders how much higher Jacobus would have had to climb. It seems a strange lie to tell.

'This women's group: it is part of this church?'

'Some of their members worship here. Others not. I provide moral and spiritual guidance to those in need.'

'They attended these demonstrations as individuals or as a group?'

'Four women run the group. They were offended by those paintings and appalled that anyone could walk in off the street to view them. Those who chose to join them did so.'

'When does this group meet?'

'Every week day. From 2 p.m. One of the conveners will open up the hall . . .' He reaches inside his robes and produces a small, gold pocket watch. 'Any minute now.'

'You didn't see Taryn Holt again after your meeting?'

'That woman lacked a moral compass; she showed no respect for her fellow human beings. We reached out to her but she spurned us . . .'

'No, then?'

'No.'

De Vries waits, but the priest says nothing more.

'Where were you last night between 10 p.m. and 4 a.m.?'

'You ask me that?'

'I ask anyone who might be a suspect that question.'

'Do you people understand who I am; who I represent?'

De Vries leans over the table at the priest.

'If you think that because you work in here, you wear dark clothes and pray to a god I do not believe in, that somehow exempts you from suspicion, you are wrong. Answer my question, Father Jacobus.'

De Vries observes contempt and anger in the man's face; he smiles inwardly.

'I was at prayer here until 10.30 p.m. I locked the church and returned to my home, four houses along the road. That is my ritual, every day.'

'And you didn't leave your home?'

'No.'

'Can anyone verify that?'

Jacobus sneers at him.

'Obviously not.'

De Vries nods, glances over his shoulder; Don February stands still and silent. He gets up and, without acknowledging the priest, lets himself out through the church door. When Don joins him on the street, he says:

'You see why I don't like these people, Don?'

'I understand you do not have faith . . .'

'We tell that man of god that Taryn Holt is dead and he asks us nothing. Instead, we have to listen to his opinion.' He begins to walk away down the street, arms swinging; turns back: 'He talks about morality, but these people, Don, these people, they fucking revolt me. Doesn't matter which fucking religion it is. They always know best and it's not enough for them to live their own lives the way they believe, they have to make others do the same, and if we don't we're condemned.'

Don says: 'He is in denial about the problems in our country.'

'I think he lied about walking to Taryn Holt's house.'

Don says quietly: 'I think he lied later too.'

De Vries walks up to him, his face close to Don's.

'When?'

Don takes a step back. Amidst his boss's mood changes, he protects his own territory. He has learnt that this is the way to operate.

'When he said that he had not heard any threats; when he did not know who had thrown the brick at the gallery.'

De Vries nods minutely.

'You did not see this, sir?'

'I wasn't watching as I should. I was too busy disliking him.'

Taryn Holt's body is uncovered, five entry wounds on her torso, the holes clean and dark and deep. Her mouth is open, empty.

Doctor Anna Jafari says: 'You can see everything there is. Five shots. No defensive wounds, no sign of movement or molestation post-mortem. She was shot where she was found, fell backwards probably from the impact of the first shot, and then shot a further four times.'

De Vries sees two holes on the left side of her chest, a third on the right side, the final two lower on her abdomen.

'Unless toxicology produce something, cause of death is simple and obvious. There is no alien material about her person. She had bathed earlier in the evening.'

'Can you narrow the time of death?'

'I will state that it occurred between 11 p.m. on Thursday evening and 1 a.m. on Friday morning. I can't be more specific.'

'Why not?'

'Because there are extenuating factors and, considering our professional history, Colonel de Vries, if I am required to testify in court, I would be unhappy moving to a narrower time-frame.'

'But, if it was off the record, would you favour the earlier or later time?'

'I would favour what I have just told you.'

De Vries sighs.

'What about what was in her mouth.'

'I extracted it and sent it to Dr Ulton in the laboratory here. It was inserted post-mortem, almost certainly within minutes of her death, since the throat constricts quickly post-mortem, and there was no sign of force or trauma.'

'What was it?'

Anna Jafari looks at him blankly.

'Twenty-four centimetres.'

De Vries gags on a smart line, stays silent.

'But I have not finished with the bullet wounds. The weapon was a nine millimetre; Dr Ulton has identified the bullets and suspects that they were shot from a Beretta, fitted with what seems to be the standard silencer. It is not clear whether she was standing when she was first hit, but it is certain that each shot was taken at a different range . . .'

'The shooter approached her firing?'

Jafari hesitates.

'That is a possible explanation. Perhaps I can explain?' She produces a silver ballpoint pen, points at the five entry wounds in turn. 'This shot is from the furthest range, probably about six metres. From the killer's point of view, it is perfect. This shot punctured the heart and caused it to explode. Death would have been instantaneous. This is the shot responsible for most of the scattered matter discovered at the scene. It is possible that she had expired seconds previously, but it would be reasonable to assume that this was the kill shot, the cause of death.' She leans forward and points at the shot on the other side of her chest. 'This shot was taken at approximately four metres from the victim. This one from perhaps three metres, this at two metres and, this final shot . . .' She indicates the entry hole just to the right of the likely kill wound. 'This entry wound suggests that the shot was taken at virtually point-blank range, perhaps thirty centimetres – you can see scorching at the perimeter of the entry wound.'

De Vries stares at the fluorescent tube above the table, lets the image go out of focus.

'The killer shoots her from six metres out – which puts him in the doorway to her bedroom . . . Then he moves towards her, shoots four further times . . .' He looks up, turns to Don February. 'I can see that.'

Don says: 'Why fire four further times when your first shot is fatal?'

De Vries shrugs.

'Perhaps you don't know for certain . . . ?'

'Doctor Jafari,' Don says, bowing minutely at the pathologist, 'told us that her heart exploded, that there was blood and organ matter exploding from her body. She would have gone down instantly.'

'If you are angry, you keep shooting . . .'

'You are assuming,' Jafari interrupts, 'that the shot from the furthest range was the first. It is possible that the killer was walking away from his victim.'

De Vries turns to Don February and back to her.

'Why?'

'It's not my job to speculate, Colonel. But, to me, it is a mistake not to consider all possibilities unless excluded by the evidence. All five shots were taken within a very few seconds, but it is unproven which shot was first.'

Don says: 'Maybe the killer crept into her room, saw her sleeping but, when he saw her waking up, began to shoot while retreating . . . ?'

'No,' De Vries says quickly. 'We think that she was standing at the end of her bed, perhaps sitting, but shot where she was. She wasn't *in* bed, and she wasn't sleeping.' He looks up at the pathologist, continues dryly: 'With respect to Doctor Jafari, it may not be proven, but we can say that it is very likely that the killer approached as he shot.'

Jafari blinks slowly.

'I will conclude my report. Doctor Ulton's team may choose to attempt a sequence with trajectory information. That is not my concern.'

'So,' Don February says. 'It seems that the killer was a good shot with his first bullet, not so good with the next three, and tried to kill his victim a second time with his last. That does not make sense.'

De Vries smiles at them both.

'No. And that's the first good news we've had.'

The woman sits. When she first saw them, she spoke curtly and continued laying out the seats in neat rows, adjusting them minutely, unnecessarily. Now, she looks at the white officer, fixes him with her eyes, knows what effect she will have.

De Vries hopes that the women's group is more welcoming to women.

'My name is Brenda Botes,' she tells them. 'I am one of the organizers here. Father Jacobus told me that you would be coming back.'

'We need to talk to you about the art exhibition, about what happened to Taryn Holt.'

'I am sorry about Taryn Holt. I am not sorry that the door is closed on her vile display.'

'The exhibition?'

'When you have been raped and abused,' she says, 'imprisoned as a slave in your own home, you do not need art to tell you that men can be cruel, can be evil even to their own wives.'

'You thought the pictures were art?'

'I thought they were exploitation.'

She pushes herself back into the orange plastic chair and tries to cross her legs. When this manoeuvre fails, she sits upright and plants her feet flat on the floor.

De Vries continues: 'Did you speak personally to Taryn Holt?'

'I went with the other ladies. When you join us here, you become part of our group. The strength is within the group; we fight for each other.'

'You approached her before the demonstration?'

'We went with Father Jacobus. We were there for different reasons but with the same aim.'

'To prevent the exhibition from opening?'

'To warn her.'

'Warn her?'

She pats her tight bun of brown hair; it is immovable.

'To explain . . . That the group would fight her; that we would not allow her to demean us.'

'How would the exhibition do that?'

'Have you seen it? Have you seen those pictures?'

De Vries speaks quietly, hoping that it will calm her.

'The painting in the window is striking, but not overtly graphic. You would have to enter the gallery to see the more . . . controversial images.'

'That is what I am saying. Our group was afraid that people would see those awful paintings and be offended, that it would reawaken memories that they are fighting to forget.'

'But you don't have to look at them . . .'

'But they can be seen. You could walk in and be confronted by them.'

De Vries opens his mouth and closes it again. He takes a breath.

'Your group; it consists of the women who meet here?'

'Yes, but we have affiliates all over the Cape. We have influential backers: professional women. We have attorneys and doctors, journalists and councillors. We have to make our voice heard.'

'And how many of you visited the gallery on the night the exhibition opened?'

Brenda Botes posits a thoughtful expression.

'Maybe eight of us.'

De Vries shakes his head; eight scandalized women.

'But there were others there?'

'A few people. I didn't know who they were. I didn't care. I was glad to see them with us.'

63

'Did you hear anyone threaten Taryn Holt?'

'At the demonstration, we were angry. Her rich, protected guests would not even look at us. This is how it is in our country now: you do not like something, you pretend not to see it; you will it not to exist. None of them spoke with us, and Taryn would not come out to speak with us. Instead, she sent out men to frighten us away.'

'Who called the police?'

'They were there already. When her security guards came out, they appeared from their cars across the way. A tall black officer and about six or seven other officers. Like they were waiting for trouble.'

De Vries frowns.

'What did they do?'

'They told us that we were causing a disturbance, blocking the highway, and that we had to disperse. It was nonsense. We were on the pavement and we were obstructing nobody.'

'Did you visit Taryn Holt's home?'

'No.'

'Before or after that night?'

'No. The group decided that she should be confronted at the gallery.'

De Vries uncrosses his legs, hesitates.

'I thought those pictures were supposed to highlight crime against women in Africa. Wouldn't you sympathize with that aim?'

She snorts.

'The artist who painted those pictures painted them to sell. She painted blood and penetration, naked men and women. She might want you to believe that they contain a message, but they don't. She and Taryn Holt knew what would sell for big bucks and that's what she went away and painted.' She looks scornfully at De Vries. 'Our group know about the art scene in Cape Town and we know that Taryn Holt was not liked. She may have given some money in grants and sponsorships, but she made damn sure she made it back again with interest. She had those artists tied to her for as long as she wanted.'

'You have had dealings with her before?'

'I had my opinion of her.'

'You didn't like her?'

'Not very much, no.'

De Vries gets up, glances at Don.

Don February gets out of his chair and squats down next to her.

'Can I ask you? Miss Holt: had she visited you here?'

Brenda Botes leans away from him, squeezes the word from her lips.

'Yes.'

'She was a member of your group?'

'She would not abide by the wishes of the majority.'

Don nods. He squats lower, so that she is looking down at him, even from her sitting position.

'But she joined you? Why did she come?'

Brenda Botes drops her head.

'I cannot tell you that.'

'But, Miss Holt is dead. Was she a victim?'

'She said she could not trust men, that they exploited her. But, when we got to know her, the group agreed: she was no victim.'

'Why did you think that?'

'She did what she wanted.'

'And you do not?'

'Do not? Can not. This is the fate of many women.'

'So she left?'

She folds her arms.

'She was asked to leave.'

'Was there bad feeling between her and your group?'

'She had promised money for the group. She withdrew it. Taryn Holt was never really part of our group; she was only interested in herself.'

Don nods at her, smiles, turns to De Vries, whose gaze seems out of focus.

'Then,' he says quietly, 'we will leave you.'

'How,' De Vries says as he opens the car door, 'did you know that Taryn Holt had been part of that set-up?'

They both get in.

'I did not know, but Miss Botes referred to her as Taryn. It was familiar in a way that she was not otherwise.'

'Very good.'

'You think that they could pose a threat? That group?'

'No. I think it is a few women who are afraid and they come together to hold each other's hands.'

De Vries nods, pulls out from the parking space, smirking.

'Even so, it seems you wouldn't want to be on the wrong side of the group?'

Don smiles.

'No, sir.'

De Vries drives up Vineyard Street, which climbs the mountain close to Kirstenbosch Botanical Gardens. It is 4.30 p.m., and he steers between the steady trickle of descending domestic workers: broad-hipped black housemaids in bright colours, leaning back to balance on the gradient; skinny coloured handymen in tight scruffy suits smoking roll-ups; and blue-boilersuited garden workers, encrusted with lawn clippings. All retrace this morning's climb, descend to the short stretch of Rhodes Drive, trudge up the main freeway towards the university and wait in a lay-by for a taxi-van to take them home to their township of Langa or Khayelitsha or Mfuleni.

He changes down a gear to take the sharp left turn and makes the vertiginous climb onto Vineyard Heights, locking eyes with a haughty ginger cat, which freezes with its paw raised to its mouth on the bonnet of a parked car, freewheels down to the end of the cul-de-sac, parks by the plain white wall of John Marantz's house.

John Marantz and he have been friends for almost ten years. Marantz worked for the British government until someone kidnapped his wife and daughter. He has never seen them since. De Vries and Marantz have drunk together, seeking salvation in oblivion. De Vries came to this house to avoid his own – his driven, demanding wife and ambitious daughters; now he is here because he is alone.

He pats Marantz's Irish terrier, Flynn, and hears his quadraphonic footsteps behind him as the lithe dog overtakes them both on the inside down the long staircase.

'What,' De Vries says at the bottom landing, 'do you know about Holt Industries?'

John Marantz gestures into his kitchen, to a perfectly straight line of six bottled beers on the marble counter.

'Nothing until I read Taryn Holt had been killed. You got that case?'

'*Ja.*'

Marantz smiles to himself.

'You get where the action is, don't you?'

'Nowhere else to go . . .'

'Holt Industries was a product of the old South Africa. Graeme Holt built his companies on the back of the Apartheid regime and the cheap labour market, expanded it throughout Southern Africa. The Nationalist government backed him and he supported them: as a growing business in an otherwise shrinking economy, and personally . . .'

67

'I thought you said you knew nothing about this . . . ?'

'It's what I was trained to do.'

De Vries levers open a bottle of East Coast Ale, tips it gently into the waiting glass. Marantz watches him. When his family was taken, and the service in London prohibited him from seeking them, he exiled himself to Cape Town to build a house and drink. He drank with De Vries for four long years, marvelled at how De Vries would be at work early the next morning, functionally sober, while he would stay in bed until mid-afternoon, when he would begin again. Now, he sips Dry Lemon and pale, weak cordials, smokes ganja, sleeps when he is not playing poker or following De Vries's cases, happy to fight battles at the green baize and involve himself in De Vries's mysteries.

'I'm still not used to you being a beer drinker.'

De Vries says: 'My life in alcohol: brandy and coke is an emotional drink; you end up angry, or you end up crying. White wine is basically piss and the red was killing me. You know I have an internal gauge that gets me to work in the morning? The Cabernets were fucking it up. Besides, as I get older, I get thirstier: this works better.'

They walk from the kitchen into the huge triple-height living space looking out over what are usually lush green suburbs close to the Mountain, beyond to the poor suburbs, townships and squatter camps on the Cape Flats and, in the far distance, the Hottentots Holland Mountains and the thin sliver of silver sea at Strand and Gordon's Bay. The fires have been burning on those mountains on and off since the beginning of the year.

'What else do you know?'

'About Holt?'

'Ja.'

'He was very vocal about what he called "De Klerk's capitulation": the decision to release Mandela, to dismantle Apartheid and hold elections. After the ANC came to power, he spent more time outside South Africa, rarely came back. Married once, one daughter – Taryn Holt. Now, they're all dead: the mother, the father and the daughter. Mother had leukemia, but Graeme Holt's death was suspicious: a collision, but the other car was never identified. And now, Taryn Holt . . . Murdered, I assume?'

De Vries snorts.

'How did you know this?'

'I told you: a news story online, some research. You know I dealt in information.' He looks down. He knows his wife and daughter must be dead, yet questions this every moment he thinks of them. There has never been confirmation, never closure. He feels the blood draining from his head. He ducks it between his legs. 'That's why, to have none for myself, it's still agony.'

'You need to get out . . . And, I don't mean those illegal fucking poker games. I mean out-out. Meet some girls, think about the next part of your life.'

'That what you're doing?'

'Never was a time when I didn't, Johnnie. Life is short. Take pleasure where you can.'

Marantz takes a sip of Dry Lemon, looks up.

'Taryn Holt: love or money?'

'I don't know . . . But I hope to God it's one of them.'

Don February rings the bell at the gate to 14 Park Terrace, opposite Taryn Holt's house. It buzzes open, and Don walks up the narrow path to the front door. The small garden is immaculate, lawn green and mown, bright bedding planted in neat rows. The front door opens as he reaches the little covered porch. He holds up his ID, and the short black woman in an apron squints to study first it and then him.

'You want to talk to my mistress?'

69

The words 'master' and 'mistress' make Don uncomfortable, remind him of how his mother would talk about her employers; he longs for those times to be nothing more than history. He is over ten years short of being a 'born-free' – an African born free of Apartheid – but in his adult life, however he chooses to present himself, he has always believed that he is the equal of the next man in the Cape Town street.

'Yes, please.'

'You wait here.'

When she closes the door, he can hear her footsteps scurry over the wooden floor, a muted exchange, and then a slim, white, middle-aged women pulls open the door, looks down at him.

'We have already spoken with you.'

'You have, madam. But when my colleague talked with you, your daughter was not available.' He looks at his notebook. 'You said that she knew your neighbour, Miss Holt.'

The woman frowns.

'Lorna does not know her. She may have seen her from her window . . . You may come in, but she is doing her homework. You must be quick.'

Don wipes his feet on the mat, steps up over the threshold into the dark hallway. The house smells both damp and clean, cool and somehow musty. The woman leads him to the back of the house, through an old fashioned kitchen and into a dining room. Three small windows overlook a tiny yard at the back, a grandfather clock ticks against the side wall, a teenaged girl sits bent over the long, dark dining table, sheets of paper lined up across the width of the surface in front of her. She is writing and does not look up when they enter the room. Her mother says nothing, waits for her to finish. When she does, she looks first at her mother and then at Don.

'This man wants to ask you about Miss Holt.'

'Miss Holt has passed on.'

Her speaking voice is staccato, mechanical.

'I am Don February.'

She stands up. He offers his hand, but she steps back and looks him up and down.

'What is your rank?'

'I am a Warrant Officer.'

The girl looks up at her mother, says: 'That is the same as an Inspector.'

'Yes,' Don says, 'that was what my rank used to be called.'

'Why are your clothes too big?'

Don stutters.

'I am . . . I suppose, because I am only small.'

'Then you should have small clothes.'

'Lorna,' the austere women says. 'Why don't you let the police-man ask his questions, then you can finish your work.'

Lorna looks from her mother to Don.

'Let me check your identification.'

Don produces his ID and passes it to her. She does not reach to take it, so he leaves it on the table in front of her. She sits back down, opens it, studies it. Don waits, hears the clock, looks around the room at the dark oil paintings, the deep turquoise velvet on the dining chairs, the ornate crucifix above the dark Victorian fireplace.

'What do you want to ask?'

'I want to ask you if you saw Miss Holt.'

'I saw her from my window, often.'

'Last Thursday night, did you see her then?'

'No.'

'When did you last see her?'

'On Wednesday night at 10.35 p.m.'

'You remember the time?'

'Yes.'

Don tilts his head; he does not doubt her.

'What was she doing?'

'She drove into her garage. I saw her in her car, but her window was closed.'

'Was there anybody else in her car?'

'No.'

'Did you see anything else?'

'There was a man waiting in a car on this side of the road. When she had gone in, he went to the door and rang on the bell. The front door opened and he went in.'

'Can you describe this man?'

'Black. He was a black man.'

'Anything else?'

'Only the police. Every day.'

'I meant, about the black man.'

'He was taller than you.'

'How tall?'

The girl hesitates.

'Taller than Miss Holt. He was on the step in front of her door. I could see them when they were both inside.'

'Anything else?'

'No. What have you found?'

'We have been investigating.'

'Have you caught the killer yet?'

'No, not yet.'

'No . . . Can I see your notepad?'

'I . . . I don't think so. It is for private notes only.'

Lorna pushes Don's ID towards him across the table.

'I am working now. Goodbye, Warrant Officer Donald February.'

She ducks her head, picks up a pencil and studies the page in front of her.

Don looks at her a moment longer, turns away. Lorna's mother gestures for him to follow her back to the hallway. The maid opens the front door.

'You have a very pretty daughter,' Don tells the woman.

'I hope,' she says, 'that this will be your last visit. If you must come again, telephone first. Lorna works on routine, and it is best not to break it.'

She turns and walks away from him. Don walks through the door, and turns to the maid. The front door closes firmly.

The light is fading by the time De Vries travels back into town. From De Waal Drive, he can see down to the docks, the Waterfront and the CBD. On the lower freeway into town, cars are backed up, locals and tourists coming into town at the start of the weekend. Lion's Head and Signal Hill are silhouetted against a phosphorescent dusk sky. Although he knows of all the ugliness on the streets, the evil which lurks in the private homes and squatter camp shacks, he still loves his city; wouldn't live anywhere else in South Africa.

He strides into his squad-room. A small group of officers are still at work. He stands in front of the whiteboard to see what further information has been accrued. Sally Frazer walks over and stands by his side.

'I'm only halfway through her cell-phone numbers. She has over a hundred and almost none of them answer our call. I'm hoarse from talking to voicemail . . .' She sniffs the air. 'A few beers, sir?'

'Liquid dinner, Sergeant.'

'Most of them seem to be artists, agents, galleries and work contacts. I've got a couple of male names I can't identify yet, but I will.'

'Good.'

'Anything to add for us on here?' She gestures at the still largely empty whiteboard.

'*Ja*. I'll type them up. None of them liked her very much, even the official boyfriend. Woman with a strong personality, liked to get her way. No one likes them.'

Sally Frazer turns to him, sees he's smiling. She says: 'I don't care what she was like.'

'Nor do I.'

'Your timing is spot on, Vaughn.'

Steve Ulton's forensic laboratory is small, very neat, dimly lit. The vast majority of forensic work gets sent to various labs within the province either through the slow official system or fast-tracked through private companies but, for the Special Crimes Unit, the work is prioritized in-house under the control of Ulton and two fellow supervisors.

He faces De Vries, says: 'Drinking mid-shift?'

De Vries scowls.

'What the fuck is this: the dog pound? I've never known so many sensitive noses. After being on duty for twelve solid hours, I had one beer.'

Ulton glances quickly at his wristwatch, silently disputing De Vries's timing, and picks up his clipboard, all business.

'I'll start with what we saw at the scene. I liaised with Doctor Jafari, and we're in agreement that the shot from the furthest range was the one that caused all the mess. I can try to calculate the exact distance if you want, but I don't think it'll tell you much. The angle suggests that the victim was standing and the shooter was in the doorway. Because of the damage, I don't think we'll get an accurate trajectory on that first shot, and any analysis of the subsequent ones is compromised because she would have been sprawled on the bed.'

'So we don't get any idea about the height of the killer?'

'I don't think so.'

'Anything special about the ammunition?'

'No. Completely standard. As I said, we found no casings, but we've studied the bullets removed from the body and from the bed, and there are defining firing striations so we'll be able to match it to the weapon, but we need it first.'

'You talked about a silencer?'

'It looks like that, and not a makeshift one either. Fitted the weapon.'

'You got my message about the outside pathway? You checked outside access to the terrace?'

'We did. There are footmarks – opposed to prints – nothing we can use. Someone has climbed up the rocks by the path and probably reached the terrace area. Could have been last night; could have been previously. Might be the gardener for all I know. There's nothing there to narrow it down, but there is disturbance.'

De Vries takes a deep breath. His meetings with Ulton are never as helpful as he thinks they will be.

'Tell me about the rubber dick?'

'Not my area of expertise, but I sent one of the guys up the road to the Adult Fantasy shop off Long Street. It sells as a novelty called 'Bestial Pleasure'. Big, muscular black guy with red horns on the packaging. All their branches sell it. Taiwanese manufactured; thousands imported into South Africa every year.'

'Anything at all to cheer me at the end of another long day in the beautiful Mother City?'

'I mentioned this morning that I wasn't convinced that the terrace door had been tampered with from the outside. I've refined my opinion. The door could have been opened from the outside, but only because the mechanism had been compromised, and that definitely took place from inside the house.'

'I don't understand.'

75

'Either the door developed a fault over time or it was tampered with, but, with the minimum of skill, it could be prised open from the outside. It is possible that someone played with the mechanism from the inside, hence allowing access at a later date.'

'So the killer, or his accomplice, could have been inside the house on a previous occasion?'

'That would make sense . . .' Ulton takes off his spectacles and wipes his face with the sleeve of his white coat. 'It's not immediately obvious from inside, either. It could have been like that for days, even weeks.'

'So we may have to look even further back. What about the alarm?'

'Okay, this is interesting. On the floor, next to the victim's bed, we found a remote-control unit for the alarm system. It's probably because there are movement sensors throughout the house. If, in the middle of the night, the owner wanted to go to the kitchen, say, she could temporarily disable this system and she would be able to go there and then re-activate it when she was back in her room.'

'But she was in her room. Why would she switch off the alarm?'

'That's what I was thinking about, so I looked at it again. Under the microscope it's clear that the unit has been extensively handled with gloves. I found the unit and I've checked no one else touched it. I picked it up by its sides and bagged it. The depression and rubbing marks which are present don't come from us, so that makes me think that someone else has been handling it – after Taryn Holt – over her existing prints.'

'Someone else examined it wearing gloves before you?'

'Look,' Ulton says. 'If my guys say they didn't touch it, I'm sure they didn't. I think someone *used* it wearing gloves.' He straightens up to face De Vries. 'Let's speculate: the alarm is disabled by the killer using the remote which perhaps he has taken previously. He gains entry to the house through the faulty window mechanism and then replaces the remote unit in the bedroom.'

De Vries narrows his eyes, tilts his head.

'Can we prove that?'

'No. But, it's a theory which might explain what I found on the unit and how the killer beat the alarm.'

'So, if that's right,' De Vries says, 'we don't have that wide a window of opportunity after all. Surely she would have missed the remote control?'

'Yes and no. I guess if she set the alarm from the main panel by the front entrance and didn't have need of the remote, she might not have missed it for a few nights.'

'Does the alarm system note the times when it was primed and deactivated?'

Ulton smiles.

'No. Does just about everything else but not that. That's more typical of commercial applications . . .'

'But he'd have to know about the remote, wouldn't he? That suggests that he's been in her bedroom, at the very least.'

'I don't think that's right,' Ulton says thoughtfully. 'We didn't find any other remote units in the house, so she could easily have taken it into other rooms. If she was watching television, for example, she could set it to guard the perimeter but then, if there was someone at the door, she could use it to switch off the system.'

'Why not use the main control panel?'

'I don't know. Ease, I guess. It's to hand.'

'But then we're back to the fact that she would have missed it sooner rather than later.'

'Yes, I guess that's right.'

'So, what have we got?' De Vries says. 'A working hypothesis:

the killer knows about the remote control, takes it, sabotages the terrace door and then re-enters the house last night between 11 p.m. and 1 a.m. He leaves the alarm disabled to allow him to leave the property. The maid sees the door open in the early hours and calls us . . .'

'It seems a sensible theory.'

'It's something.' De Vries proffers his hand. 'Thank you, Steve. I think we're looking for someone known to Taryn Holt who had been in her house in the preceding . . . say, three or four days.'

'Agreed, but you have almost no forensic help. It's still early, but we haven't found anything obvious that doesn't belong there.'

'If we're on the right track, we likely won't, because he – assuming it is a he – will have been there before, so nothing can tie him specifically to the time of the crime . . . But this points in one direction: a boyfriend. And, surely, there can't have been that many?'

As De Vries pauses in the road, waiting for his double gates to grind their way open, he sees her waiting in her car, fifty metres down the street; he feels his heart sink, breath shorten. He pulls onto the driveway, exits his car and walks back through the open gates. She is just slamming her car door. De Vries mutters under his breath. The deal had been clear, the terms explained: no strings, no promises; she had seemed to understand.

'What's the matter?'

She saunters up the road to him, smiles.

'Not pleased to see me?'

He hesitates, senses her self-confidence; he fears the emotional battle ahead, from which he has sought to free himself.

She laughs.

'Your face, man. It's a picture. I'm not here for your body. I left my lighter . . . I hope I left my lighter here. I've looked everywhere else and it was from Dickie: one of the few things he let me keep.'

De Vries tries to laugh at himself, but there is relief in his exhalation and he knows that she has sensed it. He leads her back onto the driveway, closes the gates with his remote and opens the front door of the house. He reflects that their silence now is in contrast to the noise they made two nights previously.

'I'm on a case. My mind is full.'

'Don't apologize.'

They walk into the hallway.

'Where do you think?'

'I can visualize it: on the shelf under your coffee table. I was kneeling on the floor, saw it, picked it up and slipped it in there . . . I think.'

De Vries blushes.

He met Pamela at the Forrester's Arms, let her lure him out of the dark wood-panelled bar into the evening-sun lit garden, where they talked about their married lives, stayed for *braaied* supper, each posted a nonchalant self-confidence devoid of neediness, and went home to his house. Now that his desires are empty of emotion, he is fearless in approaching women and confident in their company, so different from the stuttering, incompetent dating of his youth. She has visited him maybe five times and, each time, the sex is better.

She heads directly to the living room, pushes aside some magazines and retrieves the large gold lighter in the shape of the spirit of ecstasy on the bonnet of a Rolls Royce. She waves it at him.

He allows himself a smile.

'You want a glass of wine?'

'Why?'

79

De Vries shrugs.

'One for the road?'

'There's no point, Vaughn. I don't need to be wooed. You want to see me again: you have my cell number. We both know what we want. Let's not complicate it.'

Now De Vries laughs. She waves a finger, mock-scolding: 'You guys. You think you're the only ones who want what you want.'

She pockets the lighter, comes up to him and kisses him on the lips.

'Not that you even know what you want.'

She smiles at him again, strides to the front door and opens it. De Vries follows her, opens the gates with his remote, watches her walk quickly away from him; he wonders how she knows what he doesn't know himself.

Saturday morning dawns grey with bright slashes of white sun. As he rounds Hospital Bend, he sees the peak of Lion's Head clear of cloud. No rain yet, but Capetonians will welcome even some cloud cover. The water in the docks is choppy and matt.

De Vries has fought frustration to find sleep. As he closed his eyes, he remembered the painting in the gallery which seemed to foreshadow Taryn Holt's murder, and could then think of nothing else. At 6 a.m. he sent an SMS to Don February to set up a meeting with the artist. He has received no reply.

He drops down through the centre of Cape Town, swings into the underground garage, sees the receding figure of David Wertner, the head of the Internal Investigation Unit, who scrutinizes everything he does and has done, seeking a transgression significant enough to bring about his downfall. It reminds him that he – and his unit under Henrik du Toit – are unwelcome in the new, sanitized SAPS. Where there are old, experienced white officers, the administrators and politicians who control the service from afar crave young, university-educated black officers. As if it were not enough to fight for justice for his victims, he must be alert to the constant threat from within. It is exhausting him, but he knows that he must concentrate on each case as it comes along; he will not waste time worrying about his future.

Sally Frazer is where he left her the previous night, by the whiteboard, phone tucked under one ear and speed-reading reports. A cursory glance reveals to De Vries that little more of substance has been added. He stalks to his office, closes the door, slumps in his chair; he looks out over the squad room and notes that everyone who should be there, is. He is about to call Don February, when he sees him exit the elevators, squint in the direction of De Vries's office and then approach at speed, knocking on the glass door at the same time that he is opening it.

'I have,' Don starts, panting slightly, 'set up a meeting with Jessica Templeman, the best friend, and then after that, if you wish to travel to Franschhoek, Dazuluka Cele, the artist of the paintings in the gallery, says she will be in her studio all day and is prepared to speak to us . . .'

'Good . . .'

'But there is something more, sir. The officer Ms Botes reported as being in charge of the police officers. I made a call: there was one unit from Metro and one from Central, headed up by Lieutenant Nkosi.'

De Vries's eyes widens.

'I do not understand why he would not have told you that he attended the scene the previous evening at the gallery.'

'I don't think,' De Vries says, 'he was in a co-operative mood. I'll have to speak to him too.'

'One piece of information, sir, from last night at the neighbour's house. The girl said that she saw Taryn Holt arriving at 10.35 p.m. and that a "black man" was waiting in his car and was let into her house. No better description, and no information on when he left.'

De Vries nods.

'Okay, this is just before the estimate of time of death. Liaise with Frazer about that and, Don, find out who that is. If she let him in, she knew him.' De Vries glances at his watch. 'I want to get going, Don. Time is passing and everything is happening too slowly.' He stands up, opens a drawer in his desk and closes it again, pats his pockets. 'There's no time for distractions. You or Frazer talk to Templeman again. We need information about the boyfriends and she's the most likely person to know. I want to go see this artist woman. You'll give me directions?'

Don February hands him a handwritten note.

'She's off Main Street, a turning to the left, fifty metres before the bank.'

'Good.' He ushers Don out of his office, locks the glass door. 'If we let this stall now, we're in trouble.'

The drive to Franschhoek takes De Vries past the airport and, having turned off the freeway by the Cape Town film studios, into the Winelands towards Stellenbosch. Every time he drives this way he notices how much more development there has been, as the views of the mountains become ever more cluttered by gated communities, retail parks and golf estates. In the old days you would visit a wine estate and the owner would appear at the doorway, dogs at his feet, and invite you into his home or across the courtyard to his cellar, and personally pour you samples of his wine. Now, you are more likely to be tapped for twenty rand by a youngster with a name-badge on her uniform and herded into a tasting room via a gift shop.

He takes the ring road around Stellenbosch and heads up the Helshoogte Pass, which still boasts breathtaking views of the rolling vine-clad hillsides. The cloud cover is no more than fifty per cent here and the sun illuminates bright patches around him, moving horizontally across his field of vision.

Eventually, he reaches the turning into the Franschhoek Valley and the road that leads him into the old Huguenot Town. As he approaches, the dramatic mountains on either side of the valley converge, making the town seem nestled in their folds. He slows to look for the turn off to Uitkyk Street, notices signs on the lampposts advertising a beer festival in Greyton – a remote artist's village a few kilometres from the top of the Franschhoek Pass. De Vries likes Greyton; he and his ex-wife went there years ago, several times, to escape the city and walk the leafy streets hand in hand at dusk, eat in a romantic restaurant and retire to the soft beds of the Greyton Lodge guest house. He has a ticket for the festival, a room booked just outside the town; one afternoon, one night off after weeks without a break. On Thursday. He wonders whether it will go to waste.

Behind him, a towering SUV honks, and Vaughn realizes that he is holding up the traffic behind him. He takes the next turn, finds it is Uitkyk Street, drives up the steeply rising tree-lined street, past perfect Cape Huguenot properties with English gardens and, at the top of the road, turns right along a gravelled driveway towards a pair of modern buildings that might be barn conversions. He checks the address again, unfolds his legs from the car and rings the bell at the gates which guard the courtyard. A woman's voice answers and, when he identifies himself, the gates open. He gets back into his car, drives forward, hearing the crunching of gravel under his tyres, and parks in the shade of a Pepper tree.

★ ★ ★

Dazuluka Cele is a small, black African woman, with a slim figure and a shaven head. She proffers her hand, glances down at it, and smiles warmly.

'It is paint, but it's dry. I am Dazuluka.'

'Colonel Vaughn de Vries, SAPS.'

'It is terrible news. I cannot believe it. Only on Wednesday night, she was so full of life, so happy that so many people had come to my exhibition.'

Her voice is high, French-accented; it sings. She leads Vaughn towards the nearest of the buildings.

'Come with me. We can talk in my studio, and you can tell me what happened to Taryn.'

She leads the way into the building, up a wood and metal spiral staircase to the first floor. At the top, De Vries sees that the entire floor is a single white room, illuminated by windows on both sides, with multiple easels set up on one side, angled so that the light falls on them. On the other, there are four life-size figurative sculptures in a light wood, the last with an aluminium ladder next to it, its face only half finished. A narrow, elongated table runs down the center of the room for its entire length. It is covered in artists' materials: paint, pastels, pencils, brushes and jars of water, solvents and brush cleaners.

'You work here with others?'

'No. Only solitude provides inspiration.'

'For multiple pieces at once?'

She leads him the length of the room over broad wooden planks to the far end where she has two tiny sofas around a dark, carved wood table. She opens a cupboard behind her, pulls out two glasses and an unopened bottle of mineral water, dispenses liquid into both and places the glasses on the table. She sits lightly on one sofa, curls her legs up around her, gestures to De Vries to take the other.

'I used to paint only one canvas at a time but, as soon as I start one painting, I have an idea for the next and I cannot concentrate on what I was going to paint. So now, when I have an idea, I start the piece and then I can go back to it when my head is calm.'

'How long had you known Taryn Holt?'

'Not long. She saw my work at an exhibition I had about five years ago in Maputo, in Mozambique. She liked the work and, when I moved to South Africa, it was obvious that she should show my work here.'

De Vries glances back around the gallery.

'I want to ask you about your work.'

She smiles.

'That is unexpected. A policeman who wants to talk about art.'

'Your pictures may be connected to Taryn Holt's death.'

Dazuluka Cele stands up.

'No. No. Do not say that. How can you say that?'

De Vries gets up too, follows her towards the first of the sculptures. She runs her hand over the form and, now, De Vries can see what it represents: the carving is of a woman, doubled over, clutching her stomach, crying.

'Your paintings, this sculpture. They are very powerful. They upset a lot of people.'

Cele turns, looks up at him. He sees she is distressed, her eyes pink.

'Good. That is what art should do. For the last two years, I worked on this collection. It is what is in my heart. It shows the world how men treat women on this continent.' She takes a step back and indicates the sculpture. 'This woman was pregnant with a child her husband did not want. He had been told by some fortune teller that it would be a girl and he wanted only a boy. So, what did he do? He beat her stomach with his fists and kicked

85

her until he killed her baby and then, when he had finished, he raped her to make her pregnant with the child he wanted.'

De Vries has heard such stories before. Whenever he hears stories of deviance and evil, he reflects, he has always heard worse. He waits, out of respect for her emotion. Then, he says: 'You painted a picture, in your exhibition, which shows a white women lying on a bed. The bed is bloodied and she has a giant phallus in her mouth . . .'

'Yes. That is another story which I can tell you . . .'

'Is it about Taryn Holt?'

Cele looks confused.

'No. It is about a woman called Margaret in Maputo.' She frowns. 'Why do you ask if it is about Taryn?'

'Because Miss Holt was shot on her bed, and she had a black phallus in her mouth.'

He sees the information processed and the reaction which follows. Cele slumps back down on her chair, eyes blinking, shaking her head.

'I do not understand. That is not possible.'

Vaughn sits back down opposite her.

'What happened to this woman in Maputo?'

Cele looks up at him.

'Her husband was a drunk, a very violent man. When he suspected that his wife was having an affair with a black businessman, he took out his shotgun and killed her on their bed.'

'What about the black phallus?'

'That,' Cele says, 'was to tell the story. I only read about the woman's story in the newspaper and I was moved to paint the picture.'

Vaughn knows that any connection between the original subject of the painting and his investigation is spurious.

'Was the painting here before it was displayed at the gallery?'

'Yes. I painted it maybe . . . a year ago. It would have been here, first on an easel and then stacked against the wall there.' She indicates a series of canvases, each divided from the next by what looks like old bed-sheets.

'Who would have seen it?'

'Many people. Visitors to the studio here, and everybody who attended the gallery.'

'You notice anyone paying particular attention?'

'I notice that women look deeply at it, study the woman's eyes, examine her body. Men, they look between her legs and at her face and then they look away.'

Vaughn's mouth twitches. He takes a breath.

'Your work is passionate; personal?'

Cele nods vigorously, wiping her eyes.

'I have nothing but my gift from God. I use that to tell the story of women in Africa and what they suffer.'

De Vries gestures around her studio.

'You live here too?'

'Yes. The other building is my home. The space below is a second studio. It was used by another artist, but she died.'

'Still,' Vaughn says, 'you have done well.'

'This is not mine,' Cele says sadly. 'This belongs to Taryn. She owns the property. As one of her artists, it became mine to work in, to live in. But now, now I do not know what will happen.'

'You were fond of Miss Holt?'

'Of course, yes. Without her support, I would never have been able to mount such an exhibition, would never have sold my work to important, influential people. I owe her everything.'

'Did you know about Miss Holt's private life? About who she was seeing?'

'No. She was a private person. But, I can tell you this, all the time we were setting up the exhibition, she was excited about someone in her life.'

'A man? A boyfriend?'

'Yes,' Cele says uncertainly. 'I could see in her eyes that it was something like love . . . I think too she had plans for something that excited her. She worked hard on my exhibition, but I thought that she was thinking about something else.'

'Any idea what?'

'No. Sorry.'

'Who would want to kill her?'

'I am asking myself that. She would not let a man bully her. She was a strong woman. But I do not know.'

De Vries stands up.

'I do not understand art but, I must tell you: your paintings are very powerful. They have stayed in my mind.'

Cele leads him back across the studio. As she walks, her short dress flutters; he sees a deep scar running down the side of her left thigh. He swallows.

'That is what they should do,' she tells him. 'That is what all art should do: challenge you, stimulate you; force you to think again, to question what you think you know.'

'Well,' Vaughn says, 'you have succeeded.'

He walks back to his car, looks beyond the barn up at the mountains. It is stiflingly hot now, the air sitting in the triangular valley-floor. He gets into the car, starts the engine and switches on the air-conditioning, waiting for the cool air to permeate the cabin. He stretches his neck and glances in the rear-view mirror. His head snaps back and he blinks his eyes to focus. In the tiny screen, he can see Dazuluka Cele between the two barns. A man is gesticulating at her, shouting. He sees her shoulders slump, her head bow. De Vries releases the hand-brake and, despite facing the exit, he takes a broad turn. By the time he is facing the buildings, neither Cele nor the man are visible. He waits a moment. When no one appears, he turns again, crawls towards the gate and sees it open. He wonders whether to stop, return to the barn to check on her; he accepts that his concern is almost certainly misplaced, a product of what he judges is nothing more than childish infatuation with the eccentric artist. He looks once more in the mirror, sees no one, drives away.

'You were right about Jessica Templeman,' Don February tells De Vries. 'I took Sergeant Frazer back with me. She played her part very well, telling her that she had brought a senior officer to talk to her because she was so important as Taryn Holt's best friend.'

'Good. What did she tell you?'

'Mainly that she and Miss Holt had grown apart in the last year, that she had not seen her for the previous four months, but that Miss Holt had spoken with her on the phone – maybe just the one time – and told her she was seeing someone she was excited about, and that she had some plan which was what she had been looking for.'

'That ties in with what I heard from the artist I interviewed . . . Cele. Is that her name?'

'Dazuluka Cele.'

'Yes, her. She said that Holt was distracted by something, that she was in love.'

'With the black African man my witness says she saw?'

'Perhaps. What news on cell-phone numbers?'

'We are waiting for the activity reports from the service provider. Then we can get a better idea of who she was calling and who was calling her.'

'When will you get those?'

'Sergeant Frazer says this afternoon.'

'Good. I must speak to our reluctant Lieutenant . . . What's his name?'

'Lieutenant Nkosi.'

'Yes.'

'May I ask you, sir? Why is it that you can remember an English name, but not so much an African name?'

'Is this a test of my political correctness?'

'No, sir.'

De Vries shrugs.

'I don't know, Don. I can't say them, I can't spell them. I can't remember them. Don't ask me questions like that.'

'I see.'

'It is why,' De Vries says. 'I have you.'

He snatches at the desk phone.

'De Vries.'

'This is Mitchell Smith . . .'

'Who are you?'

'Mitchell Smith. You probably don't remember me?'

A dim light glows in the back of De Vries's mind; he recognizes the name but cannot place it.

'What can I do for you, Mr Smith?'

There is a pause.

'You were a Captain at Observatory in '93/'94?'

'Who is this?'

'Mitchell Smith. I was a Constable at Rondebosch. I worked with you on the Victoria Drinking Hall bombing.'

The glow becomes blinding; his breath catches. In an instant, his mind is flooded with images from that night. The one night he met Mitchell Smith, twenty-one years ago.

He concentrates on trying to speak.

'Are you still with the SAPS?'

'No. I left in 2000 . . . I've been trying to find you. I got your home number from an old directory, but there was no answer.'

'I don't answer that phone.'

'I need to talk to you.'

'I have a few minutes just now.'

'No ... I need to see you. I can't talk to you about this on the phone.'

De Vries sighs.

'I'm happy to talk with you, but I'm at work. A very sensitive murder enquiry. That's why I'm here on my weekend. I can't spare the time right now. Call me in a couple of weeks' time.'

'This can't wait. You need to know.'

'Know what?'

'It's about what happened.'

'Well, I can't deal with that now. I'll help you if I can. Just not now. Give me your number. I'll contact you when this case is completed.'

He notes the number on a random piece of paper.

'Please. It's urgent.'

'If you are concerned for your safety, speak to your local station. That's a Bellville number, *ja*?' He hears stuttering. 'I'll call you soon, Mr Smith.'

He puts the receiver down.

January 1994

De Vries walks stiffly towards the low building which is acting as an overflow to the main Observatory SAPS buildings, mind racing between each step, ears still reverberating from his crashing against the lockers, his brain still saturated with images from the house in Khayelitsha, nose still infested with the stench of sweat and damp, of blood newly spilt.

It was to have been so different. Mandela's release, back-channel negotiations between the ANC and the governing Nationalist party, the date set for the first free elections; all of this should have calmed and given assurance that the transfer would be orderly, scrutinized by the media, recognized by the world. Instead, extremists on both sides have threatened civil order: Afrikaners clamouring for a home state, black activists embarking on this trail of terror through the Cape, unrest in townships around Jo'burg and Pretoria. Those who predicted a bloodbath are more strident; the joy and relief after so many years of struggle now muted as the reality sets in of forming a new constitution which will avoid the disintegration of the country. The calls for reconciliation are passionate but, right now, amidst the ongoing fire-fight, hollow.

He finds Smith sitting alone on a low bench, head in hands, still in his drenched uniform; his boots heavy with thick orange mud. The lights are switched off and only the sickly yellow glow from the compound lamps outside oozes through the dirty windows above them. When he looks up at De Vries's approach, his eyes are red and swollen, his jaw locked.

He stands; De Vries puts his arm around his shoulder, leads him away from the doorway towards the back of the changing room.

'What happens now, sir? Do I go?'

De Vries sits next to him.

'We have reports to write.' He looks at Smith, sees his hands shaking. 'You need to change.'

Smith says: 'I don't have anything. Four of us came from Rondebosch. My shift ends in an hour.'

De Vries gets up, walks to the opposite corner and opens a walk-in cupboard lined with basic wooden shelves. He returns with a pair of denim jeans and a cotton sweater, two pairs of socks.

'Have a shower – if they're working. Dry off and put these on. It's lost property. They probably won't fit, but it'll do for now. I'll find us some coffee. Meet in the squad room ...' He points his chin in the direction of the far doors. 'Ten minutes. Then we have to get this done before we go home.'

Smith stands up straight, nods at him. De Vries says: 'What a fucking horrible night.'

Whether Mitchell Smith is almost illiterate or whether he is still in shock, De Vries finds himself dictating his report, watching the Constable's stiff fingers work the pen awkwardly over the forms.

'Major Nel has instructed me that we report only what we heard from outside the dwelling. We weren't inside; we didn't see what happened . . .' He pauses, makes sure he has the younger man's attention. 'You understand? Neither of us entered the building.'

Smith frowns.

'You didn't see me enter the building. *Ja*?'

Smith nods.

'*Ja* . . . I don't know what happened in there.'

'No, you don't. Just keep saying that. We waited there. When there was no further communication we returned to the station.'

De Vries sees misgivings in the man's eyes.

'Listen. We weren't inside. We don't know what happened . . .'

'It was the wrong building, the wrong address . . .'

'We followed orders, we waited, then we left.'

'They were all dead, weren't they? They killed them all?'

De Vries smacks the desk, sees Smith start. He stares him down.

'Listen to me, Constable: you don't fuck with Major Nel. Maybe neither of us are happy with what happened, but it is what it is. We won't achieve anything by crossing this man. He's a fucking hero to these guys. I don't like it, and maybe you don't either, but that's the way it is right now. We write this up, we go home.

It's the end of a war. We get out alive, go home to our families and we keep our jobs.'

Smith is watching De Vries now, focused on his words, as if they are to be held onto.

'I'll do what you say, sir.'

'Let's just do it,' De Vries says. 'That's what happened, and it stays that way. *Ja*?'

Smith snorts, shivers, nods.

'*Ja*.'

4 April 2015

Twenty-five minutes later he still sits in the same position, becomes aware that his breathing is very shallow. He swallows, shakes his head, stretches his arms behind the chair. He gets up, pulls open the stiff window and lights a cigarette, holds it outside. He sits on the ledge, staring out to the buildings across the street, up town towards the Mountain. His mind is racing; he sees nothing.

As the elevator doors open, De Vries registers Lieutenant Sam Nkosi stepping forward, but also, in the background, Julius Mngomezulu, General Thulani's bagman and attaché. De Vries already knows that he acts as a spy on his department; that, in the past, he has attempted to sabotage his investigations. Mngomezulu does not know that he knows this; it is De Vries's one advantage.

Nkosi salutes, but De Vries is still scrutinizing Mngomezulu, wondering what he is doing at work on Saturday when he is usually strictly a Monday to Friday administrator. The doors close on him; their eyes have not met.

'Follow me, Lieutenant.'

He leads him through the squad room to his office, sits him in front of his desk.

'This is the first time I have been inside this building,' Nkosi says, sitting up straight, continuing to scrutinize his surroundings. 'It is a lot more modern than our Central SAPS building, or where I was back in Pretoria.'

De Vries switches on a small voice recorder, moves a blank pad of paper in front of him.

'I don't do small talk, Lieutenant. I need to know what happened on Wednesday evening at the New Worlds Gallery, when you met Taryn Holt and what you discussed. Where do you want to begin?'

Nkosi sits up, produces some notes of his own.

'We received a call from Mr Dominic van der Merwe, the manager of the New Worlds Gallery, concerning both written and spoken threats against Miss Taryn Holt and Mr van der Merwe himself. I was allocated the follow-up. I visited the gallery on Thursday, 27 February and spoke to Miss Holt. She said she had received threats that the gallery would be targeted, and that she had also had strange letters posted to her at her private home.'

'What kind of threats?'

'To be honest, I did not think that they were serious. They looked like the work of children. Words cut out from newspapers. They said that if she did not cancel the exhibition, people would find a way to close it down.'

'What did you do?'

'At that meeting, nothing. However, on Monday, 30 March, when the exhibition was being prepared, she was visited by members of a women's group and church representatives. They told her that they would picket the gallery. She requested that officers were made available to ensure that her guests were not threatened. She also asked me to accompany her to her home to check her security as she was afraid that people might protest there or try to visit her.'

'Isn't that something her security provider should have done?'

'Yes, sir, but under the circumstances, being who she was, I thought that we should be protecting her.'

'Did you check her security?'

'Yes.'

'Did you check the windows and doors onto the terrace?'

'Yes.'

'And did you find anything wrong?'

'No, sir. Miss Holt had an effective and modern alarm system. I told her that she should keep the alarm switched on even when she was at home, and that she could call us if there was any threat to her.'

'Did you see her again?'

'Yes, sir. I visited her at the gallery on the afternoon of Wednesday, 1 April to tell her that a small unit of Metro officers would be present and I would run a unit past the road of her gallery, but that our involvement could only occur in the event of an illegal action by the demonstrators.'

'And what did happen?'

'When I was informed that there were approximately thirty demonstrators and that they were causing an obstruction, I joined the unit with three other officers. When the gallery's security men tried to move the demonstrators on, there was some threat of violence and a brick was thrown at the window of the gallery. At that point, I and my officers moved in, dispersed the crowd and secured the building.'

'Did you make any arrests?'

'No, sir. We warned the demonstrators that we considered that they were causing an obstruction and, although they argued with us at first, they then moved away.'

'You could not identify who threw the brick?'

'No, sir.'

'Did you speak with Taryn Holt then?'

'Only to tell her that it was safe for her guests and clients to continue with their party or to leave the premises if they wished . . . And, also, to give her the telephone number of an emergency company to secure the premises because of the broken window.'

'And did you see her after that?'

Nkosi looks up from his notes, hesitates.

'Yes, sir.'

'When?'

'I visited her home on Thursday, 2 April.'

'Why?'

'I wished to apologize for failing to prevent the incident at her gallery.'

'What made you think that was something you should do?'

'I . . .' Nkosi looks embarrassed. 'Knowing who she was, I wanted to make sure that there would be no complaint against me. I thought if I apologized, she would not think so poorly of me. If I had posted an officer at the entrance to the gallery, perhaps this would not have happened. Perhaps she might not even have been killed.'

'What time did you visit her house?'

'It was before my shift. I visited her house at approximately 8 p.m.'

'How long were you there?'

'Not long. Maybe five minutes.'

'What was her reaction?'

'She seemed pleased that I had visited her personally. There would be no complaint.'

'Did you notice anything about her that made you think she might be concerned about her own safety?'

'No, sir.'

'Nothing which made you at all suspicious?'

'No, sir.'

'She was alone?'

'Yes.'

De Vries sits back, wonders what else he should ask.

'How did you come to answer the call to Miss Holt's house yesterday morning?'

'It was the end of my night shift. I was the senior detective officer. When I heard the address, I took control, immediately assumed command of the scene and was reminded by my Sergeant to notify your desk, which I did. By 7.30 a.m., you had taken control of the scene and the case. That was the end of my involvement with Miss Holt.'

De Vries studies Nkosi; he is a different man to the one from whom he had taken over the murder scene not thirty-six hours previously.

Whenever he looks at black Africans, he is always filled with a mixture of innate suspicion and prejudice; he strives to counter such feelings. It leaves him doubting his interpretation, a state which he finds saps his self-confidence. Yet, there is something about Nkosi today, the efficiency and respect with which he is delivering his account, that makes De Vries suspicious. He does not know of what, but he cannot help thinking about Julius Mngomezulu in the lift with Nkosi and whether they know one another. He dismisses the notion: Mngomezulu prowls the corridors only of this building.

'The threats against Miss Holt: you have kept them on record?'

Nkosi stutters.

'The earlier ones, I told her to throw away. We have a letter from the church congregation and the later written threats.'

'Send them here straight after this meeting.'

Nkosi nods.

'With hindsight, Lieutenant. Is there any one person, or individual threat, which you think you should have taken more seriously?'

'No, sir.'

'You're sure?'

'Yes, sir. I have asked myself that question.'

'So, who killed Taryn Holt?'

'I don't know, sir.'

De Vries travels down to the building's exit with Nkosi as an excuse to walk across two side streets and towards a café which serves strong, thick coffee, the antithesis of what is available in the squad-room. He stands outside, under the canopy, with a double, double espresso and smokes three cigarettes, lighting each from the previous one. A movement catches his eye, and he realizes that it is Don February, hurrying towards him.

'I have been trying to call you.'

De Vries takes his cell-phone out of his pocket and presses a button. He tries again.

'It's dead. What is it?'

'We have identified one caller who Taryn Holt has spoken with more than any other in the last four weeks. He was the caller at 10.23 p.m. on the Wednesday night, twelve minutes before my witness said that she saw a man who could have been him entering the Holt property.'

'Who is it?'

'You are not going to like it, sir. It changes everything. We must call Mr Classon.'

'Don, who the fuck is it?'

'It is Trevor Bhekifa.'

De Vries takes a moment to process the information.

'The son of Bheka Bhekifa?'

'Yes, sir.'

The colour drains from De Vries's face.

'Jesus, Don. I thought we had ourselves a clean murder . . .' Don February recalls Taryn Holt's bedroom: the volume of blood; the walls, carpets, windows, mattress. He looks back up at De Vries, hears him say: 'But if we've got fucking politicians involved, it's going to get dirty.'

PART TWO

Bheka Bhekifa is a hero of the Struggle, a scholar from a poor family who made it all the way to Manchester University in England. He is rumoured to have been a key backroom figure in the Mandela administration of 1994, a political advisor who sought to keep that first ANC government on a more socialist footing, who argued against the free-market solutions to which Mandela soon turned. Nonetheless, he is credited with helping to mould a freedom-fighting organization into a functioning political party. Now, ostensibly away from politics, it is said that he still wields considerable influence at the highest level; that political leaders call on him for advice.

Some might question how a man devoted to the socialist cause could have graduated to living in a mansion at the very top of Bishopscourt, the smartest inland real estate in Cape Town, safe from the relentless South-Easter, surveying the Southern slopes of Table Mountain as far as Devil's Peak. A plan of his property would reveal that his house is angled towards the mountains, away from the townships and squatter-camps which were, and he might insist, remain, his constituency.

Although he has never been a businessman in the traditional sense, he has been an unofficial ambassador separate from, yet also innately connected to, the South African government. As a result, his word is said to carry some weight on the international stage.

It was his influence, commentators claim, which brought about the slashing of wholesale prices to South Africa of retro anti-viral medication for HIV sufferers; it was his name attached to NGO projects throughout the country, in education, health, opportunity for black African children, the promotion of indigenous African cultural identity. With Mandela gone, those who were part of the Struggle see him as a link to those times, when victory had come, and the future lay before them.

'As soon as Attorney Classon informed me that you were acquainted with Mr Bheka Bhekifa, sir, I came here to inform you of developments in the case.'

De Vries is standing before General Sempiwe Thulani in his relentlessly air-conditioned office, said to be the coldest place in the Southern Hemisphere save for Antarctica itself.

'We go back a long way,' Thulani says, musing. 'He is a great man who has served our country all his life . . .'

'His son left home years ago, though. It is not as if this matter will reflect on him personally.'

'There is no doubt that the maker of these calls is Trevor Bhekifa? He could not have lent his cell-phone to another party, or had it stolen?'

'We contacted him on that phone,' De Vries tells him, 'explained why we wished to speak with him, and he has agreed to return to Cape Town to be questioned. He had not, apparently, heard the news of Miss Holt's death.'

'Trevor and his father disagree on many things. I do not believe that they are even in regular communication with one another but, Colonel, we are different from you here. For us, family is everything, and anything which affects one member, affects us all.'

Thulani slips off his high chair, his girth appearing from behind his over-sized desk.

'I will visit him and inform him personally of what is happening. When you speak to Trevor, I want you to show him every respect. When you have completed your interview, take no further action until you have spoken with me. I wish to be kept informed of every development. Do you understand?'

'Yes, sir.'

'The media, the newspapers: can you imagine what a story like this would mean to them? Less than a year after the elections? Instruct your team that no information is to be leaked under any circumstances. If what you tell me is accurate, then Trevor Bhekifa was an acquaintance of the victim and is doing his duty by submitting to interview with you.' He stares at De Vries. 'You agree?'

'Yes, sir.'

Thulani dismisses him with a flick of his thick wrist.

'Colonel?'

De Vries turns back to face him.

'You are being uncommonly co-operative. I hope that this is not merely lip-service.'

De Vries mouths: 'No, sir.'

Thulani misses the jibe, and Vaughn exits the office, finds Julius Mngomezulu standing in the ante-room with Thulani's secretary. De Vries walks past him, through the outer door, into the grey but temperate corridor. Only then can he feel his jaw begin to relax.

Norman Classon says: 'The Democratic Reform Group was a think-tank set up in 2010 by political refugees from the ANC, intellectuals and public figures in South Africa, to examine the possibility of genuine multi-party politics in the country.' He looks from De Vries to Don February to Ben Thwala; all are attentive. 'Trevor Bhekifa was amongst them, a rebel to the cause. A few months back, they announced the formation of a new political party, the Democratic Reform Party – DRP. Can you imagine what a coup it was for them to have Bhekifa? Even though it is his son, that name buys hundreds of thousands of black votes. It could transform them from a fringe party to one with a real chance of upsetting the status quo. Considering the results of the 2014 election, this could blow open the entire political system. They posted an invitation to the people to join them, seeking those with expertise to become spokesmen and women on their behalf: white, coloured, black. Trevor Bhekifa is an entrepreneur; he speaks for them on business opportunity.'

'Maybe this is what he was discussing with Taryn Holt?' Don says.

De Vries turns to him.

'We'll find out.'

'Considering Miss Holt's financial weight,' Classon says, 'I would think he was discussing funding. Any political party must have considerable backing to stand any chance of making an impact.'

'Was she political?'

'Her father was no friend of the ANC. They called him and his company . . .' He consults his notes: '"Co-conspirators with the oppressive regime".'

'So,' De Vries says, 'she has been around questions of politics all her life.'

'Yes,' Classon says, 'but Bhekifa and she come from the opposite ends of the spectrum. It is a truly strange match – politically, anyway.'

'Both rebels, perhaps?'

'You don't really consider him a suspect, surely?'

'Why not?' De Vries says immediately. 'He was at Holt's house around the time she died. He obviously visited it regularly. He knew about the alarm system, had knowledge of the set-up there.'

'But if Bhekifa was lining her up as a benefactor for the party, why would he kill her?'

'We don't know anything right now, Norman. We speak to him; we see what he says. Then we can start trying to put everything together.' De Vries stands. 'Must be a treat for a lawyer like you. All the taboos in one go: money, politics, sex and violence.'

Trevor Bhekifa arrives from Stellenbosch within an hour and a half, and is sitting in the Interview Room opposite De Vries and Don February a few minutes later. De Vries likes this place, knows that cases are often made in here, feels that the surroundings alone exert a pressure on a suspect which begins to break their resolve.

Bhekifa is offered coffee or water, both of which he declines.

De Vries begins.

'We are here, sir, merely to establish some facts about the murder of Miss Taryn Holt, and the relationship which you may or may not have had with her. Do you understand?'

Bhekifa nods, says: 'Yes, I do. But, I am in shock, sir, because I did not know what happened to Taryn until I was informed by your Sergeant only two hours ago.'

De Vries pauses a moment, then says: 'We can take it in your own time.'

'Thank you, sir.'

Bhekifa is dressed in a dark suit, white shirt with gold cufflinks, and a patterned silk tie; his shoes are high quality and smartly polished.

'I need to establish first whether the calls indicated on Miss Holt's activity record in the last seven weeks, to and from your cell-phone number, were made and received by you.'

'Yes. Taryn and I were involved. We spoke often.'

'How long had you known Miss Holt?'

He leans his head back, closes his eyes.

'I suppose . . . . Maybe six or seven months ago, at the end of spring. It was at the launch of a book about the political writer and film-maker Ousmane Sembene, in a bookshop in town – and then a party at the Rust en Vreugd Museum in Buitenkant Street. We started talking, and then I suggested that we meet up again. She accepted.'

'You went out together?'

'Yes . . .' He shifts position in the small chair. 'That is . . . We met at our homes. Mainly, I would visit her at her house.'

'You didn't go out to bars or restaurants?'

'We preferred to stay private.'

'This developed into an intimate relationship?'

'Yes. We would see each other once or twice a week. We are both busy people. We have businesses to run, employees to mentor, but we became close.'

'Did you discuss politics?'

'Yes. Taryn was interested in the political alternatives that the group, the party I belong to, was discussing.'

'The . . .' De Vries looks down, reads: '"Democratic Reform Party"?'

'Yes.'

'Was Miss Holt interested in joining your party?'

'We were talking about it, yes. Taryn was very passionate in her support of the arts, of women's rights. She was a passionate woman who had much to offer.' He bows his head. 'I cannot believe it . . .'

'Was she considering donating money to the party?'

'Why do you ask this?'

'Because,' De Vries says, 'I need to know some background before we come on to the specifics of when you last saw Miss Holt, whether you had cause for concern for her safety. Matters like that.'

'Taryn and I did discuss whether she would be able to donate to the party.'

'And was she going to?'

Again, Bhekifa re-adjusts his position, frowns. De Vries smiles to himself; it is impossible to be comfortable in that chair. The legs on one side have been shortened so that the seat is at a slight angle and within minutes the back of the suspect begins to ache; the chair is too low for an adult.

'Yes. A few weeks ago, we decided that the DRP could benefit from a strong funding base. She was prepared to be our first major financial supporter, to play a role in policy formation, concentrate on areas she was an expert in.'

'Did she make a payment?'

'No. She told me that funds would have to be released, that she would investigate how soon this could be done. There were also other matters she wished to consider but, in principle, she wanted to support us.'

De Vries nods.

'At any point in the last weeks, did Miss Holt express any concern about her safety?'

'Not really . . . She told me that her exhibition was causing some problems, that some small-minded locals had objected and were calling her, meeting with her, sending her threatening letters, but she said that it was because they did not understand the art.'

'What did you think of it?'

'I did not see the letters.'

'I meant the art.'

'Oh, that . . . I only saw two or three paintings when they were in her house. They were powerful. They represented what Taryn was about. They were great art, and they conveyed a message.'

'You didn't visit her gallery?'

'No.'

'Why not?'

'I am sure that I would have, but I am busy too. I have my businesses as well as the work I do for the DRP.'

'Last week, when did you see Miss Holt?'

'We spoke a lot.' He looks De Vries in the face. 'You will know that if you have seen records of our calls to each other. I did not think that I would see her, but on Wednesday I wanted to be with her. She was upset by the demonstration and the attack on the gallery, so I drove into town, told her I would be at her home and, when she came back, I kept her company that night.'

'What time did you arrive?'

Bhekifa shrugs.

'I don't know. Ten thirty perhaps?'

'And you left the next day, when?'

'Maybe 7.30 a.m. Taryn wanted to return to the gallery, to sort out the damage. She starts every day early.'

'And that was the last time you saw her?'

'No.' He leans forward. 'I saw her just for an hour on Thursday night.'

'What time?'

'Again, I don't know exactly. I was in Cape Town meeting a client. We had a late meeting, a drink together and then, on my way back, I called in on Taryn. Maybe 9.30 p.m. I don't know.'

'Did you call her before going to her house?'

'No. I wanted to surprise her. To show her that I was concerned about her.'

'How long did you stay?'

'I said, about an hour.'

'And where did you go from there?'

'Home. I was tired. I had been working all day and then had this meeting in Cape Town in the evening.'

'Can anybody vouch for when you arrived home?'

'Maybe. I live in my own development of six apartments. I don't know if the security guard was at the desk, but there are cameras. I might be on them . . . Taryn was killed that night?'

'Yes.'

'When? What happened?'

'We think someone broke in and shot Miss Holt.'

'A robbery?'

'Probably not.'

De Vries sees pain etched on his face, is uncertain whether the expression matches what he reads in the man's eyes. There is not grief, but concern.

'I need to ask you some more questions.'

'Yes, okay . . .'

'Miss Holt had an alarm system at her home. Were you familiar with it?'

'I suppose so. She had a remote for it in her bedroom. I had not seen one of those before.'

'Did she activate the alarm after you had left?'

Trevor Bhekifa pauses.

'I don't know. Probably.'

'You didn't hear anything as you left? The sound of the alarm arming?'

'No.'

'Where was Miss Holt when you left?'

'In the house. She came to the door with me. She said good-bye; said that she was going to have a bath.'

'And you drove straight home?'

'Yes.'

Something in Bhekifa's tone makes De Vries say: 'Yes?'

'Yes . . . I sat in my car for a while after I had left her.'

'Why?'

'Because I was not sure about how I felt. I think she wanted me to stay with her, but I had meetings early the next day . . . I was deciding if I should go back to her. I needed to be home. If I had stayed with her, she would not be dead now.'

De Vries stares at him, says: 'You might both be dead.'

'Trevor Bhekifa is the last person we know who saw Taryn Holt alive. He claims he left her house at approximately 10.30 p.m. That puts him within thirty minutes of the earliest estimate of the time of death. There may be corroborative evidence at his place of residence if the video cameras recorded his return. I have already dispatched officers to investigate that.'

'So, he remains a suspect?'

'Yes, sir.'

De Vries is aware that most of the squad-room are stealing glances at General Thulani in his office. He is rarely seen on any of the operations floors; many of the elite unit team have never met him.

'What can I tell his father?'

'Whatever you choose, sir. His son has admitted to having a relationship with the victim, that he was interested in involving her in his political party, the . . . Democratic Reform Party. He wanted her to become a donor to the party.'

Thulani shakes his head slowly. De Vries wonders whether he rues Trevor Bhekifa's political actions – in direct opposition to his illustrious father – or whether it is the mingling of races in the bedroom which disturbs him. He knows little about the Assistant Deputy Provincial Commissioner beyond the fact that he has vied with De Vries's own boss, Henrik du Toit, for most of their careers, and has been overt in his desire to see Du Toit, De Vries and any other white officers he considers tainted by their service during the Apartheid era shunted into the background.

'If she was to donate to his party, what motive, then, would he have to murder her?'

112

'Nothing obvious,' De Vries says. 'If it was him, there could have been relationship problems. She was not monogamous and certainly had at least one other boyfriend at this time. Men and women become jealous; a disagreement can easily turn violent. It is still early in the investigation.'

Thulani feels under his shirt collar.

'Tread very carefully, Colonel. You are dealing with important, influential people here. Men who have connections to the highest levels of government, to the very top.'

'I am aware of that, sir.'

'Your performance will reflect on all of us.'

'I must go where the evidence takes me. But, I hear what you say.'

He sees Thulani glance at him; his is not an expression of confidence.

'You impressed on everyone the importance of keeping all elements of the investigation private, away from the press?'

'I did.'

'You do not have a reputation, Colonel, for discretion or diplomacy. This is your opportunity to impress me.'

De Vries resists a parting comment, watches Thulani strut heavily across the squad-room to the elevators.

On his return from Stellenbosch, Don February travels straight to Sergeant Joey Morten, the department's technology consultant. Attached to the Crime Scene Unit based in the building, he sits in a small office surrounded by computer screens. Don hands him the memory stick and, within moments, on screen he can see the foyer to Bhekifa's luxurious apartment building.

Above the security desk, which is located opposite the elevators, are four analogue clocks indicating the time in Cape Town, New York, London and Tokyo. In the bottom right hand corner of the screen, displayed digitally, is the date and time. Don looks around as the door to Morten's office opens and De Vries's head appears.

'I have it here,' Don tells him.

'What time did you say he got back?'

'About 12.30 a.m., but there are timing issues.'

'Meaning?'

Don indicates towards the screen.

'We are just looking at it now.'

'Where does this start and end, Don?' Morten asks.

'The security guard called the company who installed the equipment. I talked to the owner. He said that this system records digitally for a period of twenty-eight days before the records are deleted. The recording is sent electronically immediately to the company offices in central Stellenbosch. That is where I went. There was no problem in obtaining a copy. I requested the period from 9 p.m. on Thursday, second April to 6 a.m. on Friday, third.'

'What do you mean "timing issues"?' De Vries asks.

On the screen, the picture is now running at normal speed.

'Look at the clocks above the desk, sir,' Morten says. 'You can see that they all say that it is twenty-five minutes past the hour.'

'*Ja.*'

'Now look down here . . .' He points to the digital time reading on the recording. It reads thirty-seven minutes past the hour. 'It's twelve minutes out.'

De Vries says: 'Which is the correct time?'

'I did not know there was a difference until just now.' Don says.

'Just call the building,' De Vries says impatiently. 'Ask the security guard what the time is on the clocks and compare it to the correct time.'

Don nods, ducks out of the office.

'Now, just get me the moment when Trevor Bhekifa appears, Sergeant. We'll solve this time matter in due course.'

Morten fast-forwards through the recording until it reaches 12.32 on Friday, 3 April. At that moment, the camera picks up Bhekifa walking slowly into shot from behind the camera. He moves straight to the elevators. He presses a button between the two doors, the right-hand doors open and he steps inside.

'You're sure he doesn't arrive earlier and go out again?'

Morten reverses the action, running at twelve times normal speed, watching for any movement in the foyer. He stops the recording at 11.47 when a couple enter, summon an elevator and walk into the left-hand lift. He continues travelling back in time, but no one else appears. Throughout that time, no security guard appears at the desk. De Vries wonders whether this could have any significance, or whether, more likely, the guard was snoozing somewhere off camera in the building.

Don February comes back into the room.

'According to the guard on duty, the clocks were showing thirteen minutes to the hour. On my watch, it was exactly ten minutes to four, so they are three minutes slow.'

Morten says: 'If they are three minutes slow, then the surveillance system time code is nine minutes fast. Bhekifa arrived home at 12.23 on Friday morning.'

'That is almost two hours after he claimed he left Taryn Holt's house,' De Vries says. 'At that time of night, how long would it take to drive from Oranjezicht to Stellenbosch? Forty-five minutes, an hour if he drives slowly. That means he could have left Holt's house at 11.30, even 11.40 p.m. That puts him right in the time-frame.'

'We get him back in?' Don says.

'Of course . . . But maybe not just yet.' He turns to Morten.

'How solid is this timing evidence for court, if it comes to that?'

Morten contemplates for a moment.

'We should obtain a copy of the recording from the present time back to the time-frame covered here. The officer should

115

check the time against an accurate source. We can check that neither the clocks on the wall of the foyer, nor the digital display, have been altered. Then, the timing is rock solid.'

'Good. Sergeant, not one word of this goes anywhere. You understand?'

'Yes, sir.'

'I mean anywhere.'

Morten looks up at De Vries, meets his eye, nods.

They sit in silence at the back of the car. De Vries looks out of the window at the view of the Southern Suburbs anew, as a passenger now rather than as a driver watching the road; Thulani stares straight ahead. The interior of the car is cold; De Vries notes that the police driver is wearing a coat yet, outside, it is still warm. The car turns off the freeway into Bishopscourt; the peaceful, leafy streets are deserted, the plots of land extending to several hundred metres wide, most of the houses hidden from view. The car turns into a driveway, stops at a security gate. A uniformed guard appears, salutes the occupants, raises the barrier. The car drifts down a wide lane lined with olive trees under-planted with aga-panthus, and pulls up under a covered porch by the front door. Another security guard opens the car door for Thulani, and De Vries's door is opened by the driver. He walks around the car and up the steps to the house, a few paces behind Thulani. Once inside the grand hallway, a suited man greets them, leads them to the back of the house and into a formal sitting room, overlooking an expansive garden and, beyond, the breathtaking vista of the forested southern slopes of the mountainside. In a square armchair, a small, elderly man sits writing in a leather-bound folder. He wears a tweed check three-piece suit, gold cufflinks on thin wrists. As they approach him, he looks up, smiles at Thulani, leans forward in the chair and half rises. Thulani approaches, bends down to him, shakes his hand warmly.

'This is one of my senior officers, Colonel de Vries.'

Vaughn moves forward, shakes Bheka Bhekifa's hand gently. It is as if he is being granted an audience with royalty. The old man holds onto his hand, looks up at him.

'You have been with the SAPS a long time, Colonel?'

'Twenty-seven years, sir.'

'Yes . . . You have that look about you.'

Bhekifa releases his hand, nods, shifts back in his chair until he is propped up in its crook.

'Sit down, both of you.' He turns to Thulani. 'You tell me that there is news which I must hear only personally from you. This concerns me. Do not keep me waiting any longer.'

De Vries is surprised by the man's frailty, his slow delivery which reminds him of Mandela after his release, yet Bhekifa must have been at least twenty years Mandela's junior when the great man died, and is perhaps now in his early seventies. Behind the shaky words, De Vries sees bright, small eyes, and thinks that this man's brain must still be sharp amid a failing body.

'The matter,' Thulani begins, 'concerns the death of a friend of your son's – Trevor – in Cape Town two days ago.'

De Vries notices Bhekifa indicates no surprise.

'Colonel de Vries is leading the enquiry, and Trevor made himself available for questioning as it appears that the victim was a lady friend of his. The victim was the daughter of Graeme Holt, the late businessman. Her name was Taryn Holt.'

'I remember Holt. He was a friend of Botha's. My son was involved with his daughter?'

'His cell-phone number was identified by us, and we contacted him. He immediately volunteered to be interviewed and that process is now complete.'

De Vries continues to study Bhekifa; he remains silent at Thulani's statement that the process is complete, accepts that Thulani is misrepresenting him.

'What happened to this Holt woman?'

Thulani looks at De Vries, who says: 'She was shot in her home, sir, in the middle of the night between last Thursday and Friday.'

'It was a robbery?'

De Vries hesitates.

'It is too early to say, sir. The investigation is only beginning.'

Bhekifa shifts in his chair, angling himself towards Thulani.

'While so much inequality is permitted to remain in our country, it is inevitable that there will be property crimes against the wealthy and privileged. As the gap between rich and poor grows wider every day, so your job, Sempiwe, will become more difficult. The solution, as I have always said, must lie with us, the politicians.' He struggles forward, his voice stronger.

'I do not believe that people in South Africa, even the wider world, realize how lucky they have been to have had a stable ANC government for the last twenty-one years. Of course, we have made mistakes. We were not a political party . . .' He looks at De Vries. '. . . We were not permitted to be . . .' He returns his gaze to Thulani. 'We had to learn that we must sell our ideas to the people, to help them to understand. But, at least now there is hope and change all around us: better schools, better homes, more university places, workers' rights, a respect for what we do . . .'

De Vries doubts that any man in this room truly believes these words.

'I am afraid that Trevor has embraced another, more Western attitude to life, with his white girlfriends and his love of cars and celebrity. He will lose the support of his own people if they discover secrets about his life but, maybe, that is what should happen. Let them see him for what he is and, perhaps, it will help him to see himself.'

De Vries listens to the man's words and glances around the room. It is styled like an English country house, filled with antiques and oil paintings of black Africans. It is, he reflects, just as much a Western attitude to life as that of his son, about whose world he is so dismissive.

'Everything is being handled very discreetly,' Thulani says. 'I am certain that there will be the minimum of publicity.'

Bhekifa sits back, shrugs.

'It is the price of democracy. We are all prisoners of our so-called free press.'

'You have managed it well,' Thulani says, rising. 'In the unlikely event that Trevor is involved further in our investigation I will, of course, inform you personally.'

Bhekifa smiles at him, opens his palms at him. 'Thank you, my friend.'

De Vries says: 'Goodbye, sir.'

Thulani struggles in his pocket.

'Before we go, may I impose upon you?' He produces a pocket camera. 'For my family?'

'Of course, of course,' Bhekifa tells him, sitting erect on the front edge of his chair. Thulani passes the camera to De Vries, squats with shaking knees next to the old man, puts his arm around his shoulders and draws him in. Bhekifa grimaces momentarily, then smiles wanly into the lens.

Thulani says: 'The button on the top right, Colonel.'

'Is this to become a routine?' John Marantz asks, as he takes the final steps of the long staircase. 'I thought you liked drinking alone?'

De Vries walks into the kitchen, opens the fridge, selects a bottle and opens it.

'Being here with you,' he says quietly, 'it's like being alone.'

119

He looks up. Marantz stares at him. De Vries smiles.

'Well, technically, I am the only one drinking.'

They walk into the huge living area.

'I met Bheka Bhekifa this afternoon.'

Marantz raises his eyebrows.

'Well, well. You are mixing in exalted circles. Why was that?'

De Vries stops, turns to Marantz.

'You got nuts?'

'No. Tell me about Bhekifa.'

They walk through the tall doors into the garden, sit by the pool in the evening shade. De Vries takes a swig from the bottle, lights a cigarette.

'Taryn Holt was seeing Trevor Bhekifa. Our esteemed General Thulani, apparently a friend of the father, decided this warranted visiting old man Bhekifa immediately, and I was brought along as the investigating officer.'

'How does the hero seem?'

'Older than I would have expected, but very comfortable in his Bishopscourt mansion, sounding off about the inequality in our society.'

Marantz chuckles.

'You are so naïve here, thinking that politicians should be honest and true. Yours are no more hypocritical and corrupt than anywhere else. I mean, our lot wrote the rulebook: think about Blair, Bush, Cameron, even Murdoch. Your guys are amateurs.'

'You think Bhekifa is still important?'

'From what I read, yes. The ANC are under threat from splinter groups and new political parties. He seems to be working to keep them together. So, I suppose, he remains relevant for as long as you have, in effect, one-party politics. Is Trevor Bhekifa implicated?'

De Vries hesitates. He has involved Marantz before, enjoys hearing a fresh perspective but, at the back of his mind, Marantz's old profession – an Intelligence Officer and Interrogator for the British Government, the consequences for his family, the connections he seems to maintain – still bothers him.

'Yes and no. He was there, at her house, just on the edge of the time-frame estimated for time of death, but he claims he went home. There's a little doubt about timings.'

'So, he's a suspect.'

'I didn't say that.'

'You did . . . In effect. That's interesting.'

'Perhaps . . .'

'You don't think so?'

'I don't know, Johnnie. It doesn't feel right. Unless I'm missing something, there's no motivation for it, and this looks planned in advance, not a crime of passion or opportunity.'

'Very little in the papers about it. That deliberate?'

'Taryn Holt wasn't a celebrity. It has to be pretty special for murder to warrant a front page. You know how it is.'

'But the Bhekifa angle . . . ?'

'Total blackout. Not a word, John.'

'I have no contact with the press. Don't want it. I live here quietly, on my own. That's the way I intend to keep it.'

'Privately, yes. On your own, I hope not.'

'I have Flynn.'

They look up at the Irish terrier, who sits on the edge of the pool. He sees them staring and looks down, bashful.

De Vries lies in bed, head numb, mind racing. He pushes his tongue into the top of his mouth to try to loosen his jaw. It does not work. Bheka Bhekifa is not a man he had dreamed he might respect, yet something about the small man's dignity, the conviction in his people's achievements; it impresses him. He feels exhaustion overcome him, feels himself losing consciousness.

1987

He wears jeans, a Springbok rugby shirt and reflective aviator sunglasses, a pair of rip-off Ray-Bans from the Greenpoint flea market. He pushes through the double doors of the Heidelberg Tavern, spots his friends, greets them, buys a beer, sits down with them.

'Howzit?'

'Well . . .' De Vries says. 'From next week I'll be keeping my eye on you all from a patrol car from here to bloody Pinelands.'

He accepts their acclamations, but knows that several of them question his decision to join the police force. There is a sense of change in their country, as yet unquantifiable, and it will bring either violence and civil war, or a slow, painful dismantling of the system. But, from the moment he gained responsibility in the army, he knew what he would do: he knew that he was disgusted and incensed by injustice; knew that he was prepared to fight to avoid it, to speak for those whose voices had been made silent.

Already, he wishes away his period of probation, longs for the years to pass before he can transfer to plain clothes. His time in the army has tired him of undue physical exertion and use of force, but has revealed to him the benefits of using his brain to deduce and infer, to plot his way to his goal, however convoluted. He knows that he is already good at it, and will be better.

He turns back to his mates, already discussing something else, seemingly unwilling to discuss his career in public. Soon, he knows, he will drink with his new colleagues in a bar which they favour; he knows that these student friendships, born of the shared misery of National Service, will fade and decay, that everything about his life will change.

He sits back on the dirty plastic-upholstered bench, letting the hubbub of the neighbourhood beer hall retreat to the back of his mind. His thoughts turn to Suzanne Basler, his girlfriend, the woman who has supported him through his training, who speaks of making a home and building a life, and he thinks that maybe this is the moment to do it all: the career, the wife, the family.

He smiles to himself, knows that Suzanne will not hurry her own decisions. She is studying television journalism, will plan her career far more carefully than he, will live at home until the time is right – for her – to move away. For now, she visits him in his shared house in Observatory – a suburb which has always subverted apartheid and seems to welcome everyone: students and artists, the homeless, the criminal. And those hours together, in the first double bed of his life, looking out from the tall window across the narrow balcony with its wrought-iron decoration, up to Devil's Peak, they have been the making of him. They have healed his misery from his enforced time in the army, have educated him, have inspired him to take control of his life.

'Hey . . . Vaughn.'

De Vries looks up, shakes his head free of his own thoughts. 'What?'

'Constable de Vries . . .' they jeer. 'Suzie like it when you dress up in your uniform?'

'When I get out of it.'

They catcall. He feels his heart sink, knows now that everything will change . . .

2015

At the traffic lights on the crossroads between Campground Road and Rondebosch Common, even early on a Sunday, there is an array of hawkers: *Big Issue* and *Funny Money* sellers, collaged scenes of Cape Town made from tin cans, cases of fruit, beaded gifts. De Vries ignores them, shakes his head as the newspaper seller approaches. The man scowls. As he passes, De Vries sees one word on the cover of the *Cape Herald*, bold and black: Bhekifa.

He winds down his window and summons the man, pays for the paper and slaps it, face up, on the passenger seat.

Sunday Cape Herald, 5 April 2015

BHEKIFA JUNIOR LINK TO MURDERED HOLT HEIRESS

Senior SAPS officers are questioning Trevor Bhekifa regarding the murder of Holt Industries heiress Taryn Holt in Oranjezicht on Thursday night. Bhekifa is reported to have been sexually involved with the multi-millionaire patron of the arts and discussing her involvement in the new political movement supported by him, the Democratic Reform Party.

Trevor Bhekifa, the thirty-three-year-old son of ANC policy-maker and hero of the Struggle Bheka Bhekifa, has been questioned by officers of the elite Special Crimes Unit based in Cape Town's CBD. Over the years, Bhekifa junior has developed a reputation for dating high-profile women, driving expensive cars and promoting his property-development businesses and high-life style, all in stark contrast to his father's political philosophy.

Bhekifa was released without charge yesterday evening but is said to be continuing to assist police enquiries.

The lights, at last, change to green. The car behind him honks immediately.

De Vries jams his foot on the accelerator, sticks his middle finger out of the window and shouts: 'Fuck the fuck off.'

Access from the underground car park to the floors above is only by staircase to the main foyer and then by elevator, or fire escape stairs. De Vries sees a small group of reporters gathered outside the street entrance but, inside, it is quiet. He travels up to his floor alone, walks through the sparsely filled squad room to his office, where he finds Don February waiting for him.

'Calm before the storm?'

Don nods: 'General Thulani is in his office. He told me to tell you to report to him the moment you arrived.'

'Let's get it out of the way then, Don . . . No way you could have let the information about Bhekifa out?'

'No. I was thinking about it while I was waiting for you. I did not discuss it outside the team. I do not believe that they would let it out.'

'I hope not.'

'How does this affect the enquiry?'

'It doesn't, but Thulani may not see it that way.'

De Vries is not offered a seat. He stands in front of Thulani's desk.

'How many hours is it, Colonel, since I told you that I was putting my trust in you, that you had an opportunity to show me that you could control a delicate case?'

'I have checked . . .'

'I don't want to hear it,' Thulani interrupts. 'Obviously, I did not leak this information. There is no reason on earth why Trevor Bhekifa would speak to the press, so the leak comes from your department. Identify the leak in the next twenty-four hours, or I send in Colonel Wertner and his Internal Investigation Department, and I don't care how much it screws with your investigation because it cannot go on like this. Every case your department handles is sensitive: your teams must be water-tight. I have informed Brigadier du Toit and, of course, he agrees with me. His absence is proving detrimental to his unit. Clearly, it is not safe in your hands.'

De Vries feels the blood pumping in his hands at his side, Thulani's voice reverberating in his aching head. He does not even register that he has stopped speaking.

'Colonel?'

'Yes, sir?'

'Twenty-four hours.'

'Yes . . . Sir.'

De Vries feels wretched doubting his own team, but he questions each of them in turn. He picks up nothing from the interviews, believes each of them when they deny any possible indiscretion.

He feels worse that he is wasting time on a matter unrelated to finding Taryn Holt's killer. The early days of a murder investigation offer, by far, the best hope of solving it and time is racing by without a significant breakthrough. By late morning, he is convinced that the leak did not come from own team, reasons that anyone in the building seeing Bhekifa could have formed their own theory to sell to the press.

He asks himself what the motive might be for releasing such information and concludes that, if it is not money, then it is either an attempt to cause him and the enquiry trouble or that, in some way, it is political; that this was an opportunity to discredit Trevor Bhekifa. He calls a contact on the *Sunday Cape Herald* at home, traps himself into promising advance information subsequently in exchange for the journalist contacting the authors of the story and ascertaining not their source, but whether any money was paid.

At lunchtime, Don drives De Vries to Stellenbosch, retracing his route to Trevor Bhekifa's apartment building. They knock on the tall glass doors and the security guard behind the desk in the foyer buzzes them in, intercepts them with a clipboard.

'We are here,' Don tells him, showing his ID, 'to see Mr Trevor Bhekifa.'

'Yes, sir.'

'We can go up?'

'Yes, sir.'

The guard uses his clipboard to indicate the lifts.

'Were you on duty on the night of Thursday, 2 April last week?'

'No, sir. Thursday and Friday are my days off.'

'Okay.'

When the doors close, De Vries says: 'I know it's a low-paid job, but you'd think . . .'

They get out on the top floor, turn towards Bhekifa's apartment, ring on the doorbell. From behind the door, they hear laughter, then the door opens and Bhekifa is framed for a moment, barefoot in shorts and sleeveless teeshirt, muscles bulging, broad smile on his face. It fades as he registers De Vries.

'You people don't call first?'

'We need to speak to you again, Mr Bhekifa,' De Vries says. 'We came to you as a matter of courtesy. Can we come in?'

Bhekifa glances behind him, runs his hand through his hair, stands aside.

De Vries and Don walk past him into a broad living area. Their attention is distracted from the view of old Stellenbosch oaks and the little park beyond by a young black woman in denim cut-offs and a top which stops well short of her navel. She gets up, smiles at them, sits again, looks up at Trevor.

'Would you prefer,' De Vries says, turning to him, 'to discuss these matters in private?'

Bhekifa is suddenly uneasy; he stands wordless for several seconds, then walks over to a cabinet and switches off the music. He goes over to the girl and murmurs something to her. She gets up again, saunters out of the room and into another. In the awkward silence, they all hear a door opened and closed again. De Vries says nothing, stands in the middle of the room and waits. Finally, Bhekifa invites them to sit down.

'Have you seen today's *Cape Herald*?' De Vries asks.

'Yes.'

'Firstly, I want to apologize. We have no knowledge of how this information reached the newspaper. We have already begun an investigation as to who could have spoken to the press.'

Bhekifa looks sullen.

'It was inevitable. I expect it from the press and I expect it from the SAPS.'

'Well, I don't expect it from my team, and I don't believe that it was one of them. Nonetheless, we hoped that your interview with us could be discreet, and I'm sorry it has turned out not to be.'

Bhekifa raises his eyebrows.

'However,' De Vries continues, 'we have another matter of importance to discuss with you. I want you to recall what you told us when we spoke to you yesterday: that you left Taryn Holt's home at approximately 10.30 p.m.?'

'I think so, yes.'

'But you did not return to this building until 12.23 a.m. – that is seven minutes short of two hours. Can you explain what you were doing during that time?'

De Vries watches Bhekifa strain to comprehend, sees him struggle to focus.

'Mr Bhekifa? Are you all right?'

Bhekifa smiles.

'I've had a few drinks. We had a few. I shouldn't drink at lunchtime.'

'I need a proper account from you regarding the time between you leaving Oranjezicht and returning here to your apartment.'

'I told you. I was in my car for a while. I didn't know what to do.'

'How long did you sit in your car?'

'I don't know . . . Maybe ten, fifteen minutes.'

De Vries sighs.

'That doesn't explain why you took so long to make a short journey.'

Bhekifa sits staring ahead of himself, begins to nod gently as if he has come to a decision.

'I did not drive home directly. I made a detour, all right? Only across the park there. I went to see my girlfriend, Sandi. She is the girl who is with me here today.'

'You went to see this lady?'

'Yes. I called on her. We spoke for maybe half an hour and then she told me to go, that she was tired. So, I came home.'

'Right,' De Vries says. 'I want to be clear. You were in a relationship with both Taryn Holt and this young lady?'

'Yes.'

'Did Miss Holt know about the existence of your other girlfriend?'

'I don't think so.'

De Vries gestures in the direction the girl had exited the room.

'She is in another room, yes?'

'She is in our bedroom.'

'Warrant Officer February is going to take a statement from her there.'

'Okay.'

Don moves away to find Sandi; De Vries writes down what Bhekifa has told him, glancing up at the man from time to time. His eye is drawn to the man's arms, to his big hands.

'Your wrists, Mr Bhekifa?' His eyes drop to the table where they rest. Bhekifa looks down also. 'How did you get that bruising?'

Bhekifa blushes.

'It is nothing.'

'I'm afraid I need to know.'

'It is not violence. It is games.'

'Games you played with Taryn Holt?'

He says nothing.

'Your girlfriend here, Sandi? She doesn't notice?'

'It is not her business. In my culture, a man may see who he pleases.'

'And, as well as Sandi, you saw Taryn Holt. Did those bruises come from games you played with her?'

Bhekifa pushes his chair back, withdraws his arms from the table and places them in his lap. He speaks very quietly, without making eye contact with De Vries.

'Taryn liked to be in control. She knew that I could dominate her physically. She liked to dominate me. We played games. Many people do.'

'Sex games. She tied you up?'

'We would use ropes and cuffs, sometimes, yes.'

De Vries thinks about Taryn Holt, knows that he has seen no bruises on her wrists.

'How did that make you feel?'

Bhekifa frowns ostentatiously.

'That is not your business.'

De Vries smiles, meets his wide-eyed stare.

'Taryn Holt is dead, murdered by someone who knew her, someone who knew her house, her alarm system, her routine. Everything I ask you about Taryn Holt is my business.'

Bhekifa looks down.

'Did you resent this behaviour?'

'No. What lovers do in the bedroom is private. It was a game Taryn liked to play. I loved being with her and I was happy to play, or I would not have come back.'

De Vries waits for more, but Bhekifa stays silent.

'If I find that the account of your movements is still incomplete, I will prosecute you for interfering with this inquiry. Are you clear?'

Bhekifa nods. 'When I came to you, I had only just heard, sir. I did not know what I was thinking.'

'Well, think now,' De Vries says. 'I asked you before: did Taryn Holt express concern about any individual in particular when you discussed the matter of the threats against her and her gallery?'

Bhekifa shakes his head.

'No. If she had done, I would never have left her that night.'

De Vries waits, nods at him and moves away. Then he stops and turns back to him.

'I came here to apologize to you, but it is you who should apologize to me. You have wasted my time and delayed my enquiry.'

Bhekifa looks him in the eye, presses his palms together in front of himself.

'I am sorry, sir.'

Don appears from a doorway to the right of the front door, nods at De Vries who is already opening the door, follows him out. De Vries pulls the door to, puts his hand on Don's arm, waits by the door. A few moments later, they hear hushed voices then laughter.

De Vries turns away abruptly, heads for the lift.

'He'll make a fine politician. As insincere as the best of them. What did that girl tell you?'

They step into the lift, begin to descend.

'She said he arrived late, maybe a little before midnight. She was already in bed, and not happy to see him. He stayed for twenty minutes, half an hour, and then she sent him home.'

'You think it is a serious relationship or just a game?'

'She said she often stays here with him.'

'That fits,' De Vries says. 'You hear him refer to it as "our" bedroom?'

'What, then, was Miss Holt?'

The doors open onto the spacious foyer, the now unmanned security desk, the four clocks three minutes slow.

131

'I'll tell you what she was,' De Vries says bitterly. 'A publicity coup; maybe a good time but, above all, a potential donor to be wooed and coerced. The more I learn about the people around her, the less surprised I am that she trusted no one.'

As they drive back to Cape Town, De Vries receives a call from the *Sunday Cape Herald* journalist. He hangs up, turns to Don.

'Anonymous tip-off. No money involved. The more I think about it, there's no substance to the story. It's just one piece of information parlayed into an eye-catching headline. Anyone who saw me with Bhekifa could guess why he was there.'

'So why is General Thulani so concerned?'

De Vries chuckles.

'Because he and old man Bhekifa are friends, or so he likes to think. Thulani wanted to show off to him that he could keep his son's indiscretions under wraps. And now he can't, it's an embarrassment.'

'We now have two men who visited Taryn Holt shortly before she was killed. But we have no clue as to who the third visitor was.'

'No,' De Vries says, serious once more. 'And we have Wertner and the Internal Investigation Unit coming for us. It's happening again, Don. One crack in our armour and they're straight after us. We don't even have Director du Toit between us and them. We need a breakthrough: for the case, and for us.'

By the time De Vries reaches his office on Monday at 8 a.m., every member of the investigating team is present in the squad room. He wonders whether, after his questioning the previous day, this is a show of commitment and loyalty. Whatever it is, he is grateful for it.

As he reaches his desk the telephone rings and he grabs the receiver.

'De Vries.'

'This is Wertner. We have a meeting at 9 a.m. this morning. My office.'

De Vries takes a short, shallow breath.

'9 a.m., Colonel.'

He replaces the receiver, wonders how Wertner knew he would arrive at his desk at that moment, and looks at the ceiling and the four corners of his office. Whenever he has involvement with the Internal Investigation chief, he becomes paranoid.

His cell-phone rings. He sees that it is Steve Ulton from the Crime Lab. He greets Ulton, listens for almost two minutes, and hangs up. He exits his office and hurries away towards the elevators.

'We've been incredibly lucky,' Ulton says as he leads De Vries to the main bench on which a series of items are laid out.

'At approximately 2 a.m. on Saturday morning, the body of a man identified as Angus Lyle was discovered by Metro officers at the base of a hedge in De Waal Park. Lyle is known to both them and Central officers as a former mental patient, with drug problems, released into the care of a relative. Seems he preferred the street and usually escaped his relative's custody.' He looks down at his clipboard. 'Apparently, he could often be found sleeping under the overpass at the junction between Maynard Street and Mill Street.' He turns to De Vries. 'When a colleague of mine at Evidence was checking inventories of suspects, he came across these items and, because we had been discussing it previously, immediately contacted me.'

De Vries holds up a hand.

'Hang on. This Lyle is dead, right? When?'

'According to the initial readings, two to four hours previous to the discovery.'

'So, Friday evening . . . What else?'

'I'm having his body brought over here and I've asked for extra protection of the hands in case there's still a chance of residues, but it's Doctor Jafari's show and she says that she'll get to him if and when her schedule is complete.'

De Vries shakes his head.

'We need it done now.'

Ulton's chuckle is without mirth. 'She's all yours, Vaughn. She takes no prisoners.'

'You're talking about gunshot residues?'

'I am.'

'What's the point of having a mortuary here if our work doesn't take priority?'

Ulton faces him.

'Too many bodies. Way too many. . .'

'I'll go to her just now. Nothing works if we don't prioritize.'

'Be careful, man. She'll be on to you about elitism, and then you know where the argument goes . . .'

'This isn't racial . . . Not everything in this country has to be racial.' He checks himself. 'Sorry, Steve. Go on.'

He turns back to the table.

'See what we found and then make your decision.'

De Vries turns back to the bench

'This is what he found on Lyle's body,' Ulton says, indicating each item with his pen. 'Nine-millimetre Beretta. I've not run any tests yet, but it has been fired recently. Serial number's gone, but we may be able to find something. A leaflet for the New Worlds Gallery exhibition of paintings by Dazuluka Cele; a Bible . . . I've only glanced at it, but there is underlining and notes. Finally, on his sweatshirt, two blood spatters . . .'

'Whose?'

Ulton smiles.

'It's happening now, Vaughn. I'll know soon.'

'The art-exhibition flyer was what made the connection?'

'That's what my colleague said. Then the weapon.'

'Anything else known about this Lyle guy?'

'Not by me. As I said, he was known to the Metro guys and a few officers from Central. That's where he usually hung out.'

'I'll talk to Jafari now.'

He thanks him, turns towards the exit, turns back.

'The Bible: can I see it?'

'If you put on gloves, I suppose so.'

De Vries pulls on the gloves proffered by Ulton, severs the fastening to the evidence pack, picks out the small volume. He fans through the pages until he comes to some underlined writing.

The woman was arrayed in purple and scarlet, and adorned with gold and jewels and pearls, holding in her hand a golden cup full of abominations and the impurities of her sexual immorality.

He flicks through the volume again, stops once more at underlined text.

Put to death therefore what is earthly in you: sexual immorality, impurity, passion, evil, desire and covetousness, which is idolatry.

'Sex and desire and death,' Ulton says. 'I think we get the idea.'

'What gets me is how these fucking religions always target the ignorant and needy. Like they can't fight a worthy opponent.'

He flicks pages through to the front cover, reads the words from a rubber stamp, printed in faded green.

'I might have known . . .'

'What?'

'St Jerome's Chapel.'

'You know it?'

'Oh yes,' De Vries says. 'I fucking hate churches.'

'An opportunity for confession, perhaps?' Ulton says, smiling now.

'No time, man. Hours and hours and I wouldn't even have begun to scratch the surface.'

De Vries trots to the mortuary, finds the examination room empty. He moves towards the two small offices at the back of the room: one dark, the other containing the hunched form of Doctor Anna Jafari. He knocks firmly and opens her door even before he has heard a response. He finds her facing him, finger in the air. She does not look up.

'I already know why you are here, Colonel.'

'This is an ongoing murder enquiry. This could be the break-through. What can you do for me, Doctor?'

'What I can always do. Tell you that there must be order, or the system will collapse.'

De Vries feels the pressure grow inside him; he cannot under-stand why others cannot see what is obvious to him.

'This is about the murder of a woman; possibly now the death of a young, vulnerable man. Not a hit-and-run, not a drug-related killing. This is something pre-meditated and the killer is out there.'

Jafari looks up, places her pen neatly in front of her.

'I don't know how you see me. I don't care. But, I am a human being. I am trying to live my life well and do my job properly.'

'No one is asking you to compromise that . . .'

'I see women and children every single day of work, Colonel. Abused, bullied, tortured, mutilated, murdered. If I took that to heart, I would never get out of bed.' De Vries opens his mouth, but she continues, barely raising her voice yet insisting she is heard. 'I know the statistics. Very few women kill women. Men kill us. Men are weak and pathetic and anything and everything threatens them, so when they find a strong woman, a powerful woman, they are afraid and their defence mechanism kicks in, and that mechanism includes murder.' She stands up.

'If I dwelt on that, Colonel, I would prioritize every female murder victim, but the sad truth is that men will kill anything, for any reason. So, I attend to my job logically and calmly and without emotion. There is no other way.' She sits back down, picks up her pen.

'You have your way, Doctor, but we have the media all over us, we have evidence leaking from the enquiry. We need to move this on. We need results.'

Jafari looks up, her voice calm.

'Have you listened to nothing I said? You have your priorities, and I have my way. I make an exception for you, then there are three other senior investigators in your department and they will all want the same. Speak to General Thulani if you want, but I can only do what I can do.'

De Vries stares at her for a moment; he sees nothing but total assurance in her expression, such certainty in her eyes that what she says is right. He finds such hubris intolerably frustrating, finds the restriction on what he can say to her stifling. What could be more discriminatory than the fact that he must hold his tongue because she is small, coloured and a woman?

He calls Thulani's office, speaks with his secretary, leaves a message concerning post-mortem examinations. He expects nothing, but considers that the more he complains, the more there will be on record when it is proven that the system fails, as he is convinced it does.

It is 8.50 a.m., and he knows that he should report to Wertner's office and let the inevitable commence. The sooner

Wertner's team get to work, the sooner they will find nothing and leave him alone. Yet, after two days with no positive developments, he is too charged to stall the enquiry for what he knows is a waste of time. Instead, he pulls Don February from working with the collator and heads for the car park. Even Wertner cannot complain if his meeting is delayed because of a breakthrough in a murder case.

On their way across town, he updates Don on the discovery of Angus Lyle's body, the leaflet, the gun and the potential blood spatter evidence. Don listens, says nothing. They reach St Jerome Street, park outside the chapel and head immediately for the porch. De Vries pushes open the heavy door and strides inside. After a couple of steps, he stops. This morning, there are four chandeliers casting a pale, white light from bare bulbs over the pews, in which half a dozen people sit. At the altar, amidst a thick mist of blue smoke, Father Jacobus is speaking. They hear the tinkling of bells, see the thurible swinging on chains.

De Vries turns, ushers Don towards the door, leaves the church.

'What a miserable way to start the day,' De Vries says, as they get back into the car.

'Maybe, for those people, it is what helps them through the day?'

De Vries looks at his Warrant Officer, realizes that he has an empathy he lacks totally; he wonders which of them is the stronger policeman as a result of this inequality.

De Vries's cell-phone rings. He studies the screen, sees it is David Wertner, switches it to voicemail.

'Wertner has a dozen officers working for him in his office alone. Imagine how many more crimes could be solved if they were being proper policemen? The only officers we get now are Internal Investigation or Traffic. No wonder it's out of control . . .'

Don sits placidly. He has heard all these arguments before, knows that it is best to nod silently.

They wait for fifteen minutes until they see half a dozen elderly people leaving the church. Brenda Botes is the last to come out. She scans the road, sees De Vries and Don February, ducks back into the church.

They exit the car and follow her in. She is talking to Father Jacobus at the back of the church.

'I need to speak with both of you,' De Vries announces loudly.

'Why,' Jacobus starts, 'should we speak to you, when you have done nothing about that abomination?'

'Abomination?'

'That exhibition is open again. People are coming to leer at those pictures. The newspapers have made it a shrine to immorality and sinful desire.'

'You made it a shrine,' De Vries says dryly. 'No one but a few arty types knew anything about it until you came along and protested publicly.'

'It was your responsibility.'

'It isn't a police matter . . .'

'You should make it one,' Brenda Botes says. 'Our group will not let this matter drop. We have influence . . .'

'You must speak with the council . . .'

'What will they do?'

De Vries raises his hand.

'We need to talk to you about a man called Angus Lyle.'

Jacobus's eyes turn towards De Vries.

'What about Angus?'

'Angus Lyle is dead.'

Jacobus nods gravely.

'That is very sad. May God bless his soul. But, it is not unsurprising.'

De Vries turns to Brenda Botes.

'Did you know this man?'

'No.'

'No?'

'I saw him in church occasionally, but I did not know him.'

'You see him on the street?'

'No.'

'Then I must speak to Father Jacobus alone.'

Brenda Botes glances at Jacobus, turns and walks back to the main door.

'You want to sit down?'

'I want you,' Jacobus says, 'to stop coming here. You are upsetting my parishioners.'

'Upsetting them?' De Vries is shouting now, the echo from the previous word countering his next. He moderates his voice, but he can still hear his words whisper around the stone walls. 'I come here to tell you that one of them is dead, and you complain that I am upsetting other people. What kind of world do you live in? I am here to ask you about Angus Lyle, and I will continue to come here to ask you about people you know – and who subsequently die – for as long as that pattern continues.' De Vries takes a deep breath. 'So, Father, if you want rid of me, answer my questions and stop acting holier than thou.'

Jacobus says nothing. He just stares at De Vries blankly.

Don February says: 'Let us sit here and talk. Surely you are distressed that Mr Lyle has passed on?'

The priest twitches, drops into a pew; De Vries and Don take the row behind him. Jacobus twists around and faces them.

'I will tell you if you go away . . .'

De Vries and Don say nothing.

'. . . Angus Lyle was a very troubled young man. He came from a home with no father, a mother who turned to prostitution to pay her way. People do not appreciate how many whites are suffering in this country now, how many are in poverty. I will not tell you in his words what Angus told me, but I know that he witnessed these men coming to his home to have sexual intercourse with his mother, and I know that there were times he was threatened. It was one of those men who probably introduced him to drugs.'

'He came here regularly?'

'He came when he came. Once he stayed here for three days, sleeping on the floor there. At other times, I did not see him for weeks.'

'And what did you do to help him?'

'I prayed for him.'

'Was that it?'

Jacobus snorts.

'Yes. If the state could provide counselling for him, if there was a programme to tackle his addictions . . . But there was nothing.'

'Did he hate women?'

Jacobus frowns.

'That is a blunt question.' De Vries says nothing. 'I believe he came to hate his mother. I think he felt that there were other ways to survive, that prostituting herself was the ultimate sin.'

'And who gave him that idea?'

'The Bible proscribes . . .'

'Did he hate other women?'

'He read what he read and formed his own opinion. I tried to interpret and explain for him, but people will read what they will from the Holy scriptures.'

The frustration and anger wells inside De Vries; he tastes bile. He represses it.

'Did Angus Lyle ever meet Taryn Holt?'

'Not here. That woman was never here.'

'But anywhere else?'

'I don't know that. How would I know? I doubt it. I would say that they were at the furthest points of the wide divide in this country.'

'You gave him a Bible?'

'I did.'

'You ever look in it? His Bible?'

'No.'

'He seemed obsessed by immoral women. He underlined passages and made notes.'

'That is not uncommon and it is not surprising, given the man's history.'

'Was Lyle ever violent?'

Jacobus cogitates.

'He had a temper. When he did not have the drugs and he felt that the world was against him . . . But then, I suspect, you have such a temper also.'

'We're not talking about me . . .'

'And you are sensitive about it, too. I said what I did merely to illustrate that we all have things in life which disturb us, which might cause us to be bad tempered. I never saw Angus being violent.'

'What about the immoral women? What did he want to do with them?'

'I should think that depended on whether he was reading the Old Testament or the New. With the latter, he would have wanted to save them; using the former, I suspect, he would have wanted to kill them.'

De Vries turns to Don, then back to Jacobus.

'Was Angus at the demonstration on Wednesday night?'

'I don't know . . . I thought I saw him at one point, but I'm not sure.'

'But he knew about your protest?'

'I think so. We had been talking about it for a week before the event, saying that this was what we would do if the Holt woman did not cancel the exhibition.'

'Did he see the pictures himself?'

'Possibly. There were leaflets in the vestry we had collected. Angus often let himself in there, looking for me. And, for all I knew, he walked down the street and saw that hideous painting in the window.'

'When did you last speak with him?'

'Not for a while. Monday or Tuesday of last week. Possibly Tuesday.' He closes his eyes. 'So many people fall. At least now, he is in the hands of the Lord.'

De Vries thinks of the body of Angus Lyle, naked and dissected, on a bench in the mortuary, and hopes that now, right now, he is in the hands of Doctor Anna Jafari.

'You have been very quiet.'

'You do not like the priest?'

De Vries faces him.

'You don't find him arrogant and fucking annoying?'

'I think he has a difficult job. It is a matter of faith, I suppose.'

'You have faith? You are a Christian?'

'No, sir. That is not it . . .' He concentrates on pulling out into the traffic. 'It is not my place to say . . .'

De Vries studies him.

'Tell me what you think about the case?'

'I do not know what to think. A man like this Angus Lyle. It is not who we thought might have killed Miss Holt.'

'No.'

'If we find that he had met her, perhaps been to her house, then I suppose the matter is decided . . . But I cannot see why she would befriend him.'

'We don't know either of them yet.'

'Is it believable, that he is able to avoid setting off the alarm, that he picks up the shells, leaves no forensic evidence? And where does he find the weapon?'

'That we have to find out. We need to know whether this is a man with a good brain who is disturbed, or whether he is incapacitated by drugs, unable to plan and carry out something like this.'

They pull up at the traffic lights to rejoin Orange Street.

'And now he is dead, with all the evidence on him . . .'

De Vries turns to him, holds his cigarette out of the window.

'*Ja*, I agree. It would be convenient if someone wanted to implicate him to distract attention from themselves, but what bothers me is why? If someone else is responsible, they left no evidence anyway.'

'So, we follow the trail of Angus Lyle?'

'Whether Lyle is responsible or not, we follow it. Either it closes the case or we are being led somewhere for a reason. We go where it takes us . . .' De Vries looks over to Don. 'And then we find out where we are.'

Within five minutes of De Vries returning to the station, David Wertner appears in the squad room and marches over to his office. He lets himself in.

'Is this an official refusal to co-operate with my department, De Vries?'

De Vries looks up at him calmly from his chair, eyes half-closed.

'Close the door and sit down.'

'In my office, De Vries. Not here, not now. In my office at 9 a.m., that was the arrangement.'

De Vries feels composed. He has expended his wrath. His head is buzzing with possibilities at the developments of the morning. Wertner now seems no more than a minor irritation.

'We are both senior officers. I am in the middle of a serious, high-profile murder enquiry.' He sits up. 'I'm sure that you wouldn't want to be accused of hindering it?'

Wertner sits, and De Vries smiles to himself.

'What hinders your work, De Vries,' Wertner says, leaning over the desk, 'is your inability to control your team. As we have previously discussed, many times, when I am officially investigating you and your department, which I am now, I have technical rank. That is why you are insubordinate to have deliberately failed to appear before me at 9 a.m.'

'Grow up, Wertner. Insubordinate? We're not at training school now. This is the real world. I had a breakthrough in my case. It was necessary to interview a difficult witness before certain information reached him. Perhaps you have forgotten the imperatives of an investigation?'

'I haven't forgotten the way you operate. Have you questioned your team regarding this leak of crucial information?'

'First of all,' De Vries says. 'It is not crucial information. It was a report that Trevor Bhekifa was present at this station and questioned. Whoever did leak it had no information; that was invented by the newspaper. Secondly, the article included information which I didn't discuss with Bhekifa. I never overtly asked him if he was having a sexual relationship with Taryn Holt; intimate and close, maybe, but the word sex was never mentioned. Yet that's what they printed front and centre. Third, I've spoken to all my team and they deny making even a casual mention of the topic anywhere that could have been overheard, and finally, to show you that I know exactly what is happening, I used a contact at the *Sunday Cape Herald* to confirm that the tip-off received was anonymous and that no money changed hands.'

'That does not clear you or your team.'

'For fuck's sake, Wertner. Ask yourself: what is the motive for leaking the story? If it's not money, then it's troublemaking. They're trying to turn this into something it isn't. This is politics and, if you don't know by now that I don't do politics, then you know nothing.'

'You could have told me this at our agreed appointment.'

'I'm telling you now. Waste your time interviewing team members, delay my enquiry, or do some thinking and work out who gains from the leak, but it sure as hell isn't anyone on the right side of the equation.'

Wertner gets up, runs his hand over his closely shaven head, stretches stiff, thick shoulder muscles. He is still too squat to look physically threatening, De Vries thinks. He is like an elderly attack dog whose muzzle you could hold shut, keep him at arm's length.

'You always have an answer, don't you? An explanation for your deficiencies. But, know this: I am watching you all the time.'

'I know you are.'

'So, every last detail of your case had better be watertight, Colonel.'

He swivels, pulls open the door, marches out, slams it behind him.

'Colonel. You have a call from a Mr Mitchell Smith. He says it's urgent.'

De Vries sighs, glances at his watch.

'Tell him I have two minutes only. Then put him through.'

He has managed to put Mitchell Smith, the memories he

conjures, to the back of his mind; he has forced himself to focus on what gets him through each day.

'Is this secure? Is this a safe line?'

'Mr Smith. I told you I'd return your call. What is it?'

'I told you it was urgent. I need to speak to you.'

'What do you want to tell me?'

'I don't want to say on the phone.'

'Then I can't help you . . .'

'Sheldon Rich, Johan Esau, Joe Swanepoel.' He shouts the words. 'Do you remember these men?'

'This is a long time ago. I don't have time to reminisce.'

'They're dead, Colonel de Vries. Each of them is dead. In the last two weeks.'

'How?'

'They were killed. It's in the local papers.'

'We live in a violent country.'

'Three men who were there. Those three. It cannot be a coincidence.'

De Vries closes his eyes.

'It's twenty-one years ago. No one remembers any of it . . .'

'I . . .'

'No,' De Vries says firmly. 'I . . . have to go back to work. As I said before: when I have some time, I will return your call. Take care of yourself, sir.'

He puts down the phone, feels a gripe in the pit of his stomach.

1992

De Vries is a racist. He knows that this is true because when he hears Suzanne talking with her friends, he hears opinion and reasoning which, before, has eluded him. But he is not mindless. His upbringing has taught him and his training is teaching him to judge based on evidence and, for him, the evidence is clear. The white guys have built South Africa; they have the experience, the brains, the work-ethic to develop it still. He only has to look at the African countries that have demanded independence to see the corruption, the inefficiency, the violence and prejudice – their rapid decline, total regression into third world states. He fears for his future; fears for their future.

He grew up on a farm in the Overberg, saw for himself: the black farm workers arriving late each day, working slowly for a few hours, then swigging warm cool-drink and pulling the stuffing out from white loaves, snoozing in the shade until his father, or Mike du Clos, the farm manager, or, later, he himself, had to kick them awake to get them back to the fields.

But, when he was a teenager, his English mother, an immigrant herself, had told a different story. In her quiet voice, she explained that the white man might seem more intelligent, but that was because the white man wanted it that way: if you refuse to educate, you deny opportunity; if you oppress, you remain at the top. When she said this, he had listened and then forgotten her words but, now, when he hears Suzanne and her friends, they come back to him, and he thinks of them now.

The blacks are not the enemy, no matter how much his colleagues repeat their mantra. Colour is not evil. The enemy is the robber, the rapist, the murderer, the terrorist: those are the people De Vries thinks about as he prepares for his shift each day. He turns away from his colleagues at work, their overt hatred exhausting, pointless, and their pessimism for the future depressing, repetition of their blinkered beliefs closed to any challenge. He pays lip service to them, to conform, to belong.

He always resented the subjugation of childhood, the patronization of his parents and their friends. He longed for adulthood, for respect, for an understanding of the world which would allow him to be independent. Now, he longs for rank: to rise above the mere obeying of orders to the forming of them. Above all, he wants the police to police and investigate, to cease their role as paramilitaries and repressors. Amongst his peers, he is alone.

April 2015
The phone trills again. He snatches up the receiver.

'What now?'

He hears a hollow silence, like an evening wind blowing in the trees.

'I am about to begin my post-mortem examination of the man identified as Angus Lyle.'

De Vries checks his watch again. It is 11.35 a.m.

'You are?'

'It seems,' Anna Jafari says, 'that your appeal to General Thulani was heeded. I have been instructed to begin work immediately. You should know that I, too, have complained officially at this interference.' Her voice sounds even more irritating to De Vries over the phone than in person.

'Fair enough.'

'You wish to be present for the examination?'

'Not really. I want to know time of death, cause of death, anything else you consider unusual or noteworthy. And the blood work. That will be sent to Doctor Ulton's lab?'

'He already has blood samples. I will send stomach contents and other samples as required.'

'Thank you, Doctor.'

'Don't thank me, Colonel. I am acting directly on General Thulani's orders.'

'I'm grateful nonetheless. I'll call in later.'

'Very well.'

She hangs up. Vaughn chuckles, reflects that his interactions rarely end with a pleasantry.

★　★　★

149

'No one knows what is happening,' Don tells him as they travel down to the Forensics Lab. 'Angus Lyle changes everything. I do not know what to tell them to do.'

'Go to lunch?'

'That is what I did say.'

'Then you are becoming a good leader of men.'

They enter the lab. Ulton is leaning over a technician, squinting at a computer monitor. When he hears them, he looks up, murmurs something to his colleague, walks towards them.

'Let's go over here.' He leads them to the other end of the lab, looks around to check that they are alone.

'I heard you've been having some leakage problems . . . thought we'd restrict this info to the three of us.'

'That's a good idea.'

Ulton produces some papers from inside his lab coat. He snaps the papers taut.

'According to his police record, Angus Lyle was born on 18 April 1984, making him a couple of weeks short of thirty-one years old. He did not have ID on him when he was found, but he was recognized immediately by the officers who discovered him.'

'Who were they?'

Ulton reads from his notes.

'Officers Hendricks and Uzoma, Metro.'

Vaughn turns to Don, who is already writing down the names.

'Okay,' Ulton says. 'Let's start with the gun. I've run the ballistic tests and, despite missing the silencer, I can tell you for certain that this is the weapon used to kill Taryn Holt. The striations on the bullets match those seen after test firing.' He takes a breath. 'The grip bears palm and fingerprints from Angus Lyle . . .'

De Vries shakes his head.

'This is looking pretty conclusive.'

'Maybe . . .'

'Why maybe?'

'There are a few things bothering me. It's my opinion only and it's certainly open to dispute. Looking at the palm and fingerprints on the weapon, to me, it looks like his hand could have been placed on the weapon. Studying the entire weapon indicates that, apart from the marks from Angus Lyle, the rest of it is clean. That is to say: it looks as if it has been cleaned; it's devoid of any prints or dirt whatsoever. I find it hard to be certain that the gun hasn't been cleaned and then Lyle's prints overlaid.'

'Could Lyle have cleaned the weapon after firing and then held it subsequently?'

'Yes, that is exactly what could have happened, but it's a marker of oddness, that's all. It bothers me.'

'What else?'

'There are traces of animal fats on the marks made on the grip. I'm analyzing them now, but it'll take time.'

'What does that suggest?'

'That he had greasy hands and touched the weapon, possibly an otherwise clean weapon. Then, there were no casings at the scene. No casings found on or near the body of Angus Lyle. Why collect the casings and then dispose of them when you are still holding the weapon?'

De Vries says nothing. Ulton continues: 'The silencer. We know that one was used because of the markings on the bullets and also the style of entry wound. But, it's not around and I don't know why you'd discard it or hide it and keep the gun on you. Again, it's explicable but peculiar.'

'I've encountered situations like that before.'

'Me too . . .' He trails off, snaps to: 'The Bible is straightforward, covered with Lyle's fingerprints and in a fashion consistent with handling the book repeatedly over a period of time.' He looks at De Vries over his spectacles. 'As you know, he has underlined and highlighted several passages mainly, but not exclusively, referring to immoral women. Many refer to punishment, usually death or hellfire.' He looks at De Vries, smiles. 'Thought you'd like this: "*Just as Sodom and Gomorrah and the surrounding cities, which likewise indulged in sexual immorality and pursued unnatural desire, you shall serve as an example by undergoing a punishment of eternal fire.*"'

De Vries sighs.

'It's obvious and repetitive,' Ulton continues, 'but the quantity of highlighting and annotation suggests that he had been doing this for a period of months, maybe years. A cursory study of the ink and pencil marks seems to confirm this.'

He moves the top page in his hand to the back and looks over his notes before continuing.

'The leaflet about the exhibition: Lyle's prints are on the two outside plains when it was folded. Inside, there are no prints. This suggests he never opened it. He picked it up or it was given to him and, perhaps, he put it in his pocket.'

'Okay . . .'

Ulton looks up at him. 'The painting with the woman on the bed with the dildo in her mouth. It's inside the leaflet.'

'Which he might or might not have opened . . . ?'

'Finally, his clothing. We found blood traces on both his sweat-shirt and his trousers. The blood belongs to Taryn Holt . . .'

'It does?' De Vries says. 'Definitely?'

'For sure, *ja*. There are two arcs of blood spatter.'

De Vries turns to Don, raises an eyebrow.

'Note I said "spatter",' Ulton continues. 'So, we come to the science of spatter patterns. I'm going to keep it simple: if there are blood spatters on a person's clothing, as we see here, I would expect to see extensive, but minute, blood spotting. This is because if blood spurts from a wound it is, obviously, at pressure; from an explosion of an organ, as we saw with Taryn Holt, extremely high pressure. Therefore, we would expect extensive collateral spatter as well as the main arcs of spatter. My first observation is that there is virtually no collateral spatter present on Angus Lyle's clothing. Secondly, the angle of path is peculiar and emphasizes my last observation. They emanate from above and to the side of him. This is odd, because I don't see how the blood could come from that angle unless he was lying beneath her and, again, there should be blood spotting.'

De Vries is shaking his head. 'I still don't get it.'

'Okay. If he was above the body – as you would expect – when this blood got onto him, the shape of droplet would indicate that it was rising to meet him. These are drops. They have come from above.'

De Vries frowns.

'He was beneath Taryn Holt?'

'That is what the blood spatter evidence suggests – even if it is hard to imagine.'

'So, these spatters are illogical? What?'

'Put it this way: if I was asked in court if I had doubts over my findings, I would have to say yes.'

'Always doubt . . .' De Vries muses.

'Look, I may be wrong,' Ulton says. 'I've seen more dubious evidence turn out to be rock solid, but I know you want my opinion and I'm giving it to you.'

'We need to know a great deal more about Angus Lyle,' De Vries says, turning to Don. 'Find out if he had experience with firearms, if he knew Taryn Holt and had ever visited her home . . .'

'And you need to find out how he died,' Ulton says.

De Vries looks behind him now. There are three technicians only at the opposite end of the lab.

'If someone wanted to frame Angus Lyle for this killing, how would that fit?'

Ulton lowers his voice.

'I thought about that. I have to say, if that's the explanation – and, in all honesty, we both know it's not likely – whoever it was has done a pretty good job.'

De Vries sighs.

'I was afraid you might say that.'

'I am recording time of death based on my examination and the notes provided for me by Metro officers Hendricks and Uzoma, who found his body, and the medical examiner at the scene, as between 10 p.m. and midnight on Friday, 3 April 2015.'

The slender body of Angus Lyle lies between them, his face and neck, arms and hands very tanned, the rest of him pale.

'The cause of death is, in layman's terms, a sudden cardiac arrest. Although he appears generally malnourished, he is reasonably fit and his organs all seem to have been in working order. Clearly there is some damage due to historic drug use, but nothing which suggests that the heart would fail catastrophically.'

'So?'

Anna Jafari looks up at him.

'So what, Colonel?'

'So what is the cause of the death?'

'I will discuss that in due course.'

De Vries runs his tongue over the back of his bottom teeth, glances at Don. His Warrant Officer looks mildly embarrassed.

'Did he die where he was found?'

'I have not reached a final conclusion,' Jafari says forcefully. 'I want to be clear on that.'

'I understand,' De Vries says. 'Was he moved?'

'No. It is likely that he quickly lost consciousness, fell into the hedge where he was found, and died there.'

'What about stomach contents?'

'A small quantity of chicken and potato fries, very recently con-
sumed, within an hour of death. One of my assistants is analysing
it now, but the quantity found inside him suggests that he did not
eat a full meal.'

'Scavenging?'

'I can't say.'

'Anything distinguishing about the food?'

'No.'

'Chicken and fries?'

'As I said.'

'Greasy?'

'A high fat content, certainly. Why?'

'We have greasy fingerprints.'

'I see.'

'Evidence of previous drug use?'

'There are old syringe marks presenting quite clearly on the
inside of both arms. The damage I have observed is consistent with
long-term drug use. However, none of these marks is recent.

'So, a drug overdose is unlikely to be the cause of death?'

'As I have explained, the cause of death is clear; the cause of
the myocardial infarction is not.'

'Anything else?'

'Bruise marks on his left shoulder and neck. Again, recent and
probably sustained at a time close to death.'

'Any idea what caused the bruises?'

'They are consistent with hand marks, but I would need more
time. They look to me to be weight rather than impact.'

'Something I can use, Doctor,' De Vries says irritably. 'Give me
examples.'

Jafari shrugs.

'I don't give examples, Colonel. I tell you what is there.' She
hesitates. 'I would say that if . . . If the bruises were caused by hand
or hands, then they are not punches, but more likely restraining

155

bruises. A hard grip, sufficient to bruise the flesh. That is a suggestion only.'

'Thank you.' De Vries studies the wounds. 'Could they have led to his heart failing?'

'I very much doubt it. A heart does not stop beating for no reason.'

'Anything else?'

'He has a tattoo of a crucifix on his chest. It is not a professional tattoo and may even have been self-inflicted.'

They look down at his body. The blue-black outline of a crucifix, perhaps twenty centimetres in height, is positioned centrally, the horizontal axis lining up perfectly with his small, brown nipples.

'How recent?'

'It is difficult to say. Over a year, certainly.'

'You have his medical records?'

'No.'

'Have you requested them?'

'No. If you wish for them, you can request them, Colonel. I will continue to investigate this matter, including blood and other trace testing. My conclusions will almost certainly not require any further research.'

De Vries nods.

'Thank you again, Doctor. The time this early examination has bought us may prove crucial. You'll get your final report to me?'

'Yes.' She stares at him.

'What, Doctor?'

'And is there anything else I must do for you, Colonel? I wouldn't want General Thulani to have to prompt me again. Any further work in addition to my own carefully planned schedule?'

Don looks down at his feet. De Vries takes a breath, wants to explain to her the difference between crimes which can be solved – are likely to be solved – and those which cannot; priority must be given to those where the killer is still at large and possibly may strike again. In crime, there are gradations to everything; very little is generalized. As he studies her in the moment, he realizes that she probably does not care. It is not what she does.

He smiles at her, says quietly. 'That's all. Have a good day, Doctor.'

She turns away, leaves them with Angus Lyle.

'Under the circumstances,' General Thulani says, 'I accept that such an important development in a murder enquiry should take priority over a casual interview. However, be aware Colonel, that your poor relations with David Wertner and the Internal Investigation Department is a matter of concern to me – and others.' He points markedly at the chair in front of his desk. 'Now, sit down.'

De Vries sits. He is calm now; a steely resolution has descended on him and he realizes that this is how it is when he is under pressure. Although he dreads this state, he craves it also.

'It seems that you have convinced Colonel Wertner that what we thought was a serious leak of confidential information was nothing more than speculation by the newspaper journalists.'

'That seems the most likely explanation. I have spoken to all my team. It is, as you are aware, sir, only a small group. I suspect that someone in this building saw Trevor Bhekifa, recognized him, and decided to make mischief.'

'Well, they achieved that. Trevor Bhekifa is probably planning his complaint against us as we speak . . .'

'He has no complaint, sir. There is no anonymity for witnesses assisting the police in the normal course of events. I visited him at his apartment in Stellenbosch, and he is angry but accepting of the way things turned out.'

'You visited him?'

'I did, sir. Out of courtesy, and also to fill certain gaps he left in his witness statement regarding where he was at certain times.'

'Is his explanation satisfactory?'

'Up to a point. He remains a suspect in the background. Personally, based on what we currently know, I think it is unlikely that he is involved.'

'Obviously not.'

'However,' De Vries adds, 'there are questions to be resolved. It seems that the victim liked sex games which involved the domination of, as far as we know, her male partners. I cannot rule this out as being a possible motive for her death.'

Thulani raises his eyebrows.

'Trevor Bhekifa indulged in this activity?'

'He did, sir.'

'I can't imagine that.'

'I prefer not to.'

'I understand,' Thulani says, 'that there have been other significant developments?'

'There have, sir. I would also like to thank you for expediting the post-mortem examination of our latest suspect . . .'

'It is in everybody's interests to see this matter concluded efficiently. At the same time that I read your request, there was an enquiry from Pretoria about the state of the case.'

'From Pretoria?'

'I think the headlines about Bhekifa alarmed them. Tell me about this man, Lyle is it?'

'You know about him already, sir?'

'I was tasked to oversee the situation and, since Mr Classon has not been keeping me updated, I made some calls.'

De Vries wants to enquire who asked General Thulani to keep an eye on this new suspect but, instead, he delivers his report.

'Angus Lyle. Yes, sir. The evidence is pretty clear. His background, previous behaviour, the physical evidence recovered from his body. We recovered his personal Bible. It contains highlighted passages condemning immoral women. He also had on his person a leaflet for the exhibition at her gallery which, you may know, is a graphic representation of sexually compromised women . . .'

'It is conclusive?'

'His cause of death is not fully explained.'

'But his connection to Taryn Holt?'

'Still to be understood.'

'But the evidence against this man will close the case?'

'The evidence is strong.'

'How long do you anticipate it will take for you to conclude the paperwork?'

'A few days, sir. I must speak to some of the people who knew Angus Lyle, including some of our colleagues at Central and Metro. Many had dealings with him over the months and years.'

'Good work, Colonel. I hope that you can dismiss Trevor Bhekifa from suspicion and wrap this up. The moment the matter is certain, I want you to tell me personally.'

'I understand, sir.'

They pull up outside the address in Fawley Terrace. The mushroom and pink apartment buildings are dilapidated, the first floor and above looking out directly over De Waal Drive, the high road on The Mountain which takes drivers to and from the Southern Suburbs to the centre of Cape Town. Residents who can see beyond the freeway look up at the looming form of Table Mountain, this evening topped by a tablecloth of thick, perfectly white cloud, which seeps off the flat surface like dry ice from a stage.

The wind swirls around a gap between two buildings, and as they open the car doors, they snap back against their hinges. Don indicates the next building along from them and they stumble forward, trudge up the fading painted concrete steps to the second floor of the Exbury building, They ring the bell, are let in straight away by a man of about sixty. He anxiously studies their IDs, ushers them in.

'This is about Angus, isn't it?'

They walk into a dark, thickly carpeted lounge and see crucifixes on the wall, a heavy Bible on a wooden lectern.

The man stands in the doorway. They turn to him.

'Would you like to sit down, Mr Thorn?'

'Is he dead?'

De Vries hopes that the man will sit, but he remains where he is, stooped and expectant.

De Vries sighs.

'I'm afraid so.'

The man grips the doorframe, shuffles forward into his lounge, sits heavily on a blue velour sofa. He shakes his head sadly, wipes his eyes, looks up at them.

'There is only so much I could do . . .' He is pleading, head bobbing rhythmically. 'He never knew his father; his mother – my sister – she took a path he could not understand, and then she left us. He came here; there was nowhere else for him, but he needed help. Medical help, mental help. I kept asking, but without insurance, they don't even look at you.'

'We need to ask you some questions about Angus. Would that be all right?'

'Yes.'

'Mr Thorn, what was Angus's mental state in recent months?'

'What do you know?'

'Nothing, I'm afraid.'

'Angus . . . was a troubled man. Depressed and anxious. I thought that faith might see him through, but I don't think he was comforted as I have been. I am afraid it played on his fears. He was a man of great convictions. Problem was, they changed all the time. One minute he would argue almost to the death for one thing, the next, the exact opposite.'

'Did he get angry about these convictions?'

'Yes, I suppose so. He stuttered, and that frustrated him. I never knew whether it was the stutter or the subject that got him so worked up.'

'Did he get physically angry? Would he lash out?'

'When he couldn't express himself, yes, sometimes.'

'Did Angus have an education?'

'Of sorts, yes. He wasn't a fool . . . When he was clean of those cursed drugs. Only God knows what those drugs did to him, or made him think.'

'He was found with a gun on his person. Did he own a gun?'

'A gun? I never saw him with a gun. He might have wanted protection out there, but where would he get a gun?'

'We don't know, sir. We just have to tie up the loose ends.'

'Where is he?'

De Vries turns to Don.

'His body is with us at the mortuary, sir. As soon as we can, we will release him to you.'

'What happened to him?'

'He had a heart attack, sir. Did any of the professionals who dealt with Angus ever mention serious medical problems?'

'When you take drugs as Angus did, it affects your whole body. But, when I last saw him, he seemed well enough. He told me he had not taken drugs for many months.'

'There is no evidence that he had.'

'So, what killed him?'

'We don't know, sir.'

Thorn looks down, sighs deeply.

De Vries says: 'Did he stay here with you often?'

'He was supposed to stay with me all the time, but what can I offer him? He was angry at the television, he could not concentrate to read. He hated to be confined. I think he was happier outside. I would look for him, bring him home, but I was not his jailer ... And I am not well myself.' He begins to sob, hiding his face behind a church roof of interlocked fingers. 'I worried what he would do without me. Now ... It doesn't matter ...'

Don looks over to De Vries, back to Thorn, asks: 'Is there anyone who could stay with you, sir? A friend who might visit you?'

Thorn looks up.

'No, officer ... I will see my friends another day. Tonight, I will ask forgiveness for my weakness.'

He stands up shakily.

'You are finished?'

They nod at him, rise and leave the room, cross the corridor of a hallway and leave the apartment. When they open his front door, the roar of the freeway hits them. The wind lashes their faces. They walk to the car in silence, struggle to control the car doors in the unending blasts of wind. Don sits behind the wheel, De Vries next to him. For a few moments, they just wait, staring ahead at the out-sweeps of concrete supporting the raised freeway and the cars which pass above them, one after another, after another.

De Vries dreams about being old, wonders whether he will be alone. He dreams that his daughters visit him with their children, his grandchildren, but the children are afraid of him, his daughters bored and patronizing. He wakes, tries to dismiss these thoughts, rubs his eyes, turns the pillow, willing himself to dream of sex with Pamela or what he has read about Oktoberfest in Munich. Instead, half-asleep, he sees himself in a tiny apartment by the roar of the freeway, wearing a dressing gown and staring at the nails on his hands and feet. They are yellow and curling and he cannot grip the clippers, nor reach his feet. A rotund black women arrives in a gust of wind that sucks the breath from him; she washes him and cuts his nails. He hears the snipping, feels the tingle down his spine, begs her to stop. She places a tray on his lap. He sits with his hands gripping unsteadily either side of it, stares at the grey food, cannot understand how, with both his hands occupied, he can eat it.

The doorbell rings, two policemen stand in front of him. The room is suddenly silent but for the deep, heart-thumping tick of a clock. They wait for the ticking to cease. It does.

'Everyone you have ever loved,' they tell him, 'is gone.'

He wakes, feeling wretched, showers and dresses, catches himself in the mirror, wonders how soon it will be until it is not a dream.

30 December 1993
'Heidelberg Tavern . . . Under attack . . .'

De Vries reaches forward, twists the volume button on the radio-set.

'Repeat: Heidelberg Tavern, Station Road, Observatory, is under attack. Suspect gunmen in blue Volkswagen. One fatality in Station Road. All units to report to Station Road, Observatory. Reports . . . Four gunmen . . .'

He turns to the driver, Mark Edwards, frowning at the radio, checking his mirror, making a U-turn on Main Road, heading back towards Observatory.

'What the fuck do they mean "under attack"?'

'You heard,' De Vries tells him. 'Four men. What the fuck is happening?'

Edwards guns the patrol van through red traffic lights, cutting in front of cars.

'Eddy. Go easy. We want to get there.'

Edwards nods at De Vries, takes his foot off the accelerator, but still seeks space between the backed-up traffic. He lurches onto Lower Main Road, guns the accelerator once more, pulls up sharply close to Obs Café. They jump out, check their weapons, begin to jog up the street. Just short of the junction, they are stopped; orders are barked.

'Lieutenant. Stay there. Take that Constable and form a block at the intersection behind you. No cars into Lower Main Road. Seal it.'

De Vries looks past the man, sees smoke and angles to see around the corner.

'I need to see the scene.'

'Do as you're told. This is procedure. Take up position there and close the road.'

De Vries salutes briskly, turns and takes Edwards with him. By the end of January, he has been promised his Captaincy. No one will order him around on the street. Then, maybe, his work can begin.

Edwards looks at him as they stand at the intersection, waving cars in the opposite direction from the scene.

De Vries knows that he should be there; that the scene is his place.

Edwards, adrenalin rising, asks: 'Why aren't we after them? Why are we here?'

2015

Rarely has De Vries seen two better turned-out Metro officers than Officers David Hendricks and Eshi Uzoma, as Don leads them through the squad-room towards his office. Both are looking around expectantly, as if overawed to be amongst officers from an elite division. De Vries concludes that they are not long on the job.

They sit to attention in their chairs: Hendricks, Cape Coloured, narrow shouldered and thin; Uzoma, very black, bulging in her tight uniform, her hair tied tight back against her head like a helmet. Both are in their early thirties. Vaughn finds himself smiling at their eagerness to impress, almost disorientated by their enthusiasm.

'Tell me when you first encountered Angus Lyle?'

They look at one another. Hendricks speaks for them, his voice clipped.

'We saw him first about one year ago, sir. He was in the street, shouting. Not at the people in the cars, but generally. We checked his ID, spoke to him, moved him on.'

'How often did you find him under the influence of drugs or alcohol?'

Hendricks frowns.

'I don't know about drugs. Ganja sometimes, but often he would be drinking. He was intoxicated maybe half the time. We saw him often on the street or in the parks. Usually he would be reading or writing; sometimes he would stand on a bench and start preaching . . .'

'Preaching?'

'On whatever subject he was worked up about that day.'

'Was he ever violent?'

'When he was drunk, yes; otherwise, no, not really.'

'Did he strike you as coherent? Could he make a plan and carry it out?'

'Yes, sir,' Hendricks says. 'I think so. Sometimes he would be completely with it, complaining about something in the newspapers, other times, he was drunk, physically and mentally incapable.'

'You ever see him with a weapon?'

Hendricks nods. 'Yes, sir. He sometimes carried a knife. A large penknife, then another time a table knife, a serrated knife. He said it was for protection.'

'Never a gun?'

'No.'

'You ever see him up at the top of the Oranjezicht area? Serpentine Road, Park Terrace, those areas?'

Hendricks glances at Uzoma.

'In the park there, I think sometimes, but not in the streets. Eshi?'

Officer Uzoma speaks loudly and clearly, as if behind a megaphone.

'No, sir. I cannot remember seeing him up there. Usually in De Waal Park and the streets around.'

'And last Friday night. What happened then?'

Hendriks speaks quickly.

'We often drive around De Waal Park in the evenings; sometimes there are kids smoking ganja, sometimes homeless drunks. We were hailed by a resident walking his dog. He told us there was a guy who didn't look good. We parked up, went to investigate and found Mr Lyle. We called for an ambulance, but I could see that he was dead.'

'You get the name and address of the resident?'

'Yes, sir.'

'You search Lyle then?'

'No, sir. After checking for a pulse, I did not touch him.'

'You checked around where you found him?'

'Yes, sir . . . There didn't seem to be anything there.'

De Vries looks at Constable Uzoma.

'What about you, Constable?'

'I did not touch him, sir. We surveyed the scene, but we did not see anything.'

'Remains of a fast-food meal, a wrapper, box?'

They shake their heads.

'Bullet casings, a silencer for a pistol?'

They frown.

'We assumed, sir, that he had taken an overdose. We looked for equipment: a syringe, wrappers, that kind of evidence.'

'Did you go to the houses overlooking where you found him?'

'Yes, sir. We visited them. Three were empty, two others answered their doors but had not seen or heard anything.'

'You pass this on to the SAPS officers?'

'Yes, sir.'

'All right . . . How fit was Angus Lyle? Could he run? Climb?'

'Fit enough, sir,' Hendricks says. 'He was on his feet most of the day.'

De Vries breathes out slowly. Routine is only broken by the unusual, and these people have only the mundane to recount. It depresses him.

'The chapel in St Jerome Street: you know it?'

'Yes.'

'You ever have any dealings there, either with Angus Lyle or with the priest, Father Jacobus?'

'He asked to be taken there once. We drove him up the hill.'

'No other times?'

Again, Hendricks looks across at Uzoma. She shakes her head slightly.

'No, sir.'

'Before you discovered his body, when did you see him last?'

'We think it was Tuesday, 30 March,' Hendricks says, 'at the beginning of our shift, about 9 p.m.'

'What state was he in then?'

'He was quoting from his Bible. He was shouting about the immorality of women.'

'Did he know any? Immoral women?'

'I don't know, sir.'

'You ever see him with a woman?'

'No. I don't think so.'

'Did he ever meet a woman called Taryn Holt?'

'The murdered woman?'

'Yes.'

'I don't know.'

'He ever mention her name? Talk about her?'

'No, sir.'

De Vries looks at Uzoma.

'No, sir.'

De Vries looks at each of them; already they seem a little more jaded.

'Write down the dog walker's details for me, then go home. You have one less wretched citizen to worry about . . .'

Don leads them out towards the elevators. De Vries stays at his desk, thinks about what he has heard, realizes it explains nothing.

De Vries speaks with the consultant psychologist at St Anne's Hospital where, briefly, Angus Lyle was admitted.

'It is hard to specify an exact diagnosis,' the doctor tells him. 'Mr Lyle was a mild schizophrenic, but he veered from one personality and its associated character traits to another, often with little understanding of the previous one. He was deeply scarred by his childhood and the acts visited upon his mother by the men who arrived at their house. He has repressed much about that time, and I thought that he had been attacked, abused, by her clients also.'

'Why was he released?'

'He was not imprisoned here. He was free to leave at any time. His uncle had him admitted and, at first, he was happy enough to be here but, a man like him, he soon becomes bored and wants to move onto his next idea.'

THE SERPENTINE ROAD

'Was that typical of his temperament? That he moved on quickly from one thing to the next?'

'Yes . . . I would say so.'

'How was his health generally?'

'According to my notes, he was fit enough. Alcohol and narcotics abuse takes its toll eventually, but Mr Lyle was in his twenties.'

'Any family history of heart disease?'

'I can't answer that. I don't know. He was here for mental problems, not physical illness.'

'Was he violent?'

'No. I would not say so.'

'Could his schizophrenia have led to violence?'

'I don't know, Colonel. I did not have long enough to study him. He was not considered a danger to the public. When he left us for the second time, we advised his uncle to leave him.'

'I know I'm asking you to speculate, Doctor, but I must ask you: if you heard that Angus Lyle was a suspect for a shooting, what would your reaction be?'

'I can't answer that professionally.'

'That he might have chosen a high-profile woman, perhaps considered of somewhat loose morals . . . ?'

Even before the response, he can hear the desperation in the question.

'I can't answer that. I observed no vengeful or violent attributes during the short time he was assigned to me. This was five or six years ago. I have had to re-read my notes simply to have this conversation. I cannot speculate.'

De Vries considers what he might ask next, realizes that he is done; another avenue has closed. He bids the doctor goodbye, bangs down the receiver.

★ ★ ★

169

Leslie Wroughton holds the lustrous black Scottish Terrier on his lap, adjusts its front paws so that they align with his knees. When Don February leans forward, it emits a low, mellifluous growl. Otherwise, its expression remains unchanged. Don sits back, tries to remember to remain there.

'The usual characters: a couple of other dogs, a group of coloured chaps drinking something. They're often there, keeping to themselves. Never have a problem with them. I saw him on the ground, assumed he was asleep, walked by, and then something, I don't know what exactly, made me turn back. Maybe that he looked so young, and white . . . Anyway, I looked down at him, couldn't see any evidence of him breathing. When I reached my gate, the patrol car was there and I waved it down. They took my details and that was it.'

Wroughton brushes down his stained blazer. It is exactly what Don imagines Englishmen wear, and here is one, on an Englishman.

'Did you see anything around his body, sir?'

'Like what?'

'I am thinking specifically, sir, of spent ammunition, or apparatus for a weapon. A silencer: a black tube, about this long?'

Wroughton scratches his bulbous nose.

'No. I didn't see anything like that.'

'Anything else?'

'Just litter. Always litter.'

'Anything you can remember? A box or wrapper from a fast-food restaurant?'

Wroughton closes his eyes, stretches his face. The dog looks up at him, licks his neck.

'I think there was a box, yes . . . Sort of over his shoulder. Clyde made a beeline for it, of course. Pulled him back.'

'Do you remember which restaurant it came from? What it looked like?'

'Heavens, no.' He holds Clyde by the haunches and squeezes him. 'I don't know. Blue? Maybe blue and yellow?'

'Blue and yellow?'

'Maybe . . .'

Don pulls out his smart-phone, opens a new webpage, types in a search. After a few moments, a picture of a blue and yellow logo begins to open very slowly down the screen. He smiles at Leslie Wroughton, looks around the cluttered room. It is untidy and faded, but it is cosy, with squashy furniture and a grandfather clock with a slow, almost mournful tick. He glances back to his phone. Finally, when the download is complete, he holds it up to Wroughton.

'Like this?'

The dog stares at the phone above him; little yellow teeth appear beneath his nose.

Wroughton fumbles in his top pocket for glasses, puts them on and looks down at the small image. He nods, shows the screen to the dog, and looks up.

'Yes.' He gives the phone back to Don, then points at it. 'Exactly like that.'

'You got the impression that it was his?'

'Yes. Like he had been eating and just collapsed.'

'Did you see inside the box? Was there anything in it?'

'Looked like half a meal to me. Poor fellow was halfway through his dinner and then . . .' He draws a hand across his throat.

Don pockets the phone, stands.

'Thank you, sir.' He looks at Clyde, whose head is still but whose eyes are following him. 'Thank you, both of you.'

Don walks the length of De Waal Park along the side where Angus Lyle's body was found. He sees one empty brown paper bag and

171

no other litter at all. He searches in the waste-bin at the far corner, again finds almost nothing. Instead of retracing his steps, he walks further around the green space, peers down towards the fenced-off reservoirs on the tier below the park, and eventually does the best part of a circuit. There is little litter, and Don wonders who tidies it away. Just for a change, he had hoped it would be a sea of detritus.

De Vries has shut his office door, lowered the one blind that is still working over the one pane of the internal window. It gives a semblance of privacy.

'I'm reading Doctor Ulton's report and,' Norman Classon pronounces, 'I have to say, it looks pretty much done and dusted.'

'Yes.'

Classon stares at De Vries.

'That scarcely sounds like an unequivocal yes. Vaughn?'

'It's a yes, but with a nagging doubt. You do this job long enough and sometimes something just doesn't feel right.'

'In what way?'

'I don't know . . . If someone tells me that Angus Lyle knew how to handle a gun, that he had a violent and aggressive streak, even that he could concentrate on one thing for longer than a day, I'd agree with you. As it is, I'm still concerned there's doubt.'

'Well, I'm not here to comment on your investigation, only to tell you that if you were to report that Lyle was guilty of Taryn Holt's murder, I would agree that all the key elements are in place.'

'They are, aren't they?'

'They are, and I'm told that those upstairs would be happy to see this one wrapped up.'

'Another statistic in favour of the SAPS. There's never been a case I've been involved in that they haven't wanted to hurry to a conclusion. I understand why. I know that the moment this ends, the next one begins. But, after twenty years, I just know that nothing is automatic; everything requires a little more thought.'

'I won't argue with you,' Classon says. 'Call me when you need me and we can get everything written up and put away. I'll talk to Director du Toit and let him know where we're at.'

De Vries smiles at Classon until he has left the office; then the smile leaves De Vries's face. He feels it leaving, knows that this is the position his lips prefer.

Don February looks across the road, over the central reservation mound of grass and through the trees towards the Woodsman's Cabin Grill, its blue and yellow awnings shading early lunchtime diners from the noon sun. He is, according to the tachometer in his car, 0.8 km from De Waal Park. He steps out onto the road, slams his door, walks over to the restaurant.

He shows the greeter his ID, asks to see the manager. She looks him up and down, asks him to wait, and disappears into the partly open kitchen. The aroma of grilling meat fills the space and wafts onto the street. The blackboard of the day's specials advertises smoked warthog ribs, whole grilled chickens, thrice-roasted duck. Don wonders why he has never come to eat here; he realizes that his wife would not consider it a proper restaurant, that she would hate the brown paper table-coverings and wood-handled cutlery. He snorts to himself. Before he went to university, he had never been to a restaurant in town, had never imagined that he would. And now, he is almost a middle-class Capetonian.

A short, heavy-set man with a beer belly pulling a check shirt from his waist appears from the kitchen, beckons Don towards him, walks over to the corridor which leads to the restrooms.

'*Ja*, officer. What is it? We're going to be really busy today. I can't be away from the kitchen.'

'What is your name, sir?'

'I'm Henk Koeppler. I own and manage this place, last eleven years.'

'I am investigating murder. I need two minutes of your time.'

Koeppler taps his foot, folds thick hairy arms over his chest.

'Shoot, man. Do it. Ask away.'

'You offer takeaway here?'

'Yes . . .' He elongates the word.

'Is your system computerized?'

'*Ja* . . . You said murder. What is this?'

'On your system, can you recall a list of orders from last week?'

Koeppler jerks his head back and frowns theatrically.

'Why would I want to do that?'

'I want to do it, sir. I want to see the orders you gave out for takeaway last Friday, 3 April.'

Koeppler flicks his hand.

'Ask Judy, the girl you spoke with. She knows the system.' He begins to turn away.

'Sir?'

He turns back. Don holds up his smart-phone, displaying a picture of Angus Lyle.

'Do you know this man?'

Koeppler glances at it.

'Sure, that's Angus.'

'Angus Lyle?'

Koeppler shrugs.

'How do you know him?'

174

'Because he comes here sometimes, when we're closing up, asks very politely if there are any scraps. I usually give him some.'

'In one of your boxes?'

'Nah. In a baggie, man. Those things cost. I'll help the guy out but I don't want people thinking he's a customer.'

'Was he here last Friday?'

Koeppler sighs and makes a point of thinking about the question.

'I don't know. Friday and Saturday, we're packed from noon till eleven, when we have to close. I can't remember.'

'He didn't come looking for scraps, or earlier in the evening?'

'Not that I remember . . .' Koeppler takes his hand off the wall. 'Has something happened to him?'

'I'm afraid so.'

Koeppler curses under his breath, looks up.

'Now I have to go cook. Talk to Judy.' He whistles and, when the girl turns, he waves her over. 'Talk to this police officer. He wants to know about takeaway orders on Friday, *ja*?'

Judy nods, smiles momentarily at Don, leads him towards the cash desk by the entrance.

'Were you working last Friday night?'

'Sure.'

'You hand over the takeaway boxes?'

'Usually, yes. If I'm seating some people a waiter might do it, but it's one of my duties. I take payment, fetch the order from the kitchen and hand it over.'

Her intonation rises at the end of every sentence, as if she is asking a question. Don decides that she is copying an American or Australian accent, something she can surely have heard on television.

She stands behind the counter, fingers poised at the keyboard.

'What did you want to know?'

Don holds up his smart-phone again.

175

'Do you know this man?'

'Sure ... He's around from time to time. Comes round the back, asks for leftovers. I think Henk gives him some.'

'Did you see him last Friday?'

Judy freezes, eyes blinking. Then she jolts out of it.

'No. No, he wasn't here. I haven't seen him for a while, but I have Thursday off so he may have come then.'

'But not on Friday?'

'No.'

Don studies her for a moment, taken aback by her breezy manner and vague certainty. She is very tanned, made up to look happy, he thinks. Don asks: 'Can you see what takeaway orders you gave out last Friday? Chicken and fries.'

'Sure.' She taps the keyboard confidently, clucks to herself a couple of times, looks up at him. 'I don't usually look backwards ... Okay, I have them.'

'Can I see ... ? Or can you print them for me?'

'Well,' Judy says, 'there are three pages. I'll print them.' She presses a button. 'They'll come out in the office.' She hurries away and Don stands facing the road. A group of teenagers come into the restaurant, look him up and down, wait by the door.

Judy returns with three A4 pages. She sees the teenagers and walks past Don, greets them, seats them by the open window overlooking the outdoor tables and the leafy residential road. She comes back to Don and hands him the papers.

'One more question, please?'

She nods.

'Anyone ever just come in and order and then wait?'

'Sure. Sometimes, but it's best to call ahead.'

'Did anyone do that last Friday?'

She freezes again, eyes blinking.

'Can't think of anyone ... It would be a long wait on a Friday.'

Don thanks her, turns to leave.

'Officer!' She is laughing. 'I forgot. About ten, last orders for grills, we did get a walk-in. One of you guys.'

'A policeman?'

'Yes.'

'A uniformed officer?'

'No.'

'A detective, plain-clothed?'

'I guess.'

'How did you know he was a policeman?'

Judy laughs, shakes her head at him.

'I can tell. I mean, I just can.' She chortles.

'How?'

'Excuse me?'

'How can you tell, miss?'

She scrunches up her lips.

'The way you guys walk; the way you speak . . . Everything.'

Don pauses, says slowly: 'What did the policeman order?'

'Chicken, I think.'

He gestures at the sheets: 'It won't be on here?'

'Not if it's a walk-in.'

'You would remember what he looked like?'

'Yes, maybe.'

'I might ask you,' Don says.

'It is,' Henrik du Toit tells him in a hoarse whisper, 'a living night-mare. Just like these conferences always are. But, the day after tomorrow, I'm on leave, and I'm clinging to that.' De Vries hears voices in the background, Du Toit responding charmingly, ever the diplomat. 'I heard from Norman that the Holt case is pretty much concluded?'

'Possibly . . .'

'Oh, don't tell me that, Vaughn. I had some assertive Major asking me about it yesterday and then again today. I told him it was almost closed.'

'Who was that?'

'What do you mean?'

'Who was this Major?'

'Just an interested party . . .'

'Why would this case be of interest there?'

'I assumed that Taryn Holt was high-profile enough to warrant some attention.'

'Really . . .'

'What's the problem?'

'You know me, sir. It has to feel right. And it doesn't. I'm not talking on the phone about it. It's in hand.'

'It would look good to wrap this up fast. A good result.'

'I'm sure it would.'

'Keep Norman posted. He can fill me in.'

'You think I need supervision?'

'I think you need support. I gather there was talk of Wertner involved, over the newspaper thing?'

'Even he could see there was nothing in it.'

'I have to go,' Du Toit says. 'A speech on racial tension in the workplace. Just the thought induces tension. Good luck, and keep calm.'

De Vries laughs.

'Thank you, sir . . .' He listens, realizes that Du Toit has already hung up.

De Vries is smoking again, illegally, with his arm out of the window. Even the open window is against regulations; they were all sealed because of a new air-conditioning system, but he got his re-opened by a workman for the price of a packet of cigarettes.

'A box?'

Don February has laid out the three sheets of printed takeaway orders on De Vries's desk.

'I have gone through the take-out orders from Friday . . .'

'Don. These boxes get everywhere. He could have picked it out of the refuse.'

'He could have done, sir, but first of all, why would he? He went to the back of the restaurant regularly and asked for food. The owner gave it to him. He would not need to scavenge. And the boxes: this is not like a Wimpy or KFC. This is upmarket. People do not eat this food on the street. They take it home and put it on plates. I only thought of it because I passed the restaurant twice on my way up to the Holt house last week and remembered the blue and yellow awnings.'

'But who cares? He had a meal.'

'But he did not buy it. No one remembers seeing him that evening. But three people did order a half chicken and fries and somehow, maybe, the box got to Angus Lyle.'

'Don . . . ?'

'My witness said the meal was half-eaten. Doctor Jafari said that there was half a meal inside his stomach. It was a full meal. How did he get it?'

'Who cares?'

'You notice an expensive watch, or a fast car. You see things in the faces of white people I miss. But I understand the behaviour of people you know nothing about, sir. For a homeless man, a fresh dinner in a new box – that is noteworthy.'

'But why does it matter, Don?'

Don stands up.

'Sir, it matters because a short time later, Angus Lyle is dead. He has the gun that killed Taryn Holt on him, with his palm and fingerprints on it, a leaflet for the gallery, blood from the victim. You know it is all too convenient. What if someone used the promise of a meal of his favourite food to lure him to them, to plant the evidence, and try to bury the case with a disturbed addict?'

De Vries flicks the cigarette out of the window, checks that his door is closed, moves to his desk. They both sit down.

'You don't really believe that, do you?'

Don pauses.

'I am not convinced and I know you, sir, you are not convinced that Angus Lyle got past the alarm system, executed Taryn Holt with a perfect shot to the heart, left no forensic evidence at all and walked away.'

De Vries says nothing; he thinks about Henrik du Toit wanting to be able to report a concluded case, wonders why he was being asked about his case nearly two-thousand kilometres away in Pretoria.

'I agree.'

'So, if we are right . . .'

'If we are right,' De Vries interrupts, 'whoever has done this has probably killed twice. An overdose is easy to inflict. What's more, there seems too much interest in this case, and that means someone important wants it closed and forgotten. This could be conspiracy . . . Political conspiracy, and that frightens me.'

'Doctor Ulton feels that the evidence is flawed and contradictory . . .'

'Don, I know.' He rubs his temple, squeezes his eyes shut. 'I have to think about this.' He looks up at his Warrant Officer. 'I'm telling you, we have to be careful. We're going to think this over. Tell no one. No one at all. As far as everyone is concerned, we're going through the motions of concluding the case and putting it down to Lyle. Leave it like that for now.'

'Can we do that?'

'We can do whatever we want. We have one goal.'

'All right . . .'

'Trust me,' De Vries says. 'Everything we do is being scrutinized even more than usual. Before we do anything, we need to know by who, and why.'

The main forensic laboratory is dark now, a couple of Anglepoise lights over desks the only illumination.

'This my favourite time,' Steve Ulton says, gesturing at the near-empty lab. 'Do more in these few hours than in daylight hours put together.'

De Vries leads him over to the far side of the laboratory, where they had talked before.

'Have you discussed your findings on Angus Lyle with anyone?'

Steve Ulton stares at De Vries, wonders why he is speaking so quietly.

'No.'

'Good. Were you able to analyse the greasy substance on the victim's fingers?'

'Chicken fat, cooking oil. Probably scavenged from a bin somewhere.'

'That's interesting.'

De Vries looks around but, once again, they are at one end of the laboratory, while one technician sits hunched over a microscope at the other. He turns his back to him, continues quietly.

'Warrant Officer February and I are concerned that, together with your doubts, our own questions make this situation too uncertain to conclude that Lyle was responsible for the Holt killing.'

'You think he was set up?'

'If . . . that is the case, he would be an ideal candidate.'

Ulton shakes his head.

'I agree, but why use him at all? The killer has left no evidence at the scene. The forensic trail at the Holt house is dead.'

PAUL MENDELSON

'Maybe the killer wasn't certain; maybe he wanted a back-up. But I'm thinking something else: is it possible that Lyle is impli-cated not just to take the blame, but also to hide the motive?'

'Meaning?'

'I don't know yet.'

'What are we meant to be thinking?'

'Art and sex, perhaps even race, thanks to that black dildo.' He looks up. 'By the way, the dildo. Was it new?'

Ulton is taken aback by the sudden change.

'There were no other DNA traces or forensic markers on it.'

'Angus Lyle had a leaflet with the painting of the woman with the dildo in her mouth, but you said he may never have opened it. If he did this, where did he get that dildo? He has no money. If he wanted to kill this women because he knew, somehow, that she was promiscuous, why bother? The more I think about it, the less right it sounds.'

'Why couldn't it have been Taryn Holt's property?'

'The dildo?'

'Yes.'

'It sounds like she was getting enough of the real thing. Why would she want that?'

Ulton shrugs. 'Nothing surprises me any more, Vaughn, when it comes to sex.'

'Did you find any other sex aids at the property?'

'Possibly.'

'I don't understand.'

'Two sets of handcuffs. Serious things, not the kind you might find in a sex shop. Heavy duty. And a riding crop. Nothing to say she rode horses, so, again, I'm inclined to think they had another use.'

'But no dildos?'

'No.'

'Then I don't think it was hers.'

182

'So,' Ulton says. 'What? You'll re-open everything?'

'No.' He glances behind him again. 'I think we should keep this to ourselves for the moment.'

'Why?'

'Because there is a lot of interest from high up. An urge to close it down. I need to know why.'

'You have always been a conspiracy theorist, Vaughn.'

'In this country, to be a conspiracy theorist is to think with the odds. I've been right too often.'

Ulton smiles.

De Vries says: 'You think we live in a country free of conspiracy and corruption, even at the very highest level? Nothing surprises you about sex; nothing surprises me about corruption and evil. But, if this is what this is, it comes from high up. We have to be very careful.'

'My report expresses some doubts, nothing more. I'm happy to hang on to it for a while. I'm off tomorrow anyway. No one else here has dealt with more than a fraction of the analysis. Keep me posted?'

'*Ja*. Thanks.'

'I hope to God you're wrong, Vaughn. Completely bloody wrong.'

De Vries walks out of his building, turns uphill, takes a couple of cross-streets until he reaches Long Street. It is the bustling heart of Cape Town's nightlife but, even in the early evening, there are tourists sitting on the street, ambling into bars and restaurants, and locals stopping for a quick beer on the way home. He turns up Shortmarket Street and looks for the address he has been sent by SMS. He walks inside the building, nods at a security guard seated there, begins to climb a long, steep staircase.

At the top, he turns onto a glass corridor overlooking a small, modern roof terrace, then enters a tongue-and-groove panelled attic room. He sees Marantz at the bar, talking with a bartender.

'What are you doing in town, in a bar?'

'Meeting an American friend of mine. Poker player, here to play in a high-stakes game with some Chinese punters.'

'The Chinese are all over Africa.'

'They are. We should all be learning Mandarin and Cantonese.'

'You're not playing?'

'Out of my league. The buy-in is a hundred thousand dollars – million rand, give or take . . .'

De Vries raises his eyebrows, turns back to the bartender, orders a Slow Beer from the country town of Darling. They take their drinks and walk out onto the roof terrace. The view makes De Vries think of Manhattan, even though he has never been there.

'May be our last chance,' Marantz says. 'Cold front looming, apparently. At last. The Mountain is tinder dry. I'm afraid for my house.'

'You have an escape plan?'

Marantz smiles.

'Always.'

De Vries takes a long draft of beer. He rarely sees Marantz smile.

'How do you know this place?'

'Old drinking haunt . . . Well, towards the end, anyway. Cosy in winter. There used to be a lovely manager here: girl called Monique. I used to be last out, but now I'm the one leaving when everyone arrives.'

'Monique?'

Marantz sighs.

'She was just a nice girl.'

They sit alone at the far end, the bar and terrace still quiet so early in the evening.

184

'Well, I'm glad you're thinking about girls.' De Vries gulps almost half his beer, sighs, and leans back.

'What are you thinking about?' Marantz says.

'My case.'

'I can tell,' Marantz says. 'All is not well.'

Don February carries a leather briefcase; it is what his wife expects of a commissioned officer in the SAPS. He crosses the wide grey stone foyer of the building, walks out onto the street, turning towards the railway station. He has not taken more than half a dozen steps when a short, young black woman approaches him.

'Warrant Officer February?'

'Yes?'

'I met you this morning, sir. I am Officer Uzoma.'

Don looks her over. She is almost unrecognizable in casual civilian clothes, her hair down, face made-up.

'What can I do for you, Officer?'

She hesitates, then says: 'I wanted to speak with you, sir, in private . . . It concerns the man we found, Angus Lyle.'

Don is suddenly aware of how close they are to their main building. He says: 'Let us walk down here. Maybe we can have a coffee?'

'I agree, there is too much coincidence and the evidence is suspect, but if you investigate on your own, you are taking an enormous risk. You have no allies, no sympathy.'

'Who can I trust?' De Vries asks. 'The pressure is coming from high up there. I pick the wrong one, it'll be blown and God knows what happens to me.'

185

'But,' Marantz says, stirring his Virgin Mary repeatedly, 'you know the fate of a lone whistle-blower is precarious, even if what he says reveals corruption and conspiracy.'

'The conspiracy concerns me less than simply finding out who killed Taryn Holt, and why.'

'I'll tell you what I was thinking about, after we last met. The murder scene itself.'

'In what way?'

'Scenes are staged for two main reasons: the first is purely for the benefit of the perpetrator. He has an image in his head he wants to create for real, and the reality of the scene does not match his fantasy so he adjusts it to meet it. He might photograph it or store it away in his head as an enduring memory. He is likely to take a keepsake. This is an effect he wants to achieve, for himself. The second reason is also purely selfish, but the intended audience is different: you. The scene is staged to occlude the identity of the perpetrator by suggesting alternative motivations and misleading clues.'

'So, if it suggests art and sex and racism, it won't be those?'

'Probably not.'

'If the boyfriend is out of the picture, it's not likely money. The Holt board are drowning in cash.'

'Which leaves what? Politics?'

'Yep.'

De Vries drains his glass, slams it down on the table, says: 'Shit.'

They sit in the corner of the café, away from the street. Don buys her the coffee. He is not used to a junior officer wanting to confide in him.

'Tell me what is on your mind?'

'This morning, before we came to you after our shift, our supervisor spoke to us, congratulated us on finding a killer. We did not know that he meant Taryn Holt's killer. I thought it was a bit of a joke. But, when we got back afterwards, a Lieutenant from Central came up to us, shook our hands and told us we had done a good job.'

'That is all good.'

'Yes, sir,' Eshi Uzoma says uncertainly. 'But, I do not think that Angus Lyle would ever shoot somebody. I do not think he was capable.'

'Why is that?'

'Because he was a Christian, sir. He attended the chapel in St Jerome Street, and he was always reading from the Good Book.'

'Anything else?'

'I heard the Holt murder was a shot straight to the heart. Angus could not shoot straight, even if he had a gun, which I do not think he did. We saw him lots of times, searched him for drugs, but we never found a firearm.'

'Why do you think he could not shoot straight?'

'He shook. When he was angry, his whole body would shake and he would shout things. That was how he was.'

'Why did you not tell this to Colonel de Vries this morning?'

'It was my partner, Officer Hendricks. He told me only to answer the questions, not to give my opinion. He made me promise not to gossip, which I sometimes do. He said that a senior SAPS officer was not interested in what we thought, only what we did and saw.'

'Well,' Don says. 'You did well to tell me.'

De Vries does not sleep; he stays sitting in his armchair at what was the family dining table. Awake still, he reflects that Angus Lyle felt wrong the moment he saw him, the evidence on him too perfect, too signposted. Yet, if Lyle was set up, then the perpetrator has killed twice. If he can identify him, locate him, he will surely be prepared to kill again. And there is too much attention on his case, from anonymous sources high up in the SAPS in Pretoria. Perhaps it is the Bhekifa connection; perhaps that is the source of conspiracy?

Amidst circuitous contemplation, he dozes, only to wake with a stiff neck, his mouth dry and floury. His garden is black; he sees only the reflection of his room in the French windows. The man he sees depresses him. He pushes the three empty beer bottles away from him, stretching to arm's length to form a neat line out of range of his slumped body, and lays his head on top of the thick docket of Taryn Holt's murder, feels his eyes closing.

He half thinks, half unconsciously dreams, about his wife: when they were together in the beginning; the sex wherever they went; the desire to see one another when they had been apart for more than a day or two; the ritual mating to reaffirm their partnership.

He wakes, lifts his head high enough from the table to run the back of his arm and hand over his lips, lowers his head back down, the paper pile seeming as soft as a feather pillow.

Time reverses: he sees the body of Angus Lyle, opened from head to groin, flat on the dull metal table, bagged and tagged, crumpled and dusty, sprawled under a hedge. Blood squirts from a syringe over his sweatshirt and jeans; an alien hand holds his hands around the hilt of a 9mm Beretta. His face convulses in panic, in agony; he struggles for breath, starts to breathe. He fights with the man who stabs him with the syringe, struggles but cannot move. He sits up, smiles as salty food hits his taste buds, picks grilled chicken from a blue and yellow box. A shadow falls across him and he looks up.

De Vries wakes, struggles to remember the image of the man, but there is nothing but darkness. He lays his head down again, dreams of beer, smells its aroma leak from the empty open bottles in front of him. He imagines the line of bottles in Marantz's kitchen – a line which travels to an unseen horizon – the moment of anticipation as he picks one and releases the pressure from within it. It becomes clear to him: Marantz, as strange a relationship as they have, is important to him; he helps to release the pressure inside of him. From their meeting almost eight years before, they have each helped one another, gone beyond what some might consider reasonable, as if each required a greater proof of one another's loyalty. But, what he values is a friend who understands the decisions, the pressure, the absolute cost of what he does. All his friends from before he joined the police are gone; none with whom he now works are friends – decent colleagues and good acquaintances, but nothing more.

He wakes, as he does routinely now, at 3.30 a.m., climbs the stairs heavily, eyes still shut, uses the bathroom and lies on his bed, fully clothed. There, he is conscious of unconsciousness overtaking him and submits to it, sleeping fitfully until 6.30 a.m. When he wakes, he is tired.

Four missed calls from the number that Mitchell Smith left for him. He dresses, refreshed from the cool shower. He sits on the bed to put on his socks, makes a decision; he calls him back.

'I've been trying to call you.' The voice is plaintive, desperate.

'I know.'

'I have to see you. It's about you, and me. It can't wait.'

'Give me your address.' He does not have a pen by him, but commits it to his yet-to-be coffee-stimulated brain. 'I'll be there just now.'

January 1994

As he walks from the Observatory station he sees Johan Esau waiting by the gates, head down, hands in his pockets. The rain has

189

abated, but the oak trees across the road are still heavy with moisture; drops fall onto the shiny tarmac, snapping on the slick surface.

'Constable?'

Esau looks up. His face is pale, eyes hollow. He breathes out a
long trail of cigarette smoke, flicks the *stompie* across the street. De
Vries stops, walks up to him.

'You all right?'

'Yes, sir.'

'Bad call.'

'School friend of mine was in the Victoria Hall. I saw his body
on the pavement. Why can't these sick fuckers work it out? They've
won. They're getting everything. Why are they doing this?'

'It's the end of a war. Perhaps? Who knows?'

'Where did you go, sir? Major Nel was screaming down the
radio at you.'

De Vries speaks quietly.

'The radios don't work, Constable. You can't hear anything out
there. The moment we got out past Langer we were out of contact. We were ordered to guard the scene. That's what we did.
What happened at that first house? Who shot first?'

Esau recoils, shakes his head.

'I wrote my report.'

'What did it say?'

'What the major said. He told us we speak to nobody, we say
nothing. Not ever.'

'I understand. You want to talk to anyone, you come find me.
Ja?'

'That's all right, sir.'

De Vries stares at Esau. Maybe twenty-two, twenty-three. Into
the army at eighteen, fighting on the border. Now he's witnessed
a massacre; maybe he shot them, maybe he just watched Nel's rage
spew bullets into an innocent family. Five dead in a tiny concrete
room. He sees it in his head: the smoky charnel house; three

generations of one family slain. He wonders what effect this war has had on all of them, what toll it is taking.

'Fucking horrible night,' De Vries says. He walks away, begins to jog towards his home, his first tiny home, towards his wife.

2015

His drive takes him against the main rush into the city, past the airport, heading off north-east over the Cape Flats towards the satellite suburb of Bellville. Voortrekker Road is congested; he inches forward centimetre by centimetre, scrabbles with the street atlas to find a short-cut, eventually turns off towards the more industrial railway district of Belrail. He finds De Houtman Street, dusty and deserted, coated with grime from the industrial units at its sides, and is immediately depressed. The houses are small and squat, tall pitched roofs on low single-storey structures, each sur-rounded by walls of grey concrete panels, gardens of cracked salmon-pink bricks, grass bleached yellow by the unending summer.

He parks on the deserted street, smells diesel in the air, urine on the pavement, and hears the clattering of trains on the light breeze from the south. The smog from the Cape Flats extends out here now, the air thick and heavy with the beginnings of a humid day. He tries to push open the rusted garden gate, resorts to a sharp kick, walks up the concrete path to the front door. Mitchell Smith's house is heavily barred, the entrance itself protected by a steel gate in front of the wooden door. He presses the bell to no effect and knocks instead, fitting his hand through the steel bars to rap loudly.

When the door opens on Mitchell Smith, De Vries does not recognize him. He had been the youngest that night, barely more than a teenager. Now, his skin seems thin, eyes bulging. He has long sideburns, wispy and greying. He looks a lot older than De Vries, yet he knows Smith is ten years his junior.

'Colonel de Vries?'

Vaughn holds up his ID.

'You don't remember me either?'

'I remember you.'

Smith releases the chain on his front door, unlocks the steel gate and pushes it open. De Vries steps back, then enters. The interior is tatty and old; it smells of fried food, not just from the small, dark kitchen but from the walls themselves.

Behind him, Smith is re-locking the security gate, replacing the chain and locking the front door. Vaughn watches him, feeling increasingly claustrophobic. Smith wears his keys around his neck. It reminds De Vries of Father Jacobus and the ostentatious crucifix on his chest. Smith shuffles, clinking, back towards De Vries, leads him into the living room overlooking the bare yard. The three windows are barred too. He gestures for De Vries to sit at the dining table, once an elegant mahogany antique, now scratched and pocked with water marks.

'You want coffee?'

De Vries looks up at him, shakes his head.

'I don't have much time.'

Smith sits next to him, opens a green plastic folder, begins to pull out sheets of paper, newspaper cuttings. There seems no order to them. He shuffles them momentarily, then turns to De Vries.

'In January 1994, seven of us went after the Victoria Drinking Hall suspects. Do you ever think about that night?'

De Vries looks down at the sheets, turns back to Smith.

'I think you do.'

'You know what? I did for months afterwards. Then, it went away. All the new challenges, new personnel, new officers. I didn't have time for it. I had my wife and my job.'

De Vries looks around the room.

'What happened?'

Smith pauses.

'Things didn't work out. My wife left me, left the country. They got me out of the SAPS. They wanted me out and they did it. They did it to most of the white guys. Wouldn't promote me, made shit up about me. I'd taken this, or lost that; put me on all the shit assignments, made me train those lazy bastards and then watch as they'd fuck it up. They got me out.'

De Vries has heard this story before. Many times.

'What did you do then?'

'Do? There's nothing to fucking do, 'cos there's no work.' Smith is shouting now through his small, constricted mouth. 'Not for me. Not for white guys when there are fifty people looking for anything to do, and if one fucking black comes along wanting work, they give it to him.'

He is shaking, sweat on his brow and under his bottom lip.

'Why do you need to see me? You said three officers were dead.'

'None of us are with the SAPS any more. There's no place for us.'

'Tell me what's happening.'

Smith pulls a half page from a newspaper from his file, and pushes in front of De Vries.

Daily Dispatch, 11 March 2015

LOCAL MAN STABBED IN HOME

Former SAPS officer and local builder Sheldon Rich, 43, was found stabbed at his home in Maggs Street on Monday evening. Rich's wife and daughter discovered his body on their return from a visit to her parents in Port Alfred.

East London police are unsure as to the motive behind the killing as, to date, there are no reports of missing property.

Friends and co-workers have said that Rich was a hard-working family man, with no known enemies. Police are appealing for witnesses, and say that they are mystified as to why anyone would attack Rich in the evening in his own home . . .

'There's an article like that every week in every newspaper around the country. In some places every day.'

Smith stares at De Vries, searches through the papers on the table, picks one out and pushes it across to him. Then, he scratches his head with both hands, fingers digging into his scalp so that De Vries can hear the nails on his flesh.

Smith takes a deep breath and says, with forced calmness: 'Joe Swanepoel went back to live with his family in Middelburg, in the Karoo, a few years back. He was unemployed and did jobs for his father's business, trying to scrape together a living. He stayed in a room on the second floor of his family's house. Look.'

Middelburg Observer, 19 March 2015

(translated from the Afrikaans)

Joseph, the son of Oscar Swanepoel of Middelburg, was rushed to Wilhelm Stahl Hospital at 3a.m. Sunday morning, but was declared dead on arrival at the emergency room. The forty-four-year-old former SAPS officer was attacked in his flat above the family home by an unknown assailant. This latest incident, in an area previously considered safe, raises concerns for all those worried about safety in their own homes.

The SAPS would only say that he had been attacked with a knife in what they described as a 'brutal killing'.

A representative of the neighbourhood watch told our reporter that Joe, as he was widely known, did not take security very seriously and doubted that even his front door was bolted securely.

'If you do not take precautions in our country today, even here in Middelburg, you are asking for trouble.'

'I kept in contact with Johan Esau. You remember him? He phoned me two weeks ago to tell me that both of them had been killed. Then he sent these clippings. When I tried to phone him, there was no answer. I called the police in George on Friday, and they told me that Johan had been murdered. Knife attack in his yard. Maid found him in the morning when she came in to work.'

Smith is speaking fast now, mouth twitching. De Vries tries to avoid looking at him directly; Smith's anxiety is making him nervous too.

'It's not coincidence. It can't be.' Mitchell Smith is gabbling. 'Three of the men who were with Kobus Nel. Each of them murdered, with knives, in under a month.'

De Vries feels slightly dizzy, finds himself staring at the table, scrutinizing the newspaper clippings for something which might distinguish one attack from the other.

'What did you tell the police in George?'

'Nothing. I told them nothing.'

'What do you want to do?'

'You have to find Mike de Groot – he was the other guy in Nel's van. You have to warn him. You have to tell him what's happening.'

'Why can't you contact him?'

'It's gone bad for Mike,' Mitchell Smith says. 'He couldn't cope, man. He seemed okay, carried on like the rest of us. Did the new training, the courses. Worked okay with the new black guys, the fat, lazy, coloured fucks, even when they were promoted past him. Then, one day, Johan and I were driving to Forries for beers. We saw Mike under the freeway ramp, over by Settler's Way, just standing on the island between the carriageways . . .'

'Doing what?'

195

'Nothing, man. Just standing, talking to himself. We called out to him, but he looked straight through us. We stopped, got him into the car, but he was gone, man. Something in him was gone. Didn't even know where he was. Week later, he was out of the force.'

'Where is he now?'

Smith shrugs.

'Someone said they saw him over by Table View at the traffic lights, holding up a fucking sign, selling wooden beads.'

'You know if . . . ?'

'If he's still alive? No. I don't know that.'

Smith looks around his hot, stench-filled room. De Vries sees peeling paint, stained carpet, empty bottles and upturned glasses under the tatty sofa; he wonders what Smith sees.

'What do you want to do?'

'I don't know. I'm scared. Who knew we were there? Who even knew who we were?'

'No one,' De Vries says firmly. 'No one knew. No one said anything or did anything for twenty-one years . . .'

'Except for Kobus Nel.'

'What interest would he have?'

'He's a rich guy now, *ja*? Made his fortune. Lives the highlife, but they say the money isn't legitimate; that he's connected to the mafia people, the gangs, maybe the Russians.'

'It doesn't mean he has anything to do with this.'

'Who else knows?'

De Vries sighs, finds himself scratching his head hard and wonders whether it could be fleas from Smith, whether he spreads this contagion of misery and filth.

'Perhaps it should have come out at the time.' He looks up at Smith, speaks quietly. 'I doubt there would have been an investigation. It would have been swept away, but at least we would have done our duty. Nel made it pretty clear what would happen if we did speak out. I'm talking about our jobs, our safety, our family. You didn't mess with him . . .'

'I can't sleep,' Mitchell Smith says. 'I can't think about anything else.'

De Vries stands up.

'There's not much I can do. There's no viable threat to you. Even if you tell someone the story, I doubt they'll act.' He gestures at the front door. 'You have your security looking tight. Remain alert. I'll do what I can.'

'I thought . . . I thought I could go away . . . ?'

'You could. Might have to be for some time . . .'

Smith looks at him; he is exhausted.

'I haven't even got enough for a bus fare, man.'

'Is that why you wanted me here?'

Smith stands up.

'No.' He draws himself up, pushes his shoulders back gingerly. It is, De Vries thinks, a tired attempt to display some pride. 'I wanted to tell you. I wanted to warn you. I don't want your money. I've made it so far.'

'We weren't in that house. We didn't see what happened. You and I only guessed what those guys did. No one is going to bother with you, or me.'

'Johan told me.'

'I don't want to know. I thought about it long enough.'

'He just cut them down, man. They didn't know anything. They were random. He fucking shot them one by one. Children in front of parents, little kids.'

'Two kids got out.'

Smith looks up at De Vries.

'Got out? What do you mean?'

'You didn't see them? I saw them, two of them, after the shots. They got out the back of the shack, ran away.' De Vries feels his heart in his chest, his throat dry. For a split second, he is back

197

there, in the rain and the dark, the sweat thick on his face; the images of the Victoria Drinking Halls, smoking and black, disemboweled, still fresh in his mind.

'You only had to look at Johan's eyes. He remembered every day. It wasn't like the army, man. These people weren't enemies, weren't threatening us. They were just there and Nel wanted them dead.'

'Nel was a brutal fucker, but it was twenty-one years ago.'

'He put his hand in their blood and smeared it on the guys. He fucking blooded them, man, like fucking hunting dogs.'

De Vries gets up.

'All right. That's enough. This gets us nowhere . . .'

'Sheldon and Johan and Joe . . . They're all dead . . .'

'They were all SAPS. Even if they are connected, there are other reasons why someone would do this.'

Smith shakes his head.

'You don't believe that.'

'I do.'

'You're going to tell someone that these crimes are connected? That they must be connected?'

De Vries knows that this is the question he will be asked; he does not know the answer. There is little co-operation between areas and provinces, no database against which to check for similar crimes. Each of the detectives looking at these cases will not be aware of the other, such is the size of the country. Yet, if he links the crimes, he resuscitates everything that happened on that January evening twenty-one years ago: what was said and done; what was not said.

'Stay alert. Leave it with me. I'll look for Mike de Groot. We'll make sure he's safe, you're safe. It'll be okay.'

Mitchell Smith scratches himself some more, crosses the room to what could once have been a modern hi-fi unit but now stands empty except for a cracked pottery chicken in blue and white. He opens the drawer and pulls out some pictures.

'Take this, then. That was us . . . I don't know, seven, eight years ago.' He points to the man at the end of the picture. 'That's Mike. He didn't know what the fuck was happening, but we took him with us anyway.'

'Took him?'

'Beers, man. We took him for beers.'

He unlocks the door and steel gate, follows De Vries down the path to the boundary of his dusty garden. De Vries opens the gate, turns to say goodbye, but finds Smith following him.

'I'll walk to your car.'

De Vries looks at him, puzzled. Smith says: 'Last ten days, I've been out once to get food, buy some electricity. I don't feel safe here. I don't want to go out. I don't want to stay in.'

De Vries sees desperation on the man's face and cannot decide if it is justified or if a slow hysteria is taking over his mind.

'These are hard times for all of us. Change is always hard. Keep going and they'll get better.'

He gets into the car, winds down the window. Smith is on the street by the car.

'You think so?'

De Vries nods, starts his car, rolls away. A few houses down, he says out loud: 'No.'

By 9.30 a.m., Vaughn reaches his building, his mind full of three murders hundreds of kilometres away, possibly connected; possibly connected to him.

He rides up in the lift, deep in thought, and finds the squad-room almost empty, no sign of Don February. On his desk, he finds a summons from General Thulani's office. He walks back out into the squad-room, pours almost a full mug of coffee from the dregs at the bottom of the jug, adds three sugars, drinks it down like medicine. In the lift's mirror, he picks coffee grounds from the tip of his tongue, feels grittiness in his throat.

'A sexually aggravated murder of a respected clergyman and his wife in Worcester? That one sentence tells you what it will be.' De Vries shivers and looks up at haughty Thulani in full dress uniform.

'I think you should take this one. I spoke to the Captain down there. I get the feeling they are very keen to have some assistance.'

'That is an unusual position, sir.'

'It is. However, I think we should show that your department is not just here to take high-profile media cases, but that you are prepared to help, to get your hands dirty.'

De Vries smiles; he can never wash his hands free of the dirt.

'I don't see how we can take this on, sir. I would not have selected it as a case for our unit.'

'I'm listening to the word from Pretoria, Colonel. The mood is that we have to work closely together, support each other within the service.'

De Vries sighs.

'The investigative teams, as you know, are already stretched. We have one leader in physiotherapy, booked out for at least two more weeks, one on leave and Major Adams is in Paarl on the family farm murders.'

'But you have concluded the Holt case?'

'I am concluding it, yes sir, but I still have a few days on it.'

Thulani sits up, raising himself still higher.

'Could that not be undertaken in conjunction with this new case?'

'It could, sir . . .' De Vries starts slowly. 'But think how it would reflect on us if there were to be a mistake made at this point?

Brigadier du Toit is insistent that we fully complete one task before another is begun . . . For reasons of certainty in court, clarity to the media.'

De Vries feels tangible pleasure in quoting back the rule book to a man like Thulani.

'Could you at least go out there to see . . . ?'

'Sir. In the minds of the media, Trevor Bhekifa is still connected to this matter. Until everything is demonstrated to be cut and dried, there will always be rumours. I understood that this was not acceptable.'

Thulani sighs, nods reluctantly.

'It is not.'

'That is what I thought, sir.'

'Very well.'

'Why did the caseload come to you, sir? As the senior officer in my unit, I should be handling allocation of new cases. You should not have been bothered with it.'

'In the light of the protocols coming down from above, I thought it was appropriate to look out for opportunities to broaden our scope. Always, there are compromises. This matter will be another victim of our over-stretched system.'

'Protocols from Pretoria?' De Vries says casually. 'Brigadier du Toit mentioned that a Major had been enquiring about the Holt case . . . Was that the same man who contacted you?'

'Major Mabena?'

'I think it was . . .'

He has no idea, but he now has a name.

'He is an attaché between the administrators and the Police Ministry.'

'I hope the Ministry aren't unhappy with our work here in the Cape?'

Thulani shakes his head.

'No, I am sure they are not. There is no reason to question our success here in Western Province.'

De Vries relaxes. Thulani is thinking only of himself, as Assistant Deputy Provincial Commissioner. He sits silently, watching Thulani begin to wonder if the enquiries were not about De Vries at all but, instead, his own office.

Thulani looks at him, registers his demeanor.

'Go, Colonel. You look cold.'

De Vries sits in his office, waits for Don February to respond to his SMS. He looks up to see Norman Classon at the elevators, expects him to walk towards him, but instead he stands by the lift, talking to an occupant of the car. This continues for nearly two minutes. Finally, Classon turns, and begins to walk towards De Vries's squad room and office. He knocks, lets himself in.

'Good morning, Vaughn.'

'You were deep in conversation, Norman . . .'

Classon frowns, then smiles, says: 'Keeping our masters informed.'

'Who was it?'

'Julius Mngomezulu. Thulani's liaison.'

De Vries looks up.

'What were you saying to Mngomezulu? I told you before he can't be trusted.'

Classon laughs uneasily.

'Nothing. He asked me to tell him what was happening with the Holt case so he could inform Thulani. I told him we're just checking out some possible problems.'

'You did what?'

Classon holds up his hands.

'I kept it vague.'

De Vries takes a deep breath; he knows that Classon is not an enemy, even if he is not a friend. Classon has been trusted before.

'Don't say anything to that little shit. You can't know that what you say will get passed on accurately. He's not a proper policeman despite that rank. He's a secretary. You know we've had problems with him before.'

Classon slowly lifts his feet, finally takes the seat opposite De Vries.

'Sorry, Vaughn. I didn't know I was running into office politics.'

'It's not politics; it's trust. I don't trust a policeman in a tight, shiny suit and pointy shoes. Did you tell him about my interview with Bhekifa?'

'I probably did. He was in that day, wasn't he?' De Vries nods. 'You think he could have leaked that to the papers . . . ?'

'*Ja* . . . And there could be more, so we need a tight circle.'

'More?'

'Someone tried to get me moved onto another case today.'

'Someone?'

'A case elsewhere was brought to General Thulani's attention, and it was suggested that I might be sent away to deal with it. I wonder why that was?'

'Meaning?'

'The Holt enquiry requires more work and I think some-one high up doesn't want that. You know how I get when that happens?'

Classon does.

In the cool, silent room, Eric Basson sits facing the door, behind a broad polished desk. John Marantz walks across the wide par-quet floor, glancing up at the high stuccoed ceiling; he wonders why there is no furniture in the room save the desk and two arm-chairs. He meets the gaze of his host; it seems to bore through him. Basson rises slowly, offers his hand. His voice is quiet and precise.

'I knew you were here, of course, but I had understood that we were never to meet, Mr Marantz.'

'I'm sure it's inappropriate.'

'It is.' Basson gestures for Marantz to sit opposite him. 'London had mentioned that I might keep a discreet eye on you but, of late, that has seemed unnecessary . . .'

'Good.'

'But now . . . ?'

'I knew you were here too.'

Basson smiles thinly, his eyes expressionless behind spectacles, rimless but for a thick tortoiseshell frame running across the top of the lenses. Marantz assumes that he is in his seventies and admires the understated suit and quiet tie, the calmness of his demeanor.

'I'm here to ask for help, for a friend of mine: a senior officer in the SAPS.'

'Not for yourself?'

'No.'

'But there is a motive? A debt, perhaps, to be repaid?'

'No,' Marantz says. 'He is a good friend of mine. He supported me during my . . . rehabilitation.'

'And, I assume, that this assistance you seek is to be provided without my making a long-distance phone call?'

'I hope so.'

'That places me in a very difficult situation.'

'I was aware that it would, but I hoped that you would find a way.'

Basson looks at the table, stays silent. When he looks up, he says: 'What is the name of this senior SAPS officer?'

'De Vries. Colonel Vaughn de Vries.'

'Yes, I know of De Vries.' He tilts his head. 'But, regrettably, that makes your request even more difficult to fulfill.'

'Why?'

'Because Colonel de Vries is unpredictable, because he exists on the edge of alcoholism; he has character flaws which make him, in my position, difficult to trust.'

'I would argue,' Marantz says, 'that those traits you describe make him a more effective investigator. My experience of him is that he is unprepared to compromise in the pursuit of the truth.'

Basson smiles broadly now; even his eyes shine, momentarily bright.

'Since your departure, I see you have lost none of your abilities to use the English language to mould an argument. A skill sadly lacking in these times.'

'I'm sincere in what I say.'

'Of course you are.'

Basson produces a packet of cigarettes, selects one and lights it. He says casually: 'You were at Cambridge?'

'Oxford.'

'Of course.'

Marantz smiles.

'Calibrating reactions?'

Basson tilts his head.

Marantz says: 'You knew where I went to university. You wanted to see my physical reaction to an incorrect suggestion?'

'If you say so.'

'You were at Durham University.'

Basson smiles now.

'Very good.'

Marantz shifts to find a comfortable position in his chair; he stares at the man in front of him. Basson says: 'Are you considering a return to England?'

'I don't think so.'

'But you miss your work?'

'I prefer not to be personally involved. But, information still interests me.'

'And risk?'

'In a controlled setting, yes.'

'Your poker games. They allow you to fight the battle, but in safety. Am I right?'

'I suppose so.'

'But, I think you are taking a risk now: meeting me; asking me these things.'

'When you have played and lost,' Marantz says gravely, 'these stakes seem comparatively modest.'

'I heard what happened to your family. I'm sorry.'

Basson draws deeply on his cigarette, studies Marantz.

'Such action has proved unique, at least as far as London is concerned.'

Marantz scowls, feels his heart beat in his chest.

'That isn't a comfort. Perhaps it should be, but I am not that unselfish.'

'Understandably . . . It raises the question of motivation . . . Why you might have been singled out for such action.'

Marantz stares ahead, past Basson. He sees nothing.

'I had no idea that I, and they, had become a case study.'

'History de-personalizes tragedy. That which might break a man becomes no more than an event recorded.'

'Not to me.'

Basson tilts his head, studies him.

'What is the nature of the matter you wish me to assist you with?'

Marantz swallows; Basson's words impart both information and threat. He questions himself anew, whether he should have made this contact, taken a risk which is proving so personal. The wounds have been borne.

He says: 'Colonel de Vries works for the Special Crimes Unit of the SAPS, based here in Cape Town. Last week, the daughter of the late industrialist Graeme Holt was murdered in her home. I'm sure you are aware of this?'

Basson leans his head back, nods.

'The details of the investigation, the docket, I think you would say here, has not been available to me. But, based on what I know, an unlikely man – a man with a history of mental problems and drug addiction – appears to have been framed for this murder. He is dead and those above De Vries seem enthusiastic that the case should be closed. The word appears to have come from a small but influential office in Pretoria . . .'

'To be clear: you are, perhaps, suggesting a state intervention?'

'Perhaps.'

Basson stubs out his cigarette, leans back in his chair.

'As no doubt you anticipated, you have my attention.'

'That is why I came to you.'

'Yes, so you say. But, do you really know who you are speaking to?'

'I'm sure that you relish a lack of definition . . .'

'I was at *Vlakplaas* at the beginning with Dirk Coetzee. Do you know what *Vlakplaas* was?'

'Only a one sentence précis.'

'Tell me.'

Marantz hesitates.

'A farm, west of Pretoria, housing a Nationalist-government sponsored paramilitary cell, designed to turn or kill anti-government operatives, to sustain the Apartheid regime. Others might describe it as a centre for torture.'

'That was two sentences . . . But your précis is adequate. The unit was called C1 and it was formed from the existing South African Police of the time. You missed out the fact that we planned attacks on ANC terrorists: bombings, ambushes. We took the war to them.'

'And you ceased activities in 1994 . . .'

'It was, officially, closed down in 1994. And now, we are told, *Vlakplaas* operates as a centre for healing and traditional medicine.'

'Reconciliation . . .'

'Are you shocked that for so many years the British government has employed a man such as me?'

'It would have been preferable not to.'

'I can hear the apologists speaking in just such a way.' Basson leans forward, rests his hands on his desk in front of him. 'But it is a simple question: are you prepared to work with me?'

'Work?'

'Information always flows two ways.'

'I don't have any information. I am simply a private citizen.'

'Then you have nothing to fear from an alliance.'

'I've worked with worse,' Marantz says.

'I'm sure. To sustain the highest of ideals one is often forced to collaborate with those who represent the opposite. Don't you find?'

Basson smiles, continues: 'I always think it comes down to who you want protecting you. Someone who is whiter than white, or someone who understands the game?'

'I am a pragmatist. It's pointless to be anything else. Doing what we do.'

'I thought you didn't do it any more?'

'I don't.'

'Yet, your personnel file in London suggests that you are neither retired nor dismissed. An "extended sabbatical", I think, was the phrase.'

Marantz feels nauseous. Thoughts of his work bring back only memories of his wife and daughter, another life led, long ago lost.

He says: 'You read the files on the case which led to my family's abduction?'

'No.'

'I'm surprised.'

'I would have done but . . . they have become unavailable.'

'Why would that be?'

Basson says: 'A uniquely evil response to an investigation: to make the wife and daughter of the lead interrogator disappear, to leave him never knowing for certain. Nothing really gained, other than, perhaps, as a warning. Unless . . .'

'Unless?'

'Unless they had a reason. A reason personal to you?'

Marantz stares straight ahead, says blankly: 'I know of no reason.' His mind races. He has pondered the motive many times, every day. Still, he can think of nothing. He sniffs, blinks slowly, forces himself to relax.

'Will *you* ever retire?' Marantz says.

'I think I am unlikely to find relaxation and security outside my field. Doing what we do demands a simple faith: the end always justifies the means.'

'That is a very frightening prospect to many people.'

'But not to you?'

'Philosophy seems an unlikely subject matter.'

'But it proves what we believe,' Basson says. 'It encapsulates us. Every system of government demands protection and active response to threat, to protect its ideology. Many claim democracy empowers them, but it is not really so. As you know . . . Does this knowledge compromise your decision to ask me for help?'

'I'm sure you are eminently qualified. '

Basson nods.

'If I undertake some research on Colonel de Vries's behalf, it is with the understanding that neither our meeting, nor his – should it come to that – ever be revealed. Your position suggests to me that you can be trusted on this but, in the case of De Vries, I would require your word that this will be instilled in him, without fail . . .'

'I will do that.'

'. . . It is whether I deem it likely that you can control him, you see?'

Marantz waits; he knows that he has done all that he can now. Basson contemplates for several minutes, occasionally looking up at him.

'Let us leave it like this,' he says finally. 'If the information I find, assuming that it is there, warrants my taking such a risk, then I will do so. I hope you are satisfied?'

'Thank you. Yes.'

'And, it occurs to me, since we are keeping this between ourselves, there might come a time when such mutual discretion has another use. You understand me?'

'I am in your debt.'

'Potentially.' Basson rises and offers his hand, looks Marantz in the eye.

'Goodbye, John. It is most unlikely that we will meet again.'

Don February follows the two telephoned takeaway orders from the Woodsman's Grill to residential addresses within two kilometres of the restaurant. Neither are remotely suspicious. The late call-in, identified by the greeter, Judy, as a policeman, presents him with a problem. He does not try to find out from the Central Station rota who would have been free to drive to the restaurant and then, perhaps, to De Waal Park; that would raise questions he could not answer. Instead, he goes to the administration offices for Central division, speaks with a young Sergeant, obtains a black-and-white print-out of ID pictures of all officers attached to the district, and does exactly the same for Gardens district.

Then he returns to Oranjezicht, waits outside the Woodsman's Grill.

Two murder scenes, maybe, where no one has seen the killer; where there is no forensic or physical evidence. De Vries feels aimless, helpless. He longs to hunt down the perpetrator; he needs only one lead. He stares at the board in the squad room, stands smoking in his office; he wonders where Don February might be.

Judy Miles arrives in a battered white CitiGolf, parks with difficulty on the steep gradient. She gets out and walks towards him. When she sees him, she says: 'Good morning, officer.' She gestures at the door. 'Has Henk not opened up yet?'

'He is inside?'

She laughs.

'He lives above the restaurant. Henk is always here.'

She unlocks the front doors, leaves the hanging sign showing 'closed', throws down her rucksack behind the cash desk.

'You want to talk to Henk or me?'

'You, Miss Miles. I want you to look at some pictures, please.'

She looks up at the oversized clock on the far wall.

'I have to prepare for lunch service, but I have a few minutes.'

Don lays out the sheets on the counter top.

'What racial group was the police officer you saw?'

'He was black,' she says, seeming awkward. 'Maybe in his thirties. Looked quite fit.'

She starts to scan the sheets. Don notices her hesitate as her eyes fall on each black officer. She reaches the end of the first set, covering the officers from Metro; Don lays out the ones showing Cape Town Central SAPS officers. After a few minutes, she has viewed all the pictures.

'I'm sorry. I don't recognize him from any of these.'

'That is all right,' Don tells her calmly. 'Do you think you would know him if his face was there?'

'I think so.' She looks up at him.

'It is not so easy,' he says gently, 'to distinguish between those of a different racial group?'

She blushes.

'I'm not sure, but I don't think he was amongst those pictures.'

Don gathers up his papers.

'Thank you. I may need to show you some more pictures.' He nods at her and turns to leave, but twists back. 'The vehicle you saw? Was it a car or a van? Do you remember?'

She closes her eyes and concentrates, very still.

'It was big,' she declared finally. 'I don't think it was a car. Maybe a van? A tall van.'

'You didn't see any markings on it?'

'It was parked down the hill,' she says quickly. 'It was white. That's all I remember.'

She follows Don to the door, unlocks it, and lets him out.

'Thanks for coming,' she says sweetly, mechanically. 'Call again.'

'Somewhere along the line,' De Vries says, 'there has to be something that leads us in the right direction.' He holds his hand up. 'And don't mention that fucking chicken again, Don. You're an adult, you do whatever you like, but if I hear about it again, it had better be solid.' He looks at Steve Ulton. 'Anything at all we can use to get a handle on this guy?'

Ulton struggles to sit upright in De Vries's crooked visitor's chair.

'No prints or impressions of any kind outside in the garden or on the terrace. Inside, there's lots of stuff. But, you tell me that she had at least two boyfriends, visits from people protesting about her exhibition; there are half a dozen part-time domestic workers and the live-in maid. Even if we had the resources, which we don't, I can't see us finding anything significant. If there's anything there, it's hidden in the comings and goings.'

'The guy can shoot,' De Vries says. 'We think he kills Taryn Holt with the first shot. He shoots her four times more. Why? To cover the fact that he's such a good shot?'

'Possibly,' Ulton responds. 'It makes as much sense as any other explanation.'

'He collects the casings, arranges Holt with the dildo in her mouth. Again, why?'

'To make it look not like an execution,' Don says. 'To make it look like something it is not.'

Ulton nods. De Vries scratches the back of his neck.

'That's the point, isn't it,' he says, clenching his fists. 'We know it's not what it seems. We just don't know what the fuck it really is.'

He is still in his office as dusk turns to night. This is a special time for him, when the squad room goes quiet and dark, and only the lamp on his desk is on. The windows in the office buildings opposite him are mainly dark also but, beneath him, the street is a string of white and red lights as, slowly, the CBD empties out, leaving it deserted but for some sleeping forms in doorways. De Vries doesn't want to go home; he has no desire to repeat his failings to Marantz. He considers the bars of Long Street but knows that, in truth, he is happier drinking alone.

He opens his bottom drawer, fumbles in it with his left hand without looking down, feels the bottle. The previous year, he spilt whisky in the drawer, trying to hide his office tipple, just as David Wertner came into his office. He smiles at the memory. He has stayed off spirits for a while but, this evening, the thought of a warming draft suddenly overwhelms him, and he extracts the bottle. His hand fails to locate the plastic beakers which used to accompany it. He peers into the drawer, but they have gone. He gets up, strolls into the squad room and takes a mug from next to the jug of weak, tepid coffee, then wanders back again, shutting the door after him. He pours himself a modest double measure, sips it, smiles, knocks it back, and pours another, larger tot. Twenty seconds, he reflects, between pours; reminds him of how he used to be.

His thoughts turn to Julius Mngomezulu; he wonders whether it is personal with him, this need to interfere and disrupt De Vries's inquiries. He asks himself what Mngomezulu has to gain by leaking information on Trevor Bhekifa to the press, but cannot find an answer. He pours again.

By 9 p.m., he is tapping a rhythm only he hears on the surface of his desk, running through evidence which produces no answers. He stops, realizes that he has been told what to do: to dismiss what appears in front of him; to consider everything from the other side, the opposite angle. Steve Ulton's words: 'If there is anything there, it's hidden in the comings and goings.' De Vries thinks: that's the point. The killer knew the house, took the alarm remote, loosened the window. The killer knew Taryn Holt, had been there at the house – any sign of him hidden in the comings and goings? The killer shoots perfectly, then masks it; the killer kills again to hide himself, to hide the motive. None of the suspects fit this description. Yet De Vries feels that there is no one unaccounted for, no one who is hiding other than in plain view. Don February's chicken takeaway: a policeman. De Vries looks up – the room tilts and he squeezes his eyes shut. He opens them, feels suddenly sober, knows all at once: Nkosi.

He phones Don February, asks him to check whether Lieutenant Sam Nkosi appears in the mug-shots of officers from Cape Town

Central SAPS. He waits, listening to Don rummaging in his brief-case, laying out the sheets, searching for how the pictures are arranged: by rank, alphabetically?

'He is not here.'

'You're certain?'

'The print-out from Central, it is dated October 2014. Nkosi told us he had only moved from Pretoria six months ago.'

'Pretoria,' De Vries says.

'Sir?'

'If I'm right about Nkosi, there's a Pretoria link. A Major Mabena was talking to Director du Toit at his conference there, taking an interest in the Holt case, leaving messages for General Thulani. He's some kind of attaché between the Police Ministry and the SAPS top brass.'

'I do not understand.'

'Nor do I.'

'You want me to come back in?'

'No. Get some sleep, Don. If Mabena and Nkosi are linked in some way, this just got even more serious than I thought. I don't know what to do.'

'You sleep too, sir.'

Don waits, hears nothing.

'Sir?'

'Won't sleep,' De Vries says.

Vaughn de Vries wakes to the sound of a vacuum cleaner, then a knock on his door. He looks up, sees a pock-marked black face looking expectantly at him. He struggles up, waves the man in. The door opens and the mechanical noise fills the room. He acknowledges the cleaner, stumbles out of his office, sees the squad-room empty. He stretches his shoulders, waiting for the elevators, and travels down to the main foyer, out onto the street. It is still early; his body is stiff and aching. He stumbles on the pavement, laughs at himself, keeps walking towards the coffee shop he knows will be open early. The sky is darker, the air heavy. This, he thinks, still slightly intoxicated, must be what it feels like waiting for rains on the great Serengeti plains.

He orders coffee and a cooked breakfast, knows that once he is engrossed in a case, he rarely finds time to eat. He uses the men's lavatories to wash his face, tuck in his shirt. He sticks his tongue out in the grubby mirror, sees a cream-coloured coated surface to his tongue to go with the dark ringed eyes and dry lips. He blinks twice, finds his eyes harder to open again the second time; his jaw is tight. He pushes his tongue into the roof of his mouth, feels the tension ease momentarily, sees his hands shaking on the sink. He needs to be fit, needs to be well. Nkosi.

Don waits for him in his office. It is before 8 a.m. and there are still no other staff in the squad room. It smells like a bar the morning after a busy night. Don sniffs the empty mug on his desk, confirms what he thought; he jumps when he hears the voice.

'You sleep?'

'Not much.'

'I know it's him. I've been thinking about it all night. Thought about the way he was at the scene. It all makes sense. The perfect shot, his attempts to hide it. His visits to Taryn Holt to reassure her about security. Being on the scene first: any forensics are immediately compromised. He just says: "Of course I was there. I was the investigating officer until De Vries took over."'

'I will obtain a picture of him,' Don says. 'I can show the girl at the restaurant. If it was him, it links him to Angus Lyle too.'

'It'll be him,' De Vries says, nodding to himself. 'Fucking

chicken takeaway. I knew you were going to humiliate me with that.'

'Can we prove anything?'

De Vries laughs.

'Of course not. Even if you tie him to Lyle, no one saw him at the park. He can deny everything. We have to work out why he did it. We have to ask ourselves why someone higher up wants to protect him.'

'We report up to General Thulani?'

'I don't know. We can't provide evidence. Thulani won't do anything without it. Instead he may just poke around in Pretoria and alert everyone. I think this is down to us.'

'How do we do this without alerting Nkosi?'

'I don't know that either. If he's being protected from high up, even from the Police Ministry itself, there may be people who don't want us finding out. I don't know whether we want to be here at all.'

'But we are.'

De Vries nods. 'We are. Now, we have to decide whether to turn away or press on.'

'Unfortunately, sir, I already know your answer.'

The investigation is officially wound down, the squad room emptied of extra staff except for De Vries's regular team, and most have been given days off in lieu of the extra hours. The whiteboard is cleaned, notes and files brought together and stored.

De Vries ponders how he can investigate fellow officers without involving the Independent Police Investigation Department or, worse, David Wertner's Internal Investigations Unit for the elite divisions. Despite being of lower rank, both Lieutenant Sam Nkosi and a certain Major Mabena in Pretoria seem out of reach.

★ ★ ★

At lunchtime, Don February shows Judy Miles four pictures, including one of Sam Nkosi. She immediately picks him out, then expresses doubt, suggesting that the man in the picture looks like the man she served the previous week, but she cannot swear to it. Don has seen enough witnesses to know that her original gut instinct is reliable. She recalls that she did not watch him get back into his vehicle, nor the direction in which it might have gone. De Waal Park is barely 800 metres away and Don cannot lose the image of Nkosi dropping down the mountainside, parking in one of the adjoining roads, walking the poorly lit side streets with the hot chicken in its box under his arm until he finds Angus Lyle, and beginning a conversation that would result, not long afterwards, in Lyle's death.

Doctor Anna Jafari has called him. She has new information and, to conclude the phone conversation, she bids him goodbye. De Vries wonders how his behaviour towards her warrants this unusual pleasantry. He finds her by an examination table.

'What is it, Doctor?'

She gestures for him to approach the bench. The body of Angus Lyle lies under the grim lights; De Vries thinks that his body seems bluer than the last time he saw it.

'I spent many hours on this matter last night.' She does not look him in the eye. 'As far as blood, stomach and trace were concerned, there was no indication as to what might have caused the victim's heart to fail. However, I was not satisfied with this, so I re-examined the body early this morning. I believe I may have found a possible answer.'

She passes De Vries a large magnifying glass. She indicates Lyle's left foot, holds his big toe and second toe apart.

'Please look here.'

De Vries bends down, focuses the image in the glass, squints.

'You require spectacles?'

'No.'

'Your close vision seems impaired . . .'

De Vries straightens.

'It's fine, Doctor. What am I looking at?'

She takes the magnifying glass from him, places it on a desk.

'I decided that interference may have taken place, but I wasn't sure how that might have been achieved. Between his big toe and second toe, there is syringe mark.'

De Vries looks back down at Lyle's feet.

'In his foot?'

'Indeed. If I wanted to hide an injection mark, that would be a good choice of location.'

'What was injected?'

'I can't say for sure. It looks like an eight millimetre hypodermic needle was used as the delivery system, but I cannot be certain. His blood work suggests heightened readings of potassium. However, levels vary considerably over time. They may be an ambient level, or they might indicate that he was poisoned by an injection of concentrated potassium chloride. That, in turn, could lead to paralysis, heart attack and sudden death. The problem for us is that potassium chloride within the blood stream dissipates quickly.'

De Vries stares at the body, tilts his head.

'It does,' Jafari says, 'seem far-fetched but, since there is no other explanation, I am inclined to consider this a possibility.'

De Vries wonders what makes her share this possibility with him.

'How would that have panned out?'

'Now you are asking me to speculate; my previous comment was based on unexplained evidence, but evidence nonetheless. Do you see the distinction, Colonel?'

De Vries turns from the bench.

'All right. Let me ask you this, then: could the bruising you saw on Angus Lyle's shoulder and neck . . . Could that have disabled him in some way?'

Jafari hesitates.

'I don't know.'

'He starts eating. He's hungry. His assailant disables him, then injects this potassium into him via his foot. Is that possible?'

'It is possible. But it cannot be known.'

'Never any answers . . .'

'I have done my best.'

He looks up.

'You have, Doctor. I didn't mean that you do not give answers, just that people think that science can always provide the hard evidence, that the process is easy. You did exceptionally well to find those marks. Thank you.'

Jafari walks up to him. She is head and shoulders shorter than he is. She looks up at him.

'So, let us be clear, Colonel, and leave personalities out of it. You may not like me, the discipline I bring to my working life or professional women generally, perhaps even Muslims. That is your prerogative. But do not doubt my professional abilities . . .'

'I have never . . .'

'Yes, you have. I will never tell a court that I am certain about something if I am not, nor reassure them that there is no doubt when, clearly and scientifically, there is. What you think about a suspect is irrelevant, and must remain irrelevant for justice to func-tion. Justice is, I believe, something we have in common?'

'There is no need . . .'

'I worked on, despite the fact that I have my own modest life outside of work, because I felt, as I know you did, that what we saw before us did not seem right. You see, I bring more than just my qualifications to this job, as do you. But, what we bring is not the same. Not at all.'

'I don't understand you.'

'I respect you,' she continues firmly, 'for what you do – even if that is not always by the book – and, if we are to work together, you had better learn to respect me. All you have to do is suspend your prejudices.'

He opens his mouth to counter, produces no words. He nods. She smiles thinly, nods back.

'My report will be on your desk by the end of the day.'

He hears himself saying, genuinely: 'Thank you, Doctor.'

Back in the office, Don February thinks of Taryn Holt's neighbour – the teenaged girl, Lorna, watching from her bedroom window – and wonders whether she can place Nkosi at the scene at the correct time. She had said that the last time she had seen Holt had been the previous night, but it is possible that she has thought again. He telephones the house, is told that, reluctantly, they will see him before their supper, at 6.30 p.m., no later.

He looks for De Vries but, if he is in the building, he does not want to be found. He sits in the guest chair at the side of De Vries's desk, writes up what he has found and what he suspects. In the late afternoon, he sees Julius Mngomezulu peering around the wall into the squad-room, looking towards De Vries's office. It seems to Don that Mngomezulu cannot see him; that the single blind over the one window has provided cover. Mngomezulu walks into the squad-room, affecting nonchalance, glances down at the surface of the desks, up at the monitors, and scrutinizes the remains of the scrubbed writing on the whiteboard. Don stays motionless, breath held, as if witnessing the arrival of rare wildlife outside his window. He watches Mngomezulu approach his own desk in the far corner; he sees him flick through the pages in the pile, stop at one, look down for longer. Don wonders what he has left there to so enthrall Mngomezulu. Finally, the Lieutenant looks up and around, takes the sheet of paper and walks quickly but casually away.

Don waits a few moments then slowly rises from his chair and walks to his desk: one of the few with any written material on it. Atop the pile is a copy of the inventory of items found on Angus Lyle's person. Don looks hard at the pile, tries to visualize where Mngomezulu had been looking. He flicks through the papers.

He is not sure that he left the sheet in the pile, but it is possible that he left a note to himself from the day before. It would have read: 'Nkosi? Chicken from Woodsman's Grill. Friday 10 p.m.'

Don curses under his breath, wonders to whom Mngomezulu will report, knows that if it is to someone connected to Nkosi, they – and then he – will know that one part of the investigation has not ended.

'I used a contact I wasn't supposed to know about.'

'One of your people? Here, in Cape Town?'

Marantz looks up from the table. He is milling cannabis between his fingernails, flicking away the seeds. It is so still this evening, there is no danger of it blowing away.

'One of yours.'

'I don't get it.'

'Former SAPS.'

'How do you know him?'

'Connections. Leave it at that.'

'I still don't get it, and I don't like it.'

'Hopefully you will. He told me if he finds nothing, you're not even supposed to know. If he does, you'll meet him.'

'I hate this cloak-and-dagger stuff. I like it simple. A to B, as few stops along the way as possible. It's how I was taught.' De Vries looks at the bottle: Silvertree Ale. He likes the label, like its contents.

'Why do you do this, John? Why do you get involved?'

'What else is there for me to do? I sit thinking all day, play cards at night. I need something to do. Your problems distract me.'

'Why don't you stop thinking?'

Marantz laughs, eyes forlorn.

'I have never, ever been able to stop. I'm thinking until unconsciousness takes me, thinking when I wake in the night, thinking when I get up. It's exhausting.'

'I don't even know how you live. Some kind of payment, pension from your government?'

'Money? That's not my problem. I can survive here on what I have. It's not that. It's whether I can live like this any more, Vaughn. I've tried, really tried to move on. If I knew they were gone, really knew for certain, maybe then . . .'

'I thought you'd had news . . . ?'

'News? Oh yes, from my former employers: professional bullshitters. Their sources unreliable, their interpretation debatable, what they tell me unqualifiable.'

De Vries knows where his daughters are. He rarely sees them, but knows nonetheless. If he did not, he appreciates how that would feel. He recognizes the powerlessness of ignorance: about a case, about a woman, about how he will get up the next day and actually function; he knows what it is like to have to move forward but to have no idea where. This is what they share.

'You know how it feels to lose your wallet, or your keys? It's shock. Your brain can't comprehend that they are not where it is convinced they should be. The feeling that it can't have happened, that your hand will feel it at any moment, and then realizing it's been stolen. It's like that for me every day.'

'You can't live like that. Do something to distract yourself. Get yourself a job. . .'

'I'm unemployable. I was used to investigate people, assemble information, interrogate them, break them. What does that qualify me for?'

'In this country,' De Vries says, 'a whole host of jobs: bank teller, Telkom helpline, Eskom engineer, plumber, council official, planning committee chairman . . .'

'I get it.'

De Vries drains the bottle, gets up, wanders inside the house, up to the kitchen, into the fridge; he strolls back with the open bottle. Marantz runs his tongue along the long edge of the cigarette paper, wetting the gum, and begins to roll, back and forth, back and forth.

'This stillness. It's good news. Cold front's coming. It'll be raining tomorrow.'

De Vries says: 'This contact: he knows what I told you?'

'Yes.'

'What about Lieutenant Sam Nkosi?'

'His name's out there.'

De Vries frowns.

'How? Why? What did you think?'

'Information appears from places you don't even consider. And it breeds; the more you feed it, the more comes out. Besides . . .' He lights the thick joint, inhales deeply, blows the smoke out in a thin stream which drifts slowly down the pool terrace and drops over the end of his lap pool, onto the mountainside. '. . . It's quite usual: the first person who sees the victim dead is also the last person to see them alive.'

Number 14 Park Terrace is almost dark from the outside, only a dim light illuminates the porch. Don knocks and waits. Eventually, the calm, dour woman answers the door, watches him wipe his feet, leads him into the dark living area. She holds up her hand to stop him, walks on to the end of the room, stands behind the sofa where Lorna is engrossed in a television news report. She puts her hands on the girl's shoulders, waits calmly. When the item finishes, Lorna switches off the set, looks up.

'Yes, mother?'

'The policeman is here. You remember we talked about it?'

Lorna rises and walks up to Don February, looks him up and down.

'Please may I see your ID?'

'You don't know who I am?'

'I know who you are supposed to be.'

Don smiles to himself, pleased that De Vries is not here. He will ignore the strangeness, do what she asks and it will not raise his heart-rate by half a beat; De Vries, he would already be fuming. He reaches into his inside pocket, hands her the ID. She steps back. Don places it on the back of the sofa. She takes it, studies it and him, returns it, and says: 'What do you want to ask me now, Warrant Officer Donald February?'

Don wonders whether she will ask him to sit down but, instead, they both stand stiffly opposite one another, her mother a few steps away, still and silent.

'You told me the last time you had seen Taryn Holt,' Don says, 'and that you had seen police everywhere. Did you see any police on the night of Thursday second and Friday third?'

'The night the woman died.'

'Yes.'

'It wasn't a question. I know,' she says blankly. 'I only watch between 10.30 and 11 p.m., unless there is something special to see. There was a policeman in a car, parked at the corner of Serpentine Road.'

Don nods, considers, asks: 'Was is it a police car, or a police van?'

'Neither. It was a silver BMW 3 Series. I compared it with other cars of the same make.'

'So how did you know it was a policeman in the car?'

'Because I have seen him before: six times. He often watches our road from his car. And, on the morning after the lady was killed, I saw him coming out of her house, talking with other policemen.'

'What did he look like?'

'Black. He was a black man.'

'Was he tall? Maybe a little under two metres?'

'It is not possible to estimate his height from my window.'

'But tall?'

'He is taller than you; blacker than you.'

'Would you recognize his face if you saw it again?'

'Yes.'

Don produces the four pictures he showed to Judy Miles at the restaurant, lays them out on the back of the sofa. Even before he has finished, she points at the picture of Nkosi.

'That is him.'

He looks at her.

'You are certain?'

She stares back, says nothing.

'What time did he arrive?'

'10.52 p.m.'

He knows better than to question her timings.

'Did you see him leave his vehicle?'

'No.'

'But you are certain it was him?'

'Yes.'

'Why did you not tell me before that you had seen this man watching your road?'

'You didn't ask me.'

'No,' Don says ruefully, 'I did not.' He wonders what else to ask her; how to phrase the questions carefully.

'And you stopped watching out of your window at 11 p.m.?'

'Yes.'

'And you did not look out again that night?'

'No.'

'Did you see the number plate?'

'Of course.' She gives him the license number: two letters, six numbers. He writes it down carefully.

'You can remember that, too?' he says.

'Can't you?'

He smiles at her.

'No . . . Is it always the same car?'

'Yes.'

'Good. Thank you.'

'You are wearing the same suit as last time. Do you only own one suit?'

'Two suits,' Don says. 'I have two.'

'Are they both too big?'

'They are.'

'Will you catch who killed our neighbour?'

'I think so. You may even have helped.'

'Was it the man I saw watching our road?'

'Maybe.'

Lorna looks at him suspiciously.

'I don't want my picture on the news. I don't want to see myself.'

Don nods, bows gently towards her. She turns away from him, walks back to the sofa and turns the television back on. Don looks at Lorna's mother.

'Are you finished?' she says.

'It seems so.'

She leads the way to the front door. Don remembers his last visit.

Before he goes through it, he says: 'Thank you, madam. Goodnight.'

He still receives no reply.

De Vries drives out of town on the N1 past Century City, the gaudy development of apartment blocks, hotels and shopping centres which views Table Mountain from afar, and turns onto the road heading north and then onto Koeberg Road, leading past the vast industrial areas north of Cape Town, past the twisted iron and steel of the oil refineries and power distribution centres. The streets here are dark, devoid of people – the air thick and heavy. He drives to what would once have been a little green space between the groups of low-cost bungalows, but which now is no more than a dumping ground, and finds a group of white guys sitting under a copse of three windblown, almost leafless trees. The scene is lit by the dull vomit-yellow glow of the one working streetlight. He watches them a moment, passing around a bottle wrapped in a paper bag.

Before they cleared the city centre of them, the *bergies* had always been there, in the Company Gardens, on Long Street, down by the docks. At first, when he had seen more of them, the sight of destitute whites – homeless, drunk, drug-addled – had shocked and disturbed him; it had stoked an innate, inherited resentment deep within him. Now, twenty-one years on from the formation of the ANC government, they are ubiquitous. De Vries feels sickened by the reversal of fortune, but knows it is a price to be paid; he knows that, if the seemingly meaningless split-second decisions of everyday life had been different, he too could have been amongst them.

He parks up fifty metres from them, pulls two cans of Amstel from a six-pack in a carrier bag in the passenger foot-well, gets out of his car and ambles slowly towards them. When he looks up, he can see that one of them has spotted him, like a look-out for a herd of wild-buck. Their grunting conversation ceases; one by one they turn to face him. He holds up the cans, sees heads tilt up, hope challenging suspicion. He nods at them, offers the cans. No one moves to take them.

'I want to find a guy I worked with, long ago. Mike. Mike de Groot. You know him?'

They say nothing. He sees their eyes move from the alcohol to his face.

He says it again, this time in Afrikaans.

'You police?'

'*Ja*. Off duty. Looking for one of my guys, left long ago. His mates told me he needs my help. You know him? Mike de Groot?'

He produces the picture, holds it up, approaches them slowly and shows it to them.

'The guy on the right there.'

De Vries watches each of them as he turns the picture, sees little in their crusted, sunburnt eyes, bloodshot and half-open.

One holds out his hands.

'I've seen him. Stays out by the incinerator.'

De Vries stares at him, believes him, passes him the beers.

'Where?'

The *bergie* gestures with his chin.

'Past the garage, down Stella Road.'

De Vries nods.

'You have any food, man?'

De Vries shakes his head.

'Some change for food?'

'No. Beer's all I got.'

He watches them in the rear-mirror as he pulls away. They are sharing the cans around the seven or eight of them, each taking

229

a gulp and passing it on again. The pool of banana-yellow light fades as he reaches the turn back onto the main road. He wonders what those men did in their previous lives: factory workers, warehousemen; maybe SAPS. He finds his teeth gritted and his fingers tight on the wheel.

He locates Stella Road, drives past the now deserted warehouses and retail units, the sad, windblown date palms, their fronds browning in the endless summer heat. On the corner, the inside of a battered Toyota is illuminated by an orange glow. Four coloured kids are burning or cooking something, smoking and drinking. A night out. He turns left, then right, and heads towards the hulking form of the incinerator. Bungalows have become breezeblock shacks with corrugated tin roofs. Most are dark, but some display a bare bulb behind plastic-sheeting windows.

He pulls over by an illuminated shack boasting a tiny stoep, made from a continuation of iron sheeting, supported by three narrow wooden pillars. Two older men sit on a threadbare sofa smoking, gazing out across the narrow road to the lines of shacks opposite them.

De Vries gets out, pulls two more cans out with him, calls out to them in Afrikaans. The gruff reply is welcoming enough, and he approaches them. They both stand up, shake his hand. When he offers beer, he is invited to sit with them. They take the beers and open them; one offers his to De Vries. He takes a sip, tells them he must drive, hands it back. He offers them cigarettes, which are accepted eagerly.

De Vries sits back on the folding plastic chair, reflects that he is a stranger who has been welcomed into their home, and says nothing. There is no breeze now; in between the plumes of blue smoke which hang before him, he can smell the men: stale sweat and piss. He almost senses that their clothes are made brittle by the excretions. He takes a deep draw on his cigarette, lets the smoke out through loose lips, re-inhaling it through his nostrils, fighting nausea. The neighbourhood is quiet but for a distant yet insistent mechanical whirring and the sound of, maybe, fork-lift trucks coming and going.

One speaks; it makes him jump.

'You a cop?'

De Vries smiles; he knows that his demeanour is a badge.

'*Ja.*'

The man holds up his can as a toast.

'You're all right.' He nods at De Vries sagely.

'I'm Selwyn.' He thumbs the other man. 'And Danie.'

'Vaughn . . .' He sits forward. 'I'm looking for someone. A guy from the force years ago. Mate of his said he needs my help . . .'

'You didn't come here for the view.'

De Vries smiles, asks: 'What did you do? Your job?'

The silent man shrugs; Selwyn says: 'You know Pinter's factory? I was foreman there, in the packing.'

'What happened?'

'Not enough blacks, they said. They had to have blacks. It's the law now. You think there's work for guys our age? Place'll be closed down soon. They fucked it up.'

'Same in the SAPS.'

'They close you down too?'

'Trying to. Guys like me anyway.'

De Vries pulls out the picture of Mike de Groot, shows it to them. Selwyn passes it to Danie. He looks, shakes his head, tilts the beer can to his lips. Selwyn takes it back, brings it close up to his face, studies it.

'I've seen him.'

'Mike de Groot?'

'*Ja*. Mike.'

'He stays here?'

'*Ja*. Down there. I'll take you.' He gives back the picture, takes another draft of beer, sits back, waves his arm shakily from his left shoulder out into the darkness. 'Places like this all over the country now. Outside of Jo'burg, Pretoria, Durban, all over the suburbs. Whole families of white folks without work, no place to stay. It's unbelievable.' He looks at De Vries, still sitting forward. 'You want to go to Mike's now?'

'*Ja.*'

Selwyn pulls himself to his feet, steadies himself by holding onto the wooden pillar supporting the roof. De Vries looks down, sees that the man wears boots from which socks, then toes, stick out. He feels strangely ashamed, and follows Selwyn as he slowly shuffles the few steps to the pavement.

De Vries holds up a hand to Danie.

'Goodnight.'

The man just stares at him.

'Quiet guy,' De Vries says.

'He says he has nothing to say.'

'Down here,' De Vries says. 'It's all you guys staying?'

'Mainly us now, few coloured families. Funny, isn't it? Never thought we'd end up in the ghetto. Not even when we knew they were taking over. Even then, we thought we'd still be wanted.'

Selwyn laughs; a sad, strained chuckle. 'How many years, you think, till they've paid us back? My son, he says never. Builder in Dubai now. Sends me something. Only thing keeps me fed. Only thing . . .'

They walk at Selwyn's slow, lumbering pace along the road. The sky is clear, yet it seems low and heavy: an African night, a prelude to the change of seasons. The pavement narrows and deteriorates as they approach the back gates to the dominating incinerator buildings. De Vries stumbles. He looks down; the paving stones are missing.

'They take them.'

He looks up at Selwyn.

'Anything that isn't tied down.'

'People take the pavement?'

'*Ja.* Metal, stone, brick. Everything has a value.'

Selwyn looks over the road at another dark shack which, to De Vries, is indistinguishable from all the others.

'Think he stays there. Looks like he's not here, or asleep.'

'I'll take a look. You get back. Thanks for your help.'

They shake hands. Vaughn trots across the road, climbs over a fallen concrete post propping up a bowed chicken-wire fence, and approaches the shack. He pauses, listens at the door – an old glazed wooden door, salvaged. He is about to push it open, when he senses something behind him. He turns, finds Selwyn a few paces back.

'Let me check he's okay, *ja*?'

'Just stay there though.'

De Vries knocks at the door, waits. He glances back at Selwyn, pushes open the door. Immediately, he smells it, putrid and strong. Wafts of hot, fetid, rancid air hit him, flies buzz his eyes. He swallows and swallows again – tries to control his gag reflex. He reaches for the torch in his jacket pocket, switches it on. The beam illuminates a dark brown sticky pool; a slight turn of his wrist, a man on his back, his face convulsed.

'Jesus!'

De Vries jumps, unaware that Selwyn had followed him inside.

'Step back. Back through the door. This is a crime scene. I don't want you involved.'

He turns back, takes a deep breath through his mouth, puffs out his cheeks, blows it out. He looks down to check that where he steps is dry, then tilts the beam towards the man once more. The light flickers on his face in Vaughn's shaking hand. Through the stubbly beard, the wrinkled sunburnt flesh, he sees a likeness to Mike de Groot. He works the beam down his body. In his chest,

233

over his heart, there is a deep wound. Through the blood-soaked vest, he cannot see detail; he believes that there are multiple wounds in the same area.

He forces himself to examine the man's face again, knows that he is looking at Mike de Groot. He switches off the torch, stands in the dark, feeling his heart beating in his throat, at his temples – his mind racing, invaded by fear.

He draws himself up, turns and leaves the shack, pushing the door to. Selwyn stands on the pavement, not three metres away.

'It's Mike.'

'Had to be. No one else ever goes in there. They said he was mad. Used to talk to himself, sometimes sing in the street. We spoke to him. He was okay.'

They begin to walk slowly back towards Selwyn's shack.

'You see anyone out of the ordinary here the last day or two?'

Selwyn thinks a moment, says: 'Saw no one. Been out on my seat most of the last two weeks. Too hot inside. Danie's been there too. Just the guys from the incinerator – they can leave by the back. Kids, always kids; a few blacks, coloureds. Then, just us guys, a few of the wives . . .'

'Any cars?'

'Look around. No cars running here. Guys who haven't sold 'em can't afford to run 'em. They sit there out front. Might as well be on bricks.'

'Other cars. New cars?'

'No one comes down here. No reason.'

'A lot of crime?'

'Less than your neighbourhood. Nothing to take here. Anything worth having's been taken years back.'

'I need you to do something for me,' De Vries says.

'All right.'

'I need you to call the local cops.'

Selwyn stops, turns to De Vries.

'You said you were a cop.'

'I am, but this isn't my patch. I'm here because a friend of Mike's from the old days asked me to look for him, 'cos he wasn't around in his old haunts any more. If I'm here, it's hours of paperwork, questions. I can't do that. I need a favour.'

He finds his wallet, pulls out a blue hundred rand note, a red fifty, and watches Selwyn's eyes follow the coloured paper.

'Can you go up to a shop, buy you and your friend some dinner, ask one of the guys there to make the call? Just tell them you looked in on him 'cos you hadn't seen him and that's what you saw.'

Selwyn nods. Vaughn hands him the notes.

'If you mention me, it'll fuck me up. Can you keep me out of it?'

'Ja.'

'And Danie?'

'Danie doesn't say anything.'

'You're sure?'

Selwyn crosses his arms, says slowly: 'Danie and I will have tinned chicken stew and beer for dinner. If we talk, we'll talk about that a while.'

Vaughn watches Selwyn gesture to Danie and begin to walk towards the main road. De Vries waves as he drives away, but neither of them see him. He wonders whether they will keep their word and keep him out of it. He doesn't know what to tell Mitchell Smith, or what to do himself. His mind is racing, but he cannot imagine who would be killing these men twenty-one years after the event. Four of them stabbed. No doubt now: no coincidence. He wonders whether Smith and he will be next, whether Kobus Nel is tidying up history for some reason. No one knows that there is a connection between these deaths. He does not know whether he must reveal it, or whether he must play the scene out, discover the meaning behind it; keep history's secret. He feels hungry and tired but knows that he will not eat, will not sleep.

It is not raining. Still the clouds are high, forming quickly over the mountain range, disappearing again over the City Bowl. De Vries has spent the night wondering what to do about Mike de Groot and Mitchell Smith. In the early hours, it hits him that he has a major investigation with an SAPS officer as prime suspect. He feels weak and helpless.

Don February arrives in the office later than usual.

'My wife has what she calls man flu,' he tells De Vries. 'It is a cold, but she has upgraded it to stay home from work. And, as it was so serious, to keep up appearances I had to go shopping for her. I am sorry.'

'Keep 'em happy, Don. That's my advice.'

Don nods.

'What did Holt's neighbour tell you?'

'Nkosi – she identified him from the pictures immediately – has been watching the road. He arrived there at ten fifty-two on the night Taryn Holt was murdered. She says that he did not get out of his car while she was watching, but that she is sure it was the man she had seen, six times in all, she stated.'

'Why didn't she tell you this before?'

Don stutters: 'She is . . . She is a girl who only answers precisely the question she has been asked. It is an affliction, I think. I had not asked her the correct question.'

'She is certain of his identity?'

'She says she saw the same man, in the grey suit, talking with the police officers, coming out of the Holt house on the morning we arrived.'

De Vries nods, contemplates.

'So, maybe we have a witness who can place him at the scene. But, he still has room to manoeuvre.'

'I would not want the entire case to depend on her testimony . . .'

'Why?'

'She is not . . .' He searches for the words. '. . . A sympathetic witness. And I am not certain that she would be allowed, or even herself prepared, to testify.'

'How old is she?'

'Fourteen.'

De Vries shakes his head.

'She had noted the license plate. I had it checked before coming up. The registration belonged to a car which was wrecked in an accident two years ago. There is no link to a silver BMW.'

'So, he drives an anonymous car . . .'

'There is one more thing, sir . . .' Don says forlornly. 'I was working here at the side of your desk yesterday. I saw Lieutenant Mngomezulu come into the squad room, which was empty. He did not see me. He was looking around. He went to my desk and I had left papers there. He took one. I am not sure, but I think it was a note about the chicken takeaway and whether Nkosi had been to the restaurant.'

'What did it say?'

'Just that. Hand-written by me.'

'So Mngomezulu knows we have a link there . . .' De Vries sighs. 'I'm going to make a suggestion: I'm closing the case. It's over. We have what we need to tie in Angus Lyle. I am going to report to General Thulani that we have almost tied up all the loose ends and that we will conclude our report in the next two or three days. You go home to your wife. I have an appointment. If I can, I'll make sure Mngomezulu hears we're closing it down. Then, on Saturday, we can regroup and see what we have learned.'

'What will we learn at home?'

'You won't learn anything, and that's fine.' He sits at his desk, gestures Don towards him. 'Ben Thwala: he worked up in Pretoria, didn't he?'

'I think for three months.'

'That's fine. He'll know the basics of how it works up there. Call him now, Don. I want him here.'

'Now now?'

'*Ja.*'

Don turns away from the desk, faces the window and calls Thwala. De Vries sits back in his chair; he counts off names on his fingers, mouthing the words.

'He's coming just now.'

'Good. We need to brief Classon, Ulton and, God help us, Doctor Jafari. We need everything seemingly concluded.'

'The rest of the team?'

'Tell them to take leave. If we're writing it all up, that'll make sense. Nkosi didn't kill Taryn Holt on a whim. He planned it and carried it out and, since there is so much interest from above, we can assume he was acting under orders.' He pauses. They catch each other's eye, realize what the statement actually means.

'I've got an old SAPS contact too. He may be able to help us with what might be happening.'

There is a rapid knock at the office door. Ben Thwala ducks to enter the office, sits where De Vries points, sits in the low wonky chair, sits straight.

'I'll call Steve Ulton at home. He knows what's happening. He'll do whatever is needed.'

'I don't like it.'

'Of course you don't, Norman,' De Vries tells him. 'But we're not doing anything illegal. We are just conducting a private enquiry to gain information on a suspect. That must be acceptable?'

Norman Classon stretches his neck and shoulders.

'We're informing General Thulani that a case is closed and the perpetrator found when we know full well that it is not.'

'We know, yes. But until we can prove it, you think that means anything? We've discussed this before. I need you to tell no one. Not Thulani, not anyone. No one. That way, no one else is implicated and we don't have to worry about trust – on any level.'

'Does that include Brigadier du Toit?'

'With him, it is not a question of trust. It is just better not to tell him, or he will worry. Don't you think?'

'And that, I suppose, is your defence when this all comes into the open?'

'Ever the attorney . . .'

'Did you order Sergeant Thwala to Pretoria?'

'I told Thwala exactly where we were,' De Vries says. He's a good officer. He understands the position. The fact is, he was seconded to Pretoria two years ago, spent three months there, including time in Liaison with the Police Ministry. He'll stay with a relative and make some discreet enquiries. He ought to have a good idea of someone he can trust there. If he's found out, he knows what's at stake.'

'I hope he does.'

'He does.'

'And you? What will you do?'

'Nothing. I want to be seen to be doing nothing. If they're watching, they're watching me. I'm going to a beer festival, in Greyton.'

'I saw the posters.'

'You need to be in the process of drawing all the paper-work into the form it would have to be in to close the case around Lyle.'

'And Doctor Jafari?'

'I'll talk to her. I think the doctor will react positively if the right language is used. After all, she contacted me when she found the syringe mark. I'm taking that to mean she understands.'

'You trust her?'

De Vries smirks.

'You know what? Strangely, I do.'

De Vries travels to Greyton in the passenger seat, driven by the son of his neighbour for the agreed fee of the price of the fuel. The boy's girlfriend is working at one of the stalls at the beer festival and they plan to camp out for the last night in the back of the *bakkie*. Next day, the arrangement is for the girl, who is to remain moderately sober since she is at work, to drive all three of them home.

De Vries has called Anna Jafari, explained what he is doing and why, and she has accepted what he has told her. Off rotation for two days, there is no reason for her to comment on her report.

The teenager drives carefully, both hands on the wheel at all times, diligently checking his mirrors, sticking rigidly to the speed limit. He asks if he can play music; De Vries, who plans to doze for the ninety-minute journey, agrees.

He wakes as the *bakkie* struggles up Sir Lowry's Pass to drive across the Overberg, the area atop the plateau known for its forestry and fruit growing. At MacNeil's Farmstall, they pull in to pick up their renowned pies and some cool drinks. De Vries remains in the car and does not tell the boy that this is where one of his most testing cases began: the dump-site for two teenage bodies in a skip around the back. He has not stopped here since.

After another forty minutes, they turn onto the road which takes them through Genadendal, then on towards the country town of Greyton. The cloud is lower and darker now, the humidity rising. Even with both windows open the cab of the *bakkie* is warm and sticky.

Because he booked his stay late, the guesthouses in Greyton itself are full, so De Vries has opted for a country motel a couple of kilometres out of town. The deal includes a minivan to shuttle guests to and from the beer festival; an old colleague of De Vries's is staying there also.

The boy waits, engine running, as De Vries stands on the road and presses the intercom button. The outside of the Travellers' Haven is unprepossessing: a high wall painted caramel; an archway guarded by two heavy metal gates. After a moment, the gates open slowly, De Vries waves at his driver, and the boy speeds away.

The motel is set up in a rectangle, a closed courtyard of peach-coloured terraced chalets around a tarmacked central car park. The only break from the construction are three unhappy-looking pine trees growing in a line down the middle of the car park. Although there are plenty of cars, there seems to be nobody around. At almost 5.45 p.m., De Vries assumes that they are all up at the town, already drinking their way through the bars, hotels and street stalls. He hears the heavy gates clank as they shut behind him.

To his left, a small red–neon arrow flashes intermittently, advertising the reception. He trots over to the door, finds himself in a small office with a desk, some brochures on the counter, a television audible from the space behind. There is no sign of a bell. He clears his throat, hears shuffling from within, and watches as a short, stocky man with bow legs appears. He studies De Vries momentarily, smiles.

'You're Richard's friend, from Cape Town, *ja*?'

De Vries nods.

'He booked for you. I put you in adjoining rooms.' He pushes a clipboard across the counter, reaches behind him to fetch a key from the board of hooks on the wall.

De Vries signs the form, looks up to see a hand on the end of a thick arm held up at a diagonal. He shakes it.

'I'm Benny Louw.' He pushes the key across the counter at De Vries. 'You want to settle up now? Save time tomorrow when we're busy checking everyone out?'

De Vries pays cash.

'Richard say where he'd meet me?'

'*Ja*, man. Told me to tell you he'll be around the Devil's Peak stall between 6 and 7 p.m. I have a guy dropping off and collecting. You want to go up straightaway?'

De Vries looks at his watch. It is now 5.57 p.m. Why not?

'Maybe give me ten minutes?'

'Sure. No hurry, man. Almost everyone's there already. Few business people coming later. Look out for the white minibus by the front gate.'

De Vries thanks him, opens the door onto the car park and steps down.

Tracing his room from the other numbers, he walks to the furthest side of the rectangle, opens the door to his chalet. As he turns, he sees Benny Louw at the door to reception, watching the car park. De Vries ducks inside, walks through thick, stale air to examine the bathroom, peers through the small window at the rear and observes, close up, the caramel-coloured concrete wall. He sighs, runs his hand hard over his forehead, up through sweaty hair. He takes a shower in cool, brown, brackish water, puts on jeans and a polo shirt, checks that he has his wallet with him. On the back of the door, there is a big plastic sign in red letters: 'No Smoking'. He curses, re-packs his rucksack with the clothes he has taken off, scoops up his key and trots across the tarmac towards the reception. In the office, Benny Louw has been replaced by a short Cape Coloured woman. As he enters, he sees her duck around the doorway, emerge again, eyes guilty.

'Good evening.'

De Vries studies her, smells smoke on her breath, sees tar stains on her yellow-brown fingers.

'I want to do that,' he says, winking through the door behind her. 'In my room.'

He flashes the room number on the key fob.

She opens a large format binder, deliberately thumbs the pages, runs her tarred finger down the page, turns and snaps a new key on the desk.

'If you can't smoke in bed, it isn't a holiday . . .'

'No.' She winks at him. He recoils from the overt sexuality with which she instils this gesture.

He turns, steps back down into the courtyard, crosses it to his new room, throws down his rucksack, steps back out and into the door of the waiting minibus, its engine running, just outside the main gates.

Don February takes supper on a tray into the bedroom. His wife, propped up on all their pillows, gestures for it to be placed on her lap. He lays it there, checks that she has all she wants, then retreats to the kitchen to eat on his own. He is only halfway through his meal when he hears her call him. He gets up, walks down the hall and into their room. Her plate is empty.

'Is there any ice cream in the freezer? The chocolate ice cream from Pick n Pay?'

He takes her plate, serves up two large scoops of ice cream in a bowl and carries it back to her together with a spoon.

She touches his arm.

'I have had such a nice day,' she tells him. 'Having you at home. This boss of yours, maybe he is not so bad?'

Don thinks: he is an angry man; impatient, intolerant, inherently racist, with no respect for rank, or women, or the Lord.

He says, 'No, he is not so bad.'

De Vries is dropped by the Post House in town. As he exits, the air seems warmer, heavy with moisture. Over the sound of a German-style band, he hears a low rumble of thunder. He looks up at the mountains above Greyton, expecting them to be silhouettes now, but they are light grey against a background of an almost black sky, fit to burst.

Main Road runs up the centre of the nineteenth-century country town, bordered by lei-water channels from which the dwellings take a turn each week, diverting water onto their properties for irrigation, refilling swimming pools and replenishing duck ponds. The homes and businesses which line the main drag are a mixture of colloquial Cape Dutch architecture with gabled ends, simple thatched properties and modern white-painted country buildings with corrugated iron roofs and covered verandas. Well used to weekly markets and the attentions of visitors, restaurants, bars, hotels and guest houses are all offering beer-related tastings and meals. Between them, there are stalls set up under awnings from perhaps twenty-five different artisanal brewing companies: some newly formed, some a decade old – stalwarts of the craft-brewing scene in the Cape. Sun-faded bunting hangs above the street, a man dressed as a black bear dances to a three-piece brass band at the corner of Main Road and Grey Street. De Vries just makes out the smell of frankfurters and sauerkraut above the ambient aroma of freshly drawn beer.

He finds Richard Wessels, his arm around a well-built, jolly woman, a few metres down the street from the Devil's Peak Brewing Company stall. Wessels is already merry. De Vries is immediately wary; his former colleague is a notoriously boring drunk, and it is barely six thirty in the evening.

'Come with us, old friend,' Wessels says. 'Marion is going to let me taste her Flamkuchen.'

De Vries demurs, watches them walk away down the road towards the tree-lined DS Botha Street, running diagonally from the main drag, and to the stand selling the Flamkuchen. As he turns back to the Devil's Peak stall, there is a clap of thunder so strident that it halts the brass band mid-song. Then there is laughter, people toast one another, music starts again. De Vries squeezes through the line of people at the bar, waits to be served.

'I want,' he tells the barman, 'a large Silvertree but, before that, I want to taste your 'First Light' Amber Ale.'

He is handed a tot of the ale and a large plastic glass of Silvertree, and hands over his cash. He turns to push his way out into the open, catches the eye of a man standing across the street, watches him look away. He tastes the ale, immediately feels thirsty. Silvertree has been his favourite for a while and he lays into the cold beer, malty and fruity. Halfway through, he slowly turns to where the man had been standing. He is no longer there. Something from his years of experience troubles him; the man's reaction bothered him. He tries to picture what he looked like, then thinks that he could easily have been looking for a friend, seen his face and realized that De Vries was not him. He drains the glass, walks further up the street to where the buildings become private homes: cottages in perfect gardens, artists' residences and country hideaways for rich townsfolk. The old trees which line the street are shedding leaf. He has always loved this walk up towards the edge of the mountain that stands over the little town, and he walks away from the crowds into the shady peace of the upper reaches of Main Road. He turns, looks back down, drinks in the view of the strings of coloured lights bright in the night, the smoke from *braais* and grills, music, laughter. In the dappled shadows from the flickering street light on this balmy evening, he stands on the spot, wonders whether he would be happier if he was with someone. He does not miss his wife at home – he revels in his independence, does not lack sexual activity – but, he admits to himself, he sometimes misses companionship, at times such as now, at this precise moment: a warm shoulder to pull against him, a shared glance of contentment.

The street scene is illuminated by four quick flashes of lightning, raucous thunder following. He walks briskly back down to the main drag, finds another of his favourites, buys a tall glass of East Coast Ale, saunters to a grill of home-made *boerewors*, orders a coil in a huge soft bun. The hot sausage and cold beer make for a perfect combination. He struggles to eject some Mrs Ball's Chutney onto his plate from the sticky bottle on the trestle table and settles for a dab. He stands amongst a group listening to an accordion player. He looks beyond the musician, sees the same man as before, still staring in his direction. He understands what is bothering him: on each occasion he has seen him, he has not had a drink in his hand. He swallows hard, fights for a breath as he feels food stuck in his gullet, thumps the centre of his chest with his fist; De Vries places his food and beer glass on a low wall, trots around the crowd towards the man. When he reaches where he thought he had been, he sees no one like him. He stands on a plastic chair, looking over the revelry, sees no one walking away, no one suspicious. As he stands there, he hears a noise like a wave washing onto a beach, its volume increasing until the first huge drops hit him. He steps down, walks determinedly back towards his food and drink, already feeling water dripping down the back of his neck. The music has stopped and people are beginning to hunt for shelter. Within one minute, the drops have turned into a deluge. The storm rolls down the slopes of the mountains and onto the main street, pushing ahead of it the scent of steaming tarmac. He reaches his drink, feels the bread soggy on top of his *boerewors*, discards the top of the bun in the street, munches at what remains, ambling towards one of the side-street cafes with a deep awning, and joins the crowd pressed under it. He continues to eat and drink, to shelter with everyone else, his contentment stolen from him by the feeling that he is being watched, being stalked.

Just after 11 p.m., De Vries finds the white minibus where he was dropped off and, along with half a dozen others, is driven back to the Travellers' Haven. The bus smells of damp dog and belched beer, but his fellow passengers are happy despite the rain, warmed by much ale. They wait in the road, engine idling, for the gates to open, the remote control in the van failing to shift them. The driver stands hunched over the intercom, the rain falling like a heavy curtain over him and everything around. Finally, they draw inside and disembark. As Vaughn reaches the shelter of his room, he looks around the quadrangle, sees the flicker of televisions behind net curtains, wonders who would be watching television after a night of drinking and eating. He checks the window fastening, dead bolts his door, and then showers and gets into bed. He is not drunk; he is happy but for his watcher, tired yet grateful for a half day's respite from the stresses of his work. Just as he has dismissed the threat, his mind starts whirring again and he lies staring at the ceiling, resolutely awake, listening to the sound of the rain on the tin roof, cacophonous and unrelenting.

De Vries dozes sporadically, his room still sultry. He smiles to himself that he has transformed this visit into a part of his necessarily clandestine investigation. Anyone scrutinizing him must believe that the case is virtually closed. He gets out of bed, uses the toilet, switches off the rasping air-conditioning, so loud that it dominates even the sound of the rain.

As he finally loses consciousness, he hears the sound of the minibus with its rattling engine, delivering the last of the revellers back to their quarters. He hears the clang of the main gates as they close, then nothing but what, to him, now seems to be the soothing rhythm of the rain, lighter but insistent, for so long hungered after.

The minibus driver visits the reception, returns to his vehicle, drives it away. As the gates close behind him, three men jog into the quadrangle. Two wait in shadow by the main gate, the third runs to the reception area. A minute later, he rejoins the others, exchanges information and signals the direction they should travel. In a compact triangle, they trot across the centre of the car park between the two lines of parked cars, past the three pine trees. Each man wears a balaclava, dark clothes, gloves. They move in synch with one another, say nothing. They are almost invisible.

De Vries finally finds a depth of sleep which often eludes him at home. He dreams of climbing a tall wooden ladder to sever the tops of hop vines, watching them fall, heavy with warm, scented flowers. It is sunny, he is in the English countryside and, in the evening, he drinks dark, thick beer in the tiny saloons of ancient public houses; the image segues – goes home to a glamorous apartment overlooking Clifton Beaches, a tall and slender black African woman waits in the bedroom. The bed is big and soft, and he feels as if he is swimming in cool, clear water, until he pulls her towards him, feels the warmth that emanates from her, holds her in his embrace.

★ ★ ★

They collect at the doorway, eyes alert, bodies stiff, primed. One positions himself with his back to the chalet, pistol at his side: a lookout. The second man prepares to insert a short, stout crowbar level with the lock; the third waits, knife drawn, back to the left of the door, ready to spin inside. The lookout meets the eyes of both the men, signals; the crowbar rises to horizontal, gouges into the softwood door-frame, cracks open the door with ease. The knife man spins into the dark, humid room.

De Vries wakes shocked, throat dry, tongue working against the roof of his mouth, instantly alert to the screaming – heart-stopping, animal-like. He falls out of bed onto unsteady feet, ankles cracking; he grabs his gun from under the bed, stumbles to the door of his chalet, throws the bolt, barges open the door. He sees three dark figures sprint across the car park, through the open gates, disappearing from the arena of dim light into complete darkness. He exits, weapon drawn, following his line of sight as he scans the area. He sprints down the line of chalets to a door which hangs half off its hinges, to the source of the moaning, whining, begging, praying – voice high-pitched and plaintive. Two men stand outside their doors, other windows flicker light as curtains are teased open just enough to see out.

De Vries walks into the dark room, weapon drawn, fumbles with the switch until the grey ceiling light illuminates, and sees a big black African man on the bed – naked but for a pair of white Y-fronts, blood down his middle from his chest to the now stained material – clutching his torso, eyes wide, whimpering. The man sees him, cowers.

'I'm police.'

The man whispers, voice breaking: 'They stabbed me . . . I'm stabbed. Help me.'

PAUL MENDELSON

De Vries checks the bathroom, goes to the man, pulls his hands from his chest, examines the wound.

'You're okay. You're grazed. You're okay.'

Blood oozes slowly down the quivering black flesh; the man's limbs shake.

De Vries hears scurrying footsteps outside, turns to the door. Benny Louw stops perhaps five metres from the doorway.

'What's happened? Who's there?'

De Vries calls out: 'Louw. Call an ambulance. This man's been attacked. He needs medical help. Go now.'

He hears the footsteps retreat, hopes that Louw will act calmly, not panic. De Vries grabs a towel from the bathroom, bundles it up, pushes it against the wound in the centre of the man's torso.

'Hold this tight . . . You're all right. You are not in danger now.'

The man pants, grasps the shirt to himself, eyes wide.

'Masked man, had a knife. I wake up. He has this knife right here. He curses, stabs me, runs away. There were others . . .'

'Tell the local police when they come . . . I'm on vacation . . .'

He sees the man frown, close his eyes, teeth gritted.

Benny Louw comes back across the car park, peers inside the chalet.

'They're coming. What happened?'

De Vries jumps up, nods to the victim on the bed, turns away and leads Louw outside, a few paces from the chalet. The rain has dissipated, but it's still spitting. He looks around, sees a chalet door closing, mumbled sounds from within darkness, curtains twitch.

'Three men . . . I saw them escaping through the gate . . . That guest was attacked by a guy with a knife . . .' He faces Louw. 'How did they get through the gates?'

Louw swallows, knows that De Vries is studying him.

'Don't know.'

'Why are they open?'

250

Louw glances behind him, sees them open to the road. De Vries takes a step towards him.

'Don't know . . .'

'You're sure? You're sure you don't know, Benny?'

Louw cowers.

'Three men run all over your place, go to that chalet and nearly fucking slit that guy head to dick, and you don't know?'

Louw stands rigid, rooted, his eyes unable to meet De Vries', mumbles: 'Who is he? What did they want with him?'

De Vries laughs, shoots out his hand and grabs Benny Louw by the collar, drags his face up to his, smells brandy on the man's breath, oozing out of his pores.

'I don't give a fuck about him . . . And nor did they. Until I changed it for somewhere I could smoke, that fucking room was mine.'

PART THREE

The ambulance takes the victim away, curtains close, lights are switched off. It is nearly 1.30 a.m. when the local police get to talk with De Vries. Already, they have decided that it was an attempted robbery, and De Vries sees no reason to tell them differently. When the officer discovers his rank and standing, he defers to him entirely. What De Vries says, goes.

Eventually, the local officers amble away, seeming tired and aimless; there is no sign of Benny Louw. De Vries lies on his bed, gun in hand, dozing uneasily until about 6 a.m. He packs, walks around to reception, finds it deserted. He enters the office in the back. There is no one there either, but he sees that the phone to the gate intercom is there, as well as a button to open and close the gates. He drops his key on the desk, returns to the front desk, then out into the courtyard. He looks over to the room adjoining the one where the man was attacked. His acquaintance, Richard Wessels, never appeared during the night; he wonders whether he slept through the attack or was in the arms of his Flamkuchen companion under a feather duvet.

Now, the rain is light and misty, cloud cover low and dark. The main gates are still open. He walks onto the side of the road, begins to pace towards the village. Within two minutes, a van driver pulls over, offers him a lift. He takes it, feels immensely grateful to the man who does not ask him questions, drops him off outside the one café open.

De Vries finds that they have been open all night, dispensing coffee to the night owls, preparing cooked breakfasts for those camping out in cars and in the gardens of volunteer residents. De Vries accepts a full English and eats gloomily, still disorientated from his shattered night. When he has woken up some more, he sends an SMS to John Marantz, requesting information as soon as possible, hinting that he is in danger. Minutes pass with no reply, and he realizes that Marantz could have been playing poker until 4 a.m., and may not wake for hours yet.

His spirits are raised when his neighbour's son and his girlfriend walk through the door of the café, still more when they tell him that her work will end at 9 a.m., and they can then drive back to town.

At 8.50 a.m., De Vries's phone buzzes: a reply from Marantz.

'Meeting arranged, tomorrow, 5 p.m.', followed by an address in town he cannot visualize.

De Vries persuades them to take the scenic Franschhoek Pass rather than the freeway. It is a little longer but a far more pleasant drive. They travel around the Theewaterskloof Dam – a vast inland lake – observing how low the water level is, then continue on the R45 through the mountains to the top of the pass. From there, the view of the Franschhoek Valley is usually spectacular, stretching out as far as the eye can see into the thin clouds on the horizon. This morning they see only a wall of grey Tupperware. They are above the cloud over the town. When they are almost at the bottom of the winding pass, they pass through the cover and the town is revealed, misty and dank. They pass La Petit Ferme restaurant where, at this time of year, they serve De Vries's favourite pudding, 'Plum Crazy', fruit home-grown from the adjacent fields. He smiles in recognition as they sail down past the entrance, head towards the T-junction by the Huguenot Memorial.

When they reach Main Road, De Vries asks them to stop outside a café and give him twenty minutes to do something. He gives them a 200 rand note, tells them to order whatever they want. He sees the teenagers glance at one another, but cannot discern whether they are frustrated by the delay or happy enough to sit outside in Franschhoek.

He takes the *bakkie*, turns up Uitkyk Street, comes to a stop outside the two barns occupied by Dazuluka Cele. He winds down his window, presses the bell on the intercom. Only while he waits for an answer does he question why he is here, why he is checking on her.

The same cheerful voice answers and he identifies himself. At the sound of her tone, he already feels he has made a mistake but, when the gates open, he drives in, parks in the same spot, car turned ready for his departure.

'Tell me,' Dazuluka Cele shouts as she approaches him, 'that this is not police business and that you have come back to buy one of my paintings.'

De Vries smiles.

'As much as I would like that, I think they are out of my league.'

Cele smiles. 'Perhaps a deal can be done.'

They shake hands warmly.

'I came to speak to you about something. Is there somewhere private?'

She leads him across what had been the baking gravelled courtyard but which now seems damp and cold, into the bottom of her studio barn. The space is almost deserted and he can see that she has been sweeping the floor with a traditional broom made of twigs.

'It is good news: I am allowed to stay,' she says. 'Apparently Taryn left a trust to retain these buildings and allow artists to live and work here on long-term lets. I am preparing for another artist to come here too now. The lawyers say it will take time to sort everything out, but that I can remain at least until the end of the year and hopefully longer.'

'I'm pleased you can stay.'

'So am I.'

He glances around the room to see if there is anywhere to sit but, apart from two wooden easels, there is no furniture at all. He feels awkward towering over her, wonders whether to squat but fears the cracking of ankles – the struggle to get up.

'I came to check that you were okay . . .'

She smiles again.

'Yes. I am still upset about what happened to Taryn.' She stops. 'You know what did happen?'

'We think we know but there is still some work to do. We're close.'

She nods uncertainly.

He takes a deep breath, knows that he cannot waste more time, hopes that she will take his concern as a compliment.

'When I left last time, I saw you talking with a man. He seemed angry and I didn't know whether I should have intervened. I couldn't help noticing that your leg was injured. I wanted to make sure that you were safe and well.'

At first she laughs, then her expression darkens and he can see her eyes grow moist. She nods rapidly, says nothing.

'I'm sorry if I have made a mistake.'

She looks up at him.

'The man you saw was my brother. He was visiting and we were angry with one another. He stays in Maputo and there is no work for him there. He came to Cape Town, found nothing and came to me. He thought that now I was an artist with an exhibition, I would be rich. I tried to tell him that I would receive no money for many months and that it would be needed for more canvases, more materials. He did not understand. He refused to go, began drinking and got angry. That was the day before you came. When you saw him that morning, he had just woken up and he was still drunk, still wanting to argue.'

'Is he still here?'

'No. I gave him money and told him to go home. Told him that I would send money when I received it myself.'

'That is generous.'

'That is what we do. I am sure that you would give anything to your family if they had nothing?'

'If I can . . .'

'And, as for my leg . . . That is a different story, but it is over now and the man responsible is gone.'

'Then I shouldn't have been worried.'

She looks up at him.

'I am glad you were. I am not used to that. What is your name? Your given name?'

'Vaughn. I am Vaughn de Vries.'

She takes his hand.

'I want to give you something. Come . . .' She leads him out of the ground floor and back up to her studio. As he follows her up the spiral staircase, he observes the deep scarring on her leg, but also the petite body ahead of him. On the landing's left-hand wall, there is a block of twelve miniature oil paintings, a series of studies of the same small wooden carving. Each is viewed from a lightly different angle, the light casting shadows across her face, the contours of her carved body. The figure is very pregnant, but also strong. Her expression is one of confidence and health.

'This woman is a very powerful symbol to me. The carving was a gift from the mother of my husband. We wanted to have children and although we tried hard, I could not become pregnant. She told me that it had been given to her by her mother to bring her children and to protect her from the evil eyes of women who might covet her husband; once it was looking over her, it brought four sons into her life.'

She takes the picture on the top left of the block down from the wall and hands it to De Vries.

'Look at the crack which bisects her body. It is tradition amongst the artists who carve these figures for their tribe that, if the wood splits vertically like this, it increases the power of the symbol. It must never be man-made; it must be the wood itself which decides.'

'That is a wonderful story, but I cannot accept this.'

She presses it into his hand.

'I want you to have it. To thank you.'

'That's not necessary. I am doing my duty.'

She takes a few paces away from him.

'I do not have any children. Within a few days of her entering our house, I could feel that we had conceived, that I was pregnant. Ten weeks later, it was confirmed.' She drops her head. 'But I lost the baby.'

'I'm sorry.'

'My husband accused me of killing his child. He was a sick man. I know he was not true to me. When he learned of the news, he attacked me. That is how I received the wounds you saw.'

De Vries looks down at the floor.

'Perhaps she is not so lucky then?'

'Oh yes, she is good luck. My husband was a big man, strong, but I fought him, even though I was bleeding. He slipped and fell against the table, hit his head and fell unconscious. I was able to call for help.'

'When was this?'

She smiles.

'A long time ago. I was fifteen. I left my town and I went to Maputo. I started a new life, and I started to paint. Then, when I met Taryn Holt, I came here.'

'Where is the carving now?'

'I gave her to a friend of mine in Maputo. She could not have children but then, when I gave it to her, she became pregnant. She now has a daughter and a son.'

'I have two grown-up daughters.'

'I do not think you need fertility, Mr Vaughn de Vries. But, I think you need protection. She will look over you.'

He sighs.

'Let me give you something for this?'

She presses her hands against his around the small square canvas.

'It is a gift. Power like hers cannot be bought; it can only be given.'

'Thank you.'

She leads him down the spiral staircase, back to the yard.

'Visit again when you are passing. Maybe I will still be here.'

'I hope you will be.' He bows at her. 'Thank you again.'

'Thank you for thinking about me,' she tells him. 'I am not used to that. You have made me happy today.'

He looks at her swollen eyes, recalls the story she has told him, cannot believe this could bring happiness.

'If that is the case,' he tells her, 'that is a gift I usually seem to lack.'

When he reaches home, he approaches his house with caution, checks the alarm, paces his house with his gun drawn. Finally satisfied that he is safe, he puts his damp clothes by the washing machine, takes a long, hot shower and changes into a work suit.

There are fallen branches in his garden, the flat roof above his stoep is leaking and his own car is covered in damp leaves. The rain continues to fall from cloud so low and thick he cannot even see the Mountain from his window. He feels exhausted and anxious, wonders who was prepared to threaten, perhaps kill him; how they knew where he would be. He tries to form an image of the man in the crowd who, twice, he saw looking at him. He was, it seemed to him, a Cape Coloured or pale black man, but there is no one feature about the man's face around which he can form an image.

Ben Thwala seems to be shouting above the sound of a storm.

'Major Mabena is in a liaison between the Police Ministry and senior SAPS officers. My friend tells me that he is also politically active and that he has some connection to an ANC . . . I do not know if this is the right term, sir? Steering committee.'

Water splashes against the French windows to the back of the house. De Vries looks up, sees the trees and shrubs bending first one way, then the next, as the swirling wind catches wet branches.

'I have not seen him, sir, but I am told that he is considered to be a confidante to several high-ranking members of the government within, or connected to, the Police Ministry.'

De Vries scribbles notes on what Ben Thwala is telling him, his brain racing to compute this new information.

'This friend: he is trustworthy?'

'Yes, sir. I believe him to be. I worked with him and we were friends when I was here. I have told him that this is top secret.'

'What can he tell you about Nkosi?'

'This is where it is not clear. He told me he had searched for this name, but it did not appear in the files.'

'What do you mean?'

'There is no Sam Nkosi working for the SAPS. Not according

to the records. However, my friend found that this name was recognized, but as a cover name for an officer.'

'An undercover alias?'

'Maybe, sir. I do not have anybody else I can approach unless I visit the unit at which this name appeared.'

De Vries thinks, shakes his head, says: 'No, Sergeant. Definitely, no.' He hesitates, knowing that Thwala is closer to the answers than he by thirteen-hundred kilometres. He is decided: he will not risk the safety, career, the life, of another officer. 'Collect your belongings, go to the airport now, Sergeant. That's an order.'

As he climbs Hospital Bend on the way into town, the wind blows in pulses of even heavier rain. He slows, wipes the inside of his windscreen with his cuff, pushes on. As he turns towards town on De Waal drive, his car is buffeted from side to side by the wind. There is a rock-fall by the road, a thick orange morass runs from the slopes across the carriageway. Cars brake, swerve around the boulder, idle through the stream of muddy water, pick up speed again as the road drops towards the sharp turn off onto Mill Street or the descent into the CBD on Roeland Street.

By the time he reaches the car park beneath his building, he feels drained. He travels up to his floor alone, stalks down the corridor, crosses the squad-room without acknowledging anyone, slams his office door. He slumps in his chair, head in his hands. No one knocks on his door; no one even approaches. They have worked with him long enough to know when it is right to look busy.

At 2 p.m., Norman Classon strolls into the squad-room and knocks on his door, lets himself in.

263

'You disappeared.'

De Vries looks up at him.

'That was the idea . . . Sit down. Keep your voice down.'

Classon sits sheepishly.

'Heavy night?'

'In many ways,' De Vries tells him.

'I spoke to General Thulani yesterday. He told me that it was over. The message got through that you were winding it all down and moving on.'

'Good.'

'You know more now than yesterday?'

'A little, but we're playing with fire. These people have the better of us, and they have powerful allies.'

'No one to trust . . .'

'Occupational hazard for all of us. Ever since '94. When you are all one side in a war, that brings you together. Now, you have old and new enemies mixed together. What do you expect?'

'Still enemies?'

'That's what they think. You think fifty years of the system were forgotten by a few hearings? Truth and reconciliation? There's plenty of fight left in these people.'

'You think that's what this is?'

'In broad terms, probably. In detail, who knows? But I'll tell you this: pieces are falling into place for something bad. Those pieces are made up of the Police Ministry, the government – I don't know, maybe something else to do with a secret operation.'

'What is that?'

'I don't know, but there's talk of undercover identities, people walking around who should not exist.' He turns to the lawyer. 'I hope you're at the top of your game, Advocate Classon, really at the fucking top, because I may have very dire need of you any minute now.'

'I don't like the sound of that.'

De Vries chuckles.

'When was the last time I said something you people liked?'

Ben Thwala towers above the short security guard. He has to duck to pass through the metal scanner at the airport. His hand luggage is scanned and appears on the conveyor belt at the other side. He collects it and turns. Then, beneath him, he sees the guard.

'Your ID, sir?'

Thwala holds his breath, produces his ID card, watches the man read it. The guard pockets it, says: 'Come with me, please sir.'

'Why?'

'There is a message for you at Security.'

Thwala notices a second guard. He walks between them, across the crowded departure hall and through a key-coded door. The guard ahead of him stops, opens a door to a small waiting room, ushers him inside.

'Colonel Vaughn de Vries, Senior Investigator, Special Crimes Unit, Western Province. It really sounds quite impressive.'

De Vries stands in front of Eric Basson. He is in an office, formerly grand but now faded, in the centre of an anonymous building, somewhere between the SAPS Central Headquarters and the High Court.

'It isn't.'

Basson smiles dryly.

'No, it isn't, is it?'

He offers his hand. They shake over a wide polished ebony desk, their hands reflected back in the rich shine of the surface.

De Vries says: 'Why haven't we met before?'

'I really don't like meeting people.'

'I sympathize.'

'I know.' Basson gestures for him to sit, then sits himself, runs his left hand over his right arm, straightens his cuff.

'Are you one of us? You work for the SAPS?'

'Yes and no,' Basson says. 'I am a conduit to the past.'

'Meaning?'

'If we heeded the lessons of history, we might avoid the mistakes of today.'

'Unless it's too late.'

'Of course it's too late.'

De Vries studies the man. He reminds him strangely of Bheka Bhekifa: a sharp mind in a small human form.

'How do you know John Marantz?'

'I don't,' Basson says, holding up his hands. 'I met him only once.'

De Vries leans forward.

'Let's get something clear from the beginning. I appreciate what you may have to give me, but I'm not into games. John Marantz worked – maybe still works – for the British Government. I'm aware of how many British companies still operate in Southern Africa and how, therefore, there will be – how shall we put this nicely – "representatives" down here. But I won't deal with them; I can't deal with them. So, before we begin: what is your status?'

Basson's expression remains entirely calm.

'You can be reassured on that score. I've worked for my country my entire life. Thirty-two years in the SAPS. In fact, when you were a lowly Captain in Observatory, I was a Colonel right next to our leaders . . .'

De Vries stares at him, wonders whether the reference to his position in the Observatory Station refers to what happened in 1994, realizes that it must, that the man in front of him uses information as a weapon. That is what he and Marantz have in common. He says quietly: 'That was a long time ago. Everything has changed.'

'Less than you think, Colonel.'

Basson pulls out a file from beneath his desk, places it on the table.

'Shall we begin?'

De Vries nods.

'I only had what Mr Marantz provided, but it proved ample. You scarcely need my help. You have unravelled the knot yourself but, if I fill you in on the background, you will reach your conclusion sooner. That, I imagine, would be beneficial?'

He brings one sheet from the pile to the top.

'Let us start in the past and move through history.' He looks up at De Vries across the desk. 'From 1959, Graeme Holt built up his company for thirty years. During that time, he fully exploited the very favourable labour conditions in our country and exported many of those ideas to his extensive business concerns throughout Southern Africa. In return for the support he received from our government, he was able to aid in the movement of currency which, under the spurious sanctions imposed, the administration might have found difficult to arrange. Graeme Holt was a very determined man. He retained seventy-five per cent ownership of his very successful company throughout his life. Upon his death, he left a committed, experienced board to run the company and limited his daughter to control only twenty-four per cent – still representing a very significant sum of money. The potential of that fortune was, we both believe, I'm sure, the motive for her death.'

'How did Graeme Holt die?'

'Whatever we may suspect, nobody knows.'

Basson adjusts his other cufflink, waits, looks up again at De Vries.

'May I continue?'

De Vries nods.

'In April 2014, Taryn Holt meets Trevor Bhekifa at a book launch. They might have been introduced and moved on without

267

another thought, but Bhekifa mentions a think-tank, the Democratic Reform Group, and the fact that it might soon become a political party. Taryn Holt was no fan of her father's politics, nor of the way the ANC had, to her mind, abandoned the women's cause for which, it was originally hoped, it would fight. She attended some meetings, became interested in the politics and then, it seems, in Bhekifa himself. They had something strong in common: they were rebelling against their fathers' politics, their fathers' failed political ideals.'

He looks up, sees De Vries smiling.

'You are beginning to see, I imagine?'

'I think so.'

'In November last year, she visits her attorney and sets in motion the work required to free up at least some of her shareholding in Holt Industries, with a view to becoming a powerful patron of this new political party. That information leaks . . . And, now, Taryn Holt is a threat.'

'But, to who?'

Basson turns over a page.

'Imagine if you felt oppressed by a cruel regime which you had eventually overthrown to take power. How would you feel if money accrued during that time, by the blood and sweat of your people, was about to be used against you? I imagine you do not feel happy, and someone high up, influential and powerful, makes the decision that this will not be allowed to happen.'

'A state conspiracy . . .'

Basson clears his throat.

'That sounds good, doesn't it? I regret that the truth, as so often, is somewhat more prosaic.' He smiles indulgently at De Vries. 'Let's proceed chronologically, shall we? Lieutenant Sam Nkosi . . .'

'. . . Doesn't exist.'

Basson looks up at De Vries.

'He exists in so far as he is almost certainly your killer. But, I agree, he does not exist as such, at least until August 2014, when he was suddenly born. Up until then, he was a man called Sergeant Daza Xolani, a Zulu name which, ironically, translates as "bringer of peace".

'As you are aware, in August 2012 there was some trouble with workers striking at the Lonmin mine in Marikana. You can interpret the snippets of the official enquiry's findings how you wish but, simply, a vital international company required assistance in breaking that strike. Our government complied, certain members of the SAPS mishandled the situation and thirty-four workers died. Many of the policemen involved have been questioned, some even indicted, but Sergeant Daza Xolani walked away from the massacre despite being, I am reliably informed, a man with blood on his hands. When it was decided that action should be taken on the Holt matter, Xolani was promoted to Lieutenant, re-born as Sam Nkosi, transferred to Central Division, Cape Town, and began his work to terminate the threat.'

'Who in Central would have known about this?'

'That, I cannot tell you now. Those in power who use the SAPS as a method of state control . . .' He smiles. 'Not an original idea, of course – they develop networks of ambitious like-minded individuals, through coercion, bribery or political idealism, throughout the service. Unravelling that will prove impossible. It is, as the British media always like to describe racism in their police service, "endemic".'

'What about this man in Pretoria I keep hearing about: Major Mabena?'

'Mabena is a liaison between the administrators of the SAPS and the Police Ministry. I would caution you about how far you might take this. Nkosi – or Xolani – is one thing; he is disposable. But if you overreach yourself, Colonel, it will be you in the crosshairs.'

'I'm already there.'

'I know.'

'Yesterday.'

There is a discernible beat of silence.

'That, I didn't know.' Basson makes a quick note. 'This is another matter on which we should speak but, for now, I have one more element for you to consider.'

'Angus Lyle?'

'No. He is of little interest to me. He was probably set up by Nkosi as you suspected. He picked rather well. You work out what happened. I don't know or, frankly, care. What you must consider is far more interesting.'

'And that is?'

'As you are well aware, our own Nationalist government militarized the police force and used it to enforce the Apartheid ideology. Hardly a new idea, but one which was refined most effectively. The police have been used as a tool of the state in many countries, many of which would not consider themselves oppressive regimes. At some point, every government realizes that there is political imperative in suppressing opposition. It does not take them long to develop such a programme and, from there, escalation is inevitable. The question you might wish to consider is this: who, behind the scenes of the ANC, might endorse such a policy?'

De Vries shrugs.

'There was, you see,' Basson continues, clearly pleased with himself, 'a silver lining to these events for the man who I believe is ultimately behind them.'

'What was that?'

'One last connection, Colonel. Then, everything will be clear to you. General Thulani – ultimately your boss – has an attaché, a man who reports to him, but not to him alone . . .'

'That little fuck, Julius Mngomezulu,' De Vries says, mis-pronouncing the name comprehensively.

Basson actually laughs.

'Who else is he reporting to?'

Basson's expression returns to his default: emotionless.

'That is the correct question to ask. The man who placed him there originally, via his influence within the Police Ministry: the esteemed and much loved hero, Bheka Bhekifa.'

De Vries grabs his jaw, runs his hand around it slowly, mind racing.

'The leak about his son?'

'Old man Bhekifa exists only for the cause. To see his son consorting with the daughter of Graeme Holt, to hear that she would bankroll a party in direct opposition to the ANC . . . It had to stop. I have a recording of the anonymous tip-off received by the *Sunday Cape Herald*. Perhaps you would like it?'

'Yes.'

'It's in the bundle I will give you.'

'Thank you.'

Eric Basson stands.

'I rely on you, Colonel, not to divulge the source of this material. I don't wish to be coarse, but there would be a heavy price to pay if you could not keep my confidence.'

De Vries nods solemnly. Basson has impressed sufficiently for him to heed his warning.

'You will have sufficient evidence to prosecute Nkosi, if you are allowed to. Mngomezulu may be more difficult to pin down but, perhaps, you will find a way.'

Basson hands De Vries a plain brown envelope. De Vries takes it, shakes his hand, says: 'I understand that you have resources but, from a few notes given to you by Marantz, you put this all together?'

271

Basson puts his hand on De Vries's shoulder, slowly coerces him across the room to the door.

'That was easy, Colonel. When I worked for our previous government, over many years . . . The destruction of character and reputation, the placing of assets within the opposition, assassination: that was my responsibility.'

De Vries studies himself in the mirrors of the gilded lift carriage as it slowly descends to the ground floor. He knows that Basson has made the final link to Bhekifa faster than he could ever have done. A tape of Mngomezulu could prove vital to his prosecution. Whatever Marantz has promised this man, whatever debt he now owes, he feels it is justified.

His mind races: he will bring down Nkosi and Mngomezulu, poison the network. All his life he fights corruption and injustice, and the scale of this conspiracy shocks him more than he can yet register.

He walks determinedly through the bland but comfortable foyer of the building, out onto the street. After his sleepless night, the time spent in the *bakkie* this morning, in his office chair and facing Basson, he needs the walk back to his office, never mind that he will be wet again.

The rain is little more than a light, hazy mist. He breathes in the fresh, moist air and it occurs to him that he, like so many others, has been longing for winter. He turns the corner of the tree-lined street, heads back towards the centre of town. He senses something behind him and turns, feels a sudden sharp pain in his side, twists to see a broad black man, and looks down to see a pistol pushed into his hip. His mouth dries. He swallows. A second man appears to his left, puts his hand on his neck. De Vries feels a strange tingling sensation and then deep, throbbing pain, the feeling in his legs disappears; he slumps to his knees, is held up again by the two men. A black Mercedes rolls slowly towards them, stops. One of the men opens the back door and they lift him inside. He feels dizzy, very sick, his body below his neck no longer part of him, beyond his control. The men get in either side of him, close the doors. As the car moves slowly away, one of them pushes his head down so that it almost touches his thighs. He senses, more than feels, the brown envelope being pulled from his inside pocket, disappearing from his realm. The car feels cold; he feels cold. He shivers, struggles for breath. All he can see is a dark haze made up of his suit trousers, the dim interior of the car, the smell of the black men.

He senses acceleration, does not know whether it is velocity or unconsciousness.

He is aware of half walking, half being dragged from the car to a building. He smells the sea, fuel-oil, assumes that he is at the docks. Ahead of him, looming out of the dusk, is a huge oil-drilling platform. They swing him to his right, inside a warehouse smelling of oil. He can feel his feet, sense blood in his legs, is stupidly relieved: for a time, in his confusion, he had believed himself paralyzed. They march him the length of the building. He hears rain drumming on the tin roof; none of the men speak. They reach a door, push it open, hustle him through into a smaller space, dimly light by two bare bulbs. There is a wooden table and three chairs; they sit him in the chair on its own, facing two chairs across the table. One of the men walks across the room, exits through a further door; two stand opposite him, guns at their sides.

'Who are you?' De Vries's jaw seems tight, his voice strained.

The men ignore him.

'If you're SAPS, we're on the same side.'

The far door opens, crashes back against the wall. He sees Nkosi striding towards him, behind him one of the men who took him from the street.

'What are we going to do with you?' Nkosi says, pointing his chin at him.

'What are you doing here?'

Nkosi laughs, produces the brown envelope from behind him, slaps it on the table.

'I want to know who you were meeting today.'

De Vries shakes his head.

'It's not going to take long,' Nkosi says. 'I will ask questions and you will tell me answers.'

'Now I see why you didn't call me sir,' De Vries says groggily. 'You think you're in charge.'

Nkosi's eyes flare.

'Right here, right now, I am in charge.' He walks around the table, leans down to De Vries. 'You know how easily a man can get lost in the docks?'

De Vries closes his eyes, blows out his cheeks.

'The man you saw today?' Nkosi repeats.

'If I knew his name, I wouldn't tell you,' De Vries says. 'But, I don't. I was given an envelope, told it contained information about who killed Taryn Holt.'

Nkosi shakes his head.

'No, no, no, no . . . We have been watching you since you left your office yesterday morning. We know you were in that building for over an hour.'

'It's a maze.'

'Don't fuck with me, De Vries.'

'Had a nice trip to Greyton?'

Nkosi tilts back his head.

'You were a lucky man there.'

De Vries sits up as straight as he can muster, speaks calmly and firmly.

'We knew it was you. Everyone in my team knows. All you are doing now is implicating your colleagues.' He looks around, stares at each man. 'Don't know you boys. Come down from Pretoria maybe?'

Nkosi twists his arm around himself, swings it back at full force, the back of his hand smacking De Vries across the face, the force pushing him off the chair, sending him sprawling onto the cold floor. The snap of the impact echoes around the room, before a second crash, of the chair falling, as if in slow motion, next to him.

De Vries stays where he is, giving himself time to recover from the shock. The stinging pain he can bear; it has revived him, reminded him that he can still feel, still move. In the moments that follow, he looks up at Nkosi's legs, knows that the man is trapped, that he has no move to make but to do away with De Vries and make his escape. The realization sickens him.

'Your team,' Nkosi says, 'know nothing. You have a theory and now you have some information, but they don't. So, when you are gone and we are back in Guateng, everything goes back to a man in a park with the murder weapon.'

Nkosi stands over him.

'And your meeting today was secret. No one knows who you were seeing. Who was it?'

De Vries is sitting up, still shaken. He sees Nkosi above him, the two guards focused on covering him with their weapons.

'I'm not waiting.'

'I've told you . . . I was given the envelope.'

Nkosi stares at him, then suddenly lashes out with his foot, kicking De Vries hard in the neck, watching him fall backwards, hands clutching his windpipe. Nkosi takes one step over to him, slowly raises his foot and brings it down on De Vries's neck, then transfers pressure from his other leg until the weight of his body is crushing De Vries's neck, his air passage.

'Who?'

He releases his weight, watches De Vries gasp, watches him grimace as he fights to form the words.

'Why would I tell you? I'm dead anyway . . .'

'It will not only be you,' Nkosi spits. 'We have Sergeant Ben Thwala. At the airport.'

De Vries suddenly feels defeated. He could have capitulated and saved himself and his team. If this is the extent of their power, he knows he is outgunned, cornered.

'A tall man, narrow spectacles, pinstripe suit . . .'

Nkosi shouts: 'Name?'

'No name . . .'

'Name?'

'No name . . .'

'No name?' Nkosi spits. 'No name, no fucking mercy.' He kicks De Vries again, sends him sprawling.

In the fraction of the second after his body stops moving, there is a silence in which he hears a sound in the distance: something familiar, something comforting. Then, nothing. He raises his head, sees Nkosi moving back from him, hears muttered instructions. Suddenly, the door through which they entered crashes open, four men in full commando gear race through, shouting warnings. The men guarding De Vries throw down their weapons, raise their hands. De Vries presses himself flat on the ground, sees the far door open and close.

'Colonel de Vries.'

He looks up; he sees the haunting, startling sight of the commandos, clad in black, faces obscured by night-sights, staring down the sights of snub-nosed machine guns.

De Vries pulls himself up until he is on his knees and nods. Two more enter, run past them, towards the far doorway. De Vries struggles to his feet, brain racing. These must be the Hawks, the elite armed-response unit of the SAPS, perhaps? The men behind him shout an all-clear, the team-leader in front of him turns and repeats the all-clear over his shoulder. Through the door, flanked by two further men, the immense form of General Thulani appears. He strides towards De Vries.

'You're safe, Colonel.'

De Vries nods, croaks: 'Yes, sir.'

Thulani looks around.

'Where is Nkosi?'

De Vries points back to the far door.

'The door. He left just as your men arrived.'

Thulani stares across the room, until his view is obscured by De Vries rising to his feet, stumbling forwards.

'Colonel.'

He begins to run towards the door, feels his back spasm, feels his lungs draw in a huge breath. Adrenalin has him charged with energy.

'Colonel de Vries.'

He throws it open, pushes himself through it, hears Thulani barking orders behind him. Within five seconds the paramilitaries are beside him, jogging easily to keep up with his attempt at a sprint. They do not break their pace, but one shouts: 'Your orders are to return to the warehouse, Colonel, sir.'

De Vries can scarcely find the breath to reply.

'Find Nkosi. We must find Nkosi.'

He thrusts his head down, pushes himself on, his entire body charged with utter determination. Condemned, yet still alive. Not just alive: sprinting.

They reach another doorway; this time, it takes them outside. The rain clatters onto De Vries, but he scans his surroundings through the mist of his breath, hot in the mercifully cool night air. Ahead of them, across the wide expanse of water, the oil rig blazes with light. To his right, there is another hundred metres of road before it stops abruptly at a tall fence, reinforced with razor wire. To his left, the pathway around the edge of the dock follows the water towards the rig. One of the men barks: 'Suspect at eleven o'clock, on foot, running towards the rig.'

De Vries strains to see through the blurring rain, makes out a jogging form, dressed the way he thinks Nkosi was. He starts running, finds the armed men overtaking him, sprinting despite their heavy gear, accelerating away from him. Reaching the corner, he turns towards the overwhelming form of the drilling platform, hears shouts, cannot make them out over the rain and the sound of his panting. When he reaches the gate in the metal fence, a uniformed security guard tries to block his way without much conviction.

De Vries charges him aside, hears the man bellow after him: 'No guns . . . No flame, no guns.'

He reaches the long gangway, pushes himself forward, begins to pound up the steep gradient, shoes sliding despite the rough metal ridges, calves burning, lungs raw and grainy, taking an age to travel the distance across the steel grey water, each step crashing beneath him, rain and sweat pouring down his face. He finally reaches the rig entrance, screams at another security guard: 'Police!'

He pushes past him, drawn to the distant echo of boots on metal walkways, scans each face that appears in doorways, pushes himself on. He reaches a corner of the rig, stares down the next plain, sees nothing, hears nothing. He pulls himself back, falls through the doorway inside, climbs the staircase ahead of him, using the handrails to haul himself upwards. On the landing, he looks down one edge, then the other; he sees movement, hears the rhythm of drumming boots, begins to half jog, half stumble in pursuit.

By the time he has reached the next corner, his feet heavier and heavier on the cross-hatched metal gangway, he knows he is spent. He bends over the railings, retches into the darkness. He turns around, rests against the metal posts, hands on knees, thinks: there is no way off this rig but the way I came in – or down there. He pulls himself up, sees another entrance inside the rig, struggles to open it, his hands weak and greasy. He manages it, stumbles inside, over the stairway, down a level. There, he locates a bulkhead hatch, gets it open, rushes to the outside walkway. From here, he sees down towards the warehouses, the arc lights illuminating the diagonal drops which fall relentlessly, the road leading to the guarded entrance to the rig. He begins to jog in that direction.

He gets halfway there, then sees the back of a metal door swing towards him. He throws himself forward so that he is hard up against the rig's bulkhead. The door opens almost completely back on itself, but not quite. De Vries sees Nkosi, gun raised, scanning to his left, beginning to turn to his right. In the time it takes him to peer around the door, De Vries has started to move. At the moment Nkosi registers him, De Vries is half flying, half falling towards him. He tries to fire his weapon, flails with his left hand to protect himself. De Vries hits him first with his chin, then his open arms, grabbing at Nkosi, pulling him down with him, all the weight he feels in his body somehow on top of Nkosi. They hit the gangway, Nkosi first, De Vries half landing on him, then rolling off the man's body towards the railings. He spins around, crashes into the railings, feels lines of pain across his legs and side, finds his head unsupported, in free space. His body seems wedged between the icy wire railings, half into the void. Beneath him, there is only the all-encompassing black velvet water of the dock.

He pulls himself away from the edge, fingers cold and oily, their grip failing. He pushes back against the railings, hauls himself up, turns to see Nkosi struggling to get a foothold on the greasy walkway. This time, De Vries charges, head down, stumbling, collapsing into him. He feels Nkosi's hands on him, a momentary resistance, but then they are both falling; he forwards, Nkosi backwards. They crash into the metal bulkhead. Nkosi crumples, De Vries bounces backwards away from him, stops himself, sees Nkosi scrabbling to drag himself up. De Vries thuds towards him, sees him keeling, understands suddenly that the man is beaten. He stands right up to Nkosi, raises his knee viciously into the man's groin, and stands straight as he watches Nkosi double up, fall to his knees, howl.

PART FOUR

'The envelope?'

'With us.'

De Vries wants it for himself, knows that if General Thulani has it, there will be questions he cannot answer.

'The recording of the call to the newspaper?'

'Being analyzed. I have heard it. I believe it is Lieutenant Mngomezulu. We will seek proof.'

'You have him?'

Thulani smiles.

'He is under arrest.'

'He will be interrogated,' David Wertner says. 'We will find out who he works for.'

De Vries turns towards him, thinks at least his focus is elsewhere.

'Your own movements in the last forty-eight hours, Colonel, require an explanation. The source of your information is unclear. Who provided you with this material?'

De Vries sighs, turns from Wertner back to Thulani.

'Concentrate your efforts on Mngomezulu and his colleagues, Colonel,' Thulani tells Wertner. 'Colonel de Vries is to be congratulated for not capitulating in the face of intense pressure.'

De Vries looks down, disbelieving that he is receiving support from Thulani.

'Your methods, Colonel, are highly questionable, but the result achieved in this instance, I believe, justifies them.'

'Thank you, sir.'

'It's interesting how it has turned out again, that your investigations lead to one of our own?'

De Vries turns to Wertner.

'Strange how that it is, isn't it, sir.'

'General Thulani received a priority call,' Norman Classon tells De Vries and Don February in Vaughn's office. 'I can only think that the docks were already under surveillance . . .'

'Or I was.'

'Possibly. You know how keen everyone is to watch one another these days. Thulani is seen leaving in haste. After that, you probably know more than we do.'

'It was the Hawks; that or some paramilitary unit we don't know about. I don't know how they found me.'

'Networks, Vaughn. Perhaps General Thulani suspected you could be in trouble, kept an eye on you.'

'An unusually benevolent eye.'

'Nonetheless . . .'

'He will claim all the credit for exposing this.'

'Let him,' Classon says. 'Better you're not involved, officially.'

'Better for who?'

'Better for everyone, I think. You wouldn't want the reputation of going after your own, surely?'

'Nkosi isn't one of us.'

'Not any more, anyway.'

De Vries nods. Whatever Thulani does, he still retains the information to act later if he deems it necessary.

'You speak to Brigadier du Toit?'

'I did,' Classon says. 'He is concerned about you, but I told him that you still seemed your usual self.'

'I may need to see him.'

'He's in Citrusdal. You ever been to his place?'

He shakes his head, knows that Classon will have; De Vries is not considered one of the chattering classes.

'He told me to give you the address, if you wanted; if you are taking some time off now.'

'Soon, perhaps.'

Classon looks at De Vries's bruised face, his purple cheek, the dark brown marks on his neck.

'You're owed plenty, apparently.'

'I want to see what happens here first.' He turns to Don. 'Both your waitress and your strange young witness positively identify Nkosi?'

'Yes.'

'So, we have him buying the chicken. We have him at the scene at the right time. We need to know what he did to Lyle, but I want him for both murders.'

'The question will be,' Classon says. 'Is he prepared to give up his bosses in exchange for leniency?'

'I don't care. I want him and that little shit-fuck Mngomezulu taken down. All the way.'

Thulani is breathing hard, his right hand fingering his collar.

'We have confirmation that Sergeant Ben Thwala was not on the flight he checked in for. We have no information on his whereabouts. You authorized this action. Who was his contact?'

'I don't know.' De Vries shakes his head gently for Ben Thwala, for how quickly his new-found allies abandon him.

'Not one hour ago I was defending your actions, and now we

285

have an officer missing. You spread disinformation around the station, you mislead me and you send this officer into a situation without understanding the danger.'

'I understood, sir, and I informed Sergeant Thwala. He understood the risk.'

'That is not acceptable.'

'No, sir.'

'We have to accept that Nkosi was not making an idle threat,' Thulani says. 'If he and whoever he works for are holding Thwala, then they have a bargaining chip against us. And we only have one thing in exchange: Nkosi. Do you see the position you have put us in?'

'Perhaps you could put in a word with your friend, Mr Bhekifa.'

'Don't fuck with me, De Vries. The allegations contained in your mystery bundle are unbelievable and completely unproven.'

De Vries says nothing, stares ahead, seemingly over Thulani's shoulder. He catches his superior's eye movement, knows that already he is doubting what the years of loyalty have engrained in him. Nkosi, Mngomezulu, even Bhekifa: they are Thulani's own, and they have betrayed him.

'Listen to me, Colonel. Do nothing further. Nkosi and his associates are under guard, Julius Mngomezulu will be interrogated by Colonel Wertner, and I will make representations to Pretoria to see what is known about the whereabouts of Sergeant Thwala. When this matter is concluded, perhaps Colonel Wertner will, once again, feel he has due reason to examine your decisions.'

De Vries sighs. Everything is predictable in the world of the new SAPS. He will always be a target. He accepts this, is already planning his next move.

'I'm sure he will.'

★ ★ ★

Don February wants to be at work, to be assisting in locating Ben Thwala. De Vries has ordered him to stay away, to wait to be contacted in case De Vries himself needs him or there are to be further unsanctioned operations.

He realizes that this is what De Vries has warned him about: if he works on cases such as these, there will be political pressures, his decisions will affect the rest of his career; there will be threats to him and, possibly, to his family. He has agonized over whether to leave, to return to normal duties and a predictable routine, to lessen the sense of apprehension with which he greets each new case. Yet, he knows already that De Vries is fearless – heedless too – but determined to bring justice. He did not join the SAPS to earn a living; he joined because he believes in justice. It has taken him almost two years to see that, whatever De Vries is, he will do what is necessary to bring justice to the victims of his cases. Anything else, maybe almost everything else, is not enough.

'I had hoped, Colonel, that what I told you was clear. It seems not.'

'You're talking to me . . .'

'That is because,' Eric Basson tells him, 'the damage has been done. You are here, you have asked to see me, your presence has been noted. You are lucky that I am so pragmatic.'

'You helped me before. Now I need help for a colleague. A policeman.'

'I know about Sergeant Thwala.'

'What do you know?'

'No more than you, I imagine. He is held by Nkosi's supporters.'

'Where?'

Basson shakes his head.

'I don't know. I don't intend to find out. To do so would compromise my position.'

'Any suggestions?'

'Only what you already know. They will wish for the return of Nkosi and their men, you wish for the return of your colleague. Eventually, an agreement will be reached.'

'Nkosi isn't going anywhere.'

'An admirable determination, but unrealistic. If Mr Bhekifa instructs that he is to be returned, I am sure that this will subsequently occur.'

'You believe Bhekifa makes day-to-day decisions for these people?'

'I am sure not. But this is hardly "day-to-day". There is an impasse; they will eventually seek guidance from above. That above, ultimately, is Bhekifa.'

'I need more from you.'

'I possess only information. In this regard, I don't have what you want.'

De Vries grimaces, rises.

'However, I do have something else for you.'

He sits.

'I misunderstood you,' Basson says, 'when you told me you had been under threat the previous day in Greyton.'

'In what way?'

'I had thought you were nearly the victim of an attack by the man who has killed four of your colleagues already.'

'It was Nkosi's men.'

'Of course, but, at that moment, I was not aware of that.'

'I knew you knew about the Victoria Drinking Hall bombing,' De Vries says, 'when you casually mentioned my time as a Captain in Observatory.'

'It is rarely necessary to be overt.'

'Depends if you are giving orders or not.'

Basson chuckles.

'No one else has made the connection to these deaths. Unless we help them, I doubt they will. It is hard enough to pass information from one station to another; inter-provincial co-operation is still a rare commodity.'

'You don't think we should?'

'Of course not. Secret history is best left hidden.'

'You know who this is? Who is doing this?'

Basson frowns.

'No.'

'Then you have nothing to help me.'

Basson sits back in his chair, stares casually at his wedding ring, twists it. De Vries finds his fastidiousness annoying, feels that he is playing to his audience.

'I have two gifts for you.'

'Why?'

'I like you.' He studies De Vries carefully. 'I anticipated that you might wish to interview Mr Kobus Nel.'

'I can do that anytime.'

'Can you? I doubt that you would find it so easy. Mr Nel travels extensively. It is often difficult to ascertain exactly where he is at any given time.'

'So?'

'He has agreed to meet you.'

'You persuaded him?'

'Kobus Nel's heroic action during his time with the SAPS is noteworthy, especially during the mid to late 1980s. Do you know about that?'

'His legend, yes. The details, no.'

'You knew about *Vlakplaas*?'

'Of course. He was there.'

'For a time.'

'No wonder they leave him alone.'

'There is no need to sully ourselves with details. Suffice to say, Nel served his senior government masters loyally. He not only ensured the status quo, but he was publicly seen to be effective. That reputation served him well. There were never any revelations at the Truth and Reconciliation hearings. He – and the SAPS top brass – chose not to re-open those wounds. And, of course, I know about that January night in 1994. That knowledge provides me with a certain influence over Mr Nel.'

'And now, me.'

'Conceivably.'

'You think Nel is responsible?'

Basson wets his thin lips.

'It's possible. He is bidding for respectability: an international business deal which will lift him from the underworld to some kind of legitimacy. His history would certainly be examined. He might fear that one of you would seek to hurt him. Your know-ledge would buy leverage.'

'Or your knowledge?'

'Mine is kept very safely. I made it a point that Kobus Nel should know that.'

'The victims were violently stabbed in their sleep,' De Vries says. 'That doesn't sound like the work of a professional killer.'

'From what I hear, the preparation is certainly of a professional nature; the execution itself – if you'll excuse the phrase – less recognizably so. But perhaps that is intended. Misdirection is everywhere.'

'When do I get to see him?'

'I would advise soon.'

'Tomorrow?'

'You're sure?'

'Why not?'

'You're not concerned that you might not see the morning?'

De Vries says nothing; the truth he has suppressed sounds frightening spoken aloud.

'Tomorrow,' he says quietly.

'I anticipated that. Your meeting is set for 1 p.m. I have the address for you.'

Basson reaches under the table, produces a tightly wrapped package.

'My second gift.'

De Vries gauges its weight. It is light, yet it feels substantial.

'As we won't meet again, I wish you good luck.'

Vaughn nods, turns around, walks across the room, lets himself out.

When he sees it on the passenger seat of his car, just as he is about to exit the vehicle, it is as if he has not noticed it before. He opens the cardboard box in which it sits, takes it out and turns it over, so that the picture faces him. The wooden woman's eyes watch him as he scrutinizes her. It is almost photorealistic yet, close up, there are clear marks from Dazuluka Cele's brushes. The carving in the painting seems old, heavy with profound meaning. The crack is a line of longitude, bisecting her face and her body, making her seem ancient and, to him at least, calm. De Vries has no interest in art beyond that which brings him pleasure in the moment; he finds the prospect of seeing the same picture on the same wall every day strangely static and unoriginal. He opens the door, cradles the picture, walks to his house. He finds a hammer and nails, climbs the staircase to his bedroom and hangs the painting on the pillar between the two tall bow windows which overlook the garden and, further way, the edge of Devil's Peak. He stands between his bed and the picture, looks back and becomes aware that she will look at him, watch over him, as he sleeps.

★ ★ ★

He does not sleep, can't find a comfortable position. At first he hears the rain, the low rumble of thunder in the distance, so rare in Cape Town. When it seems to stop, he hears dripping and, later, silence. In the early hours he is alert to the tiniest sound, scrutinizes his interpretation until he is reassured. He turns repeatedly, sits on the edge of his bed, seeking some relief. He wonders whether he should have accepted Marantz's offer of his dog, Flynn, for the night, but knows that if he had barked, it would have scared him rigid.

He has been plagued by the four murders; he forces his eyes open when the image of Mike de Groot's contorted face will not leave the inside of his eyelids. Within a second of waking from a fitful doze, the image of de Groot floods his synapses, steals the breath from him. At 5.30 a.m., he pads downstairs to the kitchen, checks the alarm is active, substitutes his planned mug of Rooibos tea for a large whisky; he pours, drains the glass, pours again. He wonders whether to tell Mitchell Smith about de Groot, or whether to spare him. He can't see any way to help the man; he prays that whoever it is will stop with the men who entered that cursed township dwelling all those years ago. He and Smith were spectators only, unable to prevent what occurred. Yet, somehow, when he thinks of that night, he always feels guilty anew.

He looks around the darkened kitchen, feels afraid of the exposed windows, turns back up the stairs to his bedroom, walking uneasily, and slumps on the bed.

At 7 a.m., he rolls off his mattress: aching, drained, depressed – relieved.

De Vries drives across Kloof Nek, the highest pass over the Mountain, and looks over on Camps Bay. On his side of the Mountain, the sky is all dark clouds and dank, heavy air, but here, it is sunny and hot. Out at sea, however many kilometre away it is, the horizon is black. The respite may be short. He waits at the junction to turn, smiles at layer after layer of houses covering the mountainside. Thirty years ago, you could have bought land here for nothing. It was considered a windblown, sun-blasted suburb with a pretty white beach abutting sea so cold your ankles burned with pain just paddling. Now, every square metre has been built on. The main palm-lined drag on the beach consists of boutique hotels, over-priced bars, slick restaurants; at night, neon lights, thumping music, beautiful people driving their supercars at a snail's pace, acknowledging imaginary friends like desperate politicians.

He turns right atop the Nek, weaves downhill through Umbrella Pines towards the Glen, then turns again, to climb above Clifton Beaches – four perfect little beaches of white sand and blue water, watched over by apartments and mansions, just as, he imagines, in Monaco. He continues to climb, up to the highest level above the ocean, to the biggest, most vulgar architecture in Cape Town, to the grandest residences of plastic surgeons, celebrity advocates and their mutual criminal clients.

He pulls up in front of ornate iron gates. A security guard appears through a small door, asks for identity. He shows it, watches the gates open inwards.

He drives slowly into a courtyard, roofs of terracotta tiles cover parking spaces on three sides. He is guided under cover next to the latest model Bentley GT. He gets out, turns to find an escort of two guards. They walk in silence to an archway through a wall, leading to a comfortable sitting room. At the far end, he sees what appears to be a funicular railway station. He has left his weapon at home, but they pass a detector wand over and around him, check his shoes, gesture for him to sit in the smartly upholstered closed carriage. It jolts slightly as it begins to rise steeply over the roof of the covered courtyard, up the side of the rocky mountain. Twisting himself around, he catches a glimpse of the dramatic vista of the Twelve Apostles – twelve peaks down the Table Mountain range – Camps Bay, the coast road, the ocean unending. He is taken aback by the security Nel employs, but he is not surprised by the funicular railway. Several mansions here boast them, rising from the High Road up and into the mountain where, sometimes, it seems as if the owners have blasted their way through sheer rock to find their own safe havens.

At the top, he is led up some broad stone steps to a plateau, sees a wide, perfectly flat lush green lawn, bounded by mature trees, ahead of an enormous Tuscan villa, all terracotta tiles, verdi-gris copper and white columns. He is taken to the side of the house where, in a kidney shaped swimming pool, amidst loungers and parasols, backed by an ornate pool house, he sees Kobus Nel reclining in the shallows. The guard backs off. As De Vries approaches, he notices that the girl entwined with Nel is naked.

'You were thinking,' Nel's deep, coarse voice booms. 'Did I do the right thing staying in the SAPS for twenty years, or should I have followed Kobus Nel?'

'No.'

Nel laughs quietly. 'I think you were.'

De Vries approaches the water, sees Nel is also naked, notes that his physique is just as he remembers: squat and muscular, thick neck, broad head. It is accentuated by the effect of the water: Nel is big above the waterline, shrunken beneath. De Vries sees bright, distorted tattoos on the man's arms, thick gold jewelry on his wrist, around his neck.

Nel dismisses the woman; she totters towards the pool house and disappears.

'You want to talk to me?'

De Vries nods.

'Join me.'

Vaughn steps from one foot to the other.

'I'm fine here.'

Nel stares at him.

'It's Sunday. Maybe the last day of summer. I'm not having a conversation with me here and you there. Get in the pool.'

De Vries expects power games; he knows that he is here to extract information and that it will cost. He looks around to see a suited white man behind him.

'My man will take your clothes.'

He undresses slowly.

'What is it?' Nel's voice is sharper now. 'You unsure about your sexuality . . . Or maybe you don't want to get your equipment wet?'

'I've been searched thoroughly.'

'Well, I'm not getting out. Fuck, man. Too nice a day for clothes.'

Vaughn swallows, takes off his tie, his shirt — finds the guard waiting to take it all from him — and removes his shoes, socks, trousers and underpants. He walks towards the pool, looks down beyond his pink belly, white thighs, and sees steps down into the water; he takes them and walks, warm water waist high, towards Nel.

'It's the South African way . . . Kobus Nel.' He holds out his hand. De Vries knows that only capitulation will buy him answers, takes it, shakes. 'Thing about the water,' Nel says. 'Everybody's dick looks small.' He laughs loudly.

'Beer?'

De Vries nods.

'What a fucking waste,' Nel says. 'Look at you, man. Nothing more than twenty-fucking-one years older than when we last met. What have you got? What have you achieved?'

'Nothing like you.'

'No. Nothing.' He looks into the distance, into thousands of miles of sky above the ocean. 'Old Eric Basson: he's a clever fucker, isn't he? All those years with our last true government and he keeps all that information locked away. No one dares to challenge him.'

'Not even you . . .'

'We have an understanding.'

'Is that what you call it?'

Nel ignores him, his smile locked.

'He must like you. Be thankful.'

'I really don't care.'

'No pleasantries, Vaughn?'

De Vries braces himself, takes a deep breath.

'In January 1994, seven of us went to Khayelitsha. Innocent people died, and I did what you wanted: I said nothing. Now, four of them are dead. All over the country. You know that?'

Nel smiles.

'I know what is worth knowing.'

'You trying to seal up history? Make sure nothing ever comes back?'

Nel looks beyond him. De Vries hears footsteps. Two bottles of beer arrive. Nel has swallowed half of his before De Vries is served his own.

The servant moves away.

Nel says: 'You suffer pangs of guilt? That a few *kaffirs* were collateral damage? You must have been fucking useless in the army.'

'All your men, murdered in their beds, one after the other . . .'

'I don't care, De Vries. And neither should you. Crime is everywhere now and you people can't do anything about it. But, it's our fault. We knew these people couldn't run a country, keep control. They're fucking *kak*, man. All of them. Look at that corrupt, self-enriching, wife-collecting cunt Zuma; that fat little shit Malema. The only thing I wonder about him is how he fits his fat *kaffir* arse in the narrow little driver's seat of his Ferrari.' He laughs hoarsely. 'At least Ramaphosa had the guts to make the call to shoot the striking Marikana miners. At least he had balls.

But the rest of them ... They keep people like you there as trophies to show the world there might still be some hope of law and order, when we all know that's shit.'

'There's law and order where I am concerned.'

Nel sneers at him.

'Unless you're coerced.'

'That was a long time ago.'

'Fuck, yes.'

'We're making progress ...'

Nel's laugh is a bark.

'Who the fuck do you think you're talking to? I own thirty fucking businesses around this country. Every single fucking time I deal with the government, the councils, the civil servants, it's *crook*. Money changes hands. There's no rule, or statute or law, it's just fucking cash, every time.'

'That says something about you, then.'

'You think I'm going to wait while these people fuck me about? In 1994 we had three choices: we could get the fuck out of here before they destroyed our country; we could bow down to them and be thankful for what they gave us; or we could stay and play the game by our rules.' He gestures around his compound. 'Guess what I did? I have a plane, a yacht, hard currency in Europe, a fucking private army if it comes to it.'

De Vries shakes his head slowly, feels that any hope of conversation, of answers, or even hints of answers, is long gone.

'We built this fucking country. Everything good is down to us. Just because there are more of them doesn't mean we had to give it back. You look at what they do in Africa: every time you give them something, they fuck it up. So, I'm staking my claim to my land, and they can come fight me for it, 'cos the fight never ends, not if you're a South African.'

'You tell your staff that?'

Nel laughs.

297

'There's a rule around here. No fucking black faces. No coloureds. They work in the background. I see them, they're fired. Everything works here because there's order. Educated white guys tell them what to do. That's how it worked for centuries. That's how it's going to stay.'

De Vries is tired. Nel's speeches remind him how many years it is since he left the army and joined the SAPS. He wonders where that time has gone; what, in twenty years, has he actually achieved?

'Keep your head down, De Vries. You might be all right.'

De Vries squints at him, cannot read anything from his broad face. Is he telling him he is safe? He tries one more time.

'Whoever it is, is working north to south, now west, travelling down through the country . . .'

'I know,' Nel says. 'I know all about it. You come here just to talk about that?'

He laughs, tosses his empty bottle sideways, watches it roll across the lawn, and turns back to De Vries.

'You always were fucking boring. You know that?'

De Vries feels old and bellicose, body aching, deteriorating. He thinks of Kobus Nel, taut and driven, impenetrable; he knows that he has gained nothing from their meeting, yet feels that he has lost something. As he freewheels down Kloof Nek Road back into town, his mood is irritated by the trite and mundane: bad driving, unsafe vehicles smoking, swerving across the sharp curves. He engages a low gear, cuts across the road into a side street, continues his descent through suburbia until he reaches a café with a parking space directly outside. He enters the space forwards, mounts the pavement, and thumps down again into place. He sees a car guard amble towards him. He gets out, fixes him with a stare.

'Fuck off.'

The guy surrenders, stumbles back down the street. De Vries looks around, sees lunching ladies look away from him. He slams his door, crosses the street to the café. As he enters, two women leave a table. He takes a newspaper from the rack by the door, slaps it on the table, puts his dark glasses atop it. He orders a large coffee, a beer and a sandwich. He takes off his jacket, leans back with the newspaper, meets no one's eye. He starts with sport at the back, thinks better of it, scans the headlines from the front. On page nine, he reads:

Sunday Cape Herald, 13 April 2015

FORMER COP IN MYSTERIOUS MURDER

He swallows back bile; his sight begins to blur. He forces himself to breathe, aware that others might witness him. He looks back down, focuses on blurred black ink.

Former SAPS officer Mitchell Smith, of De Houtman Street, Belrail, knew to take his security seriously, but on the night of 11 April, an assailant broke into his home and stabbed him multiple times. The mystery for the current Bellville cops is this: there was no sign of forced entry or exit, and all his doors and windows were locked.

Smith, who had been in and out of work since leaving the SAPS in 2003, had expressed concern for his safety to a neighbour, but had never explained why. Other neighbours suggested a criminal who Smith had arrested might have been looking for revenge.

Captain Keith Small of Bellville SAPS said: 'The only explanation so far is that the killer gained access to Smith's residence when the alarm was not switched on, hid inside and when his victim was asleep, stabbed him repeatedly in the chest. Afterwards, the killer left the property by switching off the alarm and then re-setting it. So far, no one has come forward with information, but we remain hopeful that someone in the vicinity saw the man either on the night itself or perhaps scouting the area beforehand.'

De Vries reads the article a second time, heart-rate falling, and grunts his thanks to the waitress who delivers his drinks and cutlery for his toasted sandwich. He lays the paper down, sugars his coffee, sips it gingerly.

He thinks of Mitchell Smith, his doors and windows bolted, sensors on the perimeter, alarm primed; someone walks into his home silently, like a phantom, drives the knife into him, over and over again, walks away unseen. He feels his mouth dry within its cage of sealed lips and locked jaw, forces himself to breathe.

He thinks of Mitchell Smith's house, of how low the ceilings in the small rooms seemed. Yet, when he recalls the squat building, he remembers the pitched roof – there must be storage space above the living space, beneath the rafters. He imagines the killer getting into the house during the day when Smith is out, waiting in the crawl space there, dropping down silently in the dark, standing over his victim.

His sandwich arrives and he eats greedily, quaffs his beer and puts the bottle back down on the table, holds it there. He realizes that he is gripping it tightly, his knuckles white around the thick brown glass. He opens his fingers, orders another beer, a slice of chocolate cake.

He looks back down at the article.

'Afterwards, the killer left the property by switching off the alarm and re-setting it.'

The beer has made him think clearly. The sentence seems simple, but it is complex. The front door was locked from the inside. The alarms were switched on, the windows and doors locked. He swallows; suddenly he knows. The killer never left. He hid, killed, hid again. In the morning, the neighbour calls the cops. They force the door. They find the body, examine the scene.

They leave with the alarm off, door locked cursorily. Plastic tape guards the property now. The killer drops down from his hiding space, walks out into the dark, disappears.

De Vries wonders what to do: call this Captain Small at Bellville to share his theory? He thinks not, reasoning that if it is to be him next, he would sooner face the threat without further attention. He recalls Mitchell Smith's stuffy, scruffy house, thinks about waiting for hours in the roof, meditating on the vicious killing to be performed, climbing back and waiting again, hearing the police beneath you. He shivers. Beer arrives. He grabs it and drinks. Cake is placed in front of him. He stares at it.

As he reaches his building in the centre of town, the skies are so dark that it seems brighter in the underground car park than outside. The skies disgorge rain so torrential he can hear it even inside the massive concrete cavern of the main foyer. He travels up alone in the elevator, his mind fearful yet determined.

His squad-room is quiet, yet to begin its next investigation. He sees Don February at his desk in the corner, walks over to him. His Warrant Officer looks up at him, then stands.

'Are you all right, sir?'

De Vries balks.

'*Ja*. Why not?'

'Your meeting? It did not go well?'

Don knows nothing but that De Vries was meeting someone, for some reason. His secrecy ceases to bother him. It is his boss's way.

'No.'

'I am sorry.'

'Why are you here, Don? We agreed some home leave, just in case.'

'I was called in by Mr Classon. I wanted to come in. I love my wife, but I do not like being a nurse. Here, I am completing the report on Nkosi. General Thulani requested the docket, all the files, everything.'

De Vries furrows his brow.

'Why?'

'He said that he had been instructed to conclude matters.'

De Vries looks around the empty squad-room.

'Where is Mngomezulu?'

'I heard . . .' Don says quietly, 'that he has been taken to Pretoria with the other men.'

'What?'

'I do not know the details.'

'And Nkosi?'

'He is still in the cells. General Thulani refused to release him.'

De Vries feels anger overtake all his fears. He turns away from Don, strides towards the elevators, jabs the call button. He is about to take the stairs when the doors open. He sees Norman Classon, tries to enter the lift, but Classon pushes him back out. He is surprised by the lawyer's strength.

'Come with me.'

Classon puts his arm around De Vries's shoulders. Something in Classon's tone persuades him to acquiesce. They walk back to the squad-room, into De Vries's office. He calls for Don. They sit.

'I already know what you're thinking,' Classon says. 'Before you say anything, just hear what I have to say.'

De Vries nods.

'Thulani and I drew up charges against everyone involved. He was hands-on, Vaughn, utterly determined. Nkosi, Mngomezulu, all the men at the docks. This morning, bloody Sunday morning, I get a call at 8 a.m. The Police Ministry contacted the Provincial Commander, and Thulani received orders directly from him that all of them should be released into the custody of the Central

Independent Police Investigation Department in Pretoria. Thulani spent most of the morning with him and then on the phone to Pretoria. He fought his corner, Vaughn. I was there. I was impressed. But this comes from the Police Ministry – and above.'

'What about Thwala?'

'Nothing. The Ministry deny all knowledge, claim it is unconnected.'

'You get the CCTV footage from the airport?'

'No.'

'No?'

'They're claiming it's missing. Nothing from the security area at that time.'

'Nothing surprises me.'

'This will,' Classon says. 'Thulani refused to release Nkosi. Got me to find a legal clause which would prohibit him from being taken out of Province. Said it wasn't going to happen.'

'He's still here?'

'Yes. And it looks like he's staying. Pretoria issued an internal memorandum stating that the others have been returned for investigation but that they were likely influenced by Nkosi and were only obeying orders.'

'Sound familiar?'

De Vries looks down, shakes his head.

'We still don't have Nkosi. We don't have forensics; we don't have eyewitnesses. Not conclusive. Not so that he or some *crook* Advocate can't deny it all, wriggle free. If he uses Thwala to negotiate, he could walk. We needed Mngomezulu, perhaps even the others, to provide substantive evidence.'

Classon says: 'The guy was going to kill you. He admitted it to you.'

De Vries laughs dryly.

'You think that matters? He'll have some concocted story, the other guys will back him up. I only care about Angus Lyle and

Taryn Holt. To use your terminology, they're my clients. They deserve justice. And, for god's sake, Thwala. What does he have to do with this?'

'We put him there. We have to get him out.'

De Vries appreciates Classon's use of the word 'we'.

'We've got what we've got,' Classon says. 'We have to work with it. That's what we have to do ordinarily.'

'And the others, sir?'

Classon turns to Don.

'I don't know, Warrant . . .'

'I do,' De Vries says. 'I know exactly what will happen to the others. Nothing. Someone high up knew all about this, authorized it, and now the Police Ministry will play their game. They'll be put on leave for a few weeks, sent somewhere else. Nkosi had his name changed, for Christ's sake. You think he was an exception?'

'We don't know that,' Classon says.

'We do. We do, Norman. Is this what it's going to be like for the rest of my career?' De Vries lays his head on his desk, clenches his fists. 'We're supposed to serve the people, for fuck's sake. Not the ANC, not the Nats, not any of them. You have a state police force, you might as well have an army. I thought that's what they all fought for: a new way. You go down this route and what's the point of anything that's happened in the last twenty-five years? All you've done is change the colour of the oppressors.'

De Vries braces himself for the cold, knocks and enters General Thulani's office. Thulani has his back to him, staring out of the window. Vaughn hears the clatter of rain against the windows; Thulani may not even have heard him knock.

'Good afternoon, sir.'

Thulani turns, gestures to him to sit in the corner where there are two sofas at ninety degrees to one another. Thulani wanders over, sits heavily. Vaughn sits on the edge of his sofa, half at attention.

'This is what it comes to, Colonel. I am at work on a Sunday, and I feel ashamed by what I do. This is a sad day for us. You have been told by Mr Classon, I understand?'

'Yes, sir.'

'I want you to be clear that this is not my doing. I believe that the Commander also argued against the release of the other prisoners. This comes from the National Head Office. From the top. We are powerless.'

'We have Nkosi,' De Vries says.

'They have Thwala.'

'Without wishing to be inhumane, sir, Nkosi is far more important.'

'For now. We face a difficult problem with Nkosi. If it becomes clear that he can be convicted of his crimes, those who sent him will fear that he may testify against them. That will lead to greater pressure for his release back to them.'

De Vries says nothing.

'That is not why I have asked you here, Colonel. I wish to inform you that everything is being done to seek the release and safe return of Sergeant Thwala. You are not to be involved. If there are to be negotiations, then they will be carried out by me or the Provincial Commander. Do you understand?'

'Yes, sir.'

'Additionally, I hope that we have a chance to facilitate this officer's release at a meeting I wish you to attend this evening.'

'Sir?'

'It is impossible for you, Colonel, to understand what it was like to be part of the Struggle. Many brave, committed men died in the cause of the freedom we enjoy today. I lost my brother, shot down by the South African Police – yes, before we became what we are today – in 1983. Many of my friends were imprisoned; some disappeared. But, it was a fight which, somehow, had to be supported. Bheka Bhekifa fought. He risked his life and well-being and, when the time came, it was right that he should become a man of influence in our government. He fought for freedom and truth, and my respect for him was great.'

He meets De Vries's eyes for the first time.

'Using a contact we have with the private security company that monitors the properties in Bishopscourt, I have viewed footage of Sergeant Mngomezulu coming and going on three recent occasions at the house of Bheka Bhekifa. We have also confirmed that it is his voice on the tape you obtained.'

He stops. De Vries waits: he has no idea what is expected of him.

'Before Sergeant Mngomezulu left, he asked that the office of Major Mabena was contacted. He assumed perhaps that he would receive immediate aid. I expect his welcome back in Pretoria to be less than warm.'

Thulani hauls himself up.

'The connection is made. Bheka Bhekifa and Mngomezulu; Mngomezulu and Mabena. This evening, I intend to make a visit. I want you to come with me.'

'Sir?'

'The information we have uncovered, corroborated by your own investigation: it is quite clear. Julius Mngomezulu reported to Bhekifa, informed him of our highest-level decisions, the state of our major investigations. Bhekifa must choose either to support us, to support justice, or I will consider him the hidden hand behind these matters.'

De Vries nods at Thulani. The man has surprised him.

'This is a sad day, Colonel. It has destroyed my faith in the political struggle which we now fight. The moment the ANC became a political party, it was corrupted, slowly but surely. It is a sad day for all of us.'

De Vries suspects that he is not included in the group classified as 'us'.

'But,' Thulani adds, more in the tone to which De Vries is accustomed. 'We will behave in a civil manner. It is appropriate that you are present with me to indicate that, here in the Western Cape, we are all as one in our pursuit of justice.'

'A show of unity.'

'Indeed. This is not a racial matter. It is not a political matter. We must be above such things. I believe it is the basis of our years in the SAPS. We serve the people, not the state.'

'Yes, sir.'

'In the car, I will explain what you are to say.'

Schoolchildren, neighbours and their visitors, workmen – all walk down the road on which Vaughn de Vries's house stands. If they travel by train, they walk across the little bridge above the Liesbeek River, over the crossroads and straight on down towards the steps to the station. His successful ex-wife, Suzanne, has insisted he keep the house as a base for their daughters, in case they choose to return to Cape Town. Vaughn would be just as happy in a small apartment in the centre of town but, for now, the familiarity of his family home reassures him.

Six white school children walk down the street, each pair sharing a small, colourful umbrella. Behind them, a group of black workers in blue overalls amble, the girls under newspapers, the men letting the rain stain their boiler-suits a darker blue. As they pass De Vries's house, one drops out of sight, doubles back, searches along the base of the perimeter hedge, which is backed by a tall fence. Within moments, the figure is gone from the street. A couple walk past, chatting and laughing, their dogs sniff the fence, lift legs to tell their peers that they have been here. Nobody sees anything.

The journey out of town is long and slow, delays in the rush hour traffic compounded by flooding on the freeway, a rock fall on De Waal Drive. In the deserted side streets of Bishopscourt, shallow waves of rainwater flow downhill, drops consolidate in the trees above and fall heavily on the roof of Thulani's car. Water flows off the low grey slate walls lining the driveway to Bheka Bhekifa's house, the car's puny lights barely able to penetrate the damp gloom of what seems now like a mid-winter's evening.

Bhekifa is standing as they enter the formal drawing room, his arms open in greeting. Thulani walks up to him, but there is no embrace.

'I regret, sir, that our visit is one of official police business.'

The old man lowers his arms, his expression suspicious. He sits down, but does not invite them to do so.

'What is it that you have to tell me?'

De Vries draws level with Thulani; they stand side by side.

'You are aware of our investigation into the death of Miss Taryn Holt. Your son was a friend of hers, and was briefly involved in our investigation. Information about that part of our enquiry was leaked. You know an SAPS officer based in my offices, Sergeant Julius Mngomezulu?'

Bhekifa shrugs.

'Why should I know this man?'

'He has been observed visiting this house on three occasions in the last eight days.'

Bhekifa narrows his eyes.

'The SAPS is monitoring my visitors? This is interesting . . .'

'We believe that you are also in communication with a certain Major Mabena, in Pretoria . . .'

'Mabena,' Bhekifa interrupts, 'is a liaison between those of us in government . . .' He checks himself. '. . . Between the Police Ministry, Central government and its advisors on security matters.'

De Vries says: 'Is that what you are?'

Thulani glances at him, returns to Bhekifa.

'I think that you were aware that a unit from Pretoria was dispatched to Cape Town, headed by a man operating as Lieutenant Sam Nkosi. Acting on orders from Pretoria, he murdered Taryn Holt, implicated and murdered a man, Angus Lyle, and took prisoner Colonel De Vries.'

'How would I know this?'

'Because, sir, I believe it was at your instruction. We know that Sergeant Julius Mngomezulu was reporting confidential Western Cape Province SAPS matters to you, in direct contravention of his duty. This is not acceptable.'

De Vries sees Bhekifa's feigned expression of innocence fade, sees a determination which he had never doubted replace it. His lips thin, his teeth appear.

'Furthermore, we are aware of Lieutenant Nkosi's involvement in the Marikana Mine incident, his failure to attend the enquiries and the steps undertaken to hide this. We will not tolerate such interference in the pursuit of justice by state-sponsored operatives.'

'Enough.' Bhekifa thumps the arm of his chair, sits forward. 'You stand there in front me, next to this man . . .' He waves his hand at De Vries. 'Have you forgotten the decades of sacrifice we made to fight against men such as this? Do you think that we can allow the forces of evil to come together again to challenge us? If you think we can sit back and do nothing, then you are nothing but a traitor to all of us who have fought so hard.'

Thulani looks over to De Vries, who says: 'Taryn Holt was about to finance your son's political party in direct opposition to the ANC. We know you were aware of this. We also have Mngomezulu . . .' he does not care how badly he says the man's

name '. . . on tape, revealing to *Cape Herald* journalists the connection between him and Taryn Holt. This is a man who acts on
orders. He had come from you, and I believe that he acted on
your orders.'

Bhekifa laughs, but De Vries continues.

'You achieved both the removal of a dangerous financial backer
for a growing opposition party and you attacked the credibility of
your own son as a political force.'

'You,' Bhekifa says, 'have no right to be in my house. You talk
of state-sponsored operatives: you worked for the regime whose
agents killed tens of thousands of my people in the name of state
control. You think that because twenty-five years have passed,
people like me forget what you did . . .'

'We are not here to be lectured by you,' Thulani says firmly.
'We are here to inform you that this will not happen in Western
Province again. Our reports are on file and they will remain safe.'

'Where is Sergeant Ben Thwala?'

Thulani stares at De Vries.

'Where is Sergeant Ben Thwala?'

'Not now, Colonel.'

De Vries shouts at Bhekifa. 'He's one of your own, for fuck's
sake. Isn't that what you keep telling everyone the fight was
about? You have all your people save Nkosi, so order Thwala to
be released.'

Bhekifa sits still, smiles.

'You come here to threaten me, accuse me, and you expect my
help? You people are the traitors we have fought all our lives.'

Thulani holds up his hand.

'You call me a traitor? I uphold the law, which keeps South
Africa a democracy and a free country. If you fight against that,
you are the traitor.'

Bhekifa sits back, shakes his head, flits the air with his little hand.

'You are like all the rest of them,' he says bitterly. 'The so-called educated, the young, the complacent. You think being in government is the end. You think the fight is over.'

'That fight *is* over,' Thulani says.

'No . . . You have no idea. You see only a fraction of what exists, that is why you do not understand. The fight is not over. It never ends.'

He leans back in his chair. De Vries stares at him one last time, sees hubris and a mocking despair that others cannot see the world as he does.

'Best never to meet your idols,' John Marantz says.

De Vries laughs, opens a bottle, walks down into the living room. The rain pours down the tall windows in rivulets.

'The donga at the bottom is crumbling,' Marantz says. 'My garage is leaking and the path into the woods below is half gone. So much for wishing for rain.'

'How do you know Eric Basson?'

'From small-talk to the matter in hand, in one seamless segue.'

De Vries sits on one of the leather sofas, places his bottle on the table, hands on kneecaps, and stares at him.

'I told you,' Marantz says. 'I don't. I met him once, asked for his help. That's it.'

'That isn't the question. And you know it.'

'Barristers always say: never ask a witness a question unless you already know the answer.'

'You're not a witness,' De Vries says. 'You're the accused.'

'I gathered that.'

'Well?'

'If you think you know the answer, why ask? If I lied to you a moment ago, what makes you think I'll tell you the truth now?'

311

De Vries is too tired to fight again; he reads confirmation of his own theories in Marantz's evasion.

'Why fight all these years,' Marantz says, 'and then just do to you what you did to them?'

'Because bullying always felt better than being bullied, didn't it?'

'Not in hindsight.'

De Vries says: 'Mandela will be turning in his grave.'

Marantz smiles.

'It's funny how many white people say that.'

They both drink; Marantz opens his old marquetry box, slips a cigarette paper out, lays it flat on the table, begins to tear a narrow strip from one side. De Vries says quietly: 'You catch a small piece in the newspaper, or online, about a man called Mitchell Smith?'

'Yes.'

'I'm next.'

'What?'

'Whoever this is will kill all of us. That's what they've decided.'

'Nel?'

'My instinct tells me not. If I'm stabbed tonight, then keep it in mind, but unless Nel is employing a very unique individual, it doesn't feel right. Whoever it was hid in the eaves, waiting for hours, maybe days, then slipped down, killed him and hid there again, let the cops poke about, and still waited. Nel's way would be to shoot them in the face.'

'So, who?'

'One of them. One of the family of the people we killed.'

'*They* killed, Vaughn. They killed. Unless you've edited your role, you couldn't have stopped it; you couldn't have made it better. You are not responsible.'

'Tell him. Tell the killer.'

Marantz lights the joint, inhales deeply.

'Have some beer, stay in my guest room. At least for tonight. Flat roof, solid concrete. I'll post Flynn outside your door.'

'Maybe.'

He sleeps fitfully on the hard mattress in Marantz's spare room. Each time he wakes, he thinks not of the threat against him, but of Ben Thwala, and the position he has put him in. Dispatching him to Pretoria at the precise moment he did was reckless and selfish. He prays to anyone who will hear him that Thwala is returned.

In the morning, he opens his door and finds Flynn lying outside, wagging his tail. He pats his head, walks into the kitchen and makes coffee, carries it back to his room. The dog is on the end of the bed, looking out of the window. De Vries gets back in, puts his feet either side of Flynn and drinks his coffee; he looks over his head at the Southern Suburbs, blurred and dank.

At 8 a.m., his phone bleeps. An SMS from a withheld number. He opens the message and reads the nine letters several times.

'Nel is dead.'

'You found out quick.'

'Ears everywhere, Mike.'

'Makes you wonder . . .'

Major Mike Arends speaks abruptly, more curious to know why De Vries had visited Kobus Nel than to tell him what he has found at the scene. Arends is tight with David Wertner – a racial partnership; he and De Vries have clashed within the department.

'Stabbing, in his bed. A very sharp weapon, almost like a surgical instrument. The wounds seem deep. Doesn't look as if Nel got a chance to defend himself.'

313

De Vries shudders.

Arends says: 'What was security like when you were here?'

'Heavy. Guards at the gate on the street into the courtyard and parking area, more at the cable car, another at the top. But they knew I was coming. I made an appointment.'

'*Ja.* That's what they told us. I get the feeling there are ex-cops, ex-military here – the white guys anyway. You got that impression?'

'Yes.'

'And now several of them have disappeared. So, maybe an inside job?'

'Maybe . . .'

'I would think . . .'

'They may,' De Vries says, 'just have wanted to avoid a meeting with you. I suspect some of them may not be very sociable generally.'

'What did you discuss with Nel?'

'Better not say . . .'

'Anything relevant to his death?'

'No. Quite the contrary. Nel felt he was on the up.'

Arends squints at De Vries, knows that he is being excluded. He looks up at the grand house.

'Solid alarm system on doors and windows. Whoever it was got past his security, beat the alarm, killed him and got out. Nothing taken, as far as we know, but Nel was into all kinds of shit, knee deep. Could be underworld connected.'

De Vries hesitates; he has already decided to maintain silence, even if he doesn't truly know why.

'Nel's dirty a dozen different ways.'

He drives back to the suburbs, studying his surroundings with the eyes of a visitor who has never seen them before, or might never again. Nothing in his field of vision is clear: the precipitation blurs everything.

He views his house from the driveway, wonders if whoever it is has scoped it out, been waiting, watching for him; he knows deep down that they have. In his hallway, the air smells different. He bends to retrieve his mail, hears something and jolts upright, staggering back as he feels pain shoot down his neck. He rights himself, leans against the wall, rubs the back of his neck. He locks the front door, paces the downstairs rooms, then upstairs, considering hiding places, points of ingress. Finally, he descends the stairs, sets the alarm once more, gets back into his car.

He drives what is now grandly named the Cape-Namibia Route – the N7 highway up the West Coast of the country – for 150 kilometres, stopping once for petrol and a cold drink. When he reaches the country town of Citrusdal, he turns off the highway, drops down into the valley. The main street is busy with commerce and the exchange of information, as the mainly coloured rural community stands outside the one large supermarket, under the shelter of a wide corrugated iron roofed canopy, smoking and talking. He notices new mini-marts with Chinese names, wonders why they would come here to start their new lives. He read an article in the newspaper only weeks previously, officially dismissing as nothing more than another conspiracy theory, the stories that the Chinese government are sending these people out to South Africa, funding their start-up businesses, embedding them in every community throughout the country, so that when Chinese investment and industry begin to expand rapidly, as no one doubts they will, there are already established networks in place for the Chinese workers who follow. Change comes, he thinks, always in a way no one has anticipated.

He checks the directions Classon has provided, turns off the main street, past three blocks of simple housing and a high school, crosses onto a gravel track and begins to drive down into a lush valley of citrus farms, dams and streams, before turning towards the high hills, low mountains – the outer ranges of the mighty Cederberg.

After several kilometres, a missed turn and gingerly fording a fast-flowing swollen stream, he reaches the farmstead, continues past it for two more kilometres, and turns onto a disintegrating track towards Henrik du Toit's country house.

Du Toit waits for him under his broad stoep, which surrounds three sides of the low building, and greets him with a hug that, for twenty-five years of police acquaintance, Vaughn has never previously experienced or witnessed.

'I wait five months to get away from the sweltering city,' Du Toit says, 'and what do I find when I get here? A monsoon.'

A fire is lit in the hearth of the simple living room. De Vries smiles at Du Toit's wife: a quiet woman, baking in the dimly lit kitchen.

'I know it's business, Vaughn. We'll head for the boathouse. Had lunch?'

'On the way.'

His wife hands him a parcel in greaseproof paper, and he leads De Vries outside to the stoep. He opens a large umbrella, holds it over him through the orange grove down to the stream. A few metres further down the planked walkway, amongst the trees, a wood cabin stands overlooking the stream. Du Toit lets himself in, holds the door for Vaughn, shakes the umbrella, leaves it outside.

Inside the cabin, the brook roars, but otherwise it is peaceful. Du Toit has pictures of Arctic missions: Shackleton's huts and tents, sepia pictures of ruddy, bearded sailors, an ice-breaker frozen into the ice. Within a few seconds, De Vries has learnt more about his boss than in twenty years of conversation. Du Toit fills an electric kettle from a jug, switches it on, opens a jar of instant coffee.

'This your bolt-hole?'

'Away from the grandchildren, where I can work, and think. One holiday with them all and I swore I wouldn't come back till it was built. The boathouse.'

Two dim electric sconces illuminate another wall of old family photographs and a threadbare Persian rug.

Du Toit hands Vaughn coffee, offers him a slice of cake from the parcel. They sit in the two armchairs, listen to the rain beating on the roof, the brash rush of water outside, and say nothing.

'Bad all round, I guess?'

De Vries nods.

'Pretty much. You did well to miss it.'

'Sorry I did. That's my role these days: support. I gather Thulani surprised with his vigour to uphold the constitution?'

'He did.'

They eat, sip their tea, do not meet each other's gaze. Vaughn finds their silence acceptable: the length of their acquaintanceship, their professional journey together, lends them a mutual understanding. Silence need not be intimate; it may merely be sufficient.

'You did well on the Holt case.'

'Not really.'

'There are plenty who would have taken what was offered to them by Angus Lyle's death and walked away. You didn't.'

'I had help.'

'I gather . . .'

'What do you gather?'

Du Toit sits back.

'Classon told me that you seemed particularly well-informed; that you presented a bundle of intelligence and refused to reveal its source.'

'I didn't present it. It was taken from me.'

317

'And where did it come from?' Du Toit looks at him, folds his hands over one another in his lap. De Vries thinks he looks like a pompous teacher beginning a thorough telling off. 'Your friend from England?'

'No.'

'Wherever it came from, Vaughn, whoever supplied it: beware the cost.'

'There's always a price, sir. I'm prepared to pay. It clarified some problems.'

'You know Thulani won't be able to defy Pretoria for long. He'll send Nkosi back.'

'It's inevitable. If we want to see Ben Thwala again.'

'That's bad, Vaughn. You were naïve.'

'I was desperate for information. Thwala knew what was happening. You know him. He volunteered.'

'Spin it however you like. It still means your suspect walks.'

'I know. The man kills twice and they'll change his name so that he never existed and move him on . . . Unless I can persuade him to talk.'

'You think that's likely?'

'No.'

De Vries drains his mug, places in on the desk beside him gently.

'It's more than the Holt case, isn't it?'

Du Toit's voice, quiet and controlled, still startles him.

Vaughn nods.

'It's a story I should have told you before.'

'Why does history always encroach in our lives?' Du Toit says, swallowing cake. 'In our country, I mean?'

'It's all we have. The founding fathers, the Boer War. It's nothing. The last fifty years have shaped us now, probably will for generations.'

'What is your history lesson?'

318

De Vries is afraid and ashamed that here, in this tiny cabin, rain-sodden and cold, he must tell a story he had hoped would fade with the passing of time, only to find it consuming him, looming and completely clear.

He takes fifteen minutes; he remembers details now that he had forgotten before, yet he truly does not know the controlling emotion which made him take himself and Mitchell Smith away from Khayelitsha. When he finishes, he feels only weakness and cowardice.

Henrik du Toit stares at him, says slowly, firmly: 'You didn't give the order. You didn't take the shot.'

'I didn't speak up. Not then, not later.'

'And now, what? Why does this matter now?'

'Seven weeks ago, in East London, Sheldon Rich was killed; a week later in Middelburg, Joe Swanepoel. Then Esau, Mike de Groot and Mitchell . . .'

Du Toit views him open-mouthed, considers his words.

'So, you know the connection. You know who will be next. Stake him out, find who's doing this.'

'I know who's next,' De Vries says solemnly. 'Me.'

He sees in Du Toit a sudden fear. Vaughn comprehends instantly that it is not for himself, but for his family.

'They're always killed in their own homes, Henrik.'

'I see . . .' Du Toit fingers his earlobes, fiddles with his lips. 'Don't go home?'

De Vries laughs grimly.

'I came here to tell you, so that if he gets me, if it happens, you can tell people what they need to know.'

'If? You can't just let it happen. For God's sake, Vaughn . . .' He trails off. De Vries sees his mind working, sees the realization that while one of those seven is still alive, perhaps a secret is best kept.

'Could you go into protective custody? The whole incident then and now could be re-investigated . . .'

319

'Kobus Nel was killed yesterday. You remember him, his reputation in the SAPS after Mandela was released? I visited him the day before his death to try to find out if he was behind it. The man lived at the top of Clifton, as high as you can go – higher – with well-trained guards, a bloody funicular railway to get up there, alarms. For all I know the killer was there already, watching both of us. Whoever this is won't be caught, won't stop. Whatever I do, he'll wait, and then he'll come for me. That's why this has to end now.'

'You have anyone helping you?'

'It's not about anyone else.'

Du Toit looks moribund and helpless. Vaughn recognized long ago that his boss operates efficiently only within the strictures of the service.

'I didn't come here for help, Henrik. I came to tell you. So that you'd know.'

'What will you do?'

'This person waits in the house, hides until his victim is asleep. I can wait too.'

Du Toit nods.

'Keep off the booze, Vaughn. Stay sharp.'

De Vries smiles.

'Can't have one without the other.'

He paces around the outside of his house, checking for signs of intrusion, sees nothing. He examines the garden by the perimeter boundary, seeking footprints, broken vegetation; he finds everything overgrown and untouched. Utterly drenched, he enters with trepidation what was his familiar, comforting family home, strips naked, pulls on a dressing gown from the back of his bedroom door – an old and unloved present – and spends the next forty-five minutes examining each window, cupboard and the corners of the attic, gun in hand, holding his breath at each stage. Finally, he wanders to the cupboard under the stairs which leads to a cellar cupboard, partly subterranean, where he keeps boxes of wine; he pulls out two bottles of red and studies them intensely as he walks back to his dining room table.

Unlike the beers which sit inside him heavily, bloating his stomach and making his ears buzz, the red wine flows as if through his veins, instils his brain with a vague clarity he recognizes. The familiarity of the old sensations make him smile. He is not ashamed that his life consists now of work and wine and casual sex. He smiles more broadly. He is not happy, but he is almost fulfilled.

He pours again and finds the bottle empty. He holds it over his glass, disorientated. Even the drop on the rim seems, to him now, substantial. He waits for it to fall. When he has finished the second bottle, he is sick. It is thin and dark, and bears only grains of Mrs du Toit's cake. He studies the contents of the otherwise empty sink, recognizes that he has not felt better in weeks.

Sleeps evades him. He lies awake, back aching, neck sore, turning every few minutes, desperate to find any relief for the discomfort and pain which dog him. His arms are in the way of comfortable rest, his hips ache. When he does finally doze, it is only until the distant sound of the binmen wakes him shortly before 6 a.m. He gets up, re-checks everywhere, locks himself in what was the adult living room, and snoozes on the sofa, sitting upright, for another ninety minutes.

In the daylight, he cannot decide whether to stay at home all day and guard his property or to go out and let his assailant take his place. There is an inevitability to what must happen which pushes him to leave, drive the three or four kilometres to the Foresters Arms, sit by one of the open fires and drink from mid-morning until daylight fades once more. He drinks alone, rejecting any interaction, and slowly, he is convinced, soberly. The drive back home is treacherous. Newlands Avenue is strewn with broken branches, deep puddles; heavy drops hit the roof of his car like gunshots. The leaves fall from trees reluctantly here, and their canopy makes the road seem like a tunnel. As he drives past the President's Cape Town residence, the water pours down the sloping road in torrents; when he brakes gently at the bottom, he skids, tyres aquaplaning. By the time he reaches his street, he is exhausted. He fumbles for his gate remote, finds it in the central cubby-hole, operates the mechanism and drives slowly in. As he closes it again, he peers in his rear-view mirror, swallows hard when he sees a shadow pass between them. He jumps out of his car, stares through the rain at the gates, looks up at the streetlight and the swaying palm fronds in front of it: shadows pass this way every night.

He eats hard-boiled eggs, sliced onto toast thickly buttered. Over them, he throws salt and grinds pepper, munches them joylessly. Through his dining room windows, he sees only a dark green distortion of his garden, fragmented by the trails of water falling relentlessly down the panes. He reflects on Du Toit's words and spurns another drink, thinks: burglary incidences fall in the wet; maybe it is the same for vengeance?

He pads around his house, sees nothing out of place, dismisses the growing urge to call his daughters. He prepares for bed, hurls the blankets off, throws himself in and pulls them back up, reaches under the pillow on what was his wife's side of the bed, feels the reassuring coldness of his gun. Then, he lies rigid. His back itches and he cannot reach it to scratch it; his neck aches and no angle of head on pillow will relieve the pain. Amidst his unceasing frustration, gnawing fear and strange impatience, he falls asleep.

He screams, feels the point of the knife in his flesh, tries to move his arms but cannot. The figure is astride him. Charged, he rises at the waist, gets one arm free and strikes his assailant. His other arm free, he reaches for his weapon under the pillow, finds nothing, scrambles out of bed. Outside his room, the rain is pouring so thunderously and in such blackness, he can neither hear nor see. He registers a different dimness in the direction of the door, stumbles to it, swings around the frame, sees movement on the landing, then the stairs, gives chase. As he reaches the bottom, he sees the front door opening, a silhouette vanishing into the dark. He throws himself forward, skids on the wood floor by his front door, dashes outside. Ahead of him, he sees the figure running. Adrenalin pumps through his legs, driving him on through the deluge. He looks up, water pouring down his face, into his assailant's eyes, sees the figure climbing the gates. He charges forward, grabs at what he believes are legs, feels them jolt from between his slimy hands, like a dog withdrawing its paw from human grasp, and disappear over the gates. He starts to climb, his brain registering only that the skin he clenched was black, the legs incredibly thin, childlike, yet the strength within them was too great for him. He falls over the top of the gates, screams at the top of his voice, hears nothing over the deluge.

Ahead of him, running downhill, he sees the figure. Everything in his vision is moving away from him: the rain diagonally, the water rushing down the falling road – fast and silver in the gutters, slow in the convex shallows of the centre – leaves and branches dragged from their boughs by the gusting wind. The streetlights are working but their light does not carry far amidst so much moisture. He sprints after the figure, encumbered and

323

stiff, but feeling that his weight downhill will speed him forwards. He does not know whether he is gaining on it, suddenly sees it fall, twist sideways, scramble on the tarmac on all fours, rise to two and begin to limp – still fast but now jerky – away from him towards Liesbeek Parkway, the main road.

De Vries feels his heart struggle inside him, his breath burning in his chest. As the figure approaches the traffic lights, he is almost up with it. He sees it turn towards him, registers only a black face against black tarmac against black sky. Suddenly, eyes flare white. They gaze for a second at De Vries, a stare which takes him back twenty-one years to Pama Road in Khayelitsha; he looks around at the road behind it, sees cars speeding too fast along it, one after the other. The figure jumps sideways, disappears from view.

De Vries reaches the end of the road, turns to the side, knowing that he will see the low concrete railings to the little bridge over the Liesbeek River and, beyond this, the stepped rectangular formation of the river sides as it wends its way through the little park, planted to impress visitors to the 2010 World Cup, now a canal-side walk for locals. In the deep, dark shadows of overhanging trees, De Vries can see nothing but the river water in full flow, branches and plastic debris racing away into the darkness from beneath him. He stumbles down the side of the bridge railings to the edge of the river, looks in both directions, sees nothing. The water usually flows in the lowest section of the concrete gully but, now, it is above the step halfway up the sides and he knows that to jump in the river would be to risk his life. Amidst his panting, the water on his face, in his eyes and nose and mouth, he conjures one coherent thought: his assailant is patient, resourceful. He grasps that there is one hiding place remaining: beneath the road, under the bridge.

He takes a deep breath, begins to lower himself gingerly down the concrete sides of the river, immersing himself in the cold, dark water. Ahead, beneath the road, he sees one higher step of concrete and realizes that a man could hide there. He edges along through the water until he is under the side-road, the entrance to his own street. Ahead of him, it is pitch dark. His pyjamas, so rarely worn, adhere to his body, wet as the river, cold as the air that rushes through the crawl space beneath the bridge. He grabs a branch from the edge of the river, where it has become entangled in the overhanging bushes, and cracks off a side shoot, drops to his knees. The spray from the water exiting the tunnel soaks him; ahead, he can see nothing, knows that the tunnel runs for no more than seven, maybe eight metres, until it re-emerges on the opposite side of the road, deep in the cover of overhanging willow trees.

He edges forward, straining to form an image of what lies ahead of him, unable to hear anything but the hollow echo of rushing water. For a moment, a shard of light permeates the blackness as a car on the Liesbeek Parkway rushes past, the beam of headlight refracted dimly by the concrete lining. Ahead, on the same side as he is on, he glimpses something which could be a figure. He scrambles forward on his knees and one hand, the tree branch still held out ahead of him to warn of danger ahead. He sees nothing, hears nothing, but imagines a sudden movement, a strike, the cold agony of the blade penetrating him, gutting him.

He pushes on until he is under the centre of the road, the ceiling barely a metre above the top ledge along which he crawls. Ahead, he sees dim, pale light as the tunnel opens back out into the river-side. Suddenly, the light is obliterated; a black form scrabbles away from him. He thinks he hears a cry, but he cannot know. He pulls himself forward, slowed by the branch ahead of him. He shoves it into the river, feels one end pulled back past him even before he has released the other. Head down, he thrusts himself forward, one lurch after another. As he reaches the grey, dismal light of the Cape Town night, beside the Parkway main road, he sees ahead of him a figure limping, almost slithering up the side of the canal bank. He forces himself upright, grits his teeth and scrambles up the first tier. He looks up. Above him, the figure stands: he cannot see whether he is armed. He looks down to find a handhold, up again to see a wide, dark shape raised above the head of the figure, a shattering cry and the thick heavy log flying through space, out a little and down fast towards him. He throws himself against the side of the concrete bank, feels the air compress as the projectile crashes onto the step above him, bounces over him and lands in the foaming swell. He struggles for a breath, looks back up into the rain of silver nails which seem to assault him, sees the figure still standing above him. He blinks. The figure stumbles away.

De Vries clambers up the side and pulls himself up onto the slippery, greasy grass verge, rights himself, sees the shadow ahead of him, silhouetted against the streetlight. He watches as it seems to turn to face him, then turns away again. He hears the sound of a car changing gear and accelerating down Liesbeek Parkway towards the traffic lights, sees the figure stumble toward the road. He stands, exhausted and disorientated, and watches the figure step out in front of the car.

The car swerves away from the impact, brakes, skids, then accelerates away uphill, rear lights suddenly gone. De Vries runs up the bank towards the road, sees it now deserted, races to the fallen form, lit faintly red by the changed traffic light, yet seeming to him nothing but black against black against black. He bends down, sees something like a child's body. He picks it up, cannot comprehend its lightness, feels breath in it, stumbles to the curb, half falls, half throws the body onto the grass, and fumbles to turn it over. The speckled white light of the streetlamp at the junction illuminates her face. She wears nothing but a black leotard, a thin black belt and matching bum-bag. He sees blood on her lips, eyes flickering, mouth gaping and twisted in agony. De Vries gathers her up in his arms, holds her to him, feels a final sigh leave her body, and then a deathly, absolute slump into his own sodden body.

He looks up, around. He is completely alone: a near-naked white man, bloated by a drenched Kevlar vest – a life-saving present – and a dead black girl, so strong when alive yet, in death, almost nothing more than a shadow made real. He closes his eyes and mourns for her, mourns for the history which binds them.

De Vries has no superstitions about death, believes the human body to be a receptacle of life no more sacred than that of any living thing which might have roamed the planet for thousands of years. He unfastens the bum-bag from her belt, wonders whether to leave her body at the roadside. He looks around, bends low and pulls the body by its hands towards the canal, pitches the light, insignificant form over the edge and rolls it into the water. Within a few seconds, and without seeming to surface, the corpse is gone.

He pulls himself back up, stumbles unsteadily to the road. At the junction, he unfastens his vest, rolls it under his arm, and walks – under cover of the dark, overhanging hedges and trees weighed down low with oncoming water – back up his street to his house. He sees no one, observes no movement to suggest human scrutiny.

He closes the front gates, re-bolts his front door, throws down the vest. As he approaches the staircase, he sees the knife. It is, maybe, thirty centimetres long, shaped like a pick, tapering to the point with a double-sided blade. He touches the point to his forefinger, realizes that he has punctured the skin. A tiny drop of blood appears. He wipes it away on his saturated pajama trousers, climbs the staircase heavily.

In his bedroom, he dries himself, dresses in old clothes, switches on every light and looks around. In the bathroom, there is an old built-in cupboard. At the very top are two narrow louvered doors, long since ignored. He sees that they are open. He studies the doors closely, the bath and cabinets, the flooring. There is not a mark to be seen. No visual evidence that anyone had ever been there. He drags a chair from his bedroom into the bathroom, stands on top of it, peers inside. Behind dusty, untouched sheets, there is a tiny space, a threadbare towel flattened like an animal's nest in long grass. There, he now knows, she waited.

He unzips the small plastic bag which had been attached to her belt. It contains two tiny picks, thin rectangles of rigid rubber, hand-coiled wires and two small nine-volt batteries, a folding compact multi-tool, a narrow sharpening stone, a strapless digital watch; tools of an accomplished burglar, simple enablers of a higher, fatal cause.

He lies down on his bed, utterly spent, brain spinning, still panting twenty minutes after he has stopped all physical exertion. He hears the rain, the air in his chest, and feels every beat of his heart. He thinks of the girl moving across the country, a silhouette so dark it is invisible in the shadows; a girl beneath the water, swept away by the onset of winter.

For the next six hours he lies there, unmoving, unable to close his eyes.

'I would think,' John Marantz says, standing over him as he sits by the fire, drinking red wine, 'that your overwhelming emotion should be relief. She killed six men – but not you.'

'I was lucky.' He looks up at Marantz. 'And your friend Basson gave me the vest.'

'Not my friend.'

'Whatever.'

Marantz sits down, glances out of the tall windows of his living room, which overlook the Southern Suburbs. Everything is out of focus in the grey unending drizzle.

'I went to him because I wanted to help you. Do you regret that?'

'Not right now.'

'But later . . . ?'

'What was the cost to you, John?'

'Cost?'

'Price. Men like Eric Basson don't do anyone favours. They do it for a price, to be owed something by someone who might help them in future. What did you promise him?'

'Nothing.'

'Then you're the lucky one. The more I try for information, the more compromised I become.'

'In what way?'

'You know things about me you shouldn't . . .'

'And you, me.'

'But it doesn't matter about you, does it? I'm trying to hold on to the last vestige of honesty in the whole damn system, and all the time, I am undermined, because now I owe you something. I owe Eric Basson.'

'You don't owe me.'

'But I owe Basson and, probably, so do you.'

Marantz draws breath to speak, suddenly says nothing; he looks down silently.

After a moment, he says: 'Basson told me that he was part of *Vlakplaas*; that he was a repository of secrets from the old days, the war that was fought.'

'I knew about *Vlakplaas*,' De Vries says. 'I have some of my own sources. My mother always told me: being an adult, it's all about compromise. I just didn't think it would turn out to be every one of my ideals.'

'That's our choice of business.'

'Perhaps . . .'

'That the end always justifies the means.'

'Does it, though? Can it? The end *always* justifies the means?'

'That,' Marantz says sadly, 'depends on the end.'

De Vries sits in the Interview Room alone. In a few moments, he will be joined by Nkosi. Classon, maybe even Thulani, will sit behind the one-way mirror in the observation booth. No one is expecting anything of him, not even himself. Major Mabena is on his way with a personal instruction from the Police Ministry and the top of the top brass, ordering his release into Mabena's custody and his return to Pretoria. Thulani has capitulated, as he must. De Vries has less than two hours.

Nkosi limps into the room, cuffed, his face bruised and scratched from the pursuit on the oil rig, and sits heavily on the iron chair across the desk from De Vries. His two guards stand to the side against the wall, but they do not leave the room.

'In two hours you are to be released into the custody of Major Mabena. I imagine you are relieved?'

Nkosi says nothing, head bowed, breathing steady.

'I have an offer for you, Lieutenant. Listen carefully because my time and yours is running out. We know your connection to the Marikana Mine incident, your previous identities and operations, and what you consider to be your continuing employment. But, I hope you appreciate that now it is different for you. Your bosses don't want you back to reward you, change you, move you on. They want you to silence you, because you can provide the final link back to them which proves the conspiracy. How do people like them silence a man?'

He discerns no reaction from Nkosi, as if the man is in a trance, meditating. He realizes that this is his training: an enemy combatant on hostile territory, saying nothing.

'You've read about a place called *Vlakplaas*? That was where the Apartheid Nationalist government established a centre for state-sponsored terrorism against your people. That farm was a charnel house, a place of interrogation and torture, of mind-control. When its existence became known, it was condemned around the world. And now the ANC have power, have been in government for twenty-one years, and what do you people do? You create your own *Vlakplaas* and they make you work there. You want to be part of that?'

Nkosi looks at him.

'You know nothing about me.'

De Vries is startled at the sound of his voice, surprised that he has spoken one word.

'What should I know?'

Nkosi stares at him. A few seconds run into hundreds, but his gaze never leaves De Vries. He says slowly, quietly: 'When you first met me at Taryn Holt's house you asked who thought they were in charge. You told me that you were in charge. That's what you do not understand. You control nothing. You are nothing.'

'But you are?'

'I am a soldier.'

'You wear the badge of the SAPS, Lieutenant. Not for much longer.'

'You people never fought. You basked in absolute power and never accepted what we have known from the beginning. It is a war. It always was, and it always will be.'

Nkosi folds his arms, bows his head. De Vries knows that the conversation is over. Nkosi has loyalty to a cause which, in 2015, he misunderstands. He nods to the two guards, watches them lift Nkosi under his arms, drag him away.

To police during war, he reflects, is always harder. The value of life declines; those who have nothing to lose risk more.

★   ★   ★

331

At 4 p.m., De Vries finds himself standing behind General Sempiwe Thulani's desk, next to Norman Classon and Brigadier David Wertner. Thulani is seated in his raised position facing a tall, thin black officer in full uniform. Thulani is reading. When he has finished, he looks up at his guest.

'In response to these direct orders from the minister, Lieutenant Nkosi will be released into your custody upon your departure from this building. You will be responsible for him from that moment.'

'Yes, sir.'

'You will return with my written objection to his release from the custody of the Western Cape Province. You will present this to the Police Minister. You understand?'

'Yes, sir.'

'Furthermore, if this man, in whatever guise, re-enters the Western Cape Province, he will be arrested and detained on sight.'

'That would not be in the interest of inter-departmental co-operation, sir.'

Thulani rises.

'Do you know what, Major Mabena? I do not care a fuck what your department – whatever that might be – thinks. That is what will happen. You have information on me; I have information on you, and the ministry and the people who work for it. So, let us be completely clear on this. Distance is your best defence.'

Mabena smiles insolently.

'Whatever you say, sir.'

'I say, and I expect the meaning of my words to be conveyed to your superiors – whoever they may be.'

'Yes, sir.'

'You assure me that Sergeant Thwala is on his way home?'

'As I have stated, we located and rescued SAPS Sergeant Ben Thwala. Those holding him have been detained.'

Thulani turns to De Vries, who says: 'I spoke to him on his cell-phone from the plane. He said that the main door had been closed and that passengers had been told to turn off their handsets.'

'Perhaps we should wait for the Sergeant's arrival?'

'I, too, have a schedule, General. It has been set by the Minister himself.'

'If Sergeant Thwala does not step off that plane in perfect health, you will be held responsible, Major.' Thulani stands. 'Now, get the fuck out of my office, and never come back.'

Mabena salutes, turns smartly and leaves the room. De Vries is reminded of Julius Mngomezulu, at large elsewhere now, spinning on the spot and clacking his heels.

Classon begins to move away. Thulani is muttering to Wertner. De Vries follows Classon from the room. When they exit the ante-room, reach the corridor, Classon says: 'You want me, Vaughn?'

'No.'

He strides away down the corridor.

From the far end of the main foyer, De Vries watches Mabena and two other men escort Nkosi away. He follows them, watches Nkosi and his guards enter a police van and slowly drive away. A few moments later, Mabena gets into the driver's seat of a saloon car and moves towards the exit of the underground car park. De Vries moves to his own vehicle, starts the engine, drives towards the exit, allowing two other cars to insulate him from Mabena's rear mirror.

Mabena turns out of the headquarters and heads to the Nelson Mandela Boulevard, the freeway which leads to the airport and the Southern Suburbs. De Vries expects Mabena to fork left for the main N2 highway but, at the back of his mind, he is suspicious that Mabena has separated from Nkosi and his colleagues, that he is driving a private car on his own. At Settlers Way, Mabena forks right onto the M3 freeway to the Southern Suburbs. De Vries nods to himself. He is almost certain where Mabena is headed.

De Vries overtakes Mabena, speeds past the University and Newlands Forest. He sits with the rest of the traffic in the ubiquitous queues at the junctions and then powers up Edinburgh Drive and turns off into Bishopscourt. He positions himself across the road from the impressive entrance, hidden from the cameras. He waits little more than three minutes before Mabena's car arrives, indicates right and turns into the gates to Bheka Bhekifa's mansion. De Vries takes four photographs on his cell phone. Twenty minutes later, having listened only to the smacking of sporadic but substantial drops hitting his car roof, his front and back views obscured by sodden leaves and small, fallen twigs, he takes six further pictures of Mabena leaving the property. He does not know what can be seen in these pictures, less still what he is even doing recording such information. When Mabena turns onto the road and accelerates, De Vries follows him. After twenty-five minutes, he turns off the N2 onto the airport slip-road; De Vries drops back, but continues driving towards the terminal, badges the security guard at the special-access gate, and parks up directly outside the arrivals terminal. Officers will meet Thwala when he appears through security, but De Vries wants to see him; however immoral the process taken to retrieve him, at least he is alive.

General Thulani's heavy head pulls his neck muscles taut as he tilts it back, stretching sore muscles. He feels emasculated by the events of the afternoon, betrayed that he is not party to the secrets of the high command of whom – he knows now mistakenly – he believed to be part.

He sits up straight, faces David Wertner.

'After all this, De Vries has proven loyal to me, and useful to us. He seems able to solve crimes others might be . . . reluctant to bring to conclusion.'

'Is it worth the risk?'

Thulani smiles thinly.

'We know we do not like De Vries. Part of me despises him, but he has two traits I do admire: he wants the SAPS to be respected, and he wants to find justice for the victim. I think there are many in government, many in our own service, who might, for whatever reason, decide to compromise that goal and, if their view prevails, then what becomes of the SAPS? What becomes of our country?'

'If needs be,' Wertner says, 'De Vries can be controlled. I have sufficient material to bring his character into question.'

Thulani draws himself up.

'Listen to me. De Vries is to be left alone. Officially, he is not to be monitored, he is not to be publicly challenged – even here within this building. Keep him off your list right now. There may be scrutiny and we do not want it to reflect badly on us. Leave Brigadier du Toit to run his department and be seen to focus on other matters.'

'Be seen . . . ?'

'Be seen.' Thulani stares at Wertner, wonders if his discretion is at the cost of plain comprehension. 'Those are my words. You hear them clearly? Those are your orders.'

Wertner continues to look puzzled. Thulani sighs.

'What you may do privately is up to you. For now, we are seen to be the leaders of men, to applaud any action which roots out corruption and exposes government interference and illegality.'

'Mngomezulu?'

'Beware, Colonel. There are many more like him. I expect you to ensure that there are no more snakes in my office.'

Thulani hauls himself out of his high chair.

'I am thinking of the men and women who look forward to the weekend. I have not looked forward to a weekend in a very long time. The crime never stops, the meetings and the forms, they never end. This weekend, I have only time to prepare my presentation and reflect that, perhaps, some of my thoughts have been re-aligned.'

'In what way?'

Thulani flicks his right hand.

'You spend too much time eavesdropping and spying. You should listen more openly.'

'I am doing my job.'

'Do it well, Colonel. We have challenged the hierarchy. The time will come when we must be certain who is our friend and who is our enemy. That is, I think you will agree, a basic tenet of war.'

'Don't even think about it, Vaughn. You're pissed, the roads are treacherous.'

De Vries looks up at John Marantz.

'I'm fine.'

'Do me a favour. You can't go back home. Not yet. Not now. I'll open another bottle. Have some. Spend the night in the guest room.'

De Vries's head nods until his chin hits his chest; his eyes half close.

'One glass. I'll have one glass. I will drink to the health of my officer, the redoubtable Sergeant Thwala.'

'Redoubtable?'

'I don't know where that came from . . .'

'An education? A long, long time ago . . .'

336

Marantz walks to his kitchen, unscrews another bottle of Merlot, pours a generous measure.

'I feel happier with you back on wine. You're more predictable.'

'That's bad.'

Marantz sits opposite him, across the broad, low coffee table. The fire crackles.

'What happens to Nkosi now?'

'Who knows . . . ? My bet is that he will disappear. But, if not, he'll become someone else, move somewhere else. He's back with his own now.'

'At least everyone knows. You found him. You caught him.'

De Vries shrugs drunkenly.

'Everyone knows?'

'You can tell everyone. There are websites, newspapers, television shows.'

'You think?'

'No. Probably not. I've never considered provocation a positive tactic. Threat, now that's a different matter. You hold the evidence; you hold that threat.'

The wind blows back the blue smoke from Marantz's open fire. They both watch it ooze into the living area, then recoil against the chimney breast and meander high up to the ceiling, suddenly cut off mid-way by another gust which sucks the cloud back inside the fire and up, out, into the damp mountainside night air.

'I made the worst mistake of my life,' De Vries says blankly.

'What was that?'

'I stayed quiet, in '94, when Nel was like a rabid dog. I should have spoken out.'

'No, you shouldn't,' Marantz says. 'A man like Nel – the man you described. He would have come after you, after Suzanne, after your baby . . .'

They both seem to know at once what he has said.

'I could have protected them . . .'

'Perhaps. Or maybe we would be talking as widowers both. You have them all still. That can never equate to a mistake. Not in the long run.'

'I thought about those black kids. Lots of times.'

'How can you know it was one of them?'

'Because she stared at me and I knew she recognized me. Because it makes sense when nothing else does.'

'To kill six men?'

De Vries looks ahead, looks out of the tall windows as far as the misty vista of suburbs and the Cape Flats, the townships and squatter camps. Amidst the concertinaed perspective, he knows that Khayelitsha lies ahead of them, the sandy track once called Pama Road, the corner house with the blue car.

'To kill six men who came to her home when she was no more than a child and murdered her family. I understand that. That is not a mystery. You'd kill the men who took your family; I'd kill them too. That is what we are.'

'That's what I have become.'

'That's delusional, Johnnie. You don't become this way. This is what we are, what we always were. What we will always be. It is dormant inside us . . .' He pauses. '. . . Inside more people than we could ever contemplate. It only needs the catalyst.'

'After twenty-one years, I don't know. I don't know how she even identified each of you, found each of you.'

'I don't know either, but I think I can empathize with something, and I think you can too. It took her twenty-one years, from the moment her family was murdered to the six deaths. Can you imagine what those twenty-one years must have been like? Do you think she ever thought of anything else? Whatever she was doing, whatever she was thinking, however she tried to live her life, it always came back to this, to one moment in time when everything changed.'

'That . . . I understand that.'

'Her or me?' De Vries says. 'That was the equation. You know, I almost began to believe I deserved it. And then I thought, I don't. I don't know why, but that's all that kept me going. Just one decision, one judgement.'

Marantz sits, mouth agape, counting out the years since he last held his daughter. He nods curtly, closes his mouth and swallows.

De Vries raises his glass roughly, watches the red wine spill, spatter on the light stone floor; he smiles.

'To the next twenty one . . .'

EPILOGUE

Nqobani waits. Waits for his sister, just as he has always done. He does not keep track of the time, less still the days of the week.

Nqobani remembers. He has no recollection of time before that night. His history begins then. Nqobani remembers the four men: four white men in his family's house, the noise they bring, the shouting and spitting, the deafening fire. He still feels the moment when it is as if his body is split in two. Wendile drags him through the tiny opening at the back of the shack; half of him is burning, wet with blood, half is cold, soaked with icy rain. He feels the rusty corrugated iron catch his loose sweater, scratch his side. He wriggles free, vomits, senses Wendile urging him on in a hushed bark. Though he is younger than her, he is bigger, yet she picks him up. When they are away from their house, she goes back, leaves him panting and shivering behind a scrubby bush. When she comes back, he can see the expression on her face, knows to say nothing, knows that whatever it is she has seen, she will not forget.

'We go now,' she hisses, pulling him after her down the narrow alley between the tin and wooden shacks. Nqobani remembers the tube-like alley filled with detritus, catching his arm on the wire, feeling the blood hot on his body, crying and whining, the rain thumping like a crowd's footsteps on the roofs either side of him. He feels the sounds close in on him, the walls of the shacks

340

arching over him. Even though they are both small, they have to squeeze and shuffle to pass dwellings whose walls bulge and sub-side into the tight corridor. He hears the drumbeat of the rain, the shouting of the white men and, deep in his head, echoes of the gunfire which cut apart his mother and father, his sister, his uncle and aunt. He sees their blood: on their faces, on the walls of the shack, spattered across his own clothes. He looks down at his legs, crossed and bent. His trousers are saturated with blood, yet he feels nothing. Now, in the village, he dreams of blood; he dreams of the dark tube in the cold rain and a loom-ing wave of blood which both chases and awaits him.

Nqobani waits. Wendile should be back soon. She is his legs. With her, he can move throughout the village. He can see the outside and be free of the dark, smoke-filled hut in which he lies for so long. The villagers stoke his fire and bring him pap. But they never touch him, never hold him. Whatever it is they say is within him, they dare not come close.

Nqobani waits; days and nights pass.

Nqobani prays every night, just as he has been taught. He prays for strength in his legs, for his body to be renewed. He prays for their family, for their memories, and their place next to the Lord in heaven. He does not know why they pray since God seems so far away; since that night, He has always seemed so distant. But she insists; it is their ritual.

He wonders now where she is, away for weeks at a time, in the city. She says she is cleaning, but he sees a light in her eyes, a light absent since she was eleven years old. He wonders whether she has found a man; he wonders whether she will leave him now, abandon him in exchange for a life.

Nqobani does not know how long has passed; he does not know how long since he has seen daylight outside his hut, save when he has slithered across the earth and lain on his back with his head out of the hut, looking up at the heavens. He did not realize it then, but now, as he sits waiting for the sun to move across the sky, for the temperature to fall once more so that the air thins and he can breathe fully once more, he feels it so strongly it is as if it swims within him, in his blood, in his heart. Last night, as he lay staring up at the stars, he knew. He was alone. Wendile was absent; Wendile was not under the stars.

ACKNOWLEDGEMENTS

Huge thanks to my editor, Krystyna Green, Martin Fletcher and all at Constable who continue to support their authors so admirably.

My excellent SAPS advisor, Marianne Steyn, answers all my procedural questions, but none of the views expressed by the fictional SAPS characters within the story are necessarily a reflection of her own.

All my friends in Cape Town get press-ganged into reminiscence and fact-checking, for which I am very grateful. As ever, the amazing Birch clan deserve special thanks, as do Abbie Chetwyn and Michael Nel for medical advice, and a host of others for all manner of intriguing contributions.

To live with someone who puts up with the troughs and peaks of being a writer and can then read an early draft and make such well-judged, apposite comments is a tremendous advantage, and my love and thanks go to Gareth Hughes for doing just that.